FATHERS, SONS, *and the* HOLY GHOSTS *of* BASEBALL

Trien,

Thank you for your friendship and coming out to play tennis with us.

Bless you always!

Lorena Fleet Footed Runner on Netflix

FATHERS, SONS, *and the* HOLY GHOSTS *of* BASEBALL

Tommy Murray

BEAVER'S POND
PRESS

"*Fathers, Sons, and the Holy Ghosts of Baseball* is a well-executed story of boys, old men, and the power of the game to shape community and individual lives. Iowa native Tommy Murray has penned a solid novel set in small-town Iowa in 1974.

As with many a baseball book, *Fathers, Sons, and the Holy Ghosts of Baseball* uses the game as a jumping off point to consider other themes, including issues of faith, the relationships between fathers (and father figures) and sons, the nature of community, and the inevitability of change—sometimes for the better and sometimes for the worse. The friendship of the three coaches and their individual relationships with young men in need of guidance are at the heart of the story. Murray crafts these affiliations with care, tracing the ups and downs of vulnerable people forging strong bonds."

—Rob Cline, *The Gazette* (Cedar Rapids)

"There are plenty of characters with interesting stories in this book, descriptions of baseball games, and underlying meditation on aging as well as how important it is for boys to have older men as mentors."

—Mary Ann Grossmann, *St. Paul Pioneer Press*

"The Hawkeye State is the setting once again for a captivating baseball novel by Tommy Murray. Murray writes with the perceptiveness of one who has spent decades working with teenagers, tolerating their immaturity while refining their mettle. And he shares their precocious insight into the authenticity of the adults around them.

Murray's novel mixes Pete Hamill's pacing and characters with a touch of Mitch Albom's mysticism. It combines the down-home folksiness of W.P. Kinsella with the throw-at-their heads combativeness of Leo Durocher. Cottage Park is still a hard-drinking, quick-tempered world where men wear a sense of justice on their sleeve and never duck a fight over principle.

Such small town virtues seem a distant, nostalgic memory in these disturbing times. If literature—or baseball for that matter—has anything to teach us in this frenetic, impatient age of ours, it might be the rediscovery of restraint and humility, dedication and hard work—virtues that 'the olds' instill in all the boys of Tommy Murray's summer."

—Jim Swearingen, *National Book Review*

"The action in Murray's novel isn't limited to the diamond and its pop-up flies, bunts and double-plays. Murray leaves nobody on base or safe at home as the reader is enlightened about the private lives of high school players struggling with egos, angst, misbehavior, teen pregnancy, abuse and death."

—*The Catholic Globe*

Other Books by Tommy Murray

The Empty Set

The Author's Note is adapted from an article that appeared in the *Bancroft Register* on May 20, 2015. The poem "Tommy" by Harold Clark appears with permission from the *Bancroft Register*.

ISBN: 978-1-59298-629-3
Library of Congress Catalog Number: 2017902758
Printed in the United States of America
Third Printing: 2018
22 21 20 19 18   7 6 5 4 3

Interior layout by Athena Currier

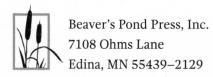

Beaver's Pond Press, Inc.
7108 Ohms Lane
Edina, MN 55439–2129

(952) 829-8818
www.BeaversPondPress.com

Fathers, Sons, and the Holy Ghosts of Baseball is dedicated to the men who taught me about baseball, love, life, and death: my grandfathers, Joe McTigue and Art Murray; my uncle Tommy Murray (see appendix), for whom I am named; and my father, John Murray.

Thank you to my uncle Dennis Pat McTigue, who gave his very all for the financing of this novel. All are residents of Cottage Park, Iowa, and remain active in the baseball community there.

Remember the days of old; consider the years of generations past. Ask your father, he will inform you; your elders, they will tell you.

—*Deuteronomy 32:7*

— CHAPTER ONE —

Countdown to the Finals: 59 Days to Go

COTTAGE PARK, IOWA, HAD BEEN BOMBED, most likely by some kind of bomb that wiped out humans but allowed all structures to remain intact. Or so it seemed to its newest resident, fourteen-year-old Timothy Jones, whom most called T. J. On his first exploration of the town's empty streets, he felt like the last person on earth. Located in the middle of nowhere, the quiet northwestern Iowa community boasted 728 residents, but it seemed as though everyone had disappeared or were dead. With each step of his trek, the gravity of his forced move from Denver slowly weighed him down. He wished he too could disappear from this town.

It was the last Sunday in May—May 31, 1974. A seething white sun, also lonely, pierced an azure ocean all the way to the bottom. It punished and beat down on T. J., pinkening his face, neck, and arms. Already he knew Cottage Park would be a hard place to live.

Main Street was three blocks of worn-out, dusty storefronts showcasing the empty memories of long-ago yesterdays when Cottage Park could support a downtown.

T. J. stopped and looked up at a tin sign swinging from a straight iron arrow protruding from a storefront. Engraved into the tin was the name "Peterson's Shoe Store." The usual cardboard sign on the door read "Sorry, we're CLOSED." On the bottom, someone had amended the standard sign with a black Magic Marker and one bold word in cursive: *Forever*.

Beneath that sign was another one, now like a tombstone, that showed the hours and days of operation for Mulroney's House of Women's High Fashion. T. J. stepped up to the door and cupped his hands around his eyes and peered into the store. This was the store his grandparents had once proudly owned. Farther back in the store were more signs for Annie's Attic

Antiques and a collection of older chairs and tables that had been neglected and denied in this setting for several years.

Like a house haunted by the ghost of each of its former occupants, this one location was the final resting place of the multiple businesses that had come and gone. In a small town with little economic stability, no one had the time, energy, or money to remove the unsold merchandise or even change the signs.

T. J. ambled down the sidewalk to the next store, Vern Van Oosbree's Variety Store, also vacant. At this store, however, someone had decorated the two large plate-glass windows with a huge multicolored banner that read: "Countdown to the Finals: 59 days to Go." Underneath the banner and plastered against the windows were several poster-sized schedules of the pride and joy of Cottage Park: the Holy Trinity High School base-ball team. The schedule listed a total of thirty-four games against schools from towns T. J. had never heard of before. The regular-season games had already begun and would continue through July 15. The schedule then showed the dates, times, and locations of the sectionals, substate quar-terfinals, and substate semifinals. Last in the list were the three games in the state tournament—or the Finals, as they were called in Cottage Park. The final game on the schedule had been circled and highlighted with a yellow marker:

> Saturday, August 1, 1974, 3:00 p.m.
> State Championship
> Sec Taylor Stadium, Des Moines

T. J. studied the team photo above the calendar. There were seventeen play-ers—some of whom looked as though they were still in grade school—and three very old men he guessed were coaches. The old men wore perpetual scowls that bled through the photo in anger.

If T. J. could have read their minds as he stared at their images, he would have learned that the old coaches hadn't seen the need for a team photo at the beginning of the season. Their team hadn't done anything to deserve a photo. What they really had needed to do at that moment was practice their defensive skills. Holy Trinity was noted for their defense. And defense—not cheery photographs—won games.

However, they had relented to the photo shoot at the repeated requests of a parent of two of their starters. Mr. Burnette had volunteered to incorporate the photo into a professional-looking schedule he would print and distribute throughout town at his own cost. He did all this because of a strong belief that something wonderful would happen that season, that a story was unfolding.

He had to have that team photo. It was part of his strategy, even part of his job, to document the season with calendars plus game recaps for the *Cottage Park Chronicle,* of which he was the editor and publisher. Mr. Burnette documented as much as he possibly could about Cottage Park, especially the Holy Trinity baseball team. He believed that story too might pass away and disappear, like the commerce that once thrived in the town.

And thus the countdown to the Finals began.

T. J. looked at the schedule and grimaced at the thought of still living in this unhappy community by August 1, the last game of the Finals. At the pace time crawled along in Cottage Park, August 1 seemed light years away.

"This place sucks!" T. J. said out loud.

He listened for an echo. There was none, only the soft murmuring of the dryers rumbling at the Cottage Park Cooperative grain elevator a few blocks away on Highway 169. His mother had promised him a new world; instead, this was the end of the world.

That wasn't the only lie she had told him about their move to Cottage Park. During the previous day's twelve-hour car ride from Denver across a labyrinth of blacktop highways to Cottage Park, she had promised he would get used to the smells that assaulted them in the Hawkeye State. There was dead skunk and a smorgasbord of manures: cow, sheep, chicken, turkey, and hog. She smiled and told him he'd eventually come to say what locals said about the whiff: "Smells like money, smells like home."

To the contrary, T. J. believed this place could never be his home and he would always be aware of its smells. He now stopped and tentatively sniffed again. He could still clearly make out the aroma of fresh hog manure. The malodor made him ill. What made him even sicker was the thought that he was possibly ingesting and absorbing the maleficent stench.

T. J. crossed the street to the Farmer Savings Bank as the scoreboard-like clock clicked off the time, 2:45 p.m., and then the temperature, 95 degrees Fahrenheit. This was followed by the price of a bushel of beans at $5.15, and corn at $2.45 per bushel.

It seemed he had been exploring for hours. In reality, he had set off on this journey forty-five minutes ago. During that time, he had seen all of Cottage Park and experienced all its emptiness.

Actually, he hadn't seen it all. His mother had begged him to visit Cottage Park's two most notable landmarks: Holy Trinity Church, a cathedral more than a church, as beautiful and spectacular as any church in Rome; and Memorial Field, an old-time ballpark that garnered as much religious zeal as the church. She had explained that he could not know and appreciate and love Cottage Park until he understood the significance of these historic houses of God and baseball gods. Both places of worship were open twenty-four hours per day.

But T. J. would not visit either of these shrines. He didn't believe in gods of any kind. He had no time for false religions in his life.

T. J. now made up his mind that he had seen everything in Cottage Park he would ever see, with one exception: he hadn't yet visited Holy Trinity High School, where his mom could probably get him placed in the tenth grade for fall. He started off in that direction.

As he slogged and sank into and amongst the tiny pebbles of the hot blacktop pavement, T. J. noticed his bell-bottom blue jeans seemed to have lengthened down over the backs of his tennis shoes and onto the street. He tried to cuff them, but they resisted any effort that constrained them from billowing unto the pavement. After giving up on cuffing, he tightened his belt to a notch he had never used before. His stomach appeared to be shrinking. That was a good thing. He wondered if kids in this town would call him Fatso and Lard-Ass as they had in Denver.

He journeyed five blocks away from downtown toward the school, which was on the same block as the church. T. J. eyed the large steeple as it grew closer and closer. The church bells were ringing solemnly.

Every day of the week, every day of the year, for as long as anyone could remember, Mrs. McCarthy rang those church bells at least three times a day. She was ninety years old and married to the town's only working barber.

Mrs. McCarthy was born with a right leg noticeably shorter than the left. Despite a specially fitted shoe with an extra-large platform, a discrepancy always remained between the two legs. Over the years, anytime she trudged from one point to another, that discrepancy ground away at her lower back, hips, knees, and ankles. Every step she now took from her home directly across the street from Holy Trinity Church was accompanied by an exclamation of severe pain.

"Ow," she'd say. "Owie. Ow. Ooh, owie."

Still, she persevered. She leaned into the pain with aluminum forearm crutches, sometimes shuffling sideways like a crab, always hoping in vain that some variation or adaptation of her gait might offer a moment's respite from the pain. Once she reached the steel railing along the steps leading up to the church, she pushed and pulled herself up each step, pausing to catch her breath and allow her body to prepare for the next jolt of pain.

Despite the pain, she came every day—whether rain, snow, or ice—to ring the bells faithfully and religiously for the Angelus at 6:00 a.m., noon, and 6:00 p.m. She also rang them to signal the start of daily Mass at 7:30 a.m. and to alert residents (nearly everyone in Cottage Park was a member of Holy Trinity Church) to the start of any other parish or school activities she deemed worthy.

Mrs. McCarthy also used the bells to notify the community of a parishioner's entrance to or passing from the world. A newborn baby earned one ringing of the bells. A departed resident earned one ring for every year of life. It was not uncommon for a group of neighbors to await her exit from the church to query her regarding the correspondence of the rung bells to who had been born or died.

On quiet days without a birth or a death, Mrs. McCarthy would ring the bells at 3:00 p.m. to remind those in earshot—on a still day the sound carried for miles—of the time Jesus was crucified. The only time the bells were silent, it seemed, was during Holy Trinity's home baseball games. Mrs. McCarthy's attendance at those games was every bit as intense as her devotion to ringing the church bells.

As T. J. reached his destination, he saw the church, a rectory, a nearly abandoned convent, and an old two-story brick school for students in grades kindergarten through twelve.

At the other end of the school, children and adults dressed up for an important occasion were entering what T. J. guessed was the gym. He gravitated in that direction and followed the people into a small gymnasium, where he observed a graduation ceremony with a class of roughly thirty students dressed in black graduation caps and gowns.

He looked around the gym. Every bleacher seat was taken. A few adults sat on the stage. A musty-smelling tarpaulin had been spread across the gym floor, with the students closest to the front. T. J. guessed the parents were in the rows of steel folding chairs right behind their children. In all, three hundred people were probably packed into the gym, with two big fans standing like sentries at each end of the gym, providing faint relief from the sweltering heat.

So this is where everybody is hanging out, T. J. thought.

He scanned the gymnasium again. Everywhere were old people—older than his mom, more like his grandparents' age. He guessed correctly that most of the men were farmers, their telltale snow-white foreheads and necks shining beneath dark brown or red faces. They were simply dressed in short-sleeved plaid shirts and gray or brown dress pants. Their wives were also simply dressed in modest, traditional skirts and blouses.

As T. J. studied the people of Cottage Park, he eventually noticed they were also studying him. An elderly woman in a billowing flowery dress waved for T. J. to come over and sit next to her. It looked as if her body had been stuffed with pillows. Her hair was an unnatural—but popular—shade of white, dark gray, and blue. T. J. glanced across the bleachers and saw several heads sporting the same hue.

He headed toward her, and she used her backside to push her husband across the bleacher seat to make room for T. J. He obeyed her order to sit down beside her.

"Who are you?" the woman whispered loudly and hoarsely. She smelled as if she had marinated herself in hamburger goulash for several days.

"I'm T. J.," he said.

"Who's your family?" the woman said with an almost urgent tone. "Who's your mom and dad?"

"My dad is . . ."

T. J. thought for some kind of explanation for his father, whom he hadn't seen for years and was rumored to be in jail or prison. He wanted to keep the insistent woman from questioning him further.

"My dad is dead," he whispered, lying. "My mom is a Mulroney. That was her maiden name. Lucy Mulroney. Monica," he added.

Monica was his mother's middle name. Many residents of Cottage Park manipulated and sometimes mangled their formal names. But T. J. didn't need to explain the name game to this old woman. In an instant, the woman worked through the calculus of generations of family trees. She determined this boy was fine—not by his merits but by the family from which he sprung.

She heartily tapped him on the knee. "That's a good family. You'll fit in good here."

Another old woman in the same gym might have worked through the same ancestry and come up with a more indifferent or wary approach to the stranger. However, this woman treated T. J. as if he were her own grandson, of which she had several, including one on the graduation stage.

She pointed to a thin stiff-backed man approaching the podium on the stage. "You know Coach Murphy? He's our baseball coach." She smiled. "You'll play baseball in Cottage Park. All our boys do."

T. J. shook his head to disagree and even tried to stand up and leave. But the woman sat him back down.

"Sh! Listen to Coach Murphy now," she ordered.

Over the last several months, school teachers, police officers, judges, and even his mother had ordered him to listen. He had ignored them, but something about the old woman broke down his defenses. Like everyone else in the tiny gymnasium, he sat back and listened to the speaker.

Coach Al Murphy had made his decision.

When he was younger, each year of teaching at Holy Trinity, each year of coaching baseball, seemed almost impossible. He had longed for the day when he would retire from it all. Five years ago, at the age of sixty-nine, he had retired from teaching, having celebrated forty years in the profession as a high school English teacher, all of it at Holy Trinity. He had decided at that time to continue coaching, as long as he felt he was making a contribution and making a difference.

Murphy thought now he was the best coach he had ever been. He might never retire from the sport and the youth he loved. He relished the challenges of this upcoming season.

The first challenge was to broach the historically taboo subject of the Finals. People in Cottage Park did not discuss problems, especially the problem of never winning the Finals, in a public setting. But today he would get it out in the open, demystify its grip on Cottage Park, and lead the community in triumph once and for all over this dreadful curse.

Murphy had told no one of his decision to address this topic. His friends and assistant coaches—Edwin Gerald Gallivan (a.k.a. Egg) and Father John Ryan—couldn't suspect him to take on such a huge task.

Murphy stepped to the microphone and then looked down at his watch. It had stopped. He shook it, but it would not continue. So he continued on, despite not being able to measure time, which was an adventurous thing for a seventy-four-year-old man to do.

He lifted the microphone to his lips, took a deep breath, and looked out across the twenty-nine graduates. They too were confused by time, but for different reasons. For them, no watch or calendar could accurately measure the rapidity from which they moved from childhood to adulthood. Time was a fleeting chaos of choice that confronted them and seemed to cheat them at every turn. Each day, they made decisions that seemed to change their lives dramatically forever. They realized that change could be terrifying. Yet having grown up in Cottage Park, where time often stood still, change could also be exciting and, most of all, liberating.

Murphy, on the other hand, feared change. If he could have, he would have frozen everyone at that very moment. No graduation. No students growing older and leaving Cottage Park for Des Moines, Omaha, and Minneapolis. Somehow he would fight against the terrible undertow that swept the youth out and away from the shore of Cottage Park.

He looked at one empty chair draped by a graduation cap and gown acting as a placeholder for an absent, grieving student whose father really had passed away a week ago. No death. Only happy, healthy boys playing the sport where no watch was needed: baseball.

It's time to begin, Murphy thought. He cleared his throat and took a deep breath.

At that moment, Hugh Wilson, the principal at Holy Trinity, crossed the stage and reached in front of Murphy to readjust his microphone. He then looked over his work, motioned for Murphy to begin, and headed back to his seat.

But beginning his speech was the very last thing in the world Murphy would do at this point. He'd been insulted—another in a litany of subtle demeaning acts that stirred up the usually stoic Murphy.

Murphy's closest friends recognized the insult in the principal's patronizing behavior. Father Ryan, seventy-nine years old, was dressed in full graduation cap and gown, as was Murphy. Egg was eighty-four years old yet seated straight and erect in the bleachers. Both of these men registered the injustice—and registered their anger and their pledge for revenge—in different ways. Egg's cold, dull eyes met Murphy's and held long and still for a moment. Ryan's eyes flittered down to the floor, then to his hands folded in front of him, and then closed as he slowly shook his head back and forth.

Murphy stared at Wilson until the principal had returned to his seat. The coach was angry enough to have waited all afternoon. Sensing that he might just do that, Murphy's wife, Katherine, cleared her throat to prompt her husband to begin his speech.

Murphy bent the microphone back to where he had first put it, and then he checked to make sure Wilson also hadn't turned the microphone off. He hadn't.

Murphy smiled at the graduates and began. "I really never know why I'm asked to speak at these graduations or what I'll say when I do speak, but I suspect my age has something to do with both of those questions. You see, I am seventy-five years old."

Murphy was, in fact, seventy-four years old. But over the last few years, he and his fellow old men frequently erred when speaking of their age or their years of service to Holy Trinity. Sometimes they intentionally added one year or more. No one quite understood why.

Katherine immediately caught the lie about Murphy's age. It upset her. She rolled her eyes and took a deep breath. She'd been married to Murphy for over fifty years (and her math was accurate). Either despite that time together or because of it, her husband could still unnerve her with his idiosyncrasies.

The old men's difficulties with time were just one of the many issues that heightened scrutiny and concern in Cottage Park. As much as the old men fretted and worried about the town's youth, the graduates seated before him were even more concerned with the old men's safety, health, happiness, and future. They were also concerned about their own inevitable future without the meddlesome, bickering old men. Especially the young men who formed the core of the baseball team.

The old men were not always so caustic. Not long ago, when the graduates had been children, they had viewed the old men as kindly and jovial grandfathers who always had time to laugh and play with them. The old men swung the children from side to side like pendulums or around in circles, like the swing ride at the Kossuth County Fair.

Over the years, though, this play—especially the play of baseball—morphed into play as preparation for life. The old men became serious and hardened about the critical importance of learning how to hold a runner on first, pop off second to complete a double play, or fake repeated throws until a runner was trapped and tagged out in a hotbox. Now they were restless, unable to ever enjoy a moment of real play with the boys. They relentlessly coached and nagged and fixed the boys to become better baseball players and, most importantly, to win. Any kindliness was set aside out of necessity.

The contentious dynamics weighed heavily on the seniors, who simply hoped Murphy's commencement address might enlighten them on how to let go of their frustrations and anxieties about the old men—how to say goodbye to them and to Cottage Park.

Despite the challenges in their relationship with Murphy and the other old coaches, each year the seniors asked one of the three to speak at their graduation ceremony. Choosing their graduation speaker was one of the very few says the seniors were afforded during their education at Holy Trinity. Like everyone else in Cottage Park, the students trusted the old men, were often exasperated by them, but in the end mostly stood in awe of them.

Murphy reasoned he had been chosen because it was his turn. Ryan had spoken at the event three years ago; Egg the previous two years. Murphy's assumption was partly right. This year, the students had actually chosen Egg. Due to a "policy change," however, Egg had been ruled out.

Egg's commencement addresses were more akin to workplace safety seminars, complete with firsthand accounts about Cottage Park residents who had been dismembered in some fashion, blinded, or even killed.

At last year's graduation, Egg spoke in excruciating detail of his experience as a gandy dancer, or track maintenance worker, for the Illinois Central Railroad in the 1940s. Ernie Richardson had hopped off the lead engine of a train snaking through Cottage Park. Ernie ducked into the depot for a cold pop. With a Coca-Cola bottle in hand, Richardson timed his jump back aboard the train via the caboose. It was a routine maneuver he had executed countless times before.

But this time, he failed to secure a strong handhold on the caboose railing. He slipped underneath the massive rolling iron wheels, which cleanly severed his right leg just below the knee. Egg had witnessed it all: the dispassionate train continued on its way, Richardson writhed on the railbed, and his torn leg lay between the steel rails.

Egg carried Richardson and his leg into the depot. Right there on the crew's break table, he assisted old Dr. McCauley in a failed operation to save the leg.

This story and similar stories from Egg's previous commencement addresses showed the ghastly consequences of not paying attention on the job. Yet they all ended with some wistful revelation. To conclude the story about Richardson's accident, Egg revealed how the mishap had motivated him to choose a different job.

Egg had taken on and quit dozens of jobs in this manner. The only job he had consistently held over his lifetime—and the only job he had never taken a penny for doing—was being the assistant baseball coach at Holy Trinity.

And Holy Trinity baseball was always the underlying message of Egg's tales of workplace woe. Egg offered these stories to explain why he and the other coaches were so severe on the baseball field. They never wanted to see similar misfortune befall their players. But that message was barely heard, let alone comprehended, by anyone in the audience. They never understood that this was as close as the old men would ever come to saying how deeply they loved and cared for the youth of Cottage Park.

When the seniors selected Egg yet again to speak at commencement, Wilson spontaneously announced a two-year consecutive limit for speakers. Thus ended Egg's illustrative reign. The graduates then decided between Ryan, to whom they listened each Sunday at Mass, and Murphy. To Wilson's chagrin, no other names were considered.

So in a way, Murphy was correct that he had been chosen because it was his turn. He also suspected he had been chosen because deep in his heart he was a poet. He had boxes of notebooks filled with longhand sonnets by the furnace in his basement. At one time in his much younger life, he excitedly read his poetry to his family and students. After years and then decades of less-than-enthused responses, he began to write only for himself and the individual(s) who would discover his work upon his death. But he still knew how to command the English language, if he so chose.

Murphy looked out over his audience. "The French composer Louis Hector Berlioz once said, 'Time is a great teacher, but unfortunately it kills all its pupils.'"

Katherine had told him not to begin with that quote. It was too depressing for such a joyous event. As she had predicted, it was met with were mostly blank stares. Somehow it still seemed right to Murphy, though. Time was a rotten thief. Murphy took every opportunity to call it for what it was.

"Maybe that means I'm not a great teacher," Murphy continued. "I haven't killed anyone . . . yet."

And now he transitioned into a subject of his expertise, something very near and dear to him, something everyone in the audience understood: baseball. In baseball Murphy found the shared love and excitement that he longed for from his fellow friends and townspeople as well as the imagery and artistry of poetry that sustained his soul.

"I guess our youth of Cottage Park have always recognized wisdom in those of us who have been around the longest. Maybe they realize we've made more mistakes than anyone else has and that we were bound to have learned something from those trials and errors. Or maybe they simply believe the elderly do not have the stamina and the long-windedness to deliver a long commencement address. Both beliefs are partially true.

"I sometimes think I am chosen to speak at graduations because the graduates believe this is it—I might not be employed next year or, worse, forget to take my heart medication and not be above ground next year. Let me assure you, I will take my medication, and I plan to be healthy for another season at Holy Trinity."

The crowd politely applauded.

"The real reason why I was invited here this year is my age. It is true that the longer you have been around, the more you learn. Thus when you reach my ripe, old age, you should be about perfect. Maybe that's true for some people, but it hasn't worked out that way for me, as my assistant coaches and especially my current and former players would be happy to explain."

Murphy removed his glasses and rubbed them with a handkerchief as he spoke. "I still make mistakes. It is more frustrating now, of course, than when I was younger, because I should know better. I've made some mistakes countless times before, and I'll probably make some of those mistakes into my future. But I hope that in the long run, I will be remembered for the good things I did that outweighed the bad."

Murphy placed his glasses on again. "People who keep records tell me I am the winningest high school baseball coach of all time. Nonsense. I don't deserve that credit. We all do."

There was scattered applause.

Murphy pointed to his friends. "I'm lucky that I have friends like Father Ryan and Egg, and a wonderful wife. My years here at Holy Trinity have truly been a blessed time in my life. I feel especially blessed by these students before us today.

"Five of the boys in this senior class have played baseball for me for four years. They have given me many of my finest moments in baseball. I have yelled and screamed at them, and amazingly they have listened to some of what I said. We all have set very high expectations for ourselves this season. Sure, we'll have our usual winning season. I expect this team will go undefeated."

The stoic Murphy made a fist and pounded it on the podium. It was now time to break the taboo. What he was about to say and do was dramatic and historic.

In the past, no one had been allowed to mention the Finals. The thought was, looking ahead to the Finals might cause the team to overlook the importance of the games leading up to the Finals. And overlooking any one of those games might mean not even making it to the big game—the only game that mattered.

Because of this tradition of not discussing the Finals, Murphy had been upset about Mr. Burnette's schedules and that banner in a storefront. But after cooling down, Murphy thought maybe it *was* time someone raised the subject and got it out in the open. The thing about the past in Cottage Park was, it was never the past. It never *passed*. The past was always very much alive and real all the time, especially in regard to baseball.

Murphy looked out over the graduates and their families until it was completely still. Then he roared, "But doggone it—this summer we're going to Des Moines, and we're going to win the Finals! I know it."

The graduates rose and cheered. Everyone else in the gym joined them.

Murphy waited several moments until cheers and conversations quieted. "I make no apologies for the pressures that might accompany that statement. I know we have to win the Finals. Like all of you, I too am counting down the days until the Finals, when we get another opportunity to win that game. And this time we will!"

Murphy looked out into the audience for Katherine. She shook her head. He knew he had infuriated her. She did not like dramatics, especially if those dramatics involved putting additional pressure on her husband. However, he had determined that these comments about winning the Finals were necessary to rid the "can't win the big one" monkey off his back—and off the back of the whole community.

Holy Trinity had made more Finals—that is, state championship tournament appearances in the spring, summer, and fall seasons—than any other school in Iowa. Yet they had never won the final summer championship game and thus had never been state champions in the most important baseball season that the best athletes and most schools competed in. It was not a subject of popular discussion, at least not in a public setting. So he put the pressure on himself and the players in hopes it would be enough to push this team over the top. What was there to lose by making the challenge?

With that challenge now issued, there was really nothing else Murphy needed to add. But he spoke for a few more minutes about seeing excitement in the fresh, clear eyes of those about to begin a journey, about how the graduates made him young again, and that in some way he was sure to join them on their journey. It was typical commencement-address fodder. He had said the same thing at previous graduation addresses and meant what he said.

However, this time when he finished his address, he knew the graduates would remember it and that this brief commencement would be the talk of Cottage Park for the rest of the summer. But even Murphy did not suspect those in attendance would remember it for the rest of their lives.

T. J. thought the frail old man at the podium might have a heart attack as he pounded the podium to make a point. His words sounded like one more lie in his lifetime of lies. Forget about a trip to the Finals. The only trip that old guy could take would be in a wheelchair or a coffin.

T. J. timed his exit to coincide with the applause at the end of Murphy's address. The elderly woman sitting next to him called out for him to come back. But this time, T. J. eluded her grasp and continued out of the gym. He headed back outside into the heat, sun, clamoring of the bells, and incessant attack of hog manure on his olfactory system.

He had counted twenty-nine graduates in this hick school, plus one empty chair for a thirtieth student. That was bush. His previous school in Denver had more than eight hundred students in his class alone. With class sizes that small in Cottage Park, everyone would be in his business, and that meant he would have no privacy.

Worse, Murphy made it sound as if everyone in town was a jock. T. J. had never played a sport; he had barely even picked up a ball of any kind. He hated jocks.

The counselors in his most recent chemical dependency program had all told him to seek progress, not perfection, one day at a time, and that's what he would do. However, he wouldn't do it at Holy Trinity High School or anywhere near Cottage Park.

Right then, he began to devise a scheme that would hasten his departure.

Spider Schmitt was the first graduate to quickly walk, then run, from the gym onto the lawn in front of the school. He was nicknamed "Spider" because he had eaten a spider on a dare in fifth grade. He joyfully spurted, skipped, and hopped across the grass exactly as he had as a kindergartener twelve years earlier. Before the life-sized statue of the Blessed Virgin Mary, he flicked his graduation cap up into the air, then watched the cap ring around her head and fall back to the ground.

His fellow male graduates—all classmates since kindergarten—gathered around him and also flicked, skimmed, and tossed their caps across the lawn. There were twelve boys in the senior class, and one of those boys was absent. The small group was not enough cover for the two boys who ached to light up their cigarettes.

After their initial giddiness, the boys conspired amongst themselves hurriedly regarding the big party they had planned for much later that evening at the quarry outside of town.

At first, the graduates of the other sex had stayed in the hallway and clung to each other in tears. As the crying let up and the girls noticed the boys were all outside, they led their friends and families in that direction.

One of those girls, Margaret Riley, observed that her boyfriend, Spider, had removed his graduation gown to reveal a bare chest. Like a centaur, he never missed an opportunity to show off rippled muscles stretched across broad shoulders that twisted down a tapered back to a buff and bubbled butt. Margaret especially always noted and appreciated that butt. Nevertheless, she yelled at him to put his clothes back on. He quickly did so.

As she approached him, she said through gritted teeth, "We need to take pictures."

When Spider made the same pained expression he might have made as a kindergartener, Margaret smiled and took his arm. He held her close.

Everyone considered them Cottage Park's official high school couple—everyone except Margaret's mother. She had never approved of Spider. She thought he was immature, and she also suspected their relationship had grown too serious.

On the other hand, Spider's parents, the owners of the Morning Sun Café, very highly approved of their son's choice to date Margaret. For some time, their son's boisterous behavior had become increasingly worrisome, and they hoped his relationship with Margaret would hasten his stability and maturity. To this point in time, though, it hadn't worked.

They wavered on how to coexist with their son's behavior. Sometimes they tried to understand it as a product of his stage of life or the time of year, in which case they reluctantly accepted or even ignored it. At other times, they reminded themselves that their son was less than three months away from leaving for Briar Cliff University in Sioux City—thank God. If they could hold out until then, surely he would mature while he was away at school.

At the moment, it was easier for Spider's parents to overlook his behaviors because he and Margaret made such an attractive couple. Spider's father snapped away at the couple with his camera, hoping that capturing enough frozen images of the two together would forge that union in reality.

Standing near the couple but safely out of the snapshots, Spider's friend Jack Burnette looked on, deep in his own thoughts. He would not be leaving for college. He would be setting forth for anywhere but Cottage Park. He planned to leave immediately after the baseball season.

Jack used to be as wild as Spider. But over the last few months, the seriousness of graduation had quieted him, in part because he really had no idea what to do next. For eighteen years, everything had been laid out in front of him and life happened. Soon it would be day-to-day, with no two days alike.

He'd once heard that taking a trip was the best way to plan your future. It put you in a somewhat objective or neutral environment with no familiar influences to guide or prejudice you toward one way of thinking over another. He hoped that was true. He was concerned about how long it would take to sort things out and get on the right path to somewhere. Actually, he was more than concerned. He was scared.

Jack's father saw the anxiousness in his son's eyes and tried to replace it with familiarity. He ordered Jack to smile and snapped a picture, then called the other boys over for a group shot. The boys huddled around Jack, who bunched in even closer when his father ordered them to squeeze together.

"One more," Mr. Burnette said.

"Wait!" Mrs. Burnette called out. "Jack, do something with that hair. Push it back."

Jack groaned and made a feeble effort at pushing the hair off his forehead.

"No," she said, quickly reaching her hand up into the mop of Jack's hair. "There!" she announced.

"I need a picture of my baseball players," Mr. Burnette said. He nudged his younger son, Jeff, a ninth grader, to stand next to his older brother. Though three years younger, Jeff was three inches taller than his brother, even when he slightly stooped and Jack stood as straight as possible.

The two boys awkwardly edged closer. Three years separated them in age, but the distance and the difference between the two boys could span almost a lifetime. Physically Jeff was taller and thinner than his older brother. Emotionally he was more cautious and reserved.

Some family members don't communicate well with each other. Others don't communicate at all. Despite sharing a bedroom in a small house, the two Burnette boys hadn't communicated in any meaningful manner since Jack became a freshman and couldn't afford to be seen playing with his little brother. They had been best friends before. Now they were like the mason jars of dill pickles that sat on the pantry shelf in the basement collecting dust and rust around the lids. Their resulting silence had become a wall, and it was easier to leave the wall standing than to tear it down.

"Closer," their father said, prodding the two together—and hoping that reality would imitate the picture of the two close, smiling brothers.

They too, like everything else in Cottage Park, seemed to be fading away before his very eyes. All too soon, they would be gone and away from home. After he had taken several pictures, the boys quickly drifted apart again, where they were more comfortable.

Seven miles southeast of Cottage Park were three small lakes that had once been gravel quarries. The lakes were actually one big lake divided by a quarter-mile inlet. At the end of the inlet, the lake nearly pinched off into the third body, shorter and rounder than the halves. These lakes had very brief shorelines that dropped off suddenly to a depth of over a hundred feet. Yet unbelievably, with all the after-hours mischief and parties so close to such a deadly location, no one had ever drowned.

This third lake was more of a marsh or wetland and hosted dozens of domed brown straw muskrat dens. This marsh was also home for countless other animals, such as frogs and turtles, both painted and snapping. Many stories about snapping turtles had been fabricated and embellished over the years in direct proportion to the amount of alcohol the teens consumed. For example, it was true that a seventy-five-pound snapping turtle had washed up on shore several years ago. But it was not true that it had chased a slow-footed Rich Orlowski until he turned and beat it to death with a sharp rock.

At sunset, the wildlife at the marsh chattered and occasionally screamed what seemed to be invitations, cries, and warnings to the young people who showed up to drink from the beer keg and mill around the water's edge. The youth of Cottage Park would have been wise to listen to the chorus of nature that warned them to stay away. But still they came, against the law, against their parents' wishes, and often against their own reason.

There were any number of ways they could die or get seriously injured during their parties at the quarry site. Only strong, confident swimmers could survive the sudden drop-off and the cool, dark waters that could swallow an unsuspecting wader or weak swimmer. If that weren't enough, brave or foolish young men practiced swan dives off the rocky cliff overlooking the water. Marijuana and alcohol clouded or shut down what little common sense young people have at that age. And even if the inebriated youth of Cottage Park avoided the deathtraps inherent at the quarries, they still had to navigate and negotiate cars and motorcycles back home in the early hours of the morning.

At 2:00 a.m. of graduation night, Orlowski and his girlfriend, Michelle, ended their assignment as the lookouts at the entrance of the quarry to warn the revelers in the event of a surprise visit from Sheriff Huffman. Of the twenty-nine graduates who had assembled a few hours earlier to sit around the bonfire and discuss the day's events, now six remained, all dating couples. One by one, they poked at the dying fire in front of them as they recounted news of their graduation parties, visiting relatives and the gifts they brought, and as always their families—especially, of late, the most unpredictable members of their families, their parents. Most specifically, their fathers (their "olds") and the old men.

Couple by couple grew tired of the chatter of the past and present. They kissed the quarries good-bye, leaving behind only Spider and Margaret.

Margaret leaned back into Spider's chest, and he placed his arms around her from behind and held her. They watched a log spit sparks from the fire out onto the sand around it.

Spider eased his hand up under Margaret's shirt until he felt her bikini top, then gently caressed her right breast. "How about a swim?" he whispered in her ear.

"At this hour of the morning?" Margaret said. "In that bottomless pit?"

Spider helped her to her feet, took off his shirt, and slowly stepped into the water until it crept up over his knees, then he dived in. When he came back up for air, he looked back to the shore, where Margaret had removed her shirt and cutoffs and was standing in her bikini.

"What are you waiting for?" he called out. "Jump in!"

Spider would always remember the vision of what happened next. Margaret undid her top, and it fell to the ground, then she wriggled her hips and dropped the bottom of her suit to the ground. Completely naked, she stretched like a cat before him.

Spider had touched much of Margaret's body but had never seen what he had touched. Now that he could see what he had previously imagined, he felt a weakness in his arms and legs. Transfixed, he stopped breathing. Suddenly he felt himself being drawn down underneath the water, and he reminded himself to tread water again until he surfaced to fill his grateful lungs with air.

Margaret was still there on the shore watching him, her hands clasped together at her waist. "Come keep me warm," she said. "I'm starting to get cold."

Spider quickly lunged from the water onto the shore and held her as she had requested. He had longed and ached for this very moment, and now that he was smack in the middle of his wildest dream, he was completely powerless and at the mercy of the woman who held him like a child. When Margaret offered her breasts to him, he sucked on each nipple like a baby.

Margaret gently pulled away, then took his hand and led him far enough out that they were blanketed by the warm water a few steps from the deadly drop-off. At that point, she reached behind, grabbed both cheeks of his butt, and brought him closer and then into her.

Both gave everything of each other, including their virginity. When they were done, Margaret quietly cried. Following her lead and rocking in her arms, Spider did the same.

It was nearly five o'clock in the morning when Orlowski drove his car up and over the curb of Jack's front yard. Orlowski cursed and jerked the steering wheel of his '71 Ford Fairlane as Jack watched on from the backseat. The vehicle took a bone-crunching bounce as it settled back down onto the street again, where he maneuvered it flush against the curb. Neither of the occupants were hurt by the mishap, though neither celebrated this accomplishment or laughed as youth often do when they cheat the fate of serious injury.

Both boys were drunk and physically tired, but moreover socially tired. They were tired of their friends, their families, and the everyday sameness of Cottage Park. They were mostly tired of rehashing about how tired they were of it all.

Orlowski turned the car off, and both boys watched as the darkness outside began to show the barest hint of a sunrise. Dawn was a little more than an hour away. After a few moments, Jack gave a half wave, opened the car door, and stumbled out. He gazed as Orlowski drove off toward downtown to open his father's grocery store.

Jack meandered up the sidewalk and nearly toppled over. When he arrived at the concrete front steps, he leaned over to steady himself, then he yanked himself up the steel railing until he could open the front door. He wondered how he would make it up the thirteen wooden steps that led upstairs to the bedroom he shared with Jeff.

Slowly he weaved up the steps until he was midway to the top. He fought the urge to lean back and fall down the steps, then continued on until he reached his bedroom. He flopped on his bed, closed his aching eyes, and kicked off his tennis shoes, dropping them like cannon balls on the wooden floor.

Jeff woke up at the sound, sitting up and trying to make sense of the scene before him. Jack had come home drunk before in the past, but he had always been quieter. Jeff never asked his brother why he came home drunk. He never really asked him anything, and his brother paid him the same respect. But on this occasion, his thoughts were on his parents.

"Did you at least tell Mom and Dad you're home?" Jeff asked.

Jack looked at his brother through the cracks of his hands. "Are you kidding? It was all I could do to make it up the stairs. They'll figure it out."

"I hope so," Jeff said. "One of them was up checking for you about a half hour ago."

"Don't worry," Jack said. "I'm a big boy. I can take care of myself."

"That's the problem," Jeff said, emboldened by a lack of sleep. "They worry . . . And I worry you guys will get caught drinking, and then you'll get kicked off the team."

"It doesn't really make a difference if I play or not," Jack said. "One way or another, we'll still get beat in the Finals. Always have. Always will."

He yawned long and deeply. "What's it matter, anyway? Baseball is a dead sport. It's dying. Iowa is dying, and Cottage Park is dying. The only way to get out of Cottage Park is to run away or be carried away in a coffin." His stomach and shoulders rose slowly, and the breath trailed from his chest. "I'm running."

Jeff watched his older brother drift off to sleep. He envied him for his upcoming freedom to run away. He wished he could run away with his older brother, sooner—now, before they ventured any further into this baseball season.

Jeff did not like baseball. His father basically strong-armed him to go out for the team. There was nothing at all fun about this sport. It hurt. And if the truth were told: whether it was screaming line drives or hopping ground balls or brush-back pitches thrown ninety miles per hour at his head, he was scared to death of the ball.

If only he could quit. But there would be no place to hide in Cottage Park. He'd have to join Jack on the road. Jeff imagined Jack and himself working on an oil rig in Louisiana or a salmon factory in Alaska. Wrapped in those dreams, he slowly joined his brother in sleep.

— CHAPTER TWO —

Countdown to the Finals: 58 Days to Go

.

"**I**'VE MADE MY DECISION," Murphy said on Monday, the day following graduation.

He sat at his kitchen table with the *Des Moines Register* in his hands, having finished breakfast.

"I'm getting out, honey. I'm all done. After this summer."

He had been looking at the newspaper, but now he stopped and looked at Katherine.

"There. That should make people happy."

Katherine stepped over from the stove with a pot of hot coffee in her hands. She poured her husband a cup, then filled her own, returned the pot to the stove, and came back to the table to sit.

"I didn't hear you," Katherine said. "Have you taken your heart pills today?"

Murphy put down his newspaper and gave his wife his full attention. Though she was the same age as Murphy, she looked several years younger. Her eyes danced when anyone showed her attention. Her hair was always made up, colored professionally in a youthful auburn. Today she had placed a pearl barrette where she had formed a bouffant. She took considerable time each morning to apply her makeup. That morning, for no reason other than to dress up for Murphy, she wore a pearl necklace with matching earrings, a silk blouse with mandarin collar, and a linen skirt, all covered with an apron adorned with the name Grandmacakes. She wore pumps with a pronounced heel to punctuate her overall appearance.

Murphy showed no understanding or appreciation of his wife's efforts to magnify her appearance. He did, however, note her keen interest in his commentary, so he continued.

"I actually made the decision yesterday, but I didn't want to take away from those kids' graduation. So today's as good as any. I'm announcing my retirement."

"Your retirement from what?" Katherine asked.

Murphy chuckled. "From baseball, of course. What else could I retire from? Baseball is all that matters in my life, and I'm getting out of it. I'm through."

Katherine sighed. "Al, how many times have you and I gone through this before? What are you really planning? Do you think this business about retiring will make your boys win all their games for you?"

"I don't know," Murphy said. "It might, but that's not why I'm retiring now."

Murphy wrested his eyeglasses from his face, huffed on them and then rubbed each lens with his shirt. His head hung down from his neck even early in the morning. Clearly visible through the strands of long gray hair was a brown, spotted balding scalp. With his glasses off he looked blinded, very old, and helpless.

"I thought that you wanted me out."

Katherine sipped her coffee. "I did while I thought you could." She shook her head. "I've wanted you out of that game for years. And I believed you each of the other three times when you said you'd get out. But no, I don't believe you now. You're married to baseball." She laughed, and he smiled. "You've been married to baseball longer than you've been married to me."

"This time you can believe me," Murphy said. "I'm through. After this season. For good."

Murphy placed his eyeglasses back on. His vision began to focus, and he studied the doubt in his wife's eyes.

"Katherine, I mean it this time. It's time to give a younger man a chance."

"And you won't come back to be his assistant?"

"No," Murphy said with a smile. "Heavens, no. Not even if everyone asks me. When I retire, I won't show my face in that ballpark for two years—or at least one year. It's been forty-five years. I think that's enough."

"This town never deserved you," Katherine said. "No one will ever do a better job." She set her chair close to Murphy's. "You know I worry about you. About the effect coaching has on your health. This would be the best for both of us." She reached out and put her hand on his. "When is your last game?"

Murphy patted his wife's hand. "At the end of the season—whenever that is. So we've got to win the Finals. That's all there is to it."

Katherine dropped her hands away. "It's such a long season. Let someone take over now."

"Now, Katherine, there really isn't much time remaining in this season. A little over a month, and I'll be all through. Forever. You can wait that long. I've been waiting forty-five years to win the Finals, and this summer I really believe we can do it." Murphy tapped his index finger against the table. "This team might be my very best. And Father, Egg, and I are the best coaches we've ever been."

Katherine laughed. "You're three silly old men!"

"No," Murphy said solemnly. "Everything is right for this summer. We really will win this thing."

Katherine shook her head. "All right, then. I know you won't stop for me. Go ahead and do what you have to do. But this season has to be the last."

Murphy nodded, and Katherine began to believe it really might be his last season.

"What will poor Father and Egg do?" she asked.

"The bishop has been after Father to retire for some time. There's a nursing home in Sioux City where he could stay and say Mass. Someone there could keep an eye on him. Sooner or later, he'll have to go there, whether he wants to or not. Might as well be now." Murphy gulped his coffee. "Egg is another one. It's not right for him to be living alone. Those two are set in their ways."

"Old men are stubborn," Katherine said.

"Well, it's not easy to start over," Murphy said.

"We'll help them. We'll all help each other. When will you break the news to Father and Egg?"

"Soon," Murphy said. "Before practice today."

"Are you going to Mass?"

"I probably should," Murphy said. "But I need to look over the field before practice today."

Katherine pressed, and tightened her apron as she stood up from the table. "Then I better start getting ready. Once you tell Father and Egg the news, everyone will be over." She strode back to the stove and lifted the top of the coffeepot. "I'll have to make more coffee and get food for tonight."

Murphy waved both hands for Katherine to sit down. She ignored him.

"What about you, Al? Are you nervous?"

"Not about retiring," Murphy said.

He picked up his newspaper again and turned to the back page of the sports section, which was called the *Peach*. He creased the paper until the high school baseball scores from the previous night were before him.

"I have to get this team prepared for the Finals."

Father John Ryan had slept uneasily during the night. After one long period of sleeplessness, he had even turned on the light and started reading from his Daily Office. Now, an hour before the daily Mass he officiated, he finished the readings, then shaved and bathed. Standing in front of his bathroom mirror, he combed thick milk-white hair straight back, showing slivers of pink scalp. He returned to the mirror a few minutes later, dressed in his priest's outfit, and sprinkled Old Spice aftershave lotion about his ears. He breathed in the aroma of nutmeg and lemon. It helped mask the subconscious essence of the holy smoke of incense Cottage Park associated with him. He took one long look into his eyes—a slow blink—then turned to go downstairs.

Though he was sure on his feet, he held onto the railing, traversing slowly and carefully down the wooden stairs. If he were to slip and fall, he would surely break a hip. He had visited too many peers in the hospital who had done that, then contracted pneumonia. Eventually, he had held their hands as he helped them pass from life to death, then officiated their funerals a few days later. That was not the way he planned to leave this world.

The solemn chime of Beethoven's "Ode to Joy" from his aging oak grandfather clock greeted him as he entered his dining room. He sidestepped around the dining room table, at which no one had eaten for several years, and headed directly to the timepiece. He began his day as he often did, by adjusting the weights and pulley to ensure its continuing life for at least another twenty-four hours.

The dining room table was covered with layers and layers of junk mail. Anything that didn't have a handwritten return address from someone he knew earned a spot on that table. The pile had been growing for years. Whenever an important letter had accidentally found its way into the mess, Ryan always proclaimed, "It has to be here someplace." Then he and a willing volunteer parishioner would look through the quagmire until they found it.

The townspeople of Cottage Park joked that maybe it was best he didn't read it. Many of the documents were from the Sioux City Diocese. For all anyone knew, his reassignment letters were probably somewhere in the paperwork maze. Most priests stayed at a location on average three to five years. Over the years, Ryan may have been reassigned many times without ever realizing it.

Another clock, this one a cuckoo, sang out for his attention from the kitchen. Ryan proceeded to the kitchen as the tiny yellow-feathered cuckoo bird retreated behind a closed door until its next scheduled appearance. He also wound that clock.

Though Ryan religiously wound the clocks and kept them in working order, he was chronically late for appointments and events. So much so that people always referred to "Ryan time" versus "McCarthy time." Like everyone else in Cottage Park, Ryan relied on Mrs. McCarthy's precise ringing of the bells to remind him of the correct time, where he needed to be, and what he should be doing at that time of the day.

"You'll be late for your own funeral!" an agitated Mrs. McCarthy would speak out whenever Ryan finally arrived to begin an event.

"I know," Ryan would say. Then he'd add a self-effacing retort that always amused those around him, even the eternally gruff Mrs. McCarthy: "And I'll probably somehow mess up the one-car procession that takes me to the cemetery."

Ryan turned away from the cuckoo clock, reached into the cupboard, and set a tall drinking glass on the table. He moved over to the sink, where a few supper dishes from the night before soaked in oily soap water. He scattered the dishes around. Then he reached for a broom and began sweeping the faded, worn linoleum, always sweeping around the chairs he encountered.

He looked behind the refrigerator and found a mousetrap that had sprung. It held a crooked dead mouse. Ryan opened the trap into the dustpan and then dumped the dustpan into the trash sack under the sink. He reset the trap with a dab of peanut butter and this time set it in front of the refrigerator, where he could easily see it.

Back at the table, he studied the glass for a few moments, then twisted it until his fingers whitened under the nails and darkened to a beet red at the tips. He looked for his own reflection in the glass but couldn't see it. He thrust the glass away to the middle of the table.

He thought, *What could one drink hurt? One little drink to get me operating.* After a few moments he convinced himself, got up, and trudged over to the liquor cabinet. Now the decision would be Scotch whisky or vodka.

He returned to the table with a bottle of vodka, unscrewed its cap, and emptied its contents into the glass. He studied the bottle, shook it to get the last few drops, capped it again before the fumes could reach him, and dropped the bottle into the trash can. Next Ryan collected a can of tomato juice and returned to his seat. He filled the glass with tomato juice and wedged it between his hands locked in prayer.

In Cottage Park, the measure of concern for whether one were an alcoholic was how much liquor he or she consumed and, to a lesser degree, how that drinking affected daily living skills and employment. For Ryan, the concern was not how much he drank but how often. Ryan began each morning with a drink or two before setting off to visit his parish families. He resumed again at lunch, then at dinner, and finally throughout the entire evening until he capped or threw away his bottles and went to bed.

Few in Cottage Park ever connected the dots of the drinks he accumulated and its impact on his health and behavior. For those who did worry about the kind but lonely old man, the concern was what might happen if he should ever stop drinking. Their consensus was that the withdrawal symptoms would kill him.

Despite his drinking, or perhaps because of it, the people of Cottage Park loved Ryan. He was a reliable and steady administer of the sacraments as well as the spiritual and corporal works of mercy. Ryan was a genuine spiritual father figure for his families. He baptized the children, gave them their First Communion, checked in on them at school each day, visited them when they were sick, heard their confessions, and confirmed them, married, and buried them. He was available at any time for any emergency—sometimes to pray for a faraway family member in a crisis situation, sometimes to anoint the sick or dying. Ryan would arrive at the scene offering wise counsel, thoughtful prayers, quick wit (when appropriate), and soothing reassurances that all would pass through the crisis and be strengthened by it. He was especially appreciated for saying Mass in less than forty minutes with sermons perhaps a mere two minutes in length.

Over his fifty-one-year tenure in Cottage Park, families understood that drinks would be served in return for Ryan's service. He had never declined this generosity at any time of the day. During these visits, he never imbibed alone. For those who were bedridden, Ryan already knew the location of the liquor cabinet and its likely contents. In addition to his role as priest, he was equally comfortable in being a bartender.

Each day, alcohol, or "spirits," orbited Ryan every three to four hours in different tumblers with ice. The spirits acted like IV bags that kept him relaxed, settled, and alive.

Ryan had no remorse for his drinking—though it did bother him immensely when he gave in and tippled before daily Mass. He mightily battled to abstain from consumption until after the holy sacrifice. More often than not, his failure to win that battle resulted in severe disappointment.

That battle already lost today, Ryan held the glass up to the light as if to toast himself and looked through it at a broken bloody rainbow. He sighed and brought the glass back to the table. He carefully tipped it and watched the liquid evenly coat its side. But before he could return the glass upright, he jolted it. The bloody mary spilled onto his fingers and from there onto the table in a dime-sized puddle.

Quickly he stood, cuffed the puddle into his palm, and carried it to the sink. He rinsed both hands and then wiped them carefully. He returned to his seat and his drink.

It was so quiet in the rectory, he could hear the grandfather clock tick-tocking from the living room. He clicked the glass with his fingernail in unison with the clock.

How long had he been living alone? Twenty-five years ago, he shared this house with another priest and a maid who took care of the cooking and cleaning. But the priest shortage required the departure of the other priest. And when the maid died, dwindling parish funds could not support the hiring of a replacement. That was ten years ago, and he'd been living alone ever since.

Out of the corner of his eye, he noticed a thin black mouse sneaking out of the space behind the refrigerator. It inched closer toward the trap, where it twitched its nose. Ryan lifted the glass to his lips, and the mouse, frightened by the movement, scampered back behind the refrigerator for safety. Ryan put the drink down and waited.

A few seconds later, the mouse was visible again—head darting in all directions, body crouched, inching toward the trap. Ryan felt the coolness of the glass against the warmth of his palms. The mouse stretched its head out over the trap for a closer look at the bait, then sat back on its hind legs and stared at Ryan. Satisfied that he posed no threat, the mouse leaned back over the trap, its nose nearly touching the peak of the peanut butter.

"Father?"

Ryan heard a voice outside the screen door at the back steps.

"Father Ryan?"

The mouse looked in the direction of the sound, then scampered between the refrigerator and the cupboard. In its wake, the trap sprang, making a loud clapping sound, and skidded off in the opposite direction.

"Coming," Ryan said. He poured the drink into the sink and turned on the water, watching it carry the contents down the drain. He marched quickly to the door.

He recognized Marty McKenna, one of his favorite players on the team. He hadn't seen McKenna since presiding at his father's funeral over a week ago. He motioned to McKenna.

"Come in and sit down. I'm finishing some dishes."

McKenna nodded and entered. "Good morning, Father," he said—as he had been brought up to say whenever addressing a priest.

"You're a little early for practice, aren't you?" Ryan asked.

"Mom and I came to Mass this morning," McKenna said. "She asked me to see if you needed an altar boy."

Ryan looked at his watch and spoke as he hurried from the rectory toward the nearby church.

"Yes. I can always use an altar boy." He looked back at McKenna and smiled. "I usually have Egg do the honors. He'll be able to take a break today."

As they found their way into the darkened church, Ryan looked for his friend Egg.

"No sign of my assistant," he said. "I hope everything is all right."

Ryan paused to think about where Egg could be—only an emergency would have prevented him from attending daily Mass.

Father Ryan was not the only one of the old men to have restless sleep. At 2:00 a.m., the primary subject of Ryan's worry, had also awoken in his La-Z-Boy rocker recliner. At that time, Egg opened his eyes and waited for them to clear.

Some people in Cottage Park knew that the name Egg was an abbreviation of his full name: Edwin Gerald Gallivan. However, more people thought the name was a description of his looks. Thin wisps of white hair were scattered over the freckled surface of an oval-shaped head. A long red-veined nose sagged like a beak between once-blue eyes, now gray with cataracts.

Egg sprung the chair from recline to rock. He yawned as he slowly recognized the room around him, his living room. Over the last several weeks, he had begun to sleep in the La-Z-Boy at night, always in his clothing, instead of climbing the stairs to his second-story bedroom.

Egg felt a cool breeze pass through the living room windows. He watched transparent white drapes hover parallel to the sill, then flutter and twist like snakes. Beneath the drapes, on the floor, were the broken shadows of the tree limbs that waved outside the windows. On his television set, a plaster statue of the Blessed Virgin glowed in the moonlight and hue of a broadcast test pattern.

Now fully awake, he smelled in the breeze the musky odor of earth, lawns, and green leaves. It seemed Egg were outside, making his daily walk. From across the alley, the clear, sharp bark of the Stanglers' collie broke the silence of Cottage Park. Then the higher, shrill bark of the McCarthys' terrier answered it.

Probably another raccoon in his garbage, Egg thought.

Egg was not alone. Across the street, his neighbor, Brigid Jensen—or Aunt B, as Egg's children had nicknamed her—was also a poor sleeper. A few years his senior, she kept a close watch on him now, as always, monitoring Egg's every movement and behavior.

Whatever bothered the dogs also bothered Egg. He reached for the potato-sized billfold in the back of his pants and quickly glanced out the window, fully expecting to surprise a burglar face to face. Though he would have had a better chance of being gored by a northern white rhinoceros in his living room than being burglarized in Cottage Park, Egg had recently begun to fear just such an intrusive theft.

Seeing no one, he stepped quickly to his secret hiding spot: the long flat drawer of an oaken china cabinet. He carefully placed his billfold between the folds of a treasured Irish linen tablecloth.

Aunt B studied his clandestine movement and smiled to herself. Though Egg always hid his precious items in that drawer, he never remembered the next day where to find them. That was her job.

From the coat closet near the front door, a cricket began to chirp. Egg walked in that direction and turned on the hallway light. Though the chirping stopped, Egg could see the cricket frantically trying to get traction on wooden flooring and escape with its life. Egg moved toward the cricket, which he could now see outside the closet door. But the cricket jumped and crawled away before he could reach it.

The cricket stayed quiet while Egg looked for it. And it remained quiet while Egg returned to the La-Z-Boy, reclined into sleep position, and arranged a light blanket over himself. Then the chirping began again.

"Hey!" Egg roared. "Quiet!"

It was no use. The cricket continued despite Egg's rant.

Egg was too upset to sleep now. He turned on the radio next to his lamp to drown out the noise from the bothersome insect. After a few moments, he turned the dial to find some baseball scores. There weren't any. Only a talk show from Des Moines. He stopped and listened.

"Hello," the host said, "on this beautiful Iowa night in June. I see we have a caller from Nemaha, Iowa. What would you like to talk about?"

"Hello," the caller said. "Are you talking to me?"

"I am, sir. And if you turn down your radio, you'll be able to hear me the first time. We're getting some feedback—"

"Hello? I'm still not connecting . . ."

"That's because you have to turn your radio down in order for us to talk . . . There you go. Now, what's on your mind?"

"I want to talk to the man who called in about an hour ago—the, uh, fellow who told how he made floating candles and gave them away as Christmas presents. I'd like to ask him if vegetable oil can be substituted for the other chemical he mentioned."

"I'll take your number. If the gentleman is still listening, he can call in now and either answer that question or call you sometime tomorrow. Okay? Next caller . . ."

Egg turned off the radio, launched himself from the La-Z-Boy again, and plodded back to the china cabinet. There he picked up and studied a picture of his nine living children, all married with children. A few of his children had grandchildren, making Egg a great-grandfather, but something of a remote one, as his grandchildren had moved far away from Cottage Park. He calculated the time for each of his children spread across each time zone of the country. All of his family had moved away from Iowa years ago, leaving Egg alone with their mother—his wife, Rose—until her death.

Egg hadn't noticed, nor had nearly any of the men of his age in Cottage Park, that their wives had mothered them almost from the day they were married. Rose told him when to go to bed, when to get up, whether to shave and shower, what to wear, what to eat and how much, what he would work on that day, and what to say when visiting with friends and family. Periodically she threw out his shoes (sometimes creatively held together by duct tape) and other worn clothing, despite Egg's desperate explanations of why each item needed to be preserved and saved.

But in every situation, Egg dutifully responded to each of her commands. Occasionally he hesitated, hoping she might change her mind. In those instances, all it took was one stern look over the top of Rose's glasses, and Egg would scurry to comply with her wishes.

Since Rose had passed away, Egg made each and every choice for himself—in ways that made perfect sense to him, to any other man his age, or to any other man who was unmarried or uninterested in securing a mate. Unfortunately these decisions often dismayed and sometimes horrified those who loved him the most—his children.

Almost the moment their mother passed away, each of Egg's children were deeply and dramatically concerned for their father. They called him daily and visited him frequently. With so many children and grandchildren, it seemed the phone calls inquiring about Egg's health and safety came almost hourly. Often his children let their own children stay behind and spend a few days of extended time with their grandfather. However, these visits and extended stays heightened their concerns and anxieties.

In April, seven of his children returned to Cottage Park and convened a family meeting to share their concerns directly with their father and, of course, to propose their solution.

One by one, each of Egg's children—sometimes between tears—read from a checklist of factors regarding whether he could or should maintain his home in Cottage Park. To a person, each of his children had reached the conclusion that Egg could no longer:

1. Live alone. On the rare occasions Egg prepared a meal for himself, his children were fearful he would forget to turn off the oven or burner.

2. Maintain such a large home with such a large lawn. It was only a matter of time before he tumbled down the stairs and broke a hip.

3. Care for himself: clean, groom, clothe, or feed himself. He did these tasks when he felt like it. And more often than not, he didn't feel like it. Specifically it bothered the children that their father sometimes smelled of urine. And it bothered them even more that they didn't know how to approach him about the matter. They found solace only in the fact that all men their father's age in Cottage Park seemed to have some variation of offensive body odor.

4. Remember to take his growing list of medications.

5. Make rational decisions about spending his money. His children accused him of being a Depression-era hobo who ate cold baked beans directly out of a can. They had frequently lectured and scolded him to spend his money on nice food and clothing—after all, he had the money and deserved it! But it was all to no avail.

6. Keep himself busy and entertained. His children thought he would be lonely, especially after the baseball season ended.

7. Be trusted to manage his anger. His children noticed that he became frustrated more easily and needed to be reminded to slow down and catch his breath. They knew that frustration could quickly fester into agitation and sometimes even rage, which could frighten or be interpreted as a threat to others.

When they had finished, Egg's oldest daughter presented him with a packet of information from a Catholic senior-living community in Spencer, Iowa. It had daily Mass and rosary, men's activities, three wonderful meals a day, and a two-bedroom apartment they were certain he would enjoy. Egg leafed through the colorful packet, took a deep breath, then set it down on a coffee table.

"What do you think?" his eldest daughter asked hopefully.

"I think," Egg said, "I would now like everyone to leave except for you four boys—I'll meet you out in the backyard in five minutes for a good old-fashioned fistfight."

While his children laughed, groaned, and cried, Egg led everyone to the front door and held it open wide while motioning for all to leave. Despite their pleas to continue the conversation, Egg shook his head and politely thanked each one of them as they departed.

When they were all milling around their cars, Egg shouted out, "I'd been saving my money to leave you for an inheritance . . . now that money will be given directly to your children!"

With that he stormed back in his home and slammed the door.

It wasn't until the next day that Egg noticed his children had taken his car—a 1971 midnight-blue Pontiac Bonneville. Egg had coddled and babied that car since he bought it new, washing and waxing it once a week and placing a plastic sheet over it in the garage so not even dust would fall on it. Egg had done all the routine maintenance himself. The engine was as clean and well cared for as the day he had driven it off the lot. The Bonneville was his pride and joy—and more importantly his freedom to go wherever he chose, whenever.

Egg called his oldest son and bitterly announced that all his children were banned from his home and property until the car was returned. That was over two months ago. Neither the car nor his children had returned.

Egg travelled over to the closet. The cricket stopped momentarily while he reached up to a shelf and brought down a cigar box—a gift from his father when Egg returned from France at the end of World War I. Egg brought the box back to the La-Z-Boy, plopped down in it, and looked inside at the World War I mementos Rose had saved.

He first rubbed cold foreign silver coins between his fingers, then balanced them in each palm until the weights were equal. Egg stacked the coins back in the box. He felt the paper currency, which was now more like skin than paper. He looked at other coins he had collected: silver dollars, Kennedy fifty-cent pieces, a 1957 plastic-wrapped collection from the Treasury Department in Philadelphia, and a one-dollar silver certificate that looked like a large one-dollar bill.

Carefully he unfolded brittle yellowed *Stars and Stripes* newspapers. He read and reread the articles, often nodding in agreement. Then he looked at the army medals he had earned, and finally he looked at loose pictures of Rose and him around the time he had returned from France.

There were also letters Egg had written to Rose during the war. She had kept them all. She had even kept the army pencils Egg had brought back from France. Egg opened a letter and tried to read the dimmed and blurred penciled words on yellowed paper. However, too many of the words had disappeared over the years. Frustrated, Egg collected the letters and placed them back in the box. He sighed and then cursed himself for not keeping the letters she had sent him.

Rose had also archived several years' worth of newspaper clippings related to the Holy Trinity baseball team—including the years when he had coached his own six boys. Rose had always underlined any mention of her sons or Egg, and occasionally she added her own notes of interest or humor in the margins. She had continued this practice long after the last of their sons had graduated.

Egg began to whistle, something he had often done in the company of Rose and his children. He now mostly whistled by himself: show tunes from classic movies, usually starring Bing Crosby; theatrical plays; and country and western songs by his favorite singer, Eddy Arnold. Egg had been raised on a farm, farmed with his brother for a short time as a young man, and now several decades later still fancied himself a cowboy. He launched into "Cattle Call" by Eddy Arnold.

Egg looked at one team photo from 1958, a team that had finished second in the state championship, losing the final game in extra innings. He stopped whistling. There was his son, Denny, the right fielder.

Egg had prayed to forget the painful memories of his life, especially those of his son. By a cruel twist of fate, he was losing his memory about everything except Denny. That memory, in fact, had been getting stronger than ever over the last few months.

Egg put the picture and the articles back in the box, then sat the box on the floor. He began to cry, gently at first, but then he sobbed.

After a few minutes, he stopped. He decided he should do something more productive and perhaps less selfish with his time. Egg pulled a pocket notebook from his front shirt pocket, then grabbed a black Bic pen. He began to fill the pages of the notebook with his beliefs regarding life and death:

> *I suppose that as I get closer to my own death, the subject of ghosts and giving up the ghost is the most logical way to start my treatise on life and death. To my way of thinking, giving up the ghost occurs at the exact moment of death. At that time, one or more of your trusted friends or family who have already given up the ghost will appear before and around you. They will guide you back to your real home, which is what I call heaven. Rapture doesn't begin to explain the feeling of being reunited again with God. Everyone—I repeat, every single individual—is welcomed back home to heaven unconditionally. No strings attached.*
>
> *I still believe God gives us the gift of free choice even after our death. Meaning, you can go directly to heaven to experience rapture or you can stay behind as a ghost. There are two kinds of ghosts: regular ghosts and holy ghosts.*
>
> *Regular ghosts continue right on with their prejudices, greed, and or whatever else separated them from their families and friends and God during their lifetime. Instead of resting in eternal bliss, they choose to wander the earth, sulking, seeking seclusion as far from human contact as possible, often in the farthest, deepest depths of the ocean or the darkest regions of never-discovered caves. Fully withdrawn*

from contact with any other being, these poor ghosts spend every second of every minute of their miserable existence mulling over what could have or should have been done for them during their short sojourn on earth. Think of the leaves blowing from the trees on a windy day in October—that's how many ghosts choose to stay behind and wallow in their misery rather than join God.

I say it's fair to call this freely chosen time away from God as hell, with the understanding that it isn't eternal and it's only as uncomfortable as they make it. In this kind of hell, there is no fire and brimstone or horned creatures jumping about in a frantic effort for you to join them. The expression "misery loves company" doesn't hold true for these creatures who revel in their utter isolation. You have nothing to ever fear from them.

A holy ghost also chooses to postpone rapture but instead stays near or around loved ones in order to watch over them. I believe holy ghosts are extremely rare. I know my son, Denny Gallivan, is a holy ghost. He is with me at all times—with me now as I write these words. I can just feel him. No one can convince me otherwise. I call Denny a holy ghost because he has sacrificed eternal joy to be with me in my sometimes-maddening frustration of struggle and suffering on earth. I'm certain Denny will be there at the hour of my death and that he will make sure I find my way to heaven. I hope he understands how much I appreciate his support. Maybe this letter will help show him my gratefulness.

I am not afraid to die. I'm looking forward to it. Whoever finds this should know I believe God is a woman. I visualize her like my grandmother Tara, very kind and patient. I know God will be happy to have me back in heaven. My life has been very good; my death will even be better.

> *Sincerely,*
> *Egg Gallivan*
> *Cottage Park, Iowa*
> *May, 1974*

When he finished writing, Egg placed the notebook and pen back in his shirt pocket, turned off the lamp, rubbed the heels of his palms against his eyes, and massaged his scalp with his fingertips. He yawned through his tears and once more prayed for his memory to leave him.

Egg started an Act of Contrition, but his mind wandered. He began to recite a hodgepodge of prayers, including the Hail Mary, Our Father, and Apostles' Creed. He never finished any prayer.

Soon his feet drooped sideways. His mouth opened wide, and his breathing became louder. His hands, mingled together on his chest, raised and lowered with each breath.

Outside, the barking stopped. Egg listened to the wind blowing through the trees and the creaking of tree limbs. The wind shifted, and the sound of the grain elevator on the north side of town quietly rumbled through the window. A few moments later, everything was quiet again. The last sounds Egg heard that very early morning were of silence.

A few hours later, Egg awoke again to birds chirping in his backyard. Outside, a rose-colored sun began its rise in a creamy-blue horizon. The air was cool and moist.

Egg awoke at this time each day and followed the same schedule. He began by washing his hands and face, then he shaved and straightened or spot-washed the clothing he wore. Next, he prepared the coffee that would not be drunk until after daily Mass, and he sat at the table to read the *Des Moines Register*.

After a few minutes, Egg closed the newspaper and heaved from the table. He fashioned his Holy Trinity baseball cap down over his head and stepped out the back door. Outside, he breathed deeply and smelled the sweet fragrance of the peonies that grew along the house and the strong, refreshing fragrance of the evergreens that stood like doormen in front of the house. Robins hopped across his front lawn, stopping and cocking their heads as if listening, then jerking night crawlers from the dew-capped grass. A squirrel clucked at Egg from a tree above, and a blue jay squawked a warning at a crow across the street.

Egg had the biggest house in the neighborhood—a Victorian model built in the 1920s, two full stories high, with five bedrooms and a huge cavernous basement. His home was also surrounded with lawns large enough to support simultaneous games of touch football, Wiffle ball, and volleyball. The backyard held a small garden and two fruit trees—one apple, the other cherry.

Most of Egg's neighbors were near his age. They vigilantly looked out for one another and their property. The neighbors' houses were smaller than Egg's. No two were alike in varying pale tints of white, yellow, pink, and blue. Almost all homes in Cottage Park featured shake siding made of a cement woven with asbestos fibers to resist wear and tear, termites, ants, and fire. To the contrary, however, Egg's home and garage were entirely wooden. Egg painted them a bright white and washed them regularly. As a result, the house and garage glowed like stars.

The neighborhood lawns, like Egg's, were fresh and full. People took pride in nurturing their grass, shrubs, flowers, and trees, which were mostly Dutch elm, oak, and maple. This pride for order and beauty bordered on envy. Competition between the neighbors was in effect twelve months of the year.

Egg saluted the American flag on the flagpole in his front yard, then started to make his way to church for daily Mass. Egg waved at Aunt B. She did not wave back but instead hurried over across the street to stop him. Her slight, frail body buffed up with the exhilaration of a big news scoop.

"Have you been out to your garage this morning?" she asked, catching her breath. Egg shook his head, so she continued. "Then you better get out there and look. Vandals got to it last night. It doesn't look good."

Aunt B followed Egg to the back of his garage, focusing entirely on Egg's reaction, which she would report verbatim to his children throughout the day. There on the large south wall in black spray paint were letters six feet high and two feet wide that spelled the expression, Die the Amerigun Way.

"God—" Egg said, his anger bursting as his face deeply reddened and also appeared ready to burst.

A number of choice curse words flashed across Egg's mind. Words he had learned sixty years ago from fellow soldiers fighting in France. He then remembered Aunt B's presence. He suspected she was one of the many spies in Cottage Park who reported worrisome stories about Egg to alarm his children. After a moment's hesitation and mental redirection, Egg softened the anger in his voice and forced a weak smile.

"God bless these teenaged kids around here!"

He slowly read the words out loud and nudged his hat up over his head.

"I don't understand this. Do you? Why would they pick on me to put up this sort of garbage?"

"It's not you," Aunt B said. "You probably got picked at random. We'll eventually find out who did it. The kids probably know. Cottage Park is so small, we all know each other's business."

Egg sighed. "I'll have to paint over it. I'll probably have to paint the whole garage to make it look good again. And I'll have to get a start on it today." Egg took off his cap and rubbed fingertips through his hair. He looked over at Brigid. "Well, now I'm late for Mass. Father Ryan will be worried about me."

"You go to Mass," Brigid said. She reached out and touched the dry spray paint, then smelled her fingers. "And pray for the souls of the little devils who did this."

"I'll do that," Egg said, retreating from Brigid to resume his trek toward church. "And you pray for my soul if I ever find out who did this."

— CHAPTER THREE —

Countdown to the Finals: 51 Days to Go

T. J.'S MOTHER WASN'T THE ONLY ONE who believed Cottage Park Memorial Field was the finest ballpark in the state. Many agreed. To Murphy, Ryan, and Egg, it was the finest ballpark anywhere.

White gravel bordered the dark-green wood planks that stood like eight-foot sentries around the ballpark. This fence kept all unwelcome, nonpaying visitors from entering the ground dedicated to the youths who had sacrificed their lives in armed conflict for the United States. But the fence and the labyrinth of wire mesh and cloth nets protecting the wooden bleachers behind home plate did not stop unwelcome visitors from leaving the ballpark. That is, foul balls regularly dented cars and shattered windshields. In a few instances, individuals who looked upward after a "Heads!" warning were subjected to the same fate as unlucky batters who faced a wild or irritated fastball pitcher.

Freshly powdered white chalk outlined the black rectangles of the batter's boxes around home plate. This black mixture, which looked so much like the fertile fields and gardens of Cottage Park, was actually a combination of dirt, sand, and gravel. The proper blend allowed a showering of rain without an ensuing mud bath. A similar barren garden isolated the pitcher's mound and second base.

First, second, and third bases fluffed up like overstuffed feather pillows along the runner's path. The path was the width of a sidewalk and extended in length from home plate to the dark-green planks that made up the fence 380 feet away in left and right fields. Chalked lines bisected each path from home plate to the white painted lines running up the fence, over the wooden scoreboard, and then unseen into infinity, forever marking foul territory.

Thick green grass grew in planned areas. Ryan, Murphy, and Egg nurtured it daily—their care and shaping like that of a manicurist for her most valued client. In the morning, the grass stood tall, clean, and shiny with dew. Intermingled in the hearty dry smell of soil were the musky odor of moisture and worms and the elusive, delicate fragrance of grass, which was heavily scented with the promise of both youth and eternity.

Fifteen feet over the right field fence, the American flag spiraled up and down, never coming to a full rest between nudging breezes. Behind the flag, five dull silver grain silos buffered endless acres of neat rows of green corn stalks. Almost ankle high, the stalks shivered and glistened in the morning sun.

The Holy Trinity dugout was along the third-base line. It was a simple two-step-down concrete shelter backed by wooden boards and covered in the front with wire mesh. A slanted roof provided relief during the occasional times when rain fell during a game. Inside the dugout, four long wooden benches seated nearly all seventeen players. However, many of the players chose not to sit on the benches but rather on the steps.

Today, Murphy sat by himself on the bench, leafing through the pages of the scorer's book and letting the recorded data from the last game show him patterns of his team's strengths and weaknesses. In the corner of the dugout, a cracked white porcelain fountain the size of a breakfast bowl bubbled water continuously. Murphy reached over and sipped the cool, sweet water.

When he heard others enter the ballpark, he set down the scorebook and waited. McKenna, Ryan, and Egg stepped through the gate onto the playing field.

Murphy studied McKenna as the trio descended into the dugout. He was always a quiet boy and a loner by choice. The death of his father had been especially grueling on McKenna. His hair had been newly cut. It was short and uneven. Wild strands spiked like shards of glass. Murphy guessed McKenna himself had done it. Dark bags shadowed the boy's sunken eyes and cast a dull stain of bloodshot.

The three old men were so comfortable with each other that they often eschewed greetings, as if their last encounters had been a few moments ago. The three were comfortable, then, with the long silence that often initiated their resumed encounters. McKenna was also aware of and comfortable with the silence. As he waited for one of the old men to speak, he focused on the gurgling sound of the fountain.

Finally Murphy broke the silence. He glanced at McKenna, then looked out into right field. "Are you ready to come back?"

McKenna sighed.

"Your father was a good baseball player," Murphy said, breaking a long silence.

"One of the best," Ryan said.

"Never saw a pitch he didn't like," Egg added.

The old men stared at and spoke to the field.

"That's true," Murphy said. "You use a lot better judgment than your dad did at the plate. Don't you think?" He looked sidelong at McKenna, in as close to a direct address as he could manage.

"I guess," McKenna said.

It was not the answer Murphy expected, mostly because it wasn't an answer. The old men lived in a black-and-white world of yes and no. McKenna's gray response called them to the cool, dark water of emotions they couldn't swim.

The old men waited in silence in hopes that McKenna would provide some clarification. When it became clear no further elaboration would be forthcoming, Murphy directed the conversation to waters in which the old men felt more confident: Holy Trinity Baseball. Ryan and Egg deftly followed Murphy's lead.

Murphy said, "We got Emmetsburg coming to town tomorrow night."

"I saw they got beat by Storm Lake St. Mary's," Egg said.

"I thought they were supposed to be tough this year," Ryan said.

"They are," Murphy said. He lugged a ball of keys from his pocket. "Marty, will you go get the equipment bag?"

He tossed the keys to McKenna and then watched the tall right fielder depart toward the equipment room underneath the bleachers. He then looked at Ryan. Now he had to ensure the old men's emotional helplessness was not exposed. Again, Ryan and Egg knew just what to do in such a situation.

"He's going to be all right," Murphy said with false bravado.

Ryan nodded. "I'll be talking to his mother," he said. "I'll keep an eye on him this season. I'm going out to visit Mom and the kids at the farm. It looks like Marty is completely taking over everything his father did."

"Those McKennas are a tough people," Egg said. "They'll come through this like they've come through every other problem they've dealt with."

The old men reflected on those problems and the wisdom in Egg's remark. He was right. The McKennas, like nearly all the families in Cottage Park, seemed to face each crisis with determined diligence and dignity. Over time, they'd overcome the crisis—and about that time, another one would take its place.

They were quiet again by the time McKenna returned with a duffel bag of bats and balls. He set the bag down at their feet, then turned it upside down. Bats cracking against each other sounded like the sweet melody of a xylophone. Baseballs and a catcher's mitt thudded a closing beat.

Ryan nodded over at Egg and said, "Egg was late to Mass today. I waited as long as I could and finally had to start Mass without him. Apparently he had some sort of artist over to his garage last night." He chuckled as Egg chewed his bottom lip in anger.

"Some little snot-nosed son of"—Egg looked at McKenna, who squashed a quick completely involuntary smile, then checked himself— "spray-painted the south side of my garage. Made a big mess. Now I'll probably have to repaint the whole garage."

"That's a rotten deal," Murphy said. "Probably somebody driving through from out of town. What did they write?"

"I can't figure it out," Egg said bitterly. "They wrote, Die the Amerigun Way."

Again, McKenna huffed back a laugh and quickly turned from the old men.

"That sounds more like one of those crazy cults," Murphy said. "Or somebody who was high on dope. You don't think it's some sort of threat, do you?"

Egg shook his head. "No. I think you're right. It's somebody driving through town who picked out my house by chance."

More players arrived. They spoke to the coaches, nodded at McKenna, who eventually joined them as they took their place along the sidelines, and paired off to play catch. The players were dressed like McKenna, in blue jeans and T-shirts. All wore black steel-cleat shoes and Holy Trinity baseball caps. After fifteen minutes of catch, Egg and Ryan counted the number of players at seventeen and signaled to Murphy that the entire team was present.

Murphy looked at his watch, then spoke to Ryan and Egg. "Everyone is here and on time. Even Moriarity. Speaking of, I have a hankering to work with our budding superstar this morning," he lamented. "Wish me luck."

Egg and Ryan grimaced as if each were simultaneously passing a kidney stone.

"Father, will you hit infield today?" Murphy asked.

Ryan nodded. Ryan always hit infield, but Murphy never failed the courtesy of asking.

"We need a good, strong practice." Murphy reached down, picked up a pebble, and put it in his pocket. "Oh, and I'll let you know first—I'm retiring."

Egg's and Ryan's eyes met and locked for a full two seconds. During that time, they silently communicated to each other.

Retiring? He didn't say the word retiring, *did he?*

No possible way. He'll never retire. Motivational ploy.

Play along.

"When?" Egg said out loud, without any expression or emotion.

"Ah . . ." Murphy began. "Probably at the end of the Finals. Or should I say when we win the Finals?"

"Well," Ryan said, "I'm not sure whether to believe you. But if you do really retire, then it's time." He shook Murphy's hand. "Congratulations on a distinguished career."

"You're the best high school baseball coach in the country," Egg said, "and it's been an honor to work with you." Egg also shook Murphy's hand. "But I don't believe you either. You say this every three to five years or so." He paused. "Unless there's something we don't know about. Are you getting out for Katherine?"

Murphy pondered the thought. "I know she's happy about me leaving, but that's only one part of the decision. I think it's best for me to move on—best for the team, the town, everybody."

Ryan looked at Egg, then looked back at Murphy. "If you leave, then we're leaving with you. We've always said that when you go, we go."

"All right, then," Murphy replied. "We'll tell these boys at the end of today's practice."

Murphy looked up at the sun through the cracks between his fingers, using that gesture to wipe the beginning of a tear in his eye.

"We've babbled on about this long enough. None of us is going anywhere until the end of the season, so let's get out there and teach these boys how to play baseball. This is it, gentlemen. This is our last chance to get the job done."

Murphy walked away from them for home plate, where he raised his right arm. Ryan and Egg followed behind. The slapping, booming sound of baseballs against gloves quickly stopped, and the boys gathered around Murphy. Suddenly it was quiet except for the nervous chirping of sparrows in the support rafters in the bleachers behind home plate.

"We'll go for about an hour and a half today," Murphy said. "We'll spend about forty minutes or so on fielding and the rest of the time on batting. We're hitting the ball well this year. I was looking over the last game against Granville-Spalding, and we had sixteen hits, which is very good."

Murphy took a deep breath and unbuttoned the top snap on his black Holy Trinity windbreaker.

"Today we'll look at everyone's follow-through, or how you follow through on every motion when you throw or bat." Murphy pretended to throw a ball in slow motion to greatly exaggerate his message. "Some of you guys watch the pros and think that because they flip and jerk the ball around—and do all sorts of other things wrong—that you can do it too. Well, we won't let you do that."

Murphy pointed to right field, and Egg called for the outfielders to join him there.

Ryan picked up a bat, stood at home plate, and prepared to hit ground balls to the infielders. Occasionally he directed an infielder to an exact location by merely pointing his fungo bat. When the infielders were set, Ryan stepped to the plate and tossed himself a ball that he tapped on the ground to Jeff, the third baseman.

As Jeff reached down to scoop up the ball, it took a bad bounce and skidded between his legs. Ryan repeated the procedure again, and this time Jeff charged in, caught the ball, and fired it back to the catcher.

Murphy stood at the warm-up pitching mound immediately behind his best pitcher, Pat Moriarity, a junior.

Moriarity was six feet seven inches tall—and still growing. He was easily the tallest and skinniest player on the team. His clothes hung baggily on him. His teeth were crowded, yellowed, crooked, and chipped, and a few hung like fangs from his gums. He showed them all in the frequent times he smiled and laughed. Freckles covered his face so densely that it looked like he had a well-browned summer tan. Rashes of pimples dotted his cheeks and chin. Bright, lively green eyes lit up his face like a happy jack-o'-lantern.

Long red hair hung like tangled vines midway down his neck. The hair hugely irritated the old men, who frequently offered to pay for his haircut. On one occasion before a game, an angry Egg actually chased Moriarity with scissors. Given the opportunity, he would have cut off the flowing tresses. But Moriarity laughed it off, as he laughed off nearly everything anyone said or did to make him more presentable.

Moriarity was the only young person in Cottage Park who did whatever he wanted whenever he wanted. His behavior was never defiant, but more like a gentle breeze that came and skittered away on its own terms. The trick was capturing that breeze and harnessing its power.

Throughout the years, nearly every adult in Cottage Park had had some kind of opinion about what to do with Moriarity and had employed a strategy of some sort to grab onto that breeze. Invariably, they had all come up empty-handed. No one was more exasperated by the futility of capturing, motivating, and molding that breeze than those who loved him the most, those who thought they knew him best: his parents, his teachers, and the old men whose faces were currently so stretched and distorted that they might snap and break.

Murphy may have understood Moriarity the best, having closely studied, monitored, and mentored him since his very first day of kindergarten. On that day, Murphy had been passing through the elementary-school hallway at Holy Trinity when he came across Moriarity, inconsolable and wrestling in the arms of his father. Murphy recognized the pair. Moriarity's father had been his star player. And Murphy had seen the father and son struggle frequently in Mass, with the father eventually picking up the son and lugging him outside until he came to peace. More often than not, the two ended up outside the church for the rest of the service.

"Coach," Moriarity's father had said that day. He turned and faced his son toward Murphy. "I'm late for work. Is there any way you could drop him off into his kindergarten class?"

Before Murphy could reply, the younger Moriarity was thrust at him. In one quick movement, the father dodged his son's desperate lunge and disappeared down the hall.

Alone, Moriarity turned and ran toward and into Murphy, burying his face into Murphy's rib cage and holding him with both arms with such vise-like intensity that Murphy feared he was being suffocated. Murphy grabbed Moriarity in turn, more to keep his balance, and the two stood there as other parents and their children detoured around them for their first day of school.

And that is where they stood for at least the next forty-five minutes. Murphy tried every trick he knew: reassuring words, songs, stories, gentle pats on the back. Nothing worked. He also tried to physically extricate himself from the boy. But even as a kindergartener, Moriarity was not much smaller than Murphy. The more Murphy squirmed to get away, the tighter Moriarity's grip intensified.

Murphy finally led Moriarity a few inches at a time, as if in a dance, until they entered the kindergarten room. Once there, the first-year teacher calmly and quietly encouraged Moriarity to join the other children. As she spoke, she gently but forcefully pried his fingers from Murphy, but Moriarity gripped even more intensely. It was no use.

"That's all that I can do," the teacher said almost shamefully to Murphy. "If you watch these students, I'll go call his mom. She'll have to come get him and take him home."

The teacher quickly stepped away toward the office. Murphy looked over the group of nearly twenty-five students sitting in their chairs. They weren't fidgeting as most children that age do. They were in awe of the scene before them. Murphy noticed immediately that Moriarity was a full ten inches taller than anyone else in the class and was probably more the size of a fourth or fifth grader.

A few of the students were noticeably frightened as they watched Murphy's struggle to shift and get comfortable inside Moriarity's embrace. To comfort the students, Murphy told them he was also a teacher and that they would learn a lot in kindergarten and in first grade, and on and on until he would see them in high school. He told them they would learn their colors and their numbers and all the things they would need to know in order to be successful in high school and college and beyond. All of that they would learn this year. Starting very soon, when their teacher returned.

"Do you have any questions for me?" Murphy asked as he finished his impromptu presentation.

Several hands shot up. One by one, each child inquired about Moriarity. What was he doing? Why was he holding Murphy like that? Was he really in kindergarten with them? When would he let go of Murphy? What would Murphy do about him?

What would he do about him? This last question would plague and dog Murphy throughout Moriarity's passage through Holy Trinity. From their very first day together, Moriarity was and would always be Murphy's problem—his responsibility.

"Pat's mother can't come and get him," the kindergarten teacher said as she hustled back into the room. "She has little ones at home. But . . ." she continued as she looked across the room and spotted a soft rubber ball in the play area. She retrieved the ball and came over and knelt beside Moriarity. "Pat's mom told me he's a baseball player, and that if we asked him he could show Coach Murphy how he can pitch. Well, Pat," the teacher continued dramatically, "let's see what you've got."

As Moriarity gazed at the ball in her hands, the teacher looked up at Murphy and rolled her eyes as if to say, *Can you believe what I have to do to work with these kids?* She loosened a few of Moriarity's fingers, and this time he let go of Murphy and grabbed onto the ball.

"Back up," Moriarity told Murphy as he stretched and wound up his arm.

He motioned for Murphy to continue backward until he was in the doorway. Murphy followed Moriarity's commands, and once at the doorway, slowly lowered himself into a catcher's squat. Moriarity had also backed up as far as he possibly could, almost up against the window.

He looked at his classmates and said, "Watch this."

Then he nodded at his teacher and started into a full pitcher's windup.

Murphy was not at all prepared for the velocity of the ball that hurtled toward him. The ball clipped him in the shoulder and bounced back into the classroom as the students squealed with laughter.

Six boys—his future teammates, as it would turn out—scrambled for the ball, fighting for it until one, Sean Powers, snatched it away. In an instant, they burst from their desks to line up behind Moriarity, all breathlessly boasting of their baseball prowess and shouting out, "I'm next!"

Moriarity smiled at Murphy, and politely stepped back to take his place at the end of the line.

However, by this time, the teacher's painstakingly detailed lesson plan for a dynamic first day of school had been derailed—as had her patience for the students who had chosen baseball over shapes and colors. There would be no more baseball or any mention of baseball for the rest of that day. She ordered the boys—including and especially Moriarity, who had now earned the seat closest to her—to sit down.

All complied immediately except Moriarity, who lingered at the window, watching Murphy. Moriarity hitched a sad smile and forced a wave much more of welcome than good-bye.

Though Murphy had to physically leave Moriarity that morning, he vowed, right then, that he would never emotionally separate himself from the boy as long as he lived. That moment, that day, seemed to have lasted forever, but the years had flown by. And today, like all the days before that, Murphy was still connected to and dealing with Moriarity.

Murphy watched Moriarity throw four windup pitches before stepping in front of him and asking for the ball.

"Here," Murphy said, edging Moriarity from the pitching rubber and taking his place. "Now watch this."

Murphy set himself as a pitcher and looked down at the catcher.

"I like the way you're setting up, and your pivot on the rubber is good, but you're not pushing off."

Murphy started a windup and followed through the entire motion, dramatically pushing away from the rubber at the very end.

"Did you see that?"

"Yeah, Coach," Moriarity said. "I saw you."

He took off his hat and parted a handful of his mane from his eyes. Satisfied with the mess, he jammed his cap back down and cocked it slightly to the right.

"But I've already been doing that," Moriarity added.

"No, Pat," Murphy said emphatically. "You have *not* been doing that, or I wouldn't have taken the time to bring this to your attention."

He handed the ball to Moriarity and stepped back off the pitching rubber.

"Let's see you try it."

Moriarity took a deep breath and stared down the pitching lane toward the catcher—his best friend, Sean Powers. Powers hunched into position and signaled for a fastball. Moriarity wound up and completed the motion with the requested fastball low and down the middle.

He looked at Murphy and smiled. "How's that, Coach?"

"It's not what I . . ." Murphy began, then abandoned. "Where's your strength?"

Moriarity tapped his right arm.

"Your *real* strength," Murphy said.

"I suppose it's my brain," Moriarity said seriously.

Murphy shook his head and motioned Moriarity off the rubber again. He took the ball and looked down at Powers as if he were taking a signal.

"Your strength comes from your butt," Murphy said, patting himself in that area. "And your upper legs. Use them! Otherwise we might as well put a chair out on the mound for you to sit on. Would you like that?"

Moriarity laughed. "No way."

Murphy handed the ball back to Moriarity, then knelt down on one knee to get a better look at Moriarity's follow-through.

Moriarity threw another strike. "Ah, there," he said.

"There nothing," Murphy said. "I don't care where you throw the ball—whether it's a strike or a ball. You're a big kid. Use your height. Don't just step off that rubber. Push it away! If you do that, you should be able to practically drop it in Powers's catching mitt. Right now, all you're doing is falling over." He sighed. "Have you ever been swimming at the pool?"

Moriarity laughed.

"Have you ever propelled off the side of the pool with your legs?" Murphy continued.

Moriarity nodded.

"Then do the same thing with this pitching rubber. Push off with all your might so that you kick this thing twenty feet into the outfield."

Moriarity shook his head and shrugged. "I'll try if you say so, Coach."

"Don't try," Murphy said as he stepped down from the mound and Moriarity resumed his place. "Come on—don't get me upset out here.

You're the one who has to be responsible for learning how to pitch. Let's go! Get your Irish up!"

Along the right field line, Egg hit short pop flies into center field for the outfielders to run in and catch and then throw back to the plate.

The group of eight outfielders had inched in from their original placement in center field—not so much with the idea of cheating on the distance they had to run to catch a ball, but for charitable reasons. They believed Egg couldn't place the ball where he had directed them to stand in deep center field.

"He can get it up, but he can't get it out," Spider said, causing the boys to break into laughter.

Egg dropped the fungo bat to his side and watched them. "None of you hot shots are using two hands!" he called out.

Then he turned to one of the younger players standing in as catcher. "It wouldn't be so funny if I gave them a good kick in the fanny," he muttered. "And I'll do it if they don't start playing baseball!"

Egg motioned for the catcher to follow him. They trekked out into the midst of the outfielders.

Egg dropped his bat to the ground and pretended to catch a ball. "After catching the ball, the most important thing is getting it out of your glove and into your relay man's glove. To do that right, you've got to have your throwing hand next to your glove. You guys who have been playing here for four years should know that by now. For God's sake, I've been telling you that since you were little kids. I would like to see you start setting a good example for the younger players who come to watch us play."

"All right, Egg," Spider said. "We get you."

"Good," Egg said. He picked up his bat and pointed it farther out into center field. "Now back up to the wall, and I'll hit you some line drives. Practice hitting the relay man. McKenna, that's you."

Egg and his catcher returned to their position along the right field line. He motioned for McKenna to stand halfway between him and the outfielders. McKenna obliged, but once again, the outfielders did not follow Egg's instructions. Egg cocked his bat on his shoulder and then looked at the catcher in disbelief.

"You'd think they'd at least have the common sense to realize they're standing too close to McKenna for him to be a relay man." Egg leaned the bat against his leg and cupped his hands. "Back up!"

The catcher also waved them back. The outfielders barely inched backward.

"Oh, well," Egg said as he flipped the ball up and cracked it off the bat.

The ball sailed three feet above Spider's outstretched glove. It clapped against the wooden fence—right where Egg had told them to stand—and rolled back several feet.

Father Ryan had hit several balls to each infielder when he held up two fingers and called out, "Take two."

Ryan hit a grounder that took a bad bounce into Jeff's shin and into foul territory. Jeff limped after it and picked it up. Ryan called for him to throw the ball back home. He did so, and another ball retraced the same path right at him.

As Jeff reached down to scoop up the ball, it again took a bad bounce and skidded up between his legs. He turned and watched the ball leave him behind, rolling out into left field.

"Let it go!" Ryan yelled out.

But it was hard for Jeff to let it go. He had no idea how to let it go. Ryan's well-intentioned counsel only caused him to dwell even more intensely on his failing. *You're too tall to be playing third base, too slow to react, too afraid of the ball . . .*

Though the hurtful words were in fact in Jeff's own voice, they could have easily come from any other player on the team. It was all true. Jeff really was slow and ponderous and error prone. Any number of his teammates riding the bench could have successfully made that play, but he stumbled and fumbled over it. Moreover, the teammates deserved the opportunity to have made that play. It wasn't fair that he was starting and they weren't.

But the last thing in the world the old men were was fair, especially when it came to matters of size. Jeff was six feet five, the second tallest player behind Moriarity. The old men, especially Murphy, were enamored with height and strength such as Jeff's. They knew it would pay off in the end. They would sacrifice that player's endless short-term mistakes for the team's eventual long-term glory, even—perhaps especially—if the player in question didn't like baseball and actually feared it.

Ryan would now hit ground balls forever, if necessary, at Jeff until he fielded one correctly. "Get down low," Ryan called out. He waited until Jeff crouched over low enough to his liking, then called out, "Now shift your feet!"

Ryan flipped the ball out and struck at it, driving it directly at Jeff, who snagged it and immediately fired it over to Orlowski at second. This time, Jeff breathed a huge sigh of relief. Done—until Ryan shot the ball around the horn at him again.

Ryan turned his attention next to Anthony at short. No one ever feared that Anthony might make an error, and no one ever questioned whether he deserved to be out there on the field. The Civilla-Orlowski double play tandem was one of the strongest combinations ever at Holy Trinity and certainly the strongest in the state of Iowa that season.

Ryan hit a hopper that Anthony chased down to his right, deep into the hole. In one yin-yang, flowing movement, he jumped high, fell backward, and adroitly threw it to Orlowski, who forwarded it on to first for what would have been a clean double play.

Even after they successfully completed a play, Ryan always hit two or three consecutive balls each to Anthony and Orlowski. Watching them together was one of the few perfect things in life. And the boys enjoyed performing together. The more difficult the play, the more graceful and artistic their dance became.

The two were best friends—the closest friends in a tightly knit senior class. Though spiritually connected on the field, they were as different as could be. Anthony's dark Italian skin stretched tightly across supple, piano-wire muscles. He quietly and effortlessly glided, sometimes stealthily, through Cottage Park in a desperate effort not to draw attention to himself.

Orlowski had bushy rust-colored hair and a moonlight complexion. Already in the morning sun, he had to be layered like an Arabian sheik. Still, the few uncovered areas, such as his face, were already turning cherry red. After fifteen to twenty minutes in direct sun, he would burn and blister. He had a beer belly—had it even before he started to drink beer. For years as a child, he had tried to rid himself of it. He finally gave up and accepted the belly and the loss of footspeed that came along with it. Though he was slower, Orlowski had more solid brute strength than Anthony. Now before a game, his belly was a pot of good luck. He laughed harder than anyone else when he allowed senior teammates to grab fistfuls of the flab or gently sink their fists into the roly-poly glob.

Where Anthony was serious, quiet, and often melancholic, Orlowski cared little for convention and immediately spoke his mind. Anthony played sports the same way he lived his life: rather than playing to win, he played as though not to lose. His meticulous grooming and reserved demeanor were frequently compared to that of a seminarian, doctor, or funeral director. Orlowski, on the other hand, knew that mistakes thrived on impulse, but he usually found that his good outweighed his bad. He was comfortable with who he was and his lot in life.

In addition to baseball the two had also paired together to make up the backcourt of the Holy Trinity basketball team. Orlowski often sought and set the ball up for Anthony, who at six feet two inches tall could dunk with the same artistry that he demonstrated on the baseball field.

Ryan hit a sharp ground ball directly up the middle. Anthony glided to it, and, without looking, backhanded it with his glove to an outstretched Orlowski. After such plays, Ryan wished he had a fresh way to acknowledge their fielding excellence. But whatever he could say, they had already heard in one shape or fashion before. So he simply paused and pointed at them as if to bless them, then he continued the infield practice.

Batting practice followed fielding practice, then Murphy directed the players into the dugout for a team meeting. Ryan and Egg shadowed a few feet behind Murphy, who stood in front of the team.

"I have a couple of announcements," Murphy said, "then we'll let you get out of here. Thursday night we play Armstrong. Meet at four o'clock in the school parking lot. If you're not here at that time, you might as well stay at home, because you won't play even if you do make it to Armstrong on your own. Any questions?"

Murphy looked over his players and then back at Ryan and Egg.

"The second announcement has to do with me. I'll be retiring as coach of the Holy Trinity baseball team at the end of this season. Egg and Father Ryan will leave with me.

"Great, Coach," Moriarity said.

He blushed as an awkward silence followed. The other players had surreptitiously glanced at Orlowski, the vocal leader of the team. He knew it was proper to reserve comment until Murphy concluded.

"At any rate," Murphy continued, "there are five seniors on this team who will be retiring at the end of this season, so Egg, Father Ryan, and I will retire with them. Now, I propose we all win our last game together before we leave. Is that a fair request?"

In unison, the boys said, "Yes!"

"That means winning the Finals. And then after that, the three of us old timers will come back to watch you younger guys keep winning it in the years to come."

Murphy again studied his team for reactions and then looked to his coaches, who nodded.

"Okay, then," Murphy said. "That's it for today." He motioned to the boys. "Get your rest," he said, his voice slightly breaking. "Let's all get ready to play baseball."

"You got it, Coach," Orlowski said.

His teammates waited until he stood up and lined up behind him to shake Murphy's hand and then Ryan's and Egg's.

— CHAPTER FOUR —

Countdown to the Finals: 51 Days to Go

Moriarity and Powers shoved open the huge wooden door at the entrance to Memorial Field and sauntered toward the Sinclair gas station on Main Street.

Powers was five inches shorter than Moriarity and almost as slender, although he didn't look nearly as gaunt as his taller friend. Powers's slight build made him something of a rarity behind the plate.

Powers preferred to play shortstop but could play any position on the field. Murphy asked him to catch because he believed a team's real strength was up the middle: the center fielder, shortstop, second baseman, pitcher, and catcher. With Powers catching, Murphy knew he would have one of the strongest combinations up the middle of any team he had ever coached. He also knew Powers could communicate and hopefully guide Moriarity through troublesome situations better than anyone else. Powers happily accepted the responsibility.

Powers took off his cap and wiped his forehead with the back of his arm, driving the sweat into his thick, curly black hair. Unlike the other players, he didn't have a band of white on his forehead or shoulders. Rather, he had a deep tan across his entire body because he was a lifeguard at the city pool. He wrung sweat from his arm and then watched it drop onto the dusty gravel parking lot.

"You really think we can win it all this summer?" Moriarity asked.

"There's no reason we shouldn't," Powers said. "We got talent, coaching, tradition, and fans. Nobody else has anything close." He nodded to himself. "Yeah, we're going to win it all this year. And I'll tell you something else: we'll be even better next year."

"Really? Without Murphy? What about when you and I and the other seniors are gone?" Moriarity asked.

"Someone else takes our place," Powers said. "These old guys built a system that can make winners out of anybody, even if they're not coaching themselves."

As they reached Sinclair's, Moriarity nuzzled the huge green plastic Dino the brontosaurus for good luck, then he carefully jumped over its long tail to the pop machine. He had performed this ritual ever since he was a little boy—as did all of Cottage Park's youth.

Powers followed suit in the exact same fashion. At the pop machine, he reached into his pocket and presented a collection of loose change.

"Good—we got enough for something to drink," he said. He dropped two quarters into the machine. "Pick your poison."

Moriarity selected an Orange Crush bottle out of the rack. Powers did the same. They continued their journey by crossing the street to Cottage Park's sole city park. The spot was a bit of a mystery. It was the only location in the community that had never been granted a formal name. And no one—not even the old-timers—seemed to know how or when it came to be filled with playground equipment.

They climbed the ancient, rusted jungle gym. At the very top, they stretched out over the steel bars, toasted each other, and looked across Cottage Park to the cornfields beyond. It was the perfect moment—except for the occasional horsefly that bit their ankles. Moriarity was skilled at clapping his hands at the pests and killing them on contact. He took out two of them, then the boys could finally relax and enjoy the moment.

"Do you remember what Sister Irenaeus said on the last day of accounting class?" Powers asked.

"She told me to turn in my missing assignments, or I wouldn't pass," Moriarity said. "I couldn't handle all those lines and boxes."

"When Sister gave us the final test, she said she was testing herself too."

"Yeah?" Moriarity asked.

"It means a teacher's success depends on how well the students do," Powers said. "I think Murphy believes his success will be measured by how kids play ten years from now, long after he's retired."

"God, I hated accounting," Moriarity said. "What a waste. I'll never use that junk."

"It's important stuff to know," Powers said. "You learned enough to know the discipline part of it. You'll never be a good businessman if you don't know the ropes."

"Nah," Moriarity said. "That's why God invented the yellow pages. I'm an idea man. That's what makes things in this country go."

"But ideas die if they don't fall into the right structure. You can have an idea for the greatest house in the world. But if you don't put up a structure to support it"—Powers tapped the steel bar his legs rested on—"it won't get started."

"You really think things won't change after Murphy leaves?" Moriarity asked.

"The important things won't," Powers said. "Kids will still learn good baseball, and Holy Trinity will still win. Murphy will make sure of that."

"I don't think Murphy likes me," Moriarity said. "He's always trying to change me."

Powers watched a cloud of doom cast its dark shadow over Moriarity's funny face. Other than Powers, few people knew how sensitive Moriarity was to people's comments and perceptions. Once injured, Moriarity could ball up and isolate himself from everyone until he thought it was safe to engage again. Powers often steered him clear of such hurt.

"He's *teaching* you," Powers said. "Everything he said today about your delivery makes sense. Now you have to do it."

"But it's all little things," Moriarity said. Powers started to shake his head in disagreement, but Moriarity continued. "No—listen to me. When I'm out on that mound, you can coach all day long. But in the end, it all boils down to me and the batter. It's a battle."

"Some of that is true," Powers said. "But it's more than you and the batter. You got eight other guys out on the field with you. You talk about battle? In the army, if you screw up, the whole platoon suffers—maybe even loses their lives. And that's what they drill into you at boot camp. Little things: make your bed the right way, polish your shoes, keep your rifle clean. You screw any of those up, and your whole platoon catches hell for it. Baseball is the same way. So much of it is mental with all the positioning, percentages, and technique."

"You can do those things for me," Moriarity said. "You're my brains."

"I am not your brains," Powers said. "You be your own brains."

Moriarity kicked his foot into the steel bars. "I try to think, and it never works out. Instead, I think what I feel." Moriarity took one last long drink to finish the pop, then belched and smiled. "Love that Orange Crush." He tossed the bottle on the sand at the bottom of the jungle gym.

"You just threw the nickel deposit away," Powers said.

"What's a nickel to us? That's gum money for the little kid who finds it and turns it in."

Powers finished his pop and dropped his bottle near Moriarity's.

"You ready to go?" Moriarity asked.

Powers nodded.

"Well, you're going down before I do!" Moriarity said.

Moriarity jerked Powers's shoulders forcefully until they slipped between the bars. Powers fell backward. Luckily, his legs hooked and locked onto the top bar, preventing him from falling on his head ten feet to the ground.

Moriarity stood at the top of the bars and beat his chest. "Today I'm the king of the mountain!"

"You crazy lamebrain!" Powers screamed in fright. "You could break my neck!" He frantically reached his hand toward Moriarity. "Help me up."

"I'll help you," Moriarity said as he clenched a fist and drove it into the muscles directly above Powers's knee. "There's a charley horse for you," he said with a laugh.

Powers howled. Despite the pain and fright, he began to laugh too. "I'll kill you! You're dead meat!"

Moriarity clumsily maneuvered through the bars to the shiny, slick fire pole. He slid gracefully down it until he reached the ground. Behind him, Powers lifted himself into an upright position and quickly scrambled down the bars to the ground.

Moriarity loped through the park as Powers raced after him. Normally Powers would have caught up to Moriarity with ease, but the pain from the charley horse attack caused him to limp.

After nearly a block, he finally caught up to Moriarity, who dropped his arms behind him to allow Powers to ride on his back, carrying him in more of an ostrich-back than horseback style. The two continued that way, laughing, until they stopped at Moriarity's home.

Mrs. Jones had been sitting in her car in Egg's driveway, crying, for nearly an hour. She had been driving to work when she first saw the graffiti on

Egg's garage. Immediately, she turned around and headed straight back home. First she called her supervisor to request an hour off. Next she had a discussion with her son. Then she got back in her car and drove straight to Egg's house, where she had been waiting ever since.

She was dressed in a blue business suit with a silk bow tie. She checked her watch and grimaced, then loosened the tie and unbuttoned the top button of her blouse. The shadow from Egg's oak tree that had once covered and cooled her car now shrank before the rising sun. A drop of sweat trickled down over the makeup on her forehead. Absentmindedly, she fingered it back up into her hair.

She thought about returning home to call Cottage Park Cooperative and take off the entire day. As she got out of her car to leave a note for Egg, she saw him in the distance, strolling down the street toward her, returning from practice.

As he neared, Mrs. Jones weakly smiled and reached out to shake his hand.

"Mr. Gallivan?" she asked. "You probably don't recognize me. I'm Monica Jones. You might remember me as Monica Mulroney."

Egg looked down in blank thought for a moment, then smiled. "Jim and Emma's daughter. Of course I remember. I haven't seen you for years. You were living out in . . ."

"Denver," Mrs. Jones said. "I don't know if my folks had a chance to tell you that I've moved back to Cottage Park."

"Is that so?" Egg said. "I understand you're doing real well for yourself."

"I was, for myself," Mrs. Jones said. "But not so well for my son." Her hands nervously locked together and began to churn as if she were wringing worry from them. After a deep breath, she opened her hands. They tapped each other in prayer. "And that's why I've come to visit with you."

Egg looked up into a barren blue prison inhabited by a solitary sun. "It's heating up out here. Let's go inside. I've got coffee ready to go."

Mrs. Jones followed Egg inside and looked around at the white cupboards and the long, polished kitchen table in front of her. The sink was filled with dirty dishes. "What a lovely kitchen," she said. "And so big."

Egg pulled a chair from the table for her, and she sat down. "It had to be a big kitchen with all the children," he said. "We had ten—now nine. You know I lost my Denny seven years ago over in Vietnam."

"Yes. I'm sorry for your loss," Mrs. Jones said. "And grateful for what Denny did for us."

He turned the burner up on the pot. After a few moments, he poured her a cup of coffee and set the pot on the *Des Moines Register* before her.

He joined her at the table. "What can I do for you today?"

Mrs. Jones rubbed her fingers across the table as if she were trying to erase something. "I really should have had my son, T. J., come over here to see you too—maybe we should be together for this. I don't know—I've been told so many different ways to handle situations like this."

She shook her head, then looked up at Egg. "This morning when I saw the writing on your garage, I knew right away that T. J. had done it. He told me everything when I returned home to ask him about it. He snuck over here last night with some spray paint that he uses for models. I didn't even know he'd been out. I'm very sorry about all this."

"I'm glad I know who did it," Egg said. "And your boy told you the truth about everything." As Mrs. Jones nodded, he continued, "That's probably more than most kids would have done."

Mrs. Jones eyes lightened, and the effect melted into a tired smile that lightened the rest of her face. "He's an honest boy. He's always been that way. But he does these things"—she gestured to the garage—"and doesn't seem to be afraid of the consequences." She bit her thumb knuckle. "I . . . I don't know."

Tears filled her eyes. One dropped out and raced the full length of her cheek, leaving a long ash trail of mascara behind.

"I haven't been a good mother."

She sniffed, and more tears welled in both eyes. She wiped her fingers at the tears, trying unsuccessfully to catch them before they fell.

"Oh, now," Egg said, getting up to reach a box of tissues for her. "Things will work out."

"I'm afraid," Mrs. Jones said. "My boy is in trouble again, and this time I don't have a plan. I've lost my boy. They're going to take him away from me."

"He's a kid who needs some direction," Egg said. He patted her hands. "Lots of boys are like that." Egg collected the coffeepot and turned down the burner. Then he returned to the table. "Now you need to remember all the good things you and your son have."

Mrs. Jones used a tissue to wipe a fallen tear from the table. Then she blew her nose with another tissue. With a sigh, she lifted her coffee cup to her lips. Her fingers quivered, and she set the cup back on the table before it spilled.

"It's hot and strong," Egg said. "And I can put something in it, if you'd like."

Mrs. Jones shook her head and took a deep breath. "T. J. is a good boy. He's very bright. He has certain energies and talents. He loves to draw. He's got dozens of comic book characters that he's drawn. He makes up his own—a lot of futuristic stuff. I don't know if you're familiar with that sort of thing."

"Not really," Egg said. "I've seen comic books at the store, but that's about it."

"And he writes little stories, mostly science fiction. He even writes songs from time to time."

"I'd like to meet him," Egg said. "I'd also like to see the things he's been working on."

"I'd like for you to see them, but T. J. doesn't show them to anyone. He doesn't have any friends. And I'm afraid he isn't interested in making friends." Mrs. Jones reached for another tissue. "I have to blame myself again for a lot of that."

Egg tried to interrupt her, but she continued.

"I didn't plan to have children. I didn't have the time to be a good mom. T. J.'s father is a piece of stool—and I'm putting it mildly. We're divorced. Have been since T. J. was four years old. T. J.'s been a mixed-up kid ever since. I'd get him straightened out, then his dad would usually pull him back down again. Now he's following in the exact same footsteps as his father—getting in trouble for little things, which eventually lead to getting in trouble for bigger and more serious things."

Mrs. Jones wiped her eyes, took a sip of coffee, then exhaled out over the steaming cup.

"T. J. has been in mental health programs, drug-treatment programs, special schools, halfway houses, even jail for short times. Two months ago, I was sitting in a courtroom in Denver, and a judge sentenced my only child to a chemical-dependency unit for the second time. That was on the condition that if T. J. didn't shape up—if he ended up back in court for any reason at all—the judge would send him to a reformatory for a long time.

But if he goes to a reformatory or anywhere else like that, I'm afraid I'll lose him forever . . . if I already haven't."

Mrs. Jones's voice shook, and her eyes filled with tears again. She quickly dabbed at them and wiped her nose.

"I can still be a good mother. I'll sacrifice anything for my boy. I'm back in Cottage Park as a last resort to save him. Having family around helps me. T. J. isn't as close to them as I am. But the more support I can get for that boy, the better."

"Your boy must know how much you care," Egg said with a gentle smile.

"I hope so," Mrs. Jones said. "I'm doing my best. But then something like this happens. I ask your forgiveness and that you allow us to clean up the mess and compensate you for all your troubles."

"Boys make mistakes," Egg said nonchalantly. "I'll paint over it. The garage needs a fresh coat of paint, anyway."

"Would you consider letting T. J. paint your garage?" Mrs. Jones said. "He's never had a job. Never finished any kind of a real project. All he does is sit around the house. I'd pay for everything, of course."

Egg nodded. "You're right. A little work might be good for him. If it all goes well, maybe I could keep him busy with lawn-mowing jobs the rest of the summer."

Mrs. Jones took a deep breath. "That would be wonderful." Her look of relief lasted a moment and then turned to anxiousness. "I must warn you. He is not an easy boy. He's determined to get out of Cottage Park and will do his best to upset you, and me, and my folks so we'll all make it easier for him to get away from here. We can't let him get the best of us."

Egg chuckled. "That's what boys do. My own boys tested me—are still testing me—a lot more than T. J. ever will. Our ball players test us too. I don't give up on these boys. They know it. They eventually"—Egg caught himself and slowed down to carefully choose each word—"they *always* come around. Your boy will come around too. I promise you." Egg reached out and gently patted her hand. "And by the way, I also promise you that your boy will be playing baseball before the summer is over."

Mrs. Jones slowly shook her head in disbelief but smiled at the thought of the upcoming battle between T. J. and Egg—and the possibility that Egg really might win. She had come to believe that her son was unbeatable in such contests. However, Egg certainly was confident.

For the first time, she began to relax in her chair and stretch her legs. She tasted and enjoyed for coffee, not simply sipped it. When she had finished, she carried her cup and saucer to the sink. Returning to the table she scooped up the mound of tissues that had accumulated. Egg rose, opened the cabinet door under the sink, and set out a wastepaper basket. Mrs. Jones dropped the tissues in.

She reached out and hugged Egg, then exited his front door. "I've got to go back home to freshen up before heading to work. I'll send T. J. over tomorrow morning about this time to meet you and work everything out."

At Orlowski's Family Grocery on Main Street, Rich Orlowski totaled Aunt B's bill at the cash register, received money for the amount, thanked her by name, then handed her a receipt. Anywhere else but Cottage Park, this transaction would be called a purchase. In Cottage Park, it was called a trade.

The residents of Cottage Park had loyally traded their money with the Orlowski family for over sixty years. In return, the Orlowski family gave them extraordinary service and attention. It was not uncommon for Orlowski to accompany loyal patrons on walks to deliver groceries to their homes in the immediate neighborhood, or to act as a chauffeur for longer deliveries that required a drive. He also was always available to hand-deliver a single item to a household in need of a missing ingredient to complete a recipe. Though the big discount grocery in Algona had cheaper prices and a larger variety of foods, the people of Cottage Park were stubbornly loyal to the Orlowski family.

Orlowski was grateful for their faithfulness. Unlike his friends, who spent their time counting down to when they could escape Cottage Park, he had no desire to ever leave, even for a vacation. He never wanted to leave the store either. Nearly everything he cared for in life—outside of baseball—could be found somewhere between the produce in aisle one and the freshly baked cookies and often-still-warm Old Home bread Mr. Moriarity brought in each day and arranged in aisle seven.

Orlowski pivoted from the cash register to help Anthony pack the last few items into grocery sacks. Each boy carried a sack out to Aunt B's car.

With one hand, Orlowski opened the driver's door for her. As she got situated behind the wheel, the boys set the sacks in the backseat. They watched her drive off, then returned to the air-conditioned comfort of the store.

"Man, it's busy today," Anthony said.

"It's all because of Coach's announcement," Orlowski replied. "My dad says that business is always good whenever something big happens—like rain or snow or a death. I guess we all eat when we're nervous."

Anthony followed Orlowski to the rack of candy bars at the checkout aisle. Orlowski's father was adamant about employees not eating in the store, let alone without paying for the product. Orlowski looked back and forth and all around. When he didn't see his father, he snatched a Walnut Crush. Orlowski had a sweet tooth he indulged—and consequently bulged—on a regular basis. He ripped off the wrapper, broke the candy bar in two, then offered a half to Anthony, who declined. Orlowski shrugged and flung one half of the bar into his mouth. He spoke while chewing.

"Really, though," he said. "People had to know this would happen someday."

"People are scared of change," Anthony said. "People around here do one of four things: drink, watch television, pray, or play baseball. Coach's leaving, then, means a lot. It could change life for a lot of people."

"I'm sure it'll be one of the topics on the agenda tonight at the quarries," Orlowski said. "We've got a lot of beer to drink, so come early."

Orlowski dropped the remaining half of the bar into his mouth. This time, he let it dissolve on his tongue and roof of his mouth.

Anthony shook his head. "I'm done with the quarries. I never told you what happened after I got home after our party at the quarries on graduation night."

Seeing there was a brief lull with no customers in line at the register, he took a deep breath and continued.

"Whatever time it was when I got home, my dad was sitting in the rocker right in front of me, staring at me. I apologized for coming home so late and waited there for him to say something—anything." He shook his head. "Not one single word. So I finally slid by him and beat it upstairs to bed. The whole thing gave me the willies."

"You afraid of him?" Orlowski asked after swallowing the last bites of the bar.

Orlowski was not afraid of his father in the least. But he was afraid his father's constant nagging about the store would break his sanity. He surveyed the area again. For the time being, his father was not breathing down his neck. This time, he snatched a Twin Bing.

The Twin Bing, produced in Sioux City and marketed almost exclusively in northwestern Iowa, was far and away his favorite. He tore the wrapper and pulled out one of the cherry-flavored nougat treats coated in chopped peanuts and chocolate. He tossed the remaining Bing still in the sack to Anthony, who juggled it like a hot potato before reaching in for the sugary delicacy and gulping it down in one bite.

Anthony immediately crumpled the wrapper and tossed it in the trash before Mr. Orlowski might come upon them and find the damning evidence of employee theft still in hand. Orlowski, on the other hand, waved his treat back and forth in front of his nose, breathing the aroma deep into his nostrils and lungs. He then bit into the bar and moaned in taste-bud ecstasy while studying the remaining fleshy, pink cherry filling.

"Manna from heaven," Orlowski said, blessing the remaining half before setting it on his tongue and letting it slowly melt into his digestive tract. "What were we talking about again? Oh yeah. Your dad."

"Nah, I'm not afraid of the old guy," Anthony said. "I could take him if he tried to get rough with me. But he was always kind of a spook with my brothers—maybe 'cause they're older. I don't know. All I know is, he's even more weird now that it's only me at home. He's constantly on my case. And then he goes and waits up for me in the middle of the night. I don't get it. It's a little spooky." He shrugged. "The way I figure it, I've got two months to go—nine days after the Finals, to be exact—and then I'm out of here and off to Iowa City."

"I still can't believe he let you go to the university," Orlowski said.

"He gave in when I told him I'd play baseball there," Anthony said. "I probably won't go through with it, but he believed me. I'll cross that bridge when I come to it."

"Sixty days . . ." Orlowski rubbed his chin in thought. "You're lucky. I've got to be with my old until he retires or until I retire. He's a strange one too. But with him, it's little things. You know how I have to hose down the sidewalk before we open every morning? Today he said he also wants me to clean the street in front of the store every morning." Both boys laughed. "He doesn't make any sense."

Anthony said, "You talk about not making sense? My old says I should throw right into the body of some poor base runner. He says, the bloodier the better." Anthony imitated the sharp, gruff voice of his father: "Make some kid a walking billboard with the message, 'Don't fool with Anthony Civilla.'"

"Jesus," Orlowski said. "Does he think that's the way we have to play to get that stupid championship monkey off our backs?"

"He's dead serious about it," Anthony said. "You heard him the other night at Humboldt."

Orlowski had indeed heard Mr. Civilla, as had everyone else at the game.

Anthony continued. "Moriarity walks the first runner, so my old gets up from his seat and stands right behind first. The next thing I know, he's yelling at me." Anthony again imitated his father. "You hit this guy, Anthony. You hit him like I told you!"

"While your old is yelling, the guy starts creeping off first. Then Moriarity throws a fireball over there that hits the poor kid right in the elbow. So the kid keels over in pain. Getting hit by Moriarity was bad enough, but then he was afraid you would hit him again if he took off for second!"

"God, I wish my dad had Moriarity for a son," Anthony said. "Me, I don't have to win that way. I won't win that way."

"If you have to hit someone," Orlowski said, "why don't you 'over-throw' next time your old is standing behind first? Let him be your walking billboard for people not to mess with you!"

"I'll think about that," Anthony said, shaking his head sadly.

When he looked up, Mr. Orlowski was approaching the front of the store from the stock room. Both boys immediately separated and looked busy cleaning.

Everyone in Cottage Park discussed Murphy's retirement announcement that day—and discussed it in great detail. No party had been planned at Murphy's home that evening. Still, they prepared for one.

Father Ryan and Egg arrived shortly after supper. Katherine situated them and Murphy with whisky sours and cocktail wieners in the living room. The three men listened to the radio broadcast of the Chicago Cubs-St. Louis Cardinals game with heightened interest until the visitors began arriving.

Cottage Park's famed baseball factory had produced two stars who had gone on to the big leagues. One had retired long ago. The other, Danny Stinson, a twenty-seven-year-old Holy Trinity graduate, was now the starting third baseman for the St. Louis Cardinals. Stinson was on a ten-game hitting streak and had raised his batting average to .316. Every radio in every home in Cottage Park tuned in whenever the Cardinals played. Any interruption to a game was always mended with two urgent questions: "How are we"—the Cardinals—"doing?" and "How is Danny doing?"

Soon, guests filed in. Katherine would bring them in one or two at a time. She'd turn down the radio and stay in the room long enough to hear her husband assure the guests that he really would retire at the end of the season. Then she would disappear into the kitchen, to reappear a short while later with a fresh platter of sandwich breads, cold meats, and cheeses. Each set of guests stayed until other guests arrived. They'd speak again with Katherine in the kitchen before leaving the house.

At the end of the evening, after the visitors bid farewell, Murphy turned up the volume so they could fully concentrate on the final inning of the game. Consequently, none of the men heard the doorbell ring.

The final visitor of the evening was Hugh Wilson, the principal of Holy Trinity School. He was in his midforties but had the air and tendencies of a much older man. He was dressed, as always, in an inexpensive business suit that was pressed stiff. Katherine escorted Wilson into the room.

"Turn that thing down," Katherine said referring to the radio. When Murphy hesitated, she stepped to the console and turned the volume down herself. "Al, you have a special guest." She got the attention of each of the three men and introduced the special guest as if the men had forgotten who he was and his role at Holy Trinity. "Mr. Wilson, the principal, has come over to see you."

Each of the three old men looked anxiously from the radio to Wilson and politely nodded. When Katherine exited, Murphy rose to turn the volume up again. He pointed to an empty chair alongside Egg and Ryan and gestured for Wilson to sit down.

"We're finishing the Cardinals game. It's a close one. What can I get you to drink?" Murphy asked as he started toward the kitchen.

Wilson shook his head, smiled, and waved him back down.

Murphy continued, "We still have a lot of food we need to eat up." He pointed to a platter on the coffee table. "And there's a lot more stuff in the refrigerator that Katherine can get right back out here."

Wilson tapped a soft round stomach. "I shouldn't. I stopped by to congratulate you on your retirement."

Murphy took a mock bow.

"It's always nice to see people retire at the right time," Wilson added.

"I think we've got a good chance to win the Finals this year," Murphy said. He looked at Egg and Ryan. "Wouldn't you two agree?"

"Yes," Egg said, glancing at Wilson briefly before giving his full attention back to the radio.

Ryan made a similar comment and gesture.

Wilson smiled. "Everyone is so positive about all this. Now we'll have to go about the task of trying to find someone to replace you, if that can even be done."

"Thank you," Murphy said. "I'd like to help you in any way I can."

"Actually, you can be of great assistance," Wilson said. "Let's visit sometime about how you can help."

"There's no better time than the present," Murphy said with a shrug. "Go ahead. What's on your mind?"

Wilson said, "Nothing much at this point. You must know it'll be a challenge to hire someone this late in the year. A good number of the coaches have already signed their contracts for the next school year."

"You'll find someone," Murphy said flatly.

Wilson seemed to relax. The tenor of his voice was hopeful. "It might be easier to find someone if I could let them start right away," he said. "Would you be willing to step aside now?"

"No," Murphy said with some irritation.

He had drifted far away to Busch Stadium. Now Wilson was dragging him back to Cottage Park for nonsense.

"This is my last season. I have to finish this one out because it's all going to happen this summer."

"But what if I could find the right person now?" Wilson asked. "Would you mind if he was your assistant coach, so he could get acquainted with our Holy Trinity system?"

"Now that," Murphy said, "is something I'd have to ask my coaches."

Murphy turned to them for their reaction, but they had fully tuned out of the conversation and were instead focusing on the drama of a Cardinal comeback on the radio.

"I'm sorry," Murphy said as he got up and turned off the radio completely. "I'm very sorry, but this is important." He looked first at Ryan and then at Egg. "What do you two think about that?"

"About what?" Egg asked, irritated. "It's the final inning for God's sake." He stared and jabbed a finger at the radio.

"Mr. Wilson here," Murphy said, "expects to bring on a new coach . . . now."

"We follow your lead," Egg said. "But I would say this . . ." He leaned forward in his seat as if to stand up. He rocked once to stand, failed, then decided to stay put. "This new fella had better know a lot about baseball—the way we play. And he better know his place, which is listening!"

"Al," he said, his eyes darting from Egg and Ryan, then back to Murphy. "I didn't intend to discuss the matter like this. I really thought I'd be visiting with only you."

"No," Murphy said. "My coaches have as much say as I do on everything. Whatever needs to be discussed can be said in front of them."

"But it does not concern them," Wilson said, his shoulders sinking. He continued patiently and tenderly. "The only reason they're on the team is because I gave my consent. They're not teachers, and they have no coaching certifications."

Everyone understood what he meant. On paper, Wilson worked at the behest of Ryan, but Ryan worked at the behest of the bishop, and Wilson was closer to the bishop than Ryan. All four men knew it.

"Father Ryan certainly has a great say in the overall school program, but we have to be careful not to mix up his roles."

"The only qualifications they need to coach with me are that they know their baseball and be gentlemen," Murphy said. Blood rushed to his face, and his eyes sharpened. "There aren't two better men for coaching jobs anywhere in Iowa, and you know it."

"No," Wilson said. "I don't know that. And I'm not the only one who disagrees with you!"

Now Wilson could feel his own temper rising. He could recite so many concerns regarding Egg and Ryan. They were liabilities and as much of a headache as Murphy. However, Wilson knew that if he even got started about Egg and Ryan, his floodgates would surely open. And no matter what temporary relief he'd feel for being honest and direct with the old men, it would end up in some kind of regret, perhaps even a fight. Besides, nothing in the world could change their minds . . . on anything. If only he were dealing with rational men.

My God, he thought to himself, *if they would just retire and go away like normal people!*

Instead of venting his rage, he changed his tact. He tried to show his compassion for them, knowing even that approach was the beginning of surrender. "Let's be honest, Al. They're older men, and we care for them. With the stress and humidity, I think we're putting them in a dangerous situation."

"I'm the same age as they are!" Murphy said.

"Yes, and you've stepped down," Wilson said. "But it's not solely about age. I listen to the people of Cottage Park, and they've told me even today"—he swallowed, as if someone else might finish his sentence for him—"that they would like to see more balance on this team. You have a tendency to run the team your way and your way only."

"Who said that?" Murphy said, raising his voice.

Egg groaned and muttered an almost-silent obscenity. "No one said anything like that except for a few sour grapes. They've always complained, and they always will."

"It's more than sour grapes," Wilson said. "It's people concerned about the image we portray at Holy Trinity. In a game last year"—Wilson pointed to Murphy and again continued respectfully—"you hit a player. Right out on the mound, in front of everyone!"

"He needed it!" Egg said.

"His father told us to keep him in line," Ryan said. "He heard what happened, and he thanked us."

"I'm proud and always have been of the way that we represent Holy Trinity and Cottage Park," Murphy said. "And that boy, Pat Moriarity, deserved to be reprimanded—right there, right then. He spoke back to me. You ask him what he said. He'll tell you he deserved more than he got. I did what I did and put the whole business behind us. Moriarity finished up and won the game for us. It's as simple as that."

As Murphy lectured him, Wilson thought to himself how easy and simple life was for the old men. In this "simple" case they were discussing, Murphy had gone from the dugout out to the mound in the fifth inning to reprimand Moriarity, who promptly said he knew what he was doing and that Murphy should return to the dugout and relax. Murphy countered by attempting to strike Moriarity across the face with a closed-fist roundhouse. But even reaching up as high as he could, he could only strike Moriarity's chest. The loud thud drew gasps of astonishment and horror from the parents and fans of the public school team Holy Trinity was beating badly. Immediately after the game, several of those parents contacted Wilson, their own school administration, and the Iowa High School Athletic Association.

Wilson probably spent a half-dozen hours over and above his thankless and time-consuming job to return phone calls and write letters to explain the basics: there was no mandatory retirement age for coaches in Iowa; and as opposed to public school staff, private school staff were still allowed to employ corporal punishment. He promised more oversight of Murphy but never believed those hopeful words even as they frantically escaped by his lips.

Making his job even more futile were the legion of Holy Trinity fans who applauded Murphy for showing that he cared enough to discipline his team in any fashion he thought most appropriate.

Wilson daydreamed again in a quick respite of ecstasy, *Oh, if I could live in their world—a world where I could say and do whatever I wanted, with no worry of repercussions!*

By virtue of their passion and their commitment, the old men had earned a begrudging respect from the community. Although Wilson heard complaints about their arrogance and eccentricity, and although people told him they recognized the need for a counterbalance to the dictatorial style, people ultimately considered the old coaches as necessary evils toward a winning program. And when Holy Trinity won, those cranky old men looked like loving and endearing grandpas. But in the wake of Murphy's retirement announcement, people were thinking and charting the future, a future of change. Wilson knew it was time to act.

Murphy took a breath, then pounded his hand against his knee. "I need these men on my team right up until the end—and that's final!"

Several seconds elapsed without a response.

Testily, Murphy spoke again. "Is there anything else I might be able to do for you tonight?"

"Yes," Wilson said as if he were letting the men in on a collaboration. "Put yourself in my position. I have to listen to the people. A lot of them think it's time for a change, and I have to agree with them. We need a younger man—a teacher and a coach. And he needs to coach the team himself or be your assistant coach this summer."

"Or what?" Murphy said snidely.

"I don't believe we need to threaten each other," Wilson said. "It's a simple and fair request. If we can work together so that you agree to take care of this, you can finish the season out."

"And Father Ryan and Egg?" Murphy asked.

"I would really prefer they step aside," Wilson said, as if it made all the sense in the world. "Step aside to open up a spot for a new coach. And do it right now."

"Because we're too old," Egg said. "That's what you're saying."

"Age has nothing to do with this for him," Murphy replied, though Wilson was sitting right there. "He orchestrated the same stunt on me to get me out of teaching a few years back. It's not a question of age. It's ego. It's full control. He can push a new guy—a younger guy—all over the place. But he won't dare try that with us."

Wilson clucked. "You want my job? You can have it." He shook his head. "I don't need this aggravation in my life. All I'm trying to do is the right thing for Holy Trinity."

"So if I'm too old to be helping at the ballpark," Ryan began, "is there anything else I'm too old for?"

"Come on, Father," Wilson said. "This is a game for young people. Coaches need to be as strong and vibrant and healthy as their players." Wilson now glared at Ryan. "They also need to set a good example."

Egg clenched his fists, stood up, and spoke quietly and dispassionately. "I think it's time for us to go out outside . . . Buster."

The name Buster was a term of endearment for men Egg felt needed to learn from him at the expense of blood, teeth, and often consciousness. As Egg saw it, Wilson had not just stepped over a line, but high-jumped over it. No one would question the character of his friend Father Ryan and get away with it without taking some lumps and bruises.

Wilson was ready to head outside, but certainly not with Egg. He stood and began to back away from the men, toward the front door.

"Al, I'd like to hear back from you in the next few days," he said as he retreated from the room.

Murphy and Ryan also got to their feet, standing between Egg and Wilson. Overhearing the entire exchange, Katherine stepped in from the kitchen to prevent Egg from starting a full-fledged fistfight.

"I can't believe what I'm seeing," Katherine said in real disbelief.

"Exhibit A," Wilson said to Katherine, pointing to Egg. "I'm leaving."

Whatever assholes want, assholes get, Wilson said to himself. He shook his head as he shut the door behind himself.

"Exhibit A? What the hell was that supposed to mean?" Egg asked, looking at everyone Wilson left behind.

Murphy reopened the door, cupped his hands over his mouth, and hoarsely yelled as loud as he could muster to an already empty sidewalk and street.

"I'll give you your answer now so you won't have to wait one bit. We stay! All of us. And if you want a fight, it'll be an ugly one. When we leave, we'll leave together. By God, mister, if you try to throw us out, the people in this town will throw *you* out for good . . . and probably on the end of a pitchfork!"

"Well, now the whole neighborhood thinks you're a kook," Katherine said, shaking her head dejectedly and heading back to the kitchen. "Or I should say a bigger kook than they already thought you were."

Once Katherine left the room, the men had sat back down again.

"He's finally gone," Egg said. "Thank you, God, for answering my prayer!" He leaned over and whispered to Ryan, "Though she still hasn't answered the other hundred prayers to drop a piano on that guy."

Murphy took his glasses off. "That is without a doubt the most miserable excuse for a human being I have ever seen."

"I agree," Egg said. "If somebody had hit *him* when he was growing up, maybe he wouldn't have turned out so bad!"

"And look," Murphy said, wincing and pointing to the radio. He reached over and turned the volume on high. Jack Buck was announcing that the Cardinals had defeated the Cubs. "We've missed our game." He turned off the radio and dropped into a chair.

Each man sipped his whisky sour.

"I don't know," Ryan said. "Maybe he's right. Maybe it would be good for a young man to come in now and start learning how we do things."

"No, Father," Murphy said matter-of-factly—his anger now dissipated. "He's never been more wrong."

"He's a bag of hot air," Egg said. "You saw him turn around and run. He wouldn't touch us. He couldn't."

"He's dead wrong," Murphy said with a steely resolve. "Now we have to show him he's wrong."

— CHAPTER FIVE —

Countdown to the Finals: 50 Days to Go

AFTER RETURNING HOME FROM MASS the next morning, Egg looked around his front yard for the young man who had spray-painted his garage. Seeing no one, Egg entered his home, poured himself a cup of coffee, and began to read his newspaper.

In a very short time, his full attention was drawn to the high school baseball scores on the back page of the sports section. Egg opened his penknife and used it as a straightedge to isolate each line of the fifty or so scores. Every single score triggered some sort of memory of a previous contest with, visit to, or friend from one of the Iowa communities. He nodded at each score. He was rarely surprised, seeing even in the upsets the possibilities that had developed into victory.

Next he looked over the sports articles and used his knife to remove one about the sudden resignation of the baseball coach at LeMars Gehlen High School. He read a few more articles, looked at the professional baseball box scores and league standings, then closed and folded the newspaper. He returned outside to take out his garbage and await his guest.

There at his garbage can, Egg saw T. J. Jones for the first time. The fourteen-year-old boy was sound asleep with his body half against the garage and half against the garbage can. He had situated himself directly under the spray-painted word *Die*. He wore white Adidas sneakers with three red stripes, blue socks, baggy flannel shorts that came down below his knees, and a black T-shirt with the name and picture of his favorite rock 'n' roll group, Deep Fried. In the middle of the picture was a button that proclaimed: I dress this way to annoy you.

Egg opened the trash can, set his garbage inside, then loudly rattled the aluminum lid as he closed the can. But T. J. still slept.

He was round and puffy, with a generous midsection. Long dust-colored strands of hair grew like weeds over his head. His chalk-white complexion was spotted with pimples and a cold sore next to his thin red lips.

Egg nudged T. J., and the boy's mouth fell open, showing gray teeth behind a wire network of braces held together by two rubber bands.

"Young man," Egg said tenderly, "you'll have to get up now."

"Oh," T. J. said, rubbing his eyes and looking into Egg's face. "Is this your garage?"

"That's right," Egg said. "Are you here to clean up your mess?"

"I'm here," T. J. said. "Barely."

"I'm very busy," Egg said. "Let's get a move on. My name is Egg."

T. J. rolled over on all fours and with great effort raised himself up to his feet.

"That's a funny nickname."

Once standing, he brought his hands to one of the rubber bands connecting his braces. Egg saw the hand movement and confused it with a greeting. He reached out to shake hands.

"Whoa," T. J. said. "Wait a minute."

He took the rubber band out of his mouth, stretched it between his fingers, and shot it toward the trash can, missing badly.

"The orthodontist put that on a few days ago before we came out here from Denver. It's been killing me."

T. J. wiped his hand dry against his pants, then finally reached out to shake hands with Egg.

Egg took it and felt a padded palm that returned little of his firmness. "I was expecting you out front of the house," Egg said. "How long have you been waiting here?"

"Beats me," T. J. said. "I'm in a grog. Mom dragged me over here on her way to work. Sorry about the z's. I'm a night owl. I can't seem to get started in the morning."

"Your mom told me a little about you," Egg said. "You're a sophomore?"

"If I'm lucky," T. J. said. "And if somebody takes the time to add up all the credits from the programs I've been in."

"Well," Egg said with a sigh, "welcome to Cottage Park." He turned and looked at the words on the garage wall. "And of course, you've already greeted me," he said with wry sarcasm.

T. J. looked at the graffiti and laughed. "I'm glad you've got a sense of humor."

Egg stated matter-of-factly, "I wasn't being funny. Now, what exactly does this literary masterpiece mean?" Egg asked.

"The words? They're a line from a comic book I wrote. Everyone thinks we'll get killed by bombs, but I think it'll be by guns. I've got a character named Armageddo, who screams out those words right before he attacks Washington, DC, with an army of giant insects that have been trained to shoot boiling liquid that can melt anything in their way."

"You have quite an imagination," Egg said. He reached over and tugged on the tiny ponytail at the back of T. J.'s head. "What is this?"

"It's funny you should ask because Mom doesn't like it either," T. J. said. "But I don't ask you about your hair."

"I think you better cut it off," Egg said incredulously. "You won't fit in Cottage Park until you do."

"I have it for exactly that reason," T. J. said. "My hair is important to me. I like to be different."

"I think you're making a mistake," Egg said. "Anyway, your mother said you'll help me paint this garage."

"Maybe," T. J. said. "If I do, I'll paint it by myself. I don't need you around to creep me out."

"Why?" Egg said in a challenging tone. His face flared. "You think I'm too old?"

"No," T. J. said. "Jeez. Because I marked it up. Man, what are you getting so red about?"

"I'm not upset about anything. But if you're doing the painting, I'll supervise."

Egg paced to the garage. T. J. followed closely behind. Egg had them lift an extension ladder, carry it out, and stand it against the garage wall.

Egg pointed to an area high on the wall below the roof. "There's one spot there. Get it first."

"What do you mean?" T. J. asked.

"Chip that off." Egg pointed again and handed the paint scraper to T. J.

T. J. climbed the first rung of the ladder and looked around, then inched up to the second rung. He began to tremble.

Egg motioned for him to go higher.

"Are you holding the ladder?" T. J. asked nervously.

Egg steadied the ladder. "Yes. You'll do fine. Get up there."

"Up into the frontiers of space," T. J. said breathlessly, as if he were narrating one of his own comic stories. He climbed the third and fourth rungs and began to wobble. "Whee-oh." He looked down at Egg. "This is about as high as I can go."

"You're hardly five feet up in the air!" Egg barked the words. "Come on. I won't let you fall. Don't be silly."

But T. J. stayed frozen on the fourth rung.

"I should have known," Egg spat. "Get down from there so I can do it!"

"No," T. J. said. "I just needed some encouragement." He looked up and climbed the next two rungs, one immediately after the other. "I have to be high enough here." His voice wavered a bit but was determined. "Now, what am I supposed to be doing?"

"There," Egg said in growing frustration. "Right in front of your face, where the paint is blistering. Scrape it off. Haven't you ever painted anything before?"

"This wall will be my first with a brush," T. J. said. "I prefer to spray my paint."

T. J. noted that Egg seemed tone-deaf to sarcasm. This robbed T. J. of his preferred, often primary mode of communication.

He slid the scraper over the paint, then dabbed at it. "Nothing's happening."

"You're not *chipping*," Egg said. "Get in there and use some elbow grease. Jab at it. Come on. Hustle your bustle, or we'll be here all day!"

T. J. increased the pressure on the chipper. Sweat dripped down over his forehead and stung his eyes. He rubbed them with the back of his wrists, causing further pain. The tiny slivers of white paint peeled from the wall and littered T. J.'s skin, clothing, socks, and shoes. His arm ached, and he was light-headed when Egg called him down. There were a few more spots to chip.

After scraping spots on the other three walls, T. J. wobbled down from the ladder. Egg had taken out a pocketknife and was diligently carving into a corner of one of the walls.

"What are you doing?" T. J. asked.

"Carving my initials," Egg said. "I keep living as long as I am remembered. I have my name written or carved into about everything around here. I pray to forget some things, but I also pray that I'll never be forgotten." Egg sighed perilously. "I'll bet you forget about me the moment I die."

"That's not true," T. J. said uneasily. "But let's not bring up the subject of death. It creeps me out."

"I do this to make sure you remember me," Egg said. "I'm putting your name on here too."

Egg carved a cross behind his name, which turned out to be an addition sign. Next to it, Egg dug the knife even deeper into the wood to engrave the initials T. and J.

"No!" T. J. cried out. "You don't have to do that. I would rather you didn't put my name there," he protested.

He had planned to work this one day with Egg, dramatically quit, then never return. Then somehow the wheels of justice would begin to turn, and he would be moved away from Cottage Park. He didn't care where. Anywhere in the world—any correctional facility—was better than being stuck in Cottage Park. But now as he watched Egg down on his knees, working so conscientiously on the common artistic signature that would tell of their story together, T. J. didn't feel right walking away from the old man and never seeing him again.

When Egg finished, he paused to admire his handiwork. He read the inscription as he touched his fingers over and into each letter.

"Egg plus T. J. 1974," Egg said. "In the end, we all become a story. This is how we will sign off on this story. This is how we will be remembered for what we did here."

He snapped the pocketknife shut and with great effort began to rise to his feet. T. J. watched him struggle, then quickly stepped over to help him up.

Egg stood stiffly, balanced himself, and then, like nearly every other older man in Cottage Park, walked as if he were doing so for the first time. Bowlegged, pigeon-toed, limping badly, and nearly but never falling, he worked the kinks from his unsteady gait.

T. J. rushed in again to assist.

"I'm fine," Egg grumbled, waving him away as he began to walk steadily.

T. J. studied Egg and concluded there was no way he could abandon the old man. He was stuck in Cottage Park, at least until the exact moment the entire garage project was completed, however long that would take. That idea depressed and fatigued him.

"Can I take a break or something?" he asked Egg. "I need a breather."

Before Egg could even nod, T. J. sank down in the shade of a maple tree in the front yard. He wiped sweat into his shirt and wrung out the ends, dripping sweat onto the roots of the tree. Egg beelined over and stood before T. J.

T. J. looked up at him. "So, are we about ready for lunch?"

"It's ten thirty in the morning!" Egg said. "Come on. Let's go to the store to get paint."

"Does your car have air conditioning?" T. J. asked, pushing himself off the ground and slapping dirt and grass off himself.

"I don't have a car," Egg said. He silently cursed whichever of his children was currently driving around in his beloved Pontiac. "I guess we won't need one here in Cottage Park. We're walking."

T. J. groaned.

His mother was right, Egg thought.

T. J. was doing his best to get under Egg's skin. It wasn't working, though. Egg promised himself that no matter how hard the boy tried to upset him, he absolutely wouldn't crack and give him the licking he obviously needed and deserved. Rather, Egg would take special delight seeing T. J. sweat and suffer with this work project. It was the perfect remedy to help him mature and become a man. Egg looked directly at T. J. and nodded in satisfaction.

"Downtown?" T. J. said worriedly. "All that way?"

"It's six blocks," Egg said.

"But carrying the paint," T. J. said. "That'll be heavy, won't it?"

"No. I'll only buy two cans," Egg said. "That should last us a while. And we'll need a couple of brushes and a roller pan. Don't let me forget."

Pigeons cooed from the eaves of tall houses as Egg and T. J. set off on the sidewalk that led to the few remaining stores in downtown Cottage Park. From darkened trees came the wistful call of Cottage Park's most numerous and vociferous birds, mourning doves. They were everywhere.

"They're singing your song," Egg said with a sarcastic chuckle. He imitated the doves: "No, no, no, oh, no, no, no."

Robins chirped across green lawns drenched by lazy but conscientious water sprinklers. On the street before them, brown sparrows wrestled and chattered, then scrambled to continue their battles in the safety of nearby thick bushes.

When the green cover of a walnut dropped from above, Egg looked into the tree and pointed out a rust-colored squirrel nervously turning and chewing a nut in its paws as if eating a buttered ear of corn.

Egg knew the names of everyone he met along the route—plus the names of their children and in many cases their grandchildren. All who greeted him called out, "Egg!" and he answered them with a wave, a crooked grin, and their appropriate name.

He introduced T. J. as a neighborhood boy whom he enlisted to help paint his garage. Many had seen T. J. before. Now all had met him. Like nearly all new residents to Cottage Park, he was initially greeted with suspicion.

Dogs barked from backyards and charged at the duo before recognizing Egg. They sniffed anxiously at T. J. before scampering along behind the two. Once they reached the railroad tracks that divided Cottage Park, the dogs stopped, cocked their heads, looked longingly at Egg and T. J. as they crossed over the tracks, then turned back toward their homes.

On the other side of the tracks, a farm implements store displayed shiny new plows, wagons, and combine equipment. Behind that new machinery stood one dozen older, obsolescent, rusted models. They were frozen forever like a collection of dinosaurs at a museum.

Other than the few farmers who had driven into town for supplies, there was no traffic downtown. Egg looked in each store window and waved to those who looked out. At the Morning Sun Café, Egg tapped on the window to attract the attention of Spider, the café's sole waiter and part-time cook, who was standing idly. He smiled and motioned for him to come in for his usual coffee and cinnamon roll. But Egg hitched his head toward T. J., pointed to his watch, and continued on to Civilla's Hardware.

Father Ryan was late for lunch with Marty McKenna and his family. He always seemed to be late for most if not all activities, even those in his ordinary daily schedule. And still, after decades of being late, he was upset with himself.

Now he was not only late but lost. He slapped his hand against the steering wheel of his 1973 Cadillac Deville. His parishioners had given him the shiny black car with the equally black plush leather interior as a gift one year ago, on the fiftieth anniversary of his ordination.

In frustration, he turned the car off the blacktop road and onto a dusty gravel road. To make up for lost time, he drove the long, wide car as fast as the road would allow—slowing periodically when the road seemed to lure the car into the ditch.

Ryan drove on in this fashion through gravel intersections and across another blacktop road before stopping his car and getting out to try a different perspective. Behind him, the gravel dust blew over and settled on a whispering field of green corn leaves beginning to poke out of the ground.

Ryan was lost—lost in space and lost in time. If someone had said he'd crossed Iowa into Missouri or Minnesota, he would have believed it. And if someone had said he'd been driving around for hours or even days, he might have believed that statement as well.

Judgment won over pride as Ryan got back into his car, drove to the nearest farmhouse, and asked for directions. For all his frustration, Ryan wasn't far from the McKenna home. He took consolation in being able to follow the newfound directions correctly to the black mailbox with the McKenna name printed on it.

Ryan maneuvered his car onto the crushed rock driveway, careful not to drive off it onto the lush green lawn on either side. Where the driveway curved to the backdoor of the McKenna home, Ryan saw freshly painted red barns with clean concrete extensions. Curious hogs stepped to a wire fence to inspect the new visitor.

Near the driveway were two full corncribs and a machine shed sheltering two tractors, a wagon, and a combine. Bolted on the shed was a basketball hoop. Beneath it, McKenna's ten-year-old brother, Marion, hoisted up shots at the rim. He waved when Ryan did.

The two-story white wooden house was nearly covered in the shade of old elms that reached out to the home as if to embrace it. Ryan cheated his car off the driveway as close to the shade as possible.

Two of six lounging cats quickly sprang from their resting positions and scampered away. A mammoth German shepherd named Sissy because she was the exact opposite of a sissy raced across the yard, barking for the first time as she jumped against the car door. Ryan instinctively slid across the bench seat to the passenger side as she stood, paws against his window, barking furiously.

Marion came running over, smiling, and opened the passenger side door. Sissy then pounced to the passenger side, but Marion grabbed her around the collar and bossed her away from the car.

"Sorry, Father," he said. "She's been a real crank since Dad died. You can get out of the car now. She won't do anything." As if to assure Ryan, the boy placed a headlock over Sissy, who wrestled playfully to back out of it.

McKenna's mother, Diane, was waiting for Ryan at the backdoor. She opened it and waved him in.

Ryan advanced to the porch. "I'm sorry I was late. I was over at Sunset Estates giving Communion, and before I knew it . . ."

"It's no problem," she said. "We needed every minute to get ready," Mrs. McKenna said. Before closing the door, she turned her attention to Marion, who was still wrestling with Sissy on the ground. "Get out of the dirt! We're eating!"

At this command, the boy released his hold, stood to brush himself clean, then ran inside the house.

Inside the kitchen, Mrs. McKenna pointed to and introduced each of her four daughters working at the table, sink, and oven. At the mention of her name, each girl smiled, then resumed their tasks.

"With me being so late, everyone must be hungry," Ryan said.

"They're always hungry," Mrs. McKenna said. "They never stop eating."

McKenna emerged from the bathroom and entered the kitchen. The underside of his large tan hands had been scrubbed pink. The fragrance of soap masked the odors of farm work. He shook Ryan's hand and offered him something to drink. Ryan quickly surveyed the kitchen for signs of something with a little alcohol in it. Seeing nothing, he tentatively agreed to ice water.

As soon as he took his seat, Ryan was attended to by members of the McKenna family, each offering him big bowls of food from the garden: green peas, asparagus, green onions, and white radishes. There was also a homemade loaf of still-warm wheat bread and a large ham, which McKenna sliced and distributed onto each plate.

"Every few months, we have one of the hogs slaughtered," Mrs. McKenna said. "There's a locker down the road, so it's all very convenient."

When each plate was filled, all said the Grace before Meals, then everyone began to eat. Two steel revolving fans blew air in all directions of the kitchen. Ryan, seated closest to the oven, occasionally mopped sweat from his brows with a napkin.

Conversation was infrequent—at times punctuated by nervous giggles from the McKenna girls. While Mrs. McKenna described the summer activities planned for her children, McKenna hunched over his plate and scooped food into his mouth, occasionally shaking his head in mild disgust at the playful antics of his younger siblings.

After a dessert of strawberry shortcake with fresh strawberries from their garden, each McKenna child assumed a role in cleanup until they were excused by their mother and burst outside to play. Mrs. McKenna wiped a wet washcloth across the table, then dried it with a dishtowel. When the table was clean, Mrs. McKenna poured coffee for Ryan and herself, then rejoined Ryan and McKenna.

"I'm sorry we never had you out more before the funeral," Mrs. McKenna said. "You've done so much for us during this whole time." She hitched her head in her son's direction. "Marty, here, is still very upset about his dad dying."

"I can understand," Ryan said. "Some time will have to pass by. Life will never be the same."

"I've told him the same thing," Mrs. McKenna said. "He knows that." She cast a glance at McKenna, who met her eyes. "He's always been such a sensible kid that I don't understand some of the things he's doing now. I'm hoping you can somehow get through to him."

"I'd like to help," Ryan said, looking from Mrs. McKenna to her son. "How can I help?"

McKenna stiffened in his chair and folded his hands together. "A lot of work needs to be done around here. I'm already behind."

"So he thinks he should quit the baseball team to help us catch up," Mrs. McKenna interjected.

"Absolutely not," Ryan said immediately. "That's out of the question."

As McKenna blinked with some surprise, Ryan took a deep breath.

"I guess if I were a good counselor," Ryan said, "I would have asked you insightful questions so you could come to a conclusion in your best interests. Well, I'll be the first to admit I'm not a good counselor—especially when it comes to baseball. And I don't believe you should even have a choice in this matter. You owe it to your team, to your town, to your family, and to yourself to play baseball." Ryan ran a finger through one of the creases in his forehead and wiped the perspiration on his pant leg. "This is it, Marty. This is the last year for all of us."

"He knows that," Mrs. McKenna interjected again. "I told him the same thing. He's got one more month of baseball with his friends before they all go away. He can do this."

"Your mother is right," Ryan said. "And your father . . ."

Ryan thought back twenty-five years, to a hot day in July when McKenna's father was playing center field for the local American Legion team against a team that had come up from Nebraska. Because of his great speed, McKenna's father could play his position very shallow, daring batters to hit the ball over him. One long fly ball did arch over the spot where he first stood. But at the crack of the bat, McKenna's father had turned and run as fast as he could, diving at the very last moment and snatching the ball inches before it hit the ground.

"Your father was fast and had a good arm," Ryan continued. "But he rarely had to show it. No one really ever tested him. Somehow they seemed to know better." Ryan looked over at the door. It was time for him to move on. "Your father would want you to finish up with this team."

"And to have some fun," Mrs. McKenna said. She smiled at McKenna and then back at Ryan. "He had fun watching Marty play too. Before he died, he was beginning to show Marion how to play the game." Now she looked directly at McKenna. "Your dad would have said baseball is more important than any of the chores around here."

"Mom," McKenna said, "things have to get done."

"They'll get done," Mrs. McKenna said. "Things will always need to be done around here. But you have your youth once. I won't let you cheat yourself out of it for anything."

McKenna shook his head and grimaced, but Mrs. McKenna continued.

"We'll work our way through this time. That's what neighbors are for. Heck— those boys on your team can come out and help with some of these chores."

"But Mom," McKenna said, "it's a *game*. I don't feel right about playing a game right now."

"It is a game," Ryan said. "But around here, from early June to early August, it's more than a game. It's everything. It's life. And that life is in you. We can't let you end it."

"Are you listening to Father?" Mrs. McKenna asked her son.

McKenna reluctantly nodded.

"Are you listening to what Father is telling you to do?"

McKenna began a groan of protest. Ignoring it, his mother turned this time to Ryan.

"Marty's a farmer." She took a drink of coffee. "His dad dreamed for him to get an agricultural degree down at Iowa State."

Ryan nodded. "Good idea."

"Everyone thought it was a good idea, even Marty," Mrs. McKenna said. "Now he tells me he can't go on to school."

"I said I've got to postpone it, Mom," McKenna corrected. "We'll see about college down the road some."

He stood briskly, excused himself, placed his chair against the table, and drop-stepped from the table to the backdoor. There he paused and pulled a DEKALB Feed Corn cap from a hat rack. The cap was yellow with a green visor, and it featured a field corncob in winged flight. McKenna pulled the cap down snugly and spoke.

"I'll finish up with the baseball season, though. I promise." McKenna nodded in Ryan's direction. "Thanks for coming out. I better get back to work." He opened the door and disappeared outside.

Mrs. McKenna shook her head and sighed. "He's angry. Anger doesn't scare me. Quitting does. Farmers can never quit."

"He's in a stage," Ryan said. "Baseball will help him pass through this."

"Thank you for coming out here today," Mrs. McKenna said with weak smile.

Ryan bowed his head and gave thanks for the meal with a quick Grace after Meals prayer, including with it a petition for the faithfully departed. In silence, he continued to appeal for the intercession of McKenna's father to help his son through this season.

But this plea was interrupted by a persistent calling for Ryan himself to reach out to McKenna. This left Ryan as deeply troubled because he feared he would fail.

Somewhere in time over the years, he had lost any connection he might have had to God. In fact, he strongly believed he may have been Cottage Park's most disconnected soul to any kind of higher power. Any advice or counsel he gave came not from timeless, all-powerful spiritual enlightenment but from whatever he could wing or fake from his own diminishing creativity. McKenna needed real spiritual solace. Surely, he would see right through Ryan's recitations and incantations. Ryan couldn't offer him the pithy-but-wise platitudes he regularly dispensed to his other parishioners.

Ryan was also troubled because the worry and time he was spending on what to do about McKenna was keeping him from moving on to his next visit, where he could locate, indulge, and refuel with the spirits.

Around two o'clock, Egg brought two glasses of ice water outside and set one next to T. J., who sprawled in the shade of the maple tree, eyes closed, listening with an earphone plugged into a transistor radio. T. J. didn't even notice Egg.

Egg patrolled the garage to measure T. J.'s progress. The entire word *Die* had been painted over, including the area around it from the ground to the roof. Upon closer inspection, however, Egg saw and felt hardening drips of paint.

Back at the maple tree, Egg leaned down to T. J., and waved his hand in front of the boy's face. T. J. turned off his radio.

"Thanks for the water," T. J. said, seeing the glass for the first time. He held the glass up to both cheeks, then splashed it across his entire face, licking whatever rolled down over his lips. "The radio said it's ninety-seven degrees in Des Moines."

"Yep. It's warm," Egg said. "But this is Iowa, and that's the way it is this time of year." He stared down at T. J. "So what happened to the painting?"

T. J. took another drink. "You're kidding, right? I'm taking a break. The humidity is too high. I can't breathe. You're working me to get heatstroke."

"You don't even know what the word *humidity* means," Egg said.

T. J. rolled his eyes. "Yes, I do. It has something to do with the air . . . like . . . I don't know. Hot air."

"No," Egg said, annoyed more with an educational system that had failed to make T. J. aware of even the very air he breathed. When Egg spoke again, he did so with the patience and precision of a caring and conscientious teacher. "It's the measure of moisture in the air."

He nodded for T. J. to get up and follow him to the garage.

"Speaking of moisture"—Egg pointed to droplets of paint—"you're dripping."

T. J. groaned. "Aren't you being kind of picky today? I swear, I can't do anything right."

"I like things to be done a certain way," Egg said informatively.

The magnitude of his new relationship with T. J. began to weigh on him. With no father and a haphazard access to education, this young man would have to have nearly everything explained to him in a number of different ways, with lots of repetition.

"I like things to be done the right way. That means you'll have to start working hard."

"But it's hot, and I'm tired—" T. J. tried to interrupt him, but Egg continued.

"You can rest and sleep at night. Right now, you need to be working. More work, fewer breaks."

"Hey, I've worked my butt off today," T. J. said. "First you marched me downtown. Then you had to show me the whole town. We visited every square inch of this town with me carrying two cans of paint."

"Halfway," Egg corrected him. "Remember, I carried them when you said your arms were paralyzed." Egg stretched his arms out to the sides and began moving them in small circles. "My arms feel fine." Egg smugly continued the arm exercises as if he could do so indefinitely.

"That's because your muscles are already formed," T. J. said. "Mine are still developing."

"Now," Egg said, "when you do finally get down to business, you better not use too much paint. That's where those drips come from. That side's a mess." Egg sighed. "I'm better off doing it myself."

T. J. took a long drink and looked at the wall. "Wait—I've got an idea. What if I change the word *Amerigun* to *American*? Then it would say: the American way." T. J. pointed to Egg's flag in the front yard. "That would save us a lot of work and time, and it would also be patriotic."

Egg shook his head. "I want my garage white again."

"You're like everyone else in this town," T. J. said. "Why is everybody here so terrified of being different?"

"No one is afraid," Egg said. "We like the way things are done here."

"Come on," T. J. said. "There must be some people here who don't think it's so great."

"Every town has bad apples," Egg said with a shrug. "But most everyone here likes things the way they are."

"Even the kids?" T. J. asked, his eyebrows raised.

"Ask them yourself," Egg said. "They'll tell you."

"Where do I find them?"

"At the park, the pool, the ballpark," Egg said. "You can come with me over to the ballpark anytime."

T. J. shook his head.

"It won't hurt to watch," Egg said. "You can chase foul balls or something."

"Never," T. J. said.

"We'll see," Egg said, with the air of a teacher getting a student on task. "Now let's get you back to painting my garage."

T. J. laughed. "I've got the rest of the summer to do that."

"This job has to be finished soon, and—"

"I'll get around to it when this heat lets up," T. J. interrupted. "And I won't put too much paint on the wall," he added.

T. J. shielded his eyes, took a look at the sun, then looked down and picked at a blister on his finger. "It's time for lunch."

Egg watched wordlessly as T. J. carried the paint can into the garage.

"I'll be back tomorrow," T. J. said.

He raised a hand to wave but dropped it in pain, then hobbled away.

— CHAPTER SIX —

Countdown to the Finals: 45 Days to Go

I T WAS EARLY MORNING. KATHERINE OPENED A SMALL tackle box and unfolded drawers and compartments until she located and collected a half dozen pills in different colors and different shapes. She placed them on a small saucer. She knew Murphy was tired of taking so many pills in the morning, afternoon, and evening, so she presented him the pills with fresh-squeezed lemonade in a frosted glass after his favorite show, *Jeopardy!* It was a pleasurable diversion from his usual tap water chaser in a plastic glass. He swallowed down the pills without complaint.

Murphy was dying, but he would not or could not die. The team of doctors who saw him regularly for his checkups at the Mayo Clinic in Rochester, Minnesota, professed utter dismay that he was still alive. Their other patients had one or maybe two health concerns for which they could develop a treatment strategy. Murphy on the other hand had arthritis, and heart disease, and chronic lower respiratory diseases—and he had also survived prostate cancer. He was a medical science experiment and a house of cards in a tornado with driving hail, yet he still kept going. Was it luck? The doctors begged him to go to Las Vegas with them to pick numbers on the roulette wheel.

Murphy responded in kind by loosening his trademark white short-sleeved dress shirt and flopping out a brown scapular with the Sacred Heart of Jesus.

"This is what keeps me alive," Murphy said. "And being ornery enough to outlive my enemies."

Murphy compared his body to an old, broken-down beater he had gotten his money out of. But he would be especially grateful if it could make one last journey—the trip to the Finals in Des Moines at the end of July.

Murphy actually knew what was keeping him alive. Two to three times each day, a near-deadly malady would strike him to a halt and force him to consider a life unfinished. No one, not even his doctors or Katherine or his fellow coaches, knew of these events.

If he were standing when a spell occurred, he would sit down. If he were sitting, he would lie down. As his heart raced or slowed, as his lungs desperately fought to expel mucous or liquid, as his blood pressure plummeted, he would close his eyes, try his best to continue breathing, and prepare for a good death.

Once he was comfortable, he would watch his life pass before him . . . childhood; his career as a good teacher and very successful coach; Katherine; four beautiful, happy, and healthy daughters; and sixteen incredible grandchildren. It was a life kings and common men alike would envy.

But then the vision of his life would continue, and he'd see the hollow, empty second-place finishes at the Finals. Finally, and most disturbingly, the vision would end with the haunting visage of Moriarity.

Each of these private showings of his life would last three to four seconds. When they passed over, Murphy would know it was still not time— not his time. At each conclusion, he would thank God for continuing his life, and he'd promise to continue to do God's work, which as best as he could make out was to win the Finals. And do something with Moriarity.

Until Moriarity's freshman year, Murphy's philosophy of coaching had been simple: He demanded that the young men who graced the Holy Trinity baseball uniforms be gods on the field and gentlemen off. Wearing that uniform was a privilege you had to earn. Those who couldn't measure up in both capacities were casually dismissed. He let the chips fall where they may without a single regret.

But Murphy discarded that philosophy the moment Moriarity stepped onto the field in his freshman year. In truth, Murphy had been preparing to discard it for years. From that day on, the usual rules did not apply.

Had he grown up in any other community than Cottage Park and with any other caring mentor than Murphy, Moriarity surely would have been labelled and medicated for some variation of an emotional or behavioral disability. He never would have discovered his salvation—baseball. God knows where the poor boy would have ended up. Even Murphy, under his old coaching approach, would have cut him loose and let the chips fall.

Murphy had dreams for the young pitcher, but he knew he couldn't achieve them alone. He needed an ally, another dealer to stack the deck so Moriarity couldn't help but win. He needed someone with whom he could openly share his thoughts and hopes about Moriarity. Murphy certainly couldn't discuss such matters with Moriarity himself, whose head was already high and far away in the clouds. The coach needed this special relationship with another player.

It was a new approach for Murphy. He didn't have such a give-and-take relationship with anyone—not Egg or Ryan, not his family, not even Katherine.

And so one day early in that freshman year, Murphy looked out over the study hall he proctored. Twenty-five freshman students worked quietly, including Moriarity. Murphy eventually focused on Sean Powers, who sat in front of the pitcher.

Powers lived with his grandparents. His father had desperately tried to piece together a variety of part-time jobs, including the family's town movie theatre business, the Five Star Theatre. But when the theater closed down, all the other balls he was juggling seemed to fall at the same time. He was forced to take his family to Mankato, Minnesota, where he was able to find a job. He kept his second oldest, Sean, behind with his parents. Although he missed his family, Sean stayed with his Cottage Park and Holy Trinity baseball families.

"Mr. Powers," Murphy had said. "Please bring your book and assignment up here for a moment."

Murphy positioned a student desk near his own for Powers to sit.

"What are you working on?" Murphy asked, pointing to the assignment the boy had been working on so diligently.

To be called on by Murphy for any kind of attention or discussion was a great privilege. Powers spoke proudly.

"This is algebra," Powers said. "We're working on different types of triangles."

"That's good work," Murphy said. Murphy looked back at the triangles and pretended to be commenting on them. "But math isn't my strong suit. I called you up here for another reason."

Murphy hesitated. It was a struggle to formulate the words he needed to communicate with Powers. As a coach, he was used to words flowing out like an instructional manual. But here he needed words that would be negotiated, shared, trusted, hopefully accepted but possibly rejected, remembered forever or forgotten a few seconds later. There was no instructional manual for such a dialogue. Murphy was setting off on a voyage to uncharted, unexplored territory.

"While we're talking," Murphy said uneasily, "keep your eyes on your assignment."

Powers was happy to comply. He stared at the page of triangles stretched into obtuse, acute, and isosceles shapes. After several seconds, he dared to look away from the page. His eyes darted for a moment to Murphy, who seemed to be struggling in thought.

Murphy broke the silence with a whisper saying one word very slowly: "Mooooreeeeeeeairrrrrriteeeeee . . ."

Again there was an uncomfortable silence. Powers guessed he was supposed to respond in some sort of fill-in-the-blank exercise.

"Is in trouble?" Powers offered.

"No," Murphy responded. He looked out across the room to see Moriarity miraculously working on an assignment. "Not at this particular moment."

"Is different?" Powers quickly responded, as if this were a game and a timer might go off at any second. He strived to convey that he knew Moriarity well, so he kept guessing with a list of adjectives. "Is crazy, wild, mixed-up . . ."

Powers anxiously looked at Murphy to see if he was getting close to the right description.

Murphy interrupted Powers. "For consistency's sake, I prefer we use the term *misunderstood*."

Powers nodded appreciatively.

"He's one of your friends," Murphy continued matter-of-factly. The ice had been broken.

Powers nodded. Moriarity was his best friend. For a boy who followed and lived by the rules, it was sometimes intoxicating to be in the presence of someone who seemingly did as he pleased whenever he pleased. By comparison, Powers seemed like the All-American boy, which he enjoyed.

"Do you pray?" Murphy asked.

"Oh yes," Powers said. "All the time. Everyday. I say the Hail Mary, Our Father, Act of Contrition, Morning Offering . . . I say the Rosary with the Glory Be, Apostles' Creed—"

"What about the Guardian Angel Prayer?" Murphy interrupted again. "Do they still teach you kids that?"

"Sure," Powers said. He continued, lying, "I say that one everyday too."

"Go ahead and say it," Murphy ordered.

Powers closed his eyes and summoned the invocation from memory.

"Angel of God . . ."

When reciting memorized supplications, Powers had to spit out the words like watermelon seeds from a machine gun. Otherwise, he would forget where he was in the prayer, then have to start over, saying the words even faster. And so the rest of the petition spewed out so fast and so connected, it could have been one long multisyllabic word.

"My-guardian-dear-to-whom-God's-love-commits-me-here. Ever-this-day-be-at-my-side-to-light-and-guard-to-rule-and-guide."

"Good. Now remember that last part," Murphy said. "That's what we need to do for Moriarity—to light and guard, to rule and guide."

"Coach," Powers insisted, "I've already been doing that."

"I know you have," Murphy said, "and I appreciate that." He continued solemnly. "But you're not alone. This is our understanding—just between us."

Murphy waited for Powers to look up from his book.

"Get it?"

Then Murphy waited for the nod of approval signifying the allegiance he knew he would receive from Powers.

Now Powers understood the purpose of this conversation. Everyone in Cottage Park knew there was a different set of rules for Moriarity. Powers understood that he would work in tandem with Murphy to help Moriarity navigate through that system of unique rules. To be included in such a pact was an incredible honor. Powers vowed to himself he would not let Murphy down.

"Back to work," Murphy said, gesturing for Powers to return to his seat with his classmates.

Since that time three years ago, the two had never spoken another word about their conversation or their collaboration. But the words they had agreed to that day seared through every trip they made together to the pitcher's mound and every other experience they had with Moriarity.

As Murphy relaxed in his kitchen with Katherine and sipped on his lemonade, he reflected on how lucky he was to be starting another day in a beautiful place like Cottage Park. Many men of his age had already passed. He had been blessed to do the Lord's work for another day.

At that time, Moriarity and Powers drove their bikes from the sidewalk up on Murphy's front lawn. Moriarity jumped from his bike while it still rolled like he had seen cowboys hop off horses in rodeo shows, then bounded up the steps and knocked on Murphy's door. Powers had to swerve to miss Moriarity's bike that toppled over in front of him. He stopped and dismounted, placed his kickstand, then joined Moriarity on the steps. Moriarity banged on the door.

Katherine opened the door and welcomed the boys in. She was happy to see them. She yelled to Murphy that they had company. "Very important company," she said as they made their way to the kitchen.

Murphy greeted his battery as they entered the kitchen.

"What do you hear?" Murphy said. "What do you say?"

The boys both answered at the same time, "Nothing," and sat down at the table with him.

In the meantime, Katherine offered the boys a choice of refreshments. Both accepted lemonade, thinking they would receive a cheap powdered drink as they did at home. A moment later, they gulped from frosty glasses filled with lemonade squeezed from actual lemons with large chunks of pulp still floating in the mix. They were amazed and appreciative.

Several moments passed in silence while they savored this treat. Periodically Katherine would ask the boys about members of their families, then they'd settle into silence again. Moriarity finally broke the silence.

"We thought we'd come over to meet with you about pitching," he said to Murphy. "I need to get a new pitch for the Finals."

"First, the season has just started," Murphy said. "We have a long ways to go before we get to the Finals. And second, you don't need anything new. Work on what you have, what God has blessed you with—a fastball. That's all you need to win. Yes, even to win the Finals."

Katherine refilled the boys' glasses. She practiced traditional Cottage Park hospitality, hovering over the boys and topping off their glasses whenever they sunk below half full. Also according to tradition, the boys showed their appreciation by finishing their drinks and politely declining her generous efforts to replenish their glasses. She politely ignored their requests to be left alone.

"Yeah, I've got a fastball," Moriarity said. "But I've also got a slider, a curve, a changeup, and a knuckleball."

"A knuckleball. I should have figured," Murphy said, shaking his head. "Where did you learn that?"

"From a book at the library," Moriarity said. "I can throw it. It works." He looked at Powers, who verified the statement with a nod, then sharply winced when he observed Murphy's disapproval.

Katherine now lugged a Blue Bunny family-size one-gallon plastic bucket of vanilla ice cream from the freezer. With great effort, she pried off its lid. Again with great effort, she strained to dig an aluminum scooper into the hardened ice cream and scrape the shavings into two huge mounds in separate bowls. Then she covered the ice cream with heaping tablespoons of hot fudge from a heated jar of Smucker's. Next she sprinkled frozen walnuts across the hot fudge. She and Murphy harvested, dried, husked, and poked black walnuts from a tree in their backyard. They stored the nuts in jelly jars in their freezer. Lastly, she sliced bananas alongside the ice cream, then carried the bowls to the boys.

"Where's mine?" Murphy said. Ice cream was his one serious indulgence.

"We're saving the rest for your wake," Katherine said sternly. Then she added, "You can have a scoop for dessert tonight."

Katherine knew that both boys were from modest households. The sundaes were an extravagance they could seldom enjoy. Her intention was to stuff them until any thought of want would be drowned in sweet satiation.

To this end, she next spread nearly half a box of Nilla wafers across a tray and set it before the boys. When they didn't immediately reach for the wafers, she plunked a handful into each of their bowls.

The boys began greedily shoveling the ice cream and wafer mix into their mouths. After several minutes, they slowed as the treat became more like a burden.

Still, Katherine continued to hover over them, insisting they allow her to drop more clumps of now-softening ice cream into their bowls. When the boys held their bowls out of reach, she grabbed onto their arms and pulled them forcefully toward her until they were in range to be bombed with more ice cream. Eventually the boys surrendered, sat back in their chairs, groaned, and gently covered their stomachs in the event a speck of dust should land on them and initiate some sort of gastrointestinal avalanche.

Murphy watched the two, somewhat surprised that Katherine had finally located the floor of their bottomless appetite pit. He turned to Moriarity.

"As I was saying, anybody can *throw* a pitch. You need consistency."

"I've got that too," Moriarity said. "Come on."

Moriarity and Powers pushed themselves from the table gingerly, groaning as they fully stood. They were not unlike Murphy, who always rose from a sitting position in that same fashion.

Moriarity motioned Murphy outside. "Even packed with ice cream, I'm going to show you."

Moriarity took one step, then immediately turned around so he and Powers could thank Katherine for the lemonade and ice cream.

Once outside, Powers grabbed his catcher's mitt from the handlebars of his bike, undid the rubber band that bound it, and opened the mitt like a clam to pull out a baseball. He tossed the ball to Moriarity, who marked off the appropriate distance. Murphy waited until Moriarity found his spot, then stood behind him.

"What do you want to see?" Moriarity asked Murphy. "You name it. I'll throw it."

"How about some catch," Murphy said. "Get good and warmed up before you do anything."

Moriarity threw a succession of pitches, some from the windup position. He started by lobbing the ball and gradually increased the speed of each pitch.

Still looking at Powers and his target, he spoke to Murphy. "There'll be pro scouts at the Finals, won't there?"

"I suppose," Murphy said. "A few."

"You know them all," Moriarity said. "You'll put in a good word for me, won't you?"

"You're my starting pitcher," Murphy said assertively. "That speaks for itself."

"Yeah," Moriarity said. "But you'll tell them the other stuff too, right? Like that I work hard. I'm a good guy and a good student." Moriarity looked over at Murphy, who looked back in doubt. "What? I am a good student. I got two Bs spring quarter."

"In gym and what else?" Murphy said.

"Geography," Moriarity said. "And that's a tough class."

Moriarity turned back to Powers and therefore never saw Murphy smirk. He would laugh out loud later, when no one was around.

"I could do better in school if I was more interested. I'd rather quit and play ball. You still think I'll make it—to the big leagues?"

Murphy folded his arms, his body language suggesting he may be covering something. "When did I ever say you'd make it to the big leagues?"

"You didn't," Moriarity said. "But you told me everything I needed to do to make it, and I've done it all."

Murphy cleared his throat.

"I mean, I'm working on it," Moriarity corrected. "And one of the things I think I really need to know is how to throw a forkball. Would you show me?"

Murphy shook his head. "I will not." He scratched his forehead. "How do you dream this stuff up? A *forkball*?"

"Come on—show me," Moriarity said. "I need a pitch that drops—like, drops off a table."

"I said I won't show you," Murphy said calmly. "And you shouldn't learn to throw pitches from a book. That's the surest way to ruin your arm."

"But it's a good pitch," Moriarity said. "I know it takes time to develop. I promise I won't use it right away."

"I've heard that before," Murphy said with a huff. "When you were in eighth grade, you asked me to show you how to throw a curve ball if you promised not to use it. And I made the mistake of showing you. You spent the whole winter working on the darn thing, and the first pitch you threw in spring baseball was a curve."

"It was a strike!" Moriarity said. He made a throwing motion that ended with a curve variation. "The guy at the plate hit the dirt. Even the umpire hit the dirt."

Murphy said impatiently, "You don't need to be monkeying around with anything like that. Your ticket is the fastball. You should be throwing that pitch almost all the time. We need to work on placing that fastball. Trust me. I know a little about baseball . . . and you."

"But how do I keep the batter off guard if all I have is one pitch?" Moriarity asked.

"That's something you can worry about at the next level!" Murphy said, his face beginning to get red.

Now he had said too much. He never should have mentioned any future beyond Holy Trinity to the boy. He took a deep breath. He could feel one of his increasingly frequent death experiences racing over him.

He slowly genuflected to the ground and wobbled for a moment, leaning forward on the one upraised knee that held him in balance.

He closed his eyes. Again his life passed before him. Again that private showing ended with Moriarity. But this time, when Murphy opened his eyes, he saw the real deal. It was Moriarity in the flesh, who by coincidence looked as if he himself had seen a ghost.

"Coach," Moriarity said worriedly. "Are you okay?" He waved for Powers to hurry over.

"Yes," Murphy said. "I've just experienced the Supreme Being."

The fright of his own death had given him courage to share his experience—as well as credence to his own craziness. He turned directly, but still dizzily, to Powers. He spoke as if the main subject of his vision wasn't also at his side, prepared to catch him if he should topple over.

"It's Moriarity," he said. "He needs to know he's at a time in his life when he doesn't have to worry what the batter thinks. I don't care if the whole world knows he's throwing a fastball. He's still the biggest kid on the field. High school boys can't hit him." Murphy waved his arm as if he were pushing something away. "All these other junk pitches could hurt his arm in the long term."

Murphy's eyes finally cleared and focused. He turned at last to Moriarity. "Now is it asking too much for you to help me up and throw a few fastballs?"

Moriarity grinned gratefully. "I'd love to," he said.

He helped Murphy back to his feet and supported him until Murphy set both feet in balance, then ordered Moriarity to let go. Powers raced back to his catcher's position, squatted down, and signaled for a fastball, jabbing his finger repeatedly to indicate that Moriarity had damn well better throw what he ordered.

Moriarity did not disappoint, winding up and delivering a fastball—straight and smooth. It popped like an M-80 firework when it pounded into Powers's mitt.

"There you go," Murphy said. He drew a long, slow, and peaceful breath. "A million pitchers would give the world to have that pitch. Use it while you can."

Moriarity smiled, then sighed passively as Powers returned the ball. After what he had witnessed, he definitely would not test Murphy's patience again today. He threw another fastball, even more searing than the first.

— CHAPTER SEVEN —

Countdown to the Finals: 43 Days to Go

EGG WAS RAKING FRESHLY CUT GRASS CLIPPINGS when Ryan drove up his driveway later that afternoon. Ryan had taken his Deville through a car wash. Water was still beaded across it. All the dust and dirt the car had accumulated during the drive to the McKenna home was gone. His car looked new again.

Egg tossed his rake near the garage and headed for the car. Ryan opened the passenger's side door, and Egg half fell, half threw himself inside.

Ryan backed his Cadillac down the driveway and slowly drove along the shaded street downtown to the Lipstick on a Pig Bar, or Lipstick for short. It was one of three bars in Cottage Park, but the only one the old men frequented.

"Your old manual mower still does the job," Ryan said.

"It's quiet—and safer too," Egg said. "It's the only way for me."

Ryan came to a stop sign and, for once, stopped instead of merely slowing down. Actually, he stopped to ponder Egg's words. Ryan was no longer strong enough to pull the cord to start his mower. A manual mower would also save on gas and oil and be quieter. A manual mower might work for him too.

From behind, a car politely honked for him to move on. Ryan lifted his right hand from the steering wheel, raised a friendly two-finger wave back, and proceeded on.

A few blocks later, Ryan angled his car into a parking spot in front of the Lipstick—with Egg's help directing and updating him on his proximity to the next car. The Lipstick was one large hall with long, heavy-duty picnic tables. The outer walls were lined with booths encased in worn-leather padding. On some, the stuffing was exposed along broken cracks of leather.

Egg and Ryan stepped inside to cheerful greetings from their many friends. The hall was filled with nearly seventy patrons—mostly of the same age group and all from the Cottage Park area. Thursday was "All You Can Eat Spaghetti Night" for one dollar, followed by bingo starting at 6:30 p.m. Other than baseball, church, and school activities, Thursday night bingo at the Lipstick was the old men's main social activity.

"My two favorite customers," O'Connor, the owner and bartender, said, joining in the greeting.

He was a bulldog of a man, with a big, thick chest and meaty, dense-muscle arms. O'Connor had been a catcher for Holy Trinity twenty-six years earlier, at a time when coaches routinely put their widest bodies at that position. O'Connor was one of the oldest men in Cottage Park to have received his entire baseball education from the old men. In gratitude for his gift of the magic of baseball, he had become a lifelong volunteer as the public address announcer for all Holy Trinity home baseball games.

He quickly waddled from around the bar with a 7 and 7—a highball of Seagram's Seven Crown and 7Up—for each man.

"Coach beat you here."

He motioned to a booth, where Murphy and Katherine were already eating and watching the Cardinals take on the Pirates. Ryan and Egg joined them. O'Connor followed behind with their drinks. He positioned the drinks before each man, then dropped bar napkins on their table.

Pointing to the napkins, he said, "These are new. What do you think?"

Egg picked up one and read it out loud: "My memory is getting worse all the time. First I began to forget faces, then names, then to zip up. Yesterday I forgot to unzip."

The men laughed.

"You have to have a sense of humor around here," O'Connor said. "Business is dying."

"Yes," Ryan said. He took a drink of his 7 and 7, and a blissful calm came over him. "All the way to heaven is heaven!"

"Thank you, Father," O'Connor said. "I'll be back in a minute with your spaghetti." He made his way to the kitchen.

"I'm starving," Egg said. "You certainly can't beat the price for this meal."

"You've got to start eating better," Katherine said to Egg. "You should come over and have your meals with Al and me."

"I've tried for months to get him to eat with me at the rectory," Ryan explained.

Katherine raised an eyebrow. Ryan relied on the casseroles thoughtful parishioners occasionally gifted to him. Otherwise, he didn't eat any better than Egg.

O'Connor returned with two plates of spaghetti, garlic bread, and salad. He dutifully helped Egg and Ryan find their silverware and napkins and didn't leave until they began to eat.

Katherine stacked her own silverware on her finished plate and began to slide from the booth. "I'll get you boys some bingo cards and daubers, then I'll sit with Rosemary and Helen so you can gab about your baseball."

Egg forked a wad of spaghetti the size of a golf ball and lifted the collection to his mouth, all the while keeping his eyes on the television. "How are we doing?" he said, his mouth full.

"No score," Murphy answered. "And Danny just struck out, so you haven't missed a thing." He slowly sipped his drink. "Nothing like a cold 7 and 7 on a hot summer night. Katherine doesn't believe that, but she gave up fighting and said I could have one. I'm savoring it."

The men watched the television in silence for a moment, each immersed in the game and his food or drink. Murphy sighed as he rubbed the inside corner of his eyes under his glasses.

"Wilson's still up to no good," he said.

"It's always Wilson," Ryan replied.

"After everything that was said the other night at your place, can't he relax until the end of the season?" Egg asked.

Murphy shook his head. "Sean Powers's grandfather said Wilson's asking people to sign a petition."

Egg took another bite, nearly finishing the spaghetti. He spoke between chews. "What's it say?"

Murphy said, "Same thing he told us—both you and Father off the bench and some new coach to replace you—and no doubt take over the team. If he can't make us step down, he'll try this petition route instead."

Ryan finished his spaghetti and twirled his salad around his plate. "I guess we'll have to see who signs the petition.'" He shrugged.

Murphy ground his fist into the table. "I don't care what anyone signs!"

He caught himself before his face reddened too much. He gave a quick glance over his shoulder.

"Of course, Katherine doesn't want me fighting back with Wilson. But this whole business stinks, and I'm sick and tired of it."

Egg said coolly, "No one will sign any petition."

"Oh, there'll be a few," Murphy said. "I expect that. I don't care about the petition itself. But I do care about having our players' full attention and keeping them concentrated on playing good baseball this summer. Now with this, they'll be wondering who's really in charge. And I don't doubt a few of them will begin to coach themselves."

"Moriarity," Egg said flatly.

The men's attention turned to the television. Danny dived and snagged a ground ball down the third-base line, then completed the play by firing a strike over to first for the out. Each looked knowingly at each other as if to say, *We had something to do with Danny Stinson . . .*

Katherine returned with the bingo equipment. "The first game is starting in one minute," she said hurriedly.

She distributed a bingo card to each man. Next she unscrewed the dauber caps and set a dauber, poised and ready, in front of each man.

"Remember—one minute before the game starts!" she said as she retreated to her friends.

Murphy continued as if he hadn't heard his wife's urgent warning. "You should have seen Danny in the first inning," he said. "Someone hit a line shot. It bounced at Danny's toes before he could catch it. He waited until the runner was nearly all the way to first, then he gunned it to first for the out. He used to do the same thing in high school."

The bingo caller spoke loudly over the microphone and introduced the first game: four corners. After asking everyone if they were ready and hearing no objections, he slowly called the first number, O67, then repeated it. Each man checked to see if he had that number. They then checked one another's card. Seeing no one had had any luck, they immediately lost interest and checked out of the game.

"Danny Stinson," Ryan said, picking up right where they had been cut off in the conversation before the bingo interruption. He nodded appreciatively. "What an arm!"

They all looked back at the television. The next batter flied out to end the inning. A beer commercial came on.

Ryan looked into his drink and stirred the ice cubes with his finger. "Wilson has been contacting more than the people in Cottage Park," he said. "The bishop called me this afternoon after Wilson contacted him."

"The bishop?" Murphy repeated.

Egg closed his eyes and sat back in the booth. All he could do was shake his head—another worthless bishop who showed little or no interest in rural parishes.

"He's all right," Ryan said, understanding the unspoken words in Egg's head shake. "He has a challenging job. I don't think he likes Wilson any more than we do. He said he trusted me whether I should continue coaching. He's praying to make sure I make the right decision for the parish."

"Did he say any more about you retiring?" Egg asked.

"He doesn't want me here another winter," Ryan said. "He suggested I consider moving soon into the nursing home there in Sioux City. He said I could stay until after the baseball season. After that point, though, he told me I've got to move on."

"Damn him," Egg said. "And I bet he doesn't send us another priest. That's how interested he is in the parish."

"He'll send a man if he can find one," Ryan said. "But there aren't enough men in the seminary. It's the same situation Wilson is facing for the coaching position. He'll never find a gentleman who knows baseball well enough to replace you, Al. With a lesser coach, I'm afraid the kids will lose interest in the sport."

"Cottage Park without baseball," Egg said, shaking his head. "Well, I guess that's already starting to happen now. The kids don't play the pickup games like they used to. They're inside watching too much television."

"Baseball, the church," Ryan said. "Pretty soon they'll have to close down Holy Trinity School." He sighed. "This whole town could dry up and blow away."

"Wait a minute," Murphy said. "Before you two read eulogies and throw dirt on our caskets, you better remember we have a fight on our hands—right now. The worst thing we can do is even consider giving up. If Wilson knew that, he'd never let up, and he'd win."

Ryan and Egg agreed.

O'Connor brought another round of drinks. Murphy declined, keeping to his one-drink limit. Instead, Ryan helped himself to Murphy's drink. O'Connor also brought a basket of salted peanuts. Each man picked at the food and nibbled indifferently.

One of Katherine's friends shrieked out "Bingo!" and leaped from her chair. She quickly made her way to the platform to have the caller check her card and, upon confirmation, collect the $15 cash prize for her efforts. A moment later, the caller announced her victory. The entire audience groaned, then applauded her as she made her way back to her seat.

The caller announced that the next game would be postage stamp bingo. The caller explained that a bingo in this game was a small square of four numbers in any corner of the card. The players tuned him out. They had heard this same tiresome explanation every Thursday night for years. The caller repeated these rules every Thursday night, however, for a reason. Despite his weekly explanation, some players continued to mistakenly believe they could call bingo only if they had the square pattern in the right hand corner of their card, like an actual postage stamp. And so it continued, week after week, year after year.

Regardless, the old men were through with bingo for the evening. As the caller announced the first number, the men turned their entire focus to the television. The Pirates had loaded the bases. The Cardinals signaled their top relief pitcher from the bullpen. The starter, shoulders drooping and seemingly defeated, made his way off the mound.

Nodding at the game, Egg said, "I think they'd be better off telling their starter at the beginning of a game, 'Do your best. If they score a couple of runs, that's okay. We're behind you.' Hell, now a guy is always looking over his back and seeing someone warming up in the bullpen. That can't do anything for your confidence."

"Actually," Murphy said, "I think those coaches know how far they can go with each pitcher. I don't like it either, but it's like everything else nowadays . . . specialization."

The relief pitcher got the next batter to hit into a double play to end the inning.

Then suddenly, the bar's front door burst open with a barrage of loud cursing. All turned to see two men wrestling in the doorway. Both were dressed in grease-dried blue jeans and unbuttoned flannel shirts. They looked to be in their late twenties. One was stocky and the other tall. It was a bit unclear, but they seemed to be friends.

The taller man broke away from the other and squeezed through the door. As he made his way to the bar, his stocky counterpart hit him in the arm with full force. The tall man groaned and slumped into the bar. The other man snorted laughter, strutted to the pool table, and dropped in a quarter.

Murphy looked at Ryan and Egg, and they all shook their heads. The other patrons in the bar looked up from their bingo cards and grimaced as the billiard balls exploded from underneath the pool table down into the tray. The stocky man collected the clacking balls from below and pounded them into the rack.

"Excuse me," Egg called to the man over the noise. When he didn't get a response, he waved his hand until he got the stocky man's attention. "I don't want any trouble here, but they've got a bingo game happening, and they can't hear over the racket you're making."

A few of the bingo players nodded as if to say, *Thanks, Egg!* for his considerate request.

The stocky man stopped and straightened. "Get a hearing aid, Gramps."

His friend returned from the bar with two beers. He set them at the table's edge, jerked his head toward Egg, and said, "What the hell's his problem?"

"Where are you two from?" Egg bellowed.

"Are you writing a story?" the tall man said.

"Hey—respect your elders," the stocky man jeered at his friend.

The stocky man looked back at Egg and started off toward the coaches' booth, chalking his cue along the way.

"We're from Schaller," he said.

The tall man also edged over to the booth.

"Well!" Egg said.

Schaller—that explained everything. In all his long life, Egg had never heard of a baseball player coming from Schaller. He viewed such communities as barbaric outposts in the wilderness. His expectations for the dirty duo decreased instantly.

"Don't they have manners in Schaller?" Egg said, stating the obvious. Still, he believed it was his responsibility to educate them. "There's people who come here to play bingo, and you're ruining it for them."

"Come on," the tall man said. "Bingo? Who cares?"

"We care!" Egg said, glaring at the men. "How about some manners, Buster?"

The stocky man bit his bottom lip. He spoke casually, but his eyes showed fury. "I get any more shit out of you, and this cue stick goes up your ass . . . sideways."

It took a moment for the words to sink into Egg. It took another moment for his response. He began to push himself out of the booth. Ryan grasped out at Egg's hands and tried to restrain him, but Egg charged ahead.

Egg was halfway out of the booth and not yet fully standing when the stocky man jerked the heel of his palm into Egg's face.

Egg gasped a breath. His dentures loosened and nearly slipped from his mouth. In a flash, Egg ripped them out and dropped them in the peanut basket. Finally freed from the booth, he stood up straight and brought his right hand back and around in a wild roundhouse swing that knocked the pool cue from his attacker's hands.

Ryan quickly stood and stepped between the men and Egg. He yelled at the men, "Stop—he's sixty years older than you!"

But the men knocked Ryan into Egg. The force sent Egg backward into another table.

Murphy reached out, though he was too far from the action to be of any help. Instead he yelled at O'Connor, "Call Sheriff Huffman!"

"He's already on his way!" O'Connor said as he speed-walked from behind the bar.

He rushed into the midst of the warring men and used his barrel chest to push the attackers toward the door. The stocky man prepared his fists but released them when O'Connor jabbed a rock-hard forefinger into his chest.

"Come on—hit me!" O'Connor cocked his own grapefruit-sized fist under the man's chin. "I called Sheriff Huffman for *your* safety, not any-body's in here. Get out of here, and don't ever come back!"

The men shoved away and turned for the door. O'Connor followed.

At the door, the stocky man looked back and gave Egg the finger, thrusting it high in the air and shaking it.

"I'm not through with you, old man."

"I'm still game," Egg said, stepping toward the men.

An enraged O'Connor now charged toward the men. As if kicking a field goal, he booted the retreating stocky man. The man collapsed forward on the ground, then hustled to his feet. Both men scurried for their lives. O'Connor chased them for a few steps out the door before returning inside, completely out of breath.

During the melee, the bingo game had stopped as everyone at the Lipstick had turned transfixed toward the action around the pool table. Then all at once, a clamor rose as patrons spread word and alarm from table to table. Already, they were adding various twists and interpretations of the affair—all complimentary to Egg.

O'Connor stepped quickly to the platform and received the microphone from the caller.

"Ladies and gentlemen," he boomed, "I present you the moral arbiter and enforcer of public decency in Cottage Park, Egg Gallivan!"

This announcement was met with loud cheering—raucous cheering, to be more precise. Egg's elderly peers were relieved and grateful for his standing up to the boorish behavior that all too often seemed to go unchecked and accepted.

O'Connor proceeded directly to Egg, embraced him, and patted him on the back. "Are you okay?" he asked.

Like many of the middle-aged men in Cottage Park, he had grown up in a time when adults looked after community children as their own. Likewise, now those children looked after the old men as if they were their own fathers.

As O'Connor released him, Egg temporarily lost his balance. He weaved like a toddler until he lurched back down inside the booth. He reached for his dentures in the peanut basket, brushed salt and shells from them, then plunked them into his highball, rinsing away the remaining residue. He finally adjusted them in his mouth and smiled.

"He blindsided you," Ryan lamented. "If I'd known he would do that, I would have let you at him in the first place."

"Yeah," Egg said. "He's *lucky* it wasn't a fair fight. I can still give a guy like that all he can handle."

"He won't be back, Egg," O'Connor said. "You showed him."

Katherine rushed over to the table. In one half of one second, she glanced at Murphy and shot him a look that distinctly said, *I step away from you three for a moment, and you get in a barroom brawl in front of everyone in Cottage Park? This is so embarrassing. Here I am, worried to death about your health, and this is how you repay me? I never should have let you have that drink!*

"Katherine . . ." Murphy implored. He understood each unspoken word and anticipated the additional words she would verbalize later that night. "We had nothing to do with this one—"

But in the second half of that one second, Katherine waved her right hand to block Murphy's explanation, then bring it lovingly to Egg's face. She gently stroked his scalp, parting his hair, and combing it with her fingernails.

"Ooh," she cooed.

Like a cut man in a boxer's corner, she plunked a napkin into Murphy's drink and dabbed it to Egg's lip, now swelling and cracking a tiny drop of blood. She looked into Egg's eyes, covered with cataracts. Her long look to him distinctly said, *It's so unrelenting getting old. You—and Father Ryan and the other old unmarried men of Cottage Park—need someone to take care of you.*

Katherine reached down and checked Egg's hands. They appeared to be okay. Her mind raced through decades of injustices, sadnesses, tragedies that had befallen Egg—especially the loss of his son in Vietnam. A wave of rage swept over her as she looked back across his face. She could see scars from fights years ago.

If those two young hooligans had returned at that moment, she herself would have attacked them: kicking, scratching, and hitting them with all her might. She glanced at the door in the lucky event she could bring her murderous blood lust to fruition. But they had not returned.

When she finally spoke, her voice trembled. "I hope you swatted those wiseacres," she said.

She picked up another napkin and dotted tears beginning in both eyes.

Egg had not channeled Katherine's unspoken messages as her husband had. Instead, as he looked back into Katherine's eyes, he simply yearned for her to know that while he hadn't picked this fight, he couldn't walk away from it.

Bingo never resumed that night. There was too much chatter—all celebratory. One by one, each of the patrons—many of them wobbling or using canes and walkers—came forth to check on and thank Egg. O'Connor arranged them in a receiving line, like that of a wedding or funeral. Egg, Ryan, and Murphy remained seated in their booth as each patron filed by and shook Egg's hand, smiling and sharing a memory of his similar exploits from the past.

"Just like the old days," one man said. "You used to be in fights all the time!"

"It's good you stood up to them," another patron said. "These young fellas think they can come right in and take over."

O'Connor brought the old men another round of drinks. Already in Katherine's doghouse, Murphy broke her one-drink rule and helped himself to another highball.

As the last of the patrons in the receiving line congratulated Egg, the old men shifted their focus back to the television. The game had ended during all the commotion. Most would read about it in the paper the next day. As it turned out, Danny knocked in the sole and winning run for the Cardinals during the bar melee. But he would have to share hero's status for the night, at least in Cottage Park—and wait for it, at that—as news spread about how Egg stood up to the younger bullying men and how those men backed down and ran out of town.

Wilson's petition—with its three names—seemed to evaporate after the fight, as did any doubts about these men's qualifications and abilities to act as coaches.

This was the old Egg, the people of Cottage Park thought. The Egg who, right along with Ryan and Murphy, had been boasting and promising a summer state championship for years. He carried a legend too many in town had forgotten—that he always had been and always would be a fighter. That sort of emotion, immune to age, would never weaken, and it was needed out there at the ballpark.

On top of it, the community knew Egg had morals, as did the other two coaches. He attended Mass, celebrated by Ryan, every morning of the week. Often Murphy joined him. None of the men had ever been known to turn down a request for help from a neighbor.

So Wilson put the petition away. Most importantly, though, he put it away because Holy Trinity was undefeated. They had won each of their four games by large margins. It was a long stretch for even their harshest critic to argue with the coaches' success—bar brawl or no bar brawl.

Disappointed but not defeated, Wilson proceeded with his next plan. He prepared help-wanted ads. Over the weekend, all of Iowa would see in the *Des Moines Register* three openings for teaching positions at Holy Trinity. Each position included the possibility of being the coach or assistant coach for the baseball team.

Wilson smiled and relaxed. The decision-making process for hiring new teachers was entirely his. Of course, the school board had to approve his nominees, but they had always trusted Wilson's judgment. Change was coming. Now, if he could be assured that Holy Trinity would make it through this season without any further drama . . .

Wilson reflected that the old men had sacrificed their time and energy to Holy Trinity for over five decades. The past and the present were theirs. But the future was so close now. He would control the future. A time of fresh, new faces with new ideas. And most importantly, new faces with a new willingness to share ideas about the management of the Holy Trinity baseball team.

— CHAPTER EIGHT —

Countdown to the Finals: 39 Days to Go

THE SAC AND FOX INDIANS WHO FIRST CROSSED OVER the Mississippi River west from what is now Illinois discovered a land of beauty and rich natural resources. They named it Iowa, which in the Fox language means, "This is the land." Those tribes would eventually fight against and be overwhelmed by the exponentially growing crush of immigrants also coming over the Mississippi River from the east. Those immigrants undoubtedly added two words to the name for this area, making it "This is the land for farming."

In 1857, the final gasp of American Indian resistance in Iowa came to an end. A band of Santee Sioux warriors escaped from Iowa for Minnesota. They were under the leadership of Inkpaduta, who avenged the murder of his brother by leading the Spirit Lake Massacre, not far from Cottage Park.

At approximately the same time, a colony of Irish families settled near Emmetsburg, named for the Irish freedom fighter Robert Emmet. All over northwest Iowa, different immigrant populations rapidly gathered and populated the land, often continuing the life and culture they brought from Europe. The Dutch, or Netherlanders, made a similar proclamation to the American Indians when they arrived in northwest Iowa announcing, "Here is the place!" They would name their settlement Orange City for the House of Orange in the Netherlands. The Bohemians, or Czechs, settled in Pocahontas.

Germans made up the largest ethnic population in Iowa. They inhabited nearly every community and accounted for approximately half the population of Cottage Park, where they formed an uneasy alliance with the Irish. At least that alliance was stabilized by the Catholic religion and cemented by their love and success with baseball. Later, when German World War II prisoners of war were interned in Algona, south of Cottage

Park on Highway 169, they were very grateful and happy to work on prosperous farms with owners who spoke their native tongue and appreciated their culture and customs.

Each nationality carried the burden of stereotypes and prejudice—some good, some bad. Germans were noted for their proficiency in farming. They planted crops with efficient precision. Yet sometimes right alongside these precise German fields were crooked crops one could immediately label as the work of Irish farmers. The Irish would take credit (and almost with pride) for these haphazard rows. They found them funny. In fact, they saw them as proof that Irish farmers' priorities were placed on more important matters than the straightness of rows of feed corn for animals. Baseball for example, was one such matter of greater importance.

Swea City was home to Swedes, Norwegians, and Danes—kind and generous peoples, but nevertheless peoples whose priorities were not considered to be in the right place. For starters, they played baseball for fun. That meant at the end of the day, they were also able to reconcile themselves with losing. When it happened—and it happened with some regularity—they accepted the inevitability and could then move on to something more important in their lives.

Not so the old men and the people of Cottage Park—largely Germans and Irishmen—for whom baseball was life.

Boys in Cottage Park were raised like Spartans. At family gatherings, they caught snippets of conversations where their fathers and grandfathers boasted of Holy Trinity baseball conquests as if winning were inevitable—a baseball paradigm of Manifest Destiny. In their minds, no one had ever really beaten them. Those few games they lost were not really *lost* but cheated from them by poor umpires or gambled away by foolish boys whose names would live forever in infamy. (Those boys often ended up in one of the town's three bars, pounding away with booze at their failure on the baseball field, or they disappeared from Cottage Park, never to return.)

So when it was time for Holy Trinity's fifth game of the season, against host Swea City, absolutely nothing was fun or funny from the Holy Trinity prospective. Winning this game, and each and every other game, was an opportunity to glorify God (i.e., the Catholic faith), Holy Trinity, Cottage Park, family, the old men and their brand of baseball, and individual pride.

It wasn't much of an exaggeration that in Murphy's nearly forty-five years of coaching, Swea City had never beaten a Holy Trinity baseball team. Players on both teams acted as if the future would continue to repeat itself. Murphy liked to schedule Swea City early in the season for this very reason. The easy victory boosted the team's confidence.

But perhaps Holy Trinity was taking it too easy this time. Murphy did not like what he saw in the warm-up routine. There were dropped and overthrown balls—and more worrisome, nonchalance about those mistakes. That was not how the old men and the boys' families had raised them in this sacred act of baseball, where the Creator's holy face was revealed in the mechanics of the game.

In the final warm-up activity, the Swea City coach fungoed the ball high and behind home plate. The Swea City catcher got dizzy spinning around, trying to track the ball. He eventually toppled over on one knee and fell to his back. The ball thudded to the ground inches from him as he covered his face to avoid injury.

Though Moriarity wasn't the only player to laugh, he was the only player Murphy noticed. Murphy wasn't picking on Moriarity. But increasingly, it seemed his attention was drawn to his pitcher, perhaps for good reason. And it wasn't entirely personal. The plain and simple truth was, baseball games were often won and lost solely by pitching.

"That's enough, you," Murphy barked. He bustled to the end of the bench and stood over the seated Moriarity. "Have you forgotten where you are?"

Moriarity shook his head.

"You're in a baseball game," Murphy said anyway. "You know how important this is. We have goals for this year." Murphy turned from Moriarity to the rest of the team. "Right now, this is the biggest game of the year. We have to win this game. Start acting like it."

Moriarity raised his hand and held it up until Murphy looked back again. He spoke after Murphy recognized him.

"Don't worry, Coach," he said sincerely. "We're not losing against these guys."

Murphy grimaced. He looked at Egg and Ryan.

"Did you hear that? These guys don't need us. We might as well retire right now and leave."

Egg and Ryan nodded.

Moriarity shook his head. "That's not what I mean—"

"You listen to me," Murphy said. "All of you." Now he addressed the entire bench. "You don't win games by comparing yourself to how bad the other team is. You win games by playing your best. I don't care who we're playing." Murphy looked at each player. "Take a good look at those uniforms you're wearing."

The players did as they were instructed.

The uniforms were actually a source of contention in Cottage Park. No one knew how old they were, not even the old men. Especially not the old men, who were so proud that they didn't know or care how old the uniforms were. Those dated, drab button-down scratchy and woolen shrouds illuminated so precisely what they preached: baseball was a tradition, a rite of passage to manhood. Those uniforms—which the mothers of Cottage Park had mended and patched over, perhaps for decades—were proof of that commitment to baseball sacrifice and excellence. Murphy proudly wore one of the uniforms himself for every game.

Those same uniforms had also retained the unique body odor of every player who had worn them over the years. Trying and failing to rid the smells, mothers often gave up in frustration and approached the old men about replacing the relics with new uniforms.

At first, several years ago, the old men laughed when they received such requests. *It was such a waste of money!* But after seeing the hurt in the mothers' faces, they changed their tactic. Rather, they encouraged the mothers to go ahead and raise money for replacements. But when the money was raised, the old men would spend it indeed on replacements—replacements for something more important and necessary for Holy Trinity, such as playground equipment or other capital improvements to the school or church. They always promised to someday get around to ordering new uniforms, yet the uniforms stayed the same year after year.

Eventually, the mothers got the idea. Their sons would have to look like ragamuffins compared to the good-looking young men from surrounding communities, who wore stylish pullover uniforms of polyester blends with bright and bold color patterns. The mothers shook their heads in disbelief and commiserated that negotiating with the old men was truly impossible.

In the old men's defense, the uniforms—and how the current players embodied them—was the first thing the alumni observed and appreciated when they came back to participate in games. Moriarity traced the red nylon stitching of the Holy Trinity name over his chest. He had been forced to take the largest uniform, though it was still too short for him. It was Number 33—Danny Stinson's number. Moriarity wore it with reverence—often continuing to wear it around his home long after the game was over.

Once the players had sufficient time to look at their uniforms, Murphy continued his lecture.

He shook his head, half annoyed and half incredulous. "I can't believe I have to waste my time like this. No one—not me, not Egg, not Father Ryan—has ever had to stand up before one of our teams and discuss such things. Your coaches here can tell you the names of every player before you who wore those same uniforms. And you better believe those players knew what it meant to wear those uniforms and what they had to do to bring pride to the program!"

From home plate, the umpire couldn't help but overhear the lecture. He knew the old men well and had umpired their games for years. As Murphy spouted, the umpire did all he could to stall the start of the game. He brushed off home again, then slowly wandered over to the Holy Trinity dugout. He waited for Murphy to pause. When he finally did, the umpire spoke.

"Coach, are you ready to go?"

The question startled Murphy. He looked at the umpire, then out to the field, and finally to his coaches.

"Are we ready to go?"

Egg and Ryan hunched their shoulders.

"I might have to leave my shoes on," Ryan said, "if we're turning around for home again."

Letting out a slow, deep breath, Murphy sat down on the bench among his players and raised his hands. "I don't know either. I'm very sorry, but I'm about ready to walk away from this whole mess." He looked back over at Ryan and Egg. "We might be leaving all this sooner than we thought."

Even from the corner of his eye, Murphy could see the boys sweat. Everything was working to perfection. Now more than ever, Murphy could successfully convince this team—and all of Cottage Park—that he was becoming slightly crazy with his advancing age and poor health and thus was capable of any kind of behavior. He enjoyed watching these boys fret that the game could end before it even started.

"We can forfeit tonight and try again next time," Egg said calmly.

It was good acting on Egg's part too. He sooner would have severed his right arm than give away a perfect night of baseball watching these young men who he regarded as his own children.

"Well, I still get paid either way," the umpire said, also playing along. Whatever lesson Murphy was imparting to the boys, he sought to be included. "But I've got to make some sort of a decision here. Are you really forfeiting?"

"I don't care," Murphy said. He casually crossed his legs and folded his arms.

"We've never had to forfeit a game," Ryan said, feigning worry.

A long silence was broken when the umpire cleared his throat.

Murphy raised his palms out and up to his players. "Why don't you ask them? Go ahead. We'll abide by what they say. Heck, everyone can go home, and these boys can watch their precious televisions."

The umpire looked over the Holy Trinity bench and asked, "What's the plan? Are we playing ball here tonight?"

"Yes!" Orlowski immediately said.

As a senior, he was embarrassed. In the four years Orlowski had been on the varsity team, Murphy hadn't ever needed to make such a presentation before.

Jack jumped from the bench and sprung out to the batting circle. Spider prepared to follow him on deck. At once, steel cleats sprang upon and scratched the concrete foundation of the dugout like the hail that periodically beat down on its tin roof.

After a knowing nod to Murphy, the umpire turned toward the plate and signaled Swea City to take the field. Uneasy cheers greeted both teams from fans who knew something of some seriousness had transpired on the Holy Trinity bench.

Now it was time for Ryan to sit back on the bench and execute the ritual he had followed for every Holy Trinity baseball game—hot or cold, wet or dry—over the nearly 2,300 spring, summer, and fall games he had participated in as first-base coach. First, Ryan rolled up his pants, cuffing them below the knee. Next, he untied his highly polished black wingtip shoes. Then he drew back the sheer black silken stockings from his wrinkled, gray, and swollen feet, finally exposing crooked toes, some of which that clung to and crossed over each other. He folded the socks and set them carefully inside his shoes, which he slid under the bench.

Ryan stretched his toes straight and breathed a sigh of relief, as if he and his feet were now free from the shackles of a dark, dank prison. He wiggled his toes—his piggies, as he called them—then gingerly placed his feet down on the cold concrete of the dugout. He stood, shakily, until his piggies were comfortable on the new surface.

Those piggies were perhaps the most famous toes in Iowa. They drew residents out to see a baseball game, some for the first time, in whichever town Holy Trinity played. As Ryan paced around the first-base coach's box in his black clerical pants, black short-sleeved shirt, white Roman collar, and bare feet, the discussion amongst those in the stands was always one of awe. Why would he do such a thing?

Though no one laughed at or ridiculed Ryan, those not from Cottage Park wondered if Ryan was aware that he was different, that everyone else was wearing shoes, that no one had ever done such a thing before. It wasn't natural. Was it even safe? What did the Catholic Church hierarchy think of his practice? What other eccentricities did the old priest practice?

Had people asked these and any other questions of anyone from Cottage Park, they would have received a simple explanation: "He's an old man who does whatever he chooses and doesn't have a wife to keep him in line."

As he hobbled to make his way from the dugout, Ryan glanced at McKenna. The young man had opened his glove and appeared to be caught in its webbing, far away and deep in thought, oblivious to his impending at bat.

Ryan reached over and patted McKenna on the back. "It's a great day for baseball," he said.

McKenna nodded, coming back from wherever his mind had taken him. He got up and began to stretch. He looked around for his bat.

"Good, good," Ryan said. "Well, relax now and treasure these moments. In the blink of an eye, this will all be over before we know it."

Ryan looked out at the pitcher. "You know, I always like to watch the pitcher and see what he's throwing—more importantly, when he throws a certain pitch."

McKenna was still listening to him, so Ryan continued, "Sometimes pitchers slip into patterns."

"Let me know what you see, Father," McKenna said respectfully. He nodded as if to thank Ryan for his attention, then turned from him to retrieve his bat.

Ryan then tiptoed from the dugout, directing the piggies across the field to the first-base coach's box.

As Jack and Spider were already swinging bats, Egg stood and peered into his *C. S. Peterson's Scoremaster* scorebook to read the lineup. He shouted out names as if he were gathering troops for a battle.

"Jack Burnette, Spider Schmitt, Marty McKenna, Rich Orlowski, Anthony Civilla, Sean Powers, Stephen Schmitt, Pat Moriarity, and Jeff Burnette."

Murphy had already taken his place directly on the chalked lines of the third-base coach's box closest to home. He studied the Swea City pitcher's last few warm-up throws, as did Jack, the leadoff batter.

When the umpire signaled for play to begin, Jack looked down at Murphy and acknowledged the take signal. He positioned himself in the batter's box, waited, then watched as the first pitch of the game set off from the pitcher's hand and sailed seven feet above home plate. The ball hit the backstop and rolled back to the plate.

"Ball one," the umpire said.

"Good eye," Orlowski called out. "Hang in there, buddy."

Each player and coach and nearly all the Holy Trinity fans joined in with similar banter.

Itching to swing, Jack resisted and took the next three pitches, which were also balls. At first base, he received the steal sign.

"Good deal," he said to the first-base coach. "Come on, Spider," he yelled. "Start us off!"

Jack led off first base. To his surprise, the pitcher stayed in his windup, allowing Jack safe passageway to second base. And then he made it to third when the ball bounced in the dirt beyond the catcher's grasp.

Spider also received the take sign. He watched the first two pitches go by as called balls. Like Jack, Spider longed to disobey and swing at one of the pitches, but he conformed his will to Murphy's.

That discipline, plus the disciplined chaos Jack was producing on third base, was enough to rattle the pitcher into throwing ball four. Now Holy Trinity players danced at first and third.

The pitcher made eye contact with the next batter, McKenna, before quickly turning away. McKenna's dark, sorrowful eyes showed anger and danger. The pitcher knew batters such as this were capable of returning a pitch with a line drive that could pound a human skull to pulp.

On the first pitch, the first strike of the game, Spider trotted from first to second. In response, the catcher made a wild throw over second. The ball bounced into the area between left and center field. Jack scored. Spider rounded third and faked toward home, drawing a throw to the plate that had he gone, would not have been in time to make an out.

McKenna received the sign to hit away. And he did, furiously cracking a ball out and high, far above the left field fence and into a farmer's hayfield for a home run. The score was three to zero with no outs.

Everyone would take a turn at bat that inning. Jeff cursed himself for breaking the string of hits and leaving men on base. He made the third out to end the side by striking out.

Moriarity's first warm-up pitch was a curve that hit the lip of the plate and bounced straight up ten feet into the air. He covered his face with his glove and laughed. Powers crouched over again at the plate, setting a good target. The rest of Moriarity's warm-ups were straight and fiery fast balls.

The umpire eventually signaled that Moriarity had thrown enough pitches. Powers threw the ball down to second, and from there the ball was fired around the horn, then the Holy Trinity infield gathered around Moriarity.

"All right," Orlowski said. "You got a good four-to-nothing lead. Let's put 'em down and ten-run rule them." Games were seven innings long, unless one team had a ten-run advantage at the end of the fifth inning.

Moriarity looked at Jeff, who showed none of the confidence and bluster of the others. Instead he registered foreboding, a sense that he was unprepared to endure whatever was about to come his way.

"Don't worry," Moriarity reassured him. "Nobody'll get any hits off me."

"Wait a minute," Anthony said. "We're out here too. You pitch your game, and we'll take care of anything they connect on."

Anthony put his hand out into the center of the group. His teammates dropped their free hands on his.

"Defense!" they shouted, then returned to their positions.

"Sean," Moriarity said, "wait up." The two met halfway between the pitching mound and home plate. The pitcher's brows knit. "I swear— Murphy picks on me. You heard him yell at me before the game."

Powers raised his face mask. He looked over at Murphy, who was keenly watching them, then looked back at Moriarity.

"Not now. We got a game to play." Seeing the concern still on their starting pitcher's face, Powers sighed. "Murphy asks a lot of you because he expects you to lead us," he said, racing his speech. "He isn't picking on you. He *picked* you. Big difference."

Powers scooted back behind the plate and called for a strike. Moriarity delivered it, then two more. The batter flailed at each pitch. He quickly exited to the dugout for the first out.

As it turned out, Murphy's longwinded soliloquy about never underestimating an opponent had been for naught. Moriarity and his short-sighted, present-tense teammates were right all along: this game was over before it started. Swea City would offer no challenge, even if the Holy Trinity players played the rest of this game at half speed and saved their energies for a more worthy opponent later. It was a blowout.

As the game progressed, the three most-detached minds in the ballpark all happened to be standing in the outfield for Holy Trinity. These minds were far away, in different directions of the past, present, and future.

In right field, McKenna kicked at the grass until a clump uprooted. He reached down and scratched a handful of dry black dirt and filtered it through his fingers. Its dust blew onto and dirtied his uniform. He looked up again and saw the second batter swinging in vain.

McKenna returned to his dreaming, to the past, when his father was as real as the warmth of the dirt that he squeezed.

"Marty," his father had once said softly, "go ahead and take over. You can do it. I trust you."

McKenna was in fourth grade. It was October, and he and his father were in the field. McKenna heard whistles and cries in the cool prairie wind that blew through the brown skeletons of cornstalks. Their leaves rattled like bones. He'd heard Halloween stories, and he was afraid. But his father was there, so nothing could happen to him.

His father edged out of the tractor seat and situated McKenna behind the steering wheel. McKenna had sat on his father's lap or stood beside him countless times, but he had never driven the tractor by himself. But now he was shifting the gear himself. He felt the tractor sway from side to side, and he braced himself for it to tip completely over. His father crouched beside him. He didn't look at his son—his full attention and delight was on the thick yellow ears of corn that were plucked and tossed into the combine behind them.

"Two outs!" Orlowski sang out from second.

McKenna waved back, then smoothed the clump of grass he had uprooted. The grass was brown. It needed rain to grow again. He smoothed it over until he noticed his teammates running from the field into the dugout.

In the top of the fourth inning, with the score seven to nothing, Jack looked over the left field fence—past the backyards of little one-story white houses and on to Highway 9, which led east to Armstrong and then Buffalo Center. He looked long and far in that direction, away from the setting sun. He looked into the future. Dark clouds hung over the horizon. He saw backbreaking work, little money, loneliness, and fear.

But those were constant worries in life. He would eventually find a job: carpentry, electrical work, handyman stuff. He learned quickly. As long as he wasn't afraid of honest work and he had his health, he knew he would always have money. As for the loneliness he saw in the swirling clouds above him, there was nothing he could do about it. Leaving his home and hometown would be daunting. Nevertheless, he had to move on. As a first step, he had recently broken up with his girlfriend, Sarah. She was the perfect girlfriend for someone who deserved her—someone willing to make a commitment to at least minimally be with her, even if it was long distance.

A loud crack made Jack focus. The batter had savagely attacked Moriarity's changeup. Jeff knelt to block it down, but the ball hopped over his shoulder.

Jack charged in toward the ball at the same time Jeff raced out toward it.

"Damn! Damn! Damn!" Jeff said with each step.

Jack, however, beat him and scooped it up with one hand. He was poised and ready to fire the ball to second for the out. But there was one obstacle— his brother, standing right in the way, head down, red faced and cursing.

"Out of my way!" Jack said.

He shifted around Jeff and charged toward second, where the runner slid, stood quickly, and pretended to be on his way toward third.

"Do it!" Jack shouted. To himself he added, *One more step from the bag either way, and I'll nail your ass.*

He set to make a throw, but the runner dived back to the bag. Jack trotted the ball into Anthony at short.

"Come on!" Moriarity said, slapping his leg with his glove hand. "Let's go. Give me the ball!"

"What's his problem?" Jack asked Anthony under his breath.

"Got a couple of hours?" Anthony replied. "He just lost his no-hitter."

Jack shook his head and started back to left field. Jeff was waiting there. He had picked up and brushed off Jack's fallen hat.

"I'm sorry," Jeff said. "I'm really sorry. You could have thrown that guy out if I hadn't been in your way."

"Don't apologize," Jack snapped. "This is a game, for God's sake. It's not that big a deal."

Jack's irritation dissolved as he saw that his remark compounded his brother's guilt.

"You're doing fine," Jack said, sighing. "Go on back to the infield." Then he yelled out loudly enough for Moriarity to hear, "And don't listen to that psycho on the mound!"

Jack watched his brother race back to third, then he glanced back at the eastern horizon. Leaving town would mean traveling lightly—with no excess worries from relationships holding him behind. But the one thing he wished he could carry with him was his relationship with Jeff—except they had no relationship.

As a big brother, it had always been Jack's responsibility to develop and grow that relationship. For the last three years, he'd ignored and dismissed Jeff, as he had just done, ordering him back to third base. And now it was nearly too late. Jack had always thought time stood still in Cottage Park, yet there it was, racing by him now, robbing him of opportunities to get to know and appreciate his little brother.

Holy Trinity kept Swea City from scoring that inning, preserving at least the shutout Moriarity coveted. By the bottom of the fifth, the score was eleven to nothing. Murphy rested all his starters, including the one who begged to stay on pitching. The ten-run rule would mercifully be enacted at the end of the inning.

As he rode the bench, Spider's mind was now even farther away than when he'd been out in center. He was trapped in the present. Margaret had come to the game, and Spider had thought of nothing else. Fever was the best description of how he felt. Or better yet, fire. Fire in his mind, heart, and seemingly every pore of his skin.

Spider looked through the wire-mesh dugout screen to the bleachers. As he gazed at Margaret, it seemed his breath was stolen from him. Only the pounding of his heart reminded him to breathe again. It had been twenty days since he had lost his virginity. Everything had fallen in place so easily and quickly, he hadn't had time to appreciate what had actually happened.

Now as he looked out at Margaret and saw her magnificent breasts rise and lower with each breath—saw the faint trace of her nipples—it was easy to undress the rest of her. Unbutton the men's white dress shirt and slip it off her shoulders, then unbutton her cutoff jean shorts and let them fall to the ground. Now he could see every muscle, smell her hair and the scent of roses in the perfume she placed behind her ears. Now he could taste her— like cream, rich and sweet.

How many other men had had this experience? If so, why did the world go on as it did? Baseball, for example—such a stupid sport. Why was he still even playing in a baseball game when he could be with her? Was he really the only guy on the team to have made love to a woman?

Now he desired more. He hungered for more. But since that time in the quarry, Margaret had limited him to kissing her, no matter how persistently he tried to go further. He longed to eat, drink, and breathe this woman.

He concentrated on taking another deep breath and noticed sweat beading above his lips. At the same time, he watched Margaret cross her legs. He followed the long, straight lines of her legs up beneath her shorts. Despite the sweat, his face suddenly felt cool, and now he also felt light-headed. He'd heard that some imaginations were so strong, men spent themselves, even when they were asleep. This was where his body was leading him, with all the control of a runaway train.

Holy Mary, Spider thought to himself, trying his best to replace his vision of Margaret with one of the Blessed Virgin statue in front of Holy

Trinity School, standing over a world of crushed snakes. *Mother of God.* He closed his eyes tightly and tried to hear heavenly music.

"Jesus," Orlowski said, reaching over and pulling Spider's hat down over his face. "What's with you? You look like you're trying to crap your pants." He shook his head in confusion and laughed. "The game's over. We're heading home."

— CHAPTER NINE —

Countdown to the Finals: 38 Days to Go

C ONTRARY TO BELIEF, THERE WAS NO VAST CONSPIRACY of spies across Cottage Park reporting on Egg to his children. The Gallivan children merely maintained communication with friends from their hometown, and those friends often shared endearing anecdotes about their father's memory lapses or inattention to detail.

Over the last few years, however, those gently amusing tales pecked away at the Gallivan children's all-consuming belief that their father would live forever. One by one, they painfully reconciled to the realization that their dad no longer was stronger and wiser than any foe, especially time. The fear of his death gave way to the fear that time would mercilessly keep him alive and bully him in his weakened, helpless state.

Egg was correct, though, about one particular spy. The main source of twenty-four-hour-seven-days-a-week updates on all things Egg lived across the street. There, most often sitting behind the picture window of her simple rambler, was Brigid Jensen.

Brigid—or Aunt B, as the Gallivan children called her—phoned at least one of Egg's children at least once a day to provide an update on Egg. The daily updates also provided Aunt B with valuable information about Egg's children and their children, whom she regarded as her own family—her only family. Her husband had passed away at a young age, and she had no children of her own.

Though stiff and formal, Aunt B had always been included in Gallivan family activities. She was invited to and attended all holiday gatherings, including Christmas, where she always received a gift, the only personal gift she would receive during that time.

The boys mowed her lawn in the summer, raked her leaves in the fall, and shoveled her driveway and sidewalks in the winter. Egg had since taken over many of those responsibilities. Aunt B returned the favor by supplying Egg with weekly dessert items: cookies, cakes, bars, and pies.

Aunt B mystified the Gallivan children. Whereas they had watched their mother and father grow old—turn gray, lose muscle tone, slow down, and forget things—Aunt B had not suffered any of those effects. In large part because it seemed she had *always* been eighty-five years old. In the case of Aunt B, time was not unkind but indifferent. Or perhaps time had forgotten about Aunt B, leaving the Gallivan children with that rare old—really old—person who had scolded and molded them into responsible adults but now engaged them as a friend and more importantly a confidante.

Aunt B kept her eye on more than Egg, though. She wrote two popular features for the *Cottage Park Chronicle*. One was "Gatherings," an account of social activity in Cottage Park. Aunt B kept readers informed about who had come back to Cottage Park to visit and for what reason, other than holidays—usually class or family reunions or funerals. Readers could also catch up on gatherings amongst the current citizens of Cottage Park. The occasion might be a club or an activity; maybe a simple neighborhood coffee. Some stories highlighted gatherings outside Cottage Park, say for a grandchild's hockey tournament in the Twin Cities or a fishing expedition for bullheads to Lake Okoboji and Spirit Lake. No gathering was too small, no reason too simple to not be included in Cottage Park's weekly social registry.

Aunt B also wrote the immensely popular "Blotter," which recorded Sheriff Huffman's weekly activity—more like meanderings—to answer calls in the neighborhoods and countryside of Cottage Park. There was very little, if any, real crime in Cottage Park, perhaps for no other reason than to see your name spotlighted in the "Blotter" was the ultimate humiliation, inviting lifelong ridicule or, at worst, banishment from the community.

Aunt B dutifully listed each of Sheriff Huffman's visits, most often about a nuisance animal: a skunk who made his home under a porch, an amorous deer frolicking in a backyard, a five-foot-long bull snake curled up in the corner of a basement. These were merely a few of the huge number of birds and animals that seemed to rub the residents of Cottage Park the wrong way. Though pest control was not in his job description, Sheriff Huffman most often had to deal with each animal himself, as frightened residents, mostly elderly, huddled inside awaiting a resolution. Aunt B described each incident, how it was resolved, and often added helpful fac-toids about that animal.

When it came to pests of the human kind, Aunt B reserved her wrath—in print—for litterbugs, vandals, and those who disturbed the peace. For each incident, she castigated the offenders, finding ever-new and inventive ways to label them: miscreants, mouth breathers, dimwits, and so on. She frequently reminded readers that Cottage Park, like the Garden of Eden, was perfect until knuckle draggers messed it up for everybody. And she strongly believed that Cottage Park, unlike the Garden of Eden, could be restored to its state of perfection.

Two of Cottage Park's most dramatic and recent episodes of crime had actually gone unreported in the *Chronicle*, because in each instance Sheriff Huffman hadn't been called. Aunt B still hadn't forgiven herself for not catching T. J. during his spray-painting spree in the middle of the night. The second episode, Egg's brawl at the Lipstick, which she had witnessed in person, had also gone unreported.

Since the fight, she had had a funny feeling. Where there's smoke, there's fire. Thus, she had stepped up her vigilance of Egg's home and their street. At least once and sometimes twice in the middle of the night, she awoke to take her seat at the window and look across the street at Egg, fully clothed and asleep on his La-Z-Boy recliner with the television showing a rainbow-colored bar chart test pattern.

And on that morning of June 15, Aunt B was looking out her window at Egg and T. J. in the garage when the peace was suddenly disturbed. A pickup truck with a broken muffler and two suspicious-looking men drove by. She made a mental note of the model and color of the truck. Fifteen minutes later, the broken muffler again announced the truck's impending arrival. This time, she picked up her binoculars and recorded the license plate number as the truck slowed to a stop in front of Egg's home. It appeared they were up to no good.

In the "Blotter," she reminded readers to "err on the side of caution and always call Sheriff Huffman when you have any concerns of suspicious activity in your neighborhood." So she called Sheriff Huffman and explained the situation, asking him to come out and take a look. He patiently and respectfully answered each and every one of Aunt B's several requests each month. He would do so again this morning, but not until after he had finished his coffee and the *Des Moines Register*. While she waited, Aunt B grabbed a large screwdriver and paced back and forth in front of her picture window.

The third time the pickup truck appeared, it drove up onto Egg's driveway. Aunt B dialed Egg's youngest daughter, the most dramatic of the Gallivans, and announced, "I'm going over to your dad's. I've got a screwdriver. Pray for us." She hung up the phone without responding to a frantic rash of questioning, then treaded out her front door across the street. Her arms were folded with the screwdriver nestled in between.

Across the street, T. J. swung a nearly full paint can around a few times and turned it upside down. Egg approached him with a mixing stick. Egg showed his displeasure with T. J.'s efforts and reached out to take the can. Instead T. J. waved him off and began to shake the can again, shaking so frantically that he became dizzy and faint.

"That's better," Egg said. "Follow me."

T. J. picked up the can and followed Egg around the garage to the wall he had vandalized. Still only the word *Die* had been painted over. Egg pried open the can and stirred it carefully, wiping the excess paint from the stick.

"Go ahead," Egg said. "And remember, no drip marks. And don't splatter on the ground."

Egg headed back inside the garage to return the paint stick but stopped at the sight of a red pickup barreling into his driveway. Egg heard beer cans rattle across the truck bed. Two men jumped out of the cab and advanced quickly toward him. Egg's smile turned to a scowl as he recognized they were the deadbeats who had sucker-punched him at the Lipstick a week earlier.

"I told you I'd be back," the stocky man said. He rolled up his shirt and made a fist. "Time to kick your ass, Grandpa."

His partner laughed.

"Egg?" T. J. asked as he came around the corner.

Egg quickly motioned him away. "Go on. Go home!"

Egg turned back to give the intruders the same admonition, but he never got the chance. A punch in the stomach knocked the wind out of him and sent him staggering backward until his knees buckled and he collapsed.

T. J. dived toward Egg and caught him, helping him slowly to the ground.

"You bastards!" T. J. screamed. "Get out of here!"

"You should have gotten out of here when the old man told you to," the stocky man said to Egg.

He tossed T. J. to the ground. T. J. scrambled to get back up, but the taller man pinned him down.

"Maybe it's good you see this," the stocky man said. "Your old man here is supposed to be a big hero." He slapped Egg repeatedly against the jaw one way and then the other. He grabbed him by the scalp. "Isn't that right?" He lifted Egg's head up and down.

"Fuckers!" T. J. screamed. He began to cry. "Leave him alone!"

The taller man who held T. J. mimicked his words. He slammed T. J.'s head to the ground and jammed a handful of grass into his mouth. T. J. spit it out.

"Shut up, pussy!"

The taller man shoved his knuckles against T. J.'s mouth until his lips cut into his braces and blood trickled onto his chin.

Egg had fallen to his stomach. Despite his strongest efforts, he was unable to move. He was aware of pain, and he knew he was in danger. But he was more worried about T. J.

Again he used all his might to push toward T. J., but the stocky man grabbed him by the scalp again and turned him over on his back. He kicked Egg and stepped on him as he made his way to the side of the garage. A moment later, he came back with the can of paint, raised like a trophy. He looked at his partner and smiled broadly.

"Should I?"

"Not yet," the taller man said.

He got off T. J., who lunged over to cover Egg. The taller man kicked him.

"Now," the taller man said. The stocky man raised the can over the pair on the ground.

"That's enough!" someone said.

Aunt B waited until she had both men's attention. She dug her screwdriver as deeply as she could into the side of the pickup as she passed from the rear to the front, leaving a deep and jagged scratch. Then she turned and did the same, starting at the front of the hood and walking backward.

The men had hoped to make a spectacle of Egg, drowning him in his own paint. Instead, the stocky man tossed the can, hitting T. J. in the head. About half the contents spilled out over the two before T. J. righted the can.

The taller man grabbed Aunt B's hand holding the screwdriver and twisted it behind her back until she dropped it. He jammed her head down and into the truck hood.

"You're paying for every penny of this!" he shouted with fury.

Both men stopped, however, when they saw a police car racing toward them with its lights flashing. The taller man released Aunt B. No strangers to trouble, the men lowered themselves to the ground with their arms in handcuff position. The police car pounded up and over the curb, at which point Sheriff Huffman exploded out of the car to steady Aunt B. He then helped Egg to his feet.

T. J., his eyes partially covered by paint, rolled on the ground and swung out his arms wildly. He reached out and grasped Sheriff Huffman's feet, mistakenly believing he was tackling one of the assailants.

"It's all right, young man!" Sheriff Huffman said, blocking the blows and gently restraining T. J. "It's me—Sheriff Huffman."

He helped T. J. to his feet over by Egg, then looked at the men laying before him. He undid a foot-long billy club from his belt and slowly wrapped his fingers into and around the leather strap.

"Here's how we do things in Cottage Park," Sheriff Huffman announced to the men. "We can either press charges," he said. "Or you can take your beating this morning and be done."

Before either of the two men could respond, Sheriff Huffman brought the billy club down as mightily as he could, alternatively hitting each man in the upper back, buttocks, and calves, while walking around in a circle. After each blow, he announced a single word that eventually formed a complete sentence: "In . . . this . . . case . . . I . . . am . . . going . . . to . . . do . . . both."

The men were groaning when Sheriff Huffman stopped the beating and handcuffed them to each other. He lifted them to their feet, then escorted them in a professional manner to his car and helped them into the backseat. He opened his door, one foot into the car, then turned back to Egg and his counterparts.

"I apologize for all this," Sheriff Huffman said. "I'll talk to these two again at the station. By the time I'm done with them, I promise you'll never see them again." Sheriff Huffman gave a long wave. "I'll have a tow come get this truck out of the way later today."

He looked over to see a crowd of about twenty neighbors gathering in Aunt B's front yard. He gave them a similar wave, then drove away, turning off his lights as he made his way downtown.

Aunt B. picked up her screwdriver and stood before Egg and T. J.

"If you two are okay," she said, "I think I'll go back home."

Before she exited the crime scene to go home and write about it, Aunt B took her screwdriver to the opposite side of the truck. This time she started at the front and scratched it the entire length. Satisfied, she headed back across the street to the group gathered in her yard.

T. J. could feel paint stiffening over his skin.

"We should probably clean ourselves up," T. J. said. "Huh, Egg?"

Egg looked at the paint and blood across T. J.'s face. "You've got a few nasty cuts around your mouth. Let's get you over to the doctor."

"I'm all right," T. J. said. "They didn't hurt me. I'm just sorry I didn't hurt them."

Egg headed to the back of the house to the garden hose, and T. J. followed. T. J. undressed down to his underwear. Egg used the hose to rinse the paint out of T. J.'s hair, and together they peeled off strips of paint from T. J.'s skin.

When T. J. was clean, he held the hose for Egg, who had also stripped down to his boxer shorts. Egg cupped his hands together and splashed water across his face and the rest of his body. Not a word was said. When they were both clean, they entered Egg's home to towel down and put their clothes back on.

T. J. dressed quickly and returned outside. He resealed the paint can and wiped as much of the paint as he could from the lawn. If ever there was an excuse to cancel painting for the day, an attack by a crazed pickup gang would be it.

Needing a moment, he found his favorite tree, the slim maple, and slid down its trunk until he rested on the ground in the cool shade of its rich dark-purple leaves. He half smiled as he thought to himself, *If only there could be action like this every day in this quiet old town.*

T. J.'s seat gave him a perfect view of the truck. It was very slowly dripping oil onto Egg's clean driveway. He prepared to get back up again to alert

Egg when one of Egg's neighbors strolled by with a brick. The middle-aged man paused and respectfully returned T. J.'s look, then he nodded at Aunt B perched in her usual seat across the street.

He reared the brick back and tossed it through the driver's side window, breaking the glass and hitting the steering wheel so forcefully that it tapped the horn. The man continued on his way as if nothing had happened.

A minute later a woman of about the same age visited with a paper bag of trash. She too looked at T. J and caught Aunt B's attention before turning the bag upside down and emptying the trash across the pickup bed almost solemnly, as if she were dropping off canned goods at the church food drive. Like the previous man, she continued on her way.

Next a car drove up and parked in front of Aunt B's. Two young men emerged with crowbars. They nodded in the direction of Aunt B and this time actually spoke to T. J.

"How are you doing?" one said.

"Need some hubcaps?" the other man asked.

When T. J. shook his head, one man pried off all four of the truck's hubcaps and slammed his crowbar into them until they either cracked or punctured. Meanwhile, his partner swung away at the windows and the windshield. The door windows shattered immediately, but the front windshield and the back window required more effort.

"See ya," the men said and waved. A moment later, they were in their car and gone.

After the men drove away, a couple of high school boys arrived on bikes. T. J. had seen them around but had never spoken to them. They waved to Aunt B, smiled at T. J., then began to work together. One of the boys let the air out of each tire; the other followed behind, hacking at the deflated tires with a hatchet until slivers of rubber could be peeled back and away.

Inspired, T. J. rolled over and up from the ground to the back of the truck. He considered his own contribution to the destruction of the vehicle. He fished around his pocket until he located a disposable lighter he once used to light smokes, joints, and anything else he could get his hands on. That suddenly seemed like so long ago. Turned out he had been saving the lighter for this sort of occasion.

He looked up and down the street and saw no more visitors. T. J. flicked the lighter and offered it up to Aunt B, as if holding a torch that would light the way for them all out of the darkness. She stared at him.

That doesn't mean no, T. J. thought.

T. J. turned and lit several ends of the trash, which seemed to drink up the flame. He tossed the lighter into the fire, then crossed the street to Aunt B's lawn, where he found a new seat to observe his arson artistry.

He watched flames lick up along the sides of the truck and raise like a dragon, dancing with all its might onward and upward. Then it tired, gasping and flickering back to the flatbed. Soon black smoke billowed up, lazily spiraling and billowing to the heavens. Ash floated up and down like butterflies before falling to the street, turning to embers and dying.

The smoke attracted neighbors again. A part of T. J. hoped and braced for the dying flames to ignite the gasoline line and blow up the pickup. However, a bigger part of him wanted everyone to be safe.

For the first time he could remember, T. J. felt responsible for someone else—in fact, for everyone coming to see the source of the long tower of black smoke. He politely motioned for those joining the crowd on Aunt B's lawn to stand behind him, and he held his arms up and out like a safety patrol boy.

"Wait—I have a special gift for the truck," said a man not much younger than Egg. He held up a paper bag for all to see. "Six months of dog poop I collected from my backyard!"

The crowd cheered. T. J. volunteered to deliver it. Making sure no one followed him, he trotted up to the truck and lowered the sack in the bed, prodding it until the flame stripped the sack, exposing the dog feces.

"Where's Egg?" a man asked when T. J. returned to the crowd.

"He's changing into new clothes," T. J. said. "I'll go get him as soon as the fire goes out."

The size of the crowd shrunk proportionately to the size of the fire. By the time a feeble wire of smoke zigzagged from the truck, everyone had gone away except T. J. and, of course, Aunt B. She still watched from her window, conversing on her phone, probably explaining the action to one of Egg's children.

T. J. crossed the street and pounded on Egg's door. Three more times he pounded, and still no answer. He also tried the backdoor and pounded several times.

T. J. began to worry—another emotion he hadn't felt for any human being other than his mother over the last few years. He knew Egg was still in the house. He circled it twice, all the while peering through windows and searching for movement or sound. He finally stopped at the kitchen and poked his face against the screen.

There at the kitchen table sat Egg in his bathrobe and boxer shorts, staring blankly at his hands, which lay across the top of the table.

"Come on, Egg," T. J. said. "Open the door. Let me in."

Egg continued to stare blankly at his hands.

"Egg," T. J. said determinedly, "either open your door, or I'll tear the screen and come through your window.

Egg finally stood and let T. J. in. T. J. joined Egg at the table.

T. J. studied Egg's appearance, which really hadn't changed since he and Egg cleaned up in the backyard. Egg looked sad and pale. Blue veins stood out like byways on a roadmap across his gray skin sprinkled with brown spots. Swollen, bloodshot eyes peered through blackened, dried blood still caked above Egg's right eyebrow. Egg's pure-white hair, which was usually carefully combed straight back, now seemed to be celebrating its newfound freedom. It stood independently in any and many directions, resembling the spiked hairstyles high school students wore at the time.

"Damn, Egg," T. J. said. "You're scaring me. What's going on?"

Egg shook his head.

"Are you okay?"

Egg continued to show no emotion.

T. J. knew he could get him out of his funk by initiating a conversation about his seemingly only love and passion. "You've got a game coming up tonight, don't you?"

"Fonda Our Lady of Good Counsel," Egg said, breaking his silence. "But I'm not going."

"Come on, man. You're the guy who tells me baseball is everything," T. J. said.

"Look at me," Egg said with resignation. "I'm one hundred years old. I'm an old man of no use to myself or anyone else. I was helpless against those ding-a-lings today. Completely helpless." He shook his head, then spoke to himself: "When did I become a burden?"

"Is this about the fight?" T. J. asked in disbelief. "Haven't you ever got your ass kicked before?"

"I did not get my 'ass kicked,'" Egg said angrily. "I got *jumped*. I've been jumped before, but I've never been beaten like that, by the likes of that." His voice trembled. "I couldn't move. I couldn't help you." His eyes fell to the table. "I don't care about me, but I've never let anyone lay a hand on someone I care for."

"I don't need anyone looking out for me," T. J. said. "I can take care of myself. How do you think I felt watching those jerks hit you?" T. J. bit his lip. "But we've got to get up again." From a pants pocket, he produced a pocketknife and switched open one sharp blade. "We'll be able to take care of those guys the next time."

"Put that away," Egg said softly. "We fight with our fists around here. But those guys won't be back. Hell, I wish they would come back. They're good-for-nothings."

"If they're good-for-nothings, then they're not worth worrying about," T.J said. "Right?"

Egg nodded.

"Good. Then let's get you ready. I know everybody's expecting you at the game."

"No," Egg said. "I'm sitting this one out tonight. Probably hang around here."

"Okay," T. J. said, trying another tactic. He stood from the table. "Then I won't go either. My mom said I could go to the game tonight. I've been thinking about maybe playing—you said you could get me on the team. If you're not there, l can stay home and work on my comics."

"You'd really play?" Egg said.

He remembered his promise to Mrs. Jones that T. J. would play baseball. His prophecy was coming true. Excitement brought color to Egg's face. But he cautioned himself not to show excitement. Rather, he had to carefully and subtly set the hook.

"I don't know if I'm ready to play," T. J. said. "But maybe I could start off by helping out with stuff on the bench."

"You could help me keep score," Egg said. "Sometimes I miss things. I can use an extra set of eyes."

T. J. nodded.

"But you really will have to play sometime," Egg continued. "We'll start getting you ready. Baseball is such a fun sport for a young man." He stood up and made his way toward the bathroom. "I've got to go get dressed. You get us something to eat."

With a small smile, T. J. opened Egg's nearly empty refrigerator. He pulled out everything, beginning with a carton of milk he sniffed to determine freshness. The resulting smell made him nearly vomit. He plugged his nose as he dumped the entire contents into the sink, ran hot water to chase the mess down the drain, then carried the offending carton out to Egg's trash can.

T. J. also sniffed the other four items from the fridge: saltine crackers, sweet pickle slices, a crinkled and nearly empty silver-wrapped sleeve of Blue Bonnet oleomargarine, and a yellow-wrapped roll of braunschweiger. It appeared that he could mix and match these four ingredients to make something for them to eat.

There was also ice cream in the freezer. Lots of it—three different containers. They could have that for dessert along with some of Aunt B's peanut butter cookies, still very fresh on a Saran Wrapped plate in the middle of the table.

— CHAPTER TEN —

Countdown to the Finals: 38 Days to Go

A T THE GAME LATER THAT NIGHT, MURPHY GATHERED all the players toward him in the dugout. Ryan and Egg joined in as well. T. J. stayed behind at the other end of the dugout on the bench. Egg motioned for him to join the team, but T. J. ignored the invitation. He had agreed to help Egg with scorekeeping, whatever that entailed. He had not agreed to join the team.

Egg motioned a second time for T. J. to join the huddle. This invitation was made with anger and a veiled threat to physically pull T. J. off his seat if he didn't immediately join the group. T. J. cursed to himself, rolled his eyes, and stood to join the old men and players.

"All right," Murphy said, noticing T. J. and believing he could now begin. "If you haven't yet met the young man standing alongside Egg, his name is T. J. He's already enrolled at Holy Trinity in the . . . uh . . . what grade, T. J.?"

"Tenth," T. J. said.

Murphy continued. "T. J. is here to help us with our scorekeeping, and as such, that makes him an extremely valuable member of our team."

Murphy called T. J. over. The players stepped aside for T. J. to make his way. Murphy positioned T. J. directly in front of him. He placed both arms around T. J.'s shoulders as if he were anointing him.

"I'm really proud of this young man, and I want it understood that whatever he needs from now on, you will all take care of it for him."

Players nodded. T. J. tried to head back toward Egg, but Murphy held him.

"We've never been a team for dedicating games to people, but tonight's as good a night as any to start." Murphy again placed both hands on T. J.'s shoulders. "Let's play this one tonight for T. J."

How did I get myself into this mess? T. J. thought to himself. Less than three weeks ago, his plot to escape Cottage Park had failed. Since then, each day he found himself being swallowed deeper and deeper into the town—and worse, into its vortex of baseball. Now he was surrounded by guys on the first team he had ever been on in any way. But after thirty seconds, he was more desperate than ever to get away from here and quit.

Everything about Cottage Park was closing in on him, and it seemed as though he couldn't do anything about it. He'd lost all control to outside forces taking over his life. Some of those forces he couldn't even explain at that moment. Others he could see, feel, and smell—such as the baseball team currently squeezing on him from all sides and separating the breath from his body.

Without a word, players kept crowding in and unto T. J. They each placed a hand or glove on T. J. and bowed their heads. They had never done anything like this before. They awaited Murphy's next direction.

"We are in for a fight tonight," Murphy said. He motioned with his head to the opposing dugout. "These guys did not drive all the way up here from Fonda to lose this ball game. They're hardheaded and believe they can beat anybody. As far as they're concerned, they have no respect for our tradition here and what we've accomplished. Well, fellas, we've got to do this every year. Let's introduce ourselves again to the boys from Fonda and show them how we play baseball out here. More importantly, let's show T. J. here how we play baseball."

There was another long silence. This time, Orlowski raised his right hand to T. J.'s head and palmed it. Again the players tightened even closer around him. T. J. noticed Egg and Ryan making a valiant effort to reach in and be included on this laying of the hands.

"Get in here," Orlowski ordered.

The players and coaches jostled against T. J., who strained to take a breath.

"T. J. on three," Orlowski said. He counted out, "One, two, three . . ."

All replied in unison, "T. J.!"

The players then lifted their hands and burst from the dugout, taking their positions in the field. But as Moriarity motioned to leave, Murphy reached out to him and put his arm around Moriarity's waist. To Murphy's surprise, Moriarity in turn put his arm around Murphy's shoulder. They travelled together in this fashion for a few steps toward the third-base line before Murphy stopped and looked at Moriarity.

"All right, young man. What's wrong with you?"

Moriarity momentarily looked surprised. On instinct, he grinned. Then the grin grew cold on his face until it finally wore away to sadness.

"It's sort of a bunch of things."

"Let's go throw a few pitches," Murphy said.

At the mound, Moriarity picked up the ball and threw a flaming fastball over the plate, where Powers waited. A hush came over the Fonda dugout. It never failed—seeing Moriarity in action always had that effect on opponents. Murphy had several players who could pitch. They were all good. But when Moriarity reared back and threw smoke, opposing teams quieted as if the air had been sucked out of them.

"These are warm-ups, Pat," Murphy said. He took a step back and studied Moriarity's form on the next pitch. "Better," he said. "Now, what's bothering you?" He chose to ignore the next pitch, which was Moriarity's attempt at a knuckleball.

Moriarity took a deep breath. "Look out into the stands." He stopped and scanned the bleachers surrounding the field. "Everybody's dad is here except mine."

Murphy nodded and sighed. "I know."

Moriarity threw another fastball. "You know how many times my dad has seen me play this year?" He made the sign for zero. "In three years, he's come to maybe two games. And each time, he didn't even stay the whole game. It's sad. It gets to me every once in a while."

"I have noticed that," Murphy said. "I can understand why that would upset you. But your dad cares for you. He's a good dad. By the way, do you realize he came to all your basketball games?"

Moriarity stopped and looked at Murphy. "Huh," he said. He took off his hat and stared out into the outfield. "Why is that, Coach?"

"I coached your dad from the time he was in first grade until the day he took leave to play semi-pro," Murphy said. He motioned for Moriarity to throw another pitch. "All I know is that you two are like peas in a pod. He loves you. He probably loves you more than he should. When it's time, you'll know more why your dad doesn't come to watch you play baseball."

The umpire ordered Powers to throw the ball down to second base to end the warm-up pitches. The ball then made its way from infielder to infielder around the horn. Powers ran out to join Moriarity and Murphy at the pitcher's mound, and the rest of the Holy Trinity infield closed in around them as well.

"Fastballs," Murphy said to Powers. "No monkey business. Let's put the fear of God in these boys right from the start."

It's that simple, Murphy thought to himself as he exited the mound to the dugout.

And it was. One after another, the Fonda batters came up to hit the ball, then sunk back to the dugout frightened, frustrated, and empty-handed. That's what good pitchers do to batters. They take away their very soul and their reason for living. Moriarity wasn't merely fast. His ball had a mind of its own and swerved and twisted where it pleased, a God-given intangible movement baseball players called by different names: shlop, slick, goop . . . The less comprehensible the name, the better it explained his pitches—and for that matter, the better it explained Moriarity himself.

Egg called out the batting lineup for the bottom of the first inning, simultaneously pointing to each name in the scorebook so T. J. could follow along.

"Egg," Jack said, laying out an open palm. "How about a slap for good luck?"

"You don't need good luck against this guy—he's nothing," Egg said, dismissing the request. "We save luck for when we actually need it."

Spider came up to Egg next. "You think I should try to pull the ball more?" he asked.

Damn kids, Egg thought to himself.

Opposing pitchers rarely intimidated the Holy Trinity batters. Egg had taught his players how to be aggressive, how to be the intimidators. So were they now going out of their way to make him feel needed after the incident with the two punks in the truck?

Egg was still angry and miserable about the fight earlier in the day, but he knew they wouldn't leave him alone until he at least acted happier. He had to make an effort to humor them. Besides, he had T. J. sitting beside him, taking in all the action. No matter what had happened earlier that day, it was all worth it to get T. J. this close to baseball.

Thank you, God! Egg thought.

Suddenly Egg transformed back to his normal self, remembering that T. J. could be his "eyes" to help him with the scorekeeping duties. Egg took this responsibility very seriously, as he explained to his young helper.

Egg pointed to the official scorekeeping guide. "In here, we collect information on every single action during the game," he said in dramatic fashion. "It's like the Holy Bible. And in it, God speaks to us—about everything from who's up to bat next, to stats, to who's hot, pitch count . . . very serious matters."

T. J nodded, looking over the myriad of rows with little boxes.

"Careful recording of the past helps us predict our future," Egg continued. "And winning baseball all boils down to predicting the future. When it comes to capturing the information we need to predict the future, I don't think anybody does a better job than yours truly." Egg proudly pointed two thumbs back at himself.

T. J. heard more—much, much more—from Egg about the scorekeeper's critical role on a championship baseball team. In theory, everything Egg said was true. However, there was one major fallibility in his pontification. Once the game began, it took T. J. but a few moments to see that Egg was a terrible scorekeeper. He was guilty of a scorekeeper's greatest sin: he was so immersed in the game that he couldn't take his eyes off it, even for a moment. Occasionally he remembered he was supposed to be keeping score, most often between innings. By then, he had to rely on his memory—or more realistically, the memory of those around him—to record what he had only a few moments earlier been so wound up about.

For three innings, T. J. observed Egg's growing frustration and the players' growing anxiety as he continually asked them to recall game situations. It didn't help matters that Egg was hard of and hardly hearing. Often he angrily yelled at the players to speak up. It was a mess. In fact, T. J. came to the conclusion that Egg's entire life was a mess. He needed almost constant surveillance and follow-up assistance. No one in the whole world seemed able to help Egg, T. J. thought, except himself.

So once again that day, he decided to step in and make Egg's life easier. "Hey, Egg, could I maybe keep score?"

Egg's response was immediate and severe. "You could never do this without a lot more training."

"You're probably right," T. J. said, donning his most humble voice. "But let me try it. You can watch me to make sure I do it correctly."

Soon T. J. was keeping score, with Egg looking on skeptically as T. J. quickly, intuitively, and most importantly accurately recorded each action on the field. He was the ideal person for this task. He could be thorough and objective because he wasn't emotionally tied to the drama unfolding before him. His entire interest was seeing a frustrated old man find some joy in his increasingly challenged life. Unfortunately, this meant he was now further tied to Cottage Park—at least until the end of the baseball season.

And Egg really did enjoy his new role as the play-by-play "eyes" for the action on the field. It combined his two greatest passions in life: devouring the drama of a baseball game and breaking it down so the uninitiated could benefit from his wisdom. Egg occasionally explained to T. J. terms such as fielder's choice, balk, passed ball, and sacrifice. Egg followed these mini lessons with stern admonitions that he would be watching T. J. like a hawk to ensure accurate scorekeeping.

"The last thing we need is to give up an out in a crucial situation because the batting order is screwed up," Egg said. What he didn't say was that he himself had made this very mistake on more than one occasion over the years.

As the game progressed, T. J. settled into his new role, and the Holy Trinity team settled in right along with him. Players substituting into the game politely checked in with T. J., and each starter who came out eventually came over to T. J. to introduce himself and thank him for taking on such a huge responsibility. All were grateful for the new quiet and calm in the dugout.

Murphy had a similar reaction, though he never said a word. His face lit up in delight as he glanced down at T. J.'s handiwork. For the first time in a long time, he could accurately read through the scorekeeper guide without wondering if a smudged-over erasure was in fact an accurate depiction of that game's activities. When T. J. looked up at Murphy, the old coach gave him a nod of approval.

T. J. was glad his new responsibilities demanded complete focus. It kept him from dwelling on how that same overwhelmed sensation was returning, the one he had felt earlier when the team crowded around him. T. J. had never really fit into any group. Groups he might have fit into—those that matched his interests in art, science fiction, or music—didn't seem to exist. As a result, he had become a loner. Over the years, he had tried to convince himself that his lonely ways were best for him, that he would develop faster and know himself better than any of his peers. In reality, the isolation had created a void, which he then tried to fill in all the wrong ways. But here, now, for the first time in forever, he was fitting in nicely.

It was the fifth inning. From the stands, Mr. Burnette focused his binoculars on his youngest son, Jeff, standing in the dugout. Jeff focused his own attention on his brother, Jack, who stood at the plate with his bat nonchalantly laid down on his shoulder.

You're nothing, Jack said to the pitcher in words of silence.

But everyone in the ballpark—especially the pitcher—understood the message. Murphy certainly did. That was why he chose Jack to be his lead-off man in the lineup. Jack challenged every pitcher, every pitch.

Mr. Burnette very clearly understood Jack's message. He also knew it was highly unlikely for Jeff to ever impart such a message to a competitor. His sons were so different in their approach to the game of baseball.

As Jack stepped into the batter's box, he purposely kept the pitcher waiting. He casually knocked dirt from his cleats. He looked at Murphy for a sign. Then he finally got into his stance and signaled the umpire that he was ready. Jack's whole body wrapped around like a coil.

Mr. Burnette turned his binoculars back to the dugout to study Jeff's reaction as the bat swung around and cracked against the ball. The ball shot like a bullet right into the pitcher's kneecap.

As gasps of fright escaped from the crowd, Jack dropped his bat and raced to first base. The catcher tore off his mask and took several quick steps out to pick up the ball. He threw it to first base, but Jack beat the throw.

Mr. Burnette had seen none of this, though he didn't need to. With the binoculars still on his youngest son, he had understood it all through Jeff's reaction.

With rapt attention, Jeff watched Murphy hurry to the mound, where the pitcher writhed in pain on his back. The Fonda coach was already there, kneeling by the boy.

When Mary Agnes Connelly, the ninety-six-year-old medic for Holy Trinity, made her way from the backstop bleacher seats to the field, everyone became fully aware of the gravity of the situation. Mary Agnes always waited for an injured player to eventually make his way up into the stands for her diagnosis and remedy. If she was making this trip to the pitcher's mound, surely it was a serious injury.

Murphy signaled for an ambulance, then helped settle the hysterical boy. It took a few minutes for the boy's shrieks of pain to turn to gentle sobbing.

Soon the wail of a siren made its way to the ball park. There was polite applause as the boy was carried off the field on a stretcher.

Mr. Burnette watched Jeff shake his head and drop down on the dugout bench. Jeff closed his eyes and froze in that position until a new pitcher came in to warm-up. Mr. Burnette then turned his attention to Jack on first base, who greeted the new pitcher with the same unspoken aggression. Mr. Burnette shook his head and handed the binoculars to his wife for her to study their sons' behaviors.

Katherine saw everything that had happened without binoculars—in fact, without even being at the ball park. She was at home, listening to the radio broadcast of the game. As she looked out her kitchen window, she imagined the scene. It sickened her. This sort of mishap always seemed to happen at baseball games. Someone was always getting hurt. The broadcaster had guessed the pitcher had suffered a broken kneecap. What he hadn't said was that the boy could be crippled for the rest of his life. Katherine knew boys like that—they were men now, hobbling the streets of Cottage Park. Some of them were lucky to be alive.

Her husband would not be as lucky. Murphy's health was so fragile that simply getting out of bed in the morning might wear him down and take his life. And there he was, at his age and with his health, out on a baseball field. Baseball was played with unforgiving weapons such as balls and bats, and every single call could be argued to the death—all under the blazing sun of a hot, humid Iowa summer. Baseball must have been the grim reaper's favorite sport.

"You can bury me right out under the third-base coach's box," Murphy had said to the delight of his friends. They spoke as if they were martyrs hoping to glorify themselves in battle. But Katherine saw them not as martyrs in a noble war but as selfish little boys who enjoyed their game time. In her mind, there certainly was no war, so no one needed to sacrifice anything, especially his life. Her husband had given the very best years of his life to baseball. He shouldn't have to die for it as well.

Katherine knew this to be true, yet her fears and worries only seemed to amuse her husband and his fellow coaches. The old men half listened to her arguments, nodding at the appropriate times. Ten thousand times she had explained this to her husband, and each time the words had fallen on deaf ears. He and the other old men would never give up.

But neither would she.

The game came to life again as play resumed. Spider drove Jack in for the first run of the game.

Katherine turned off the radio. Tonight she would try once again to convince Murphy to retire from baseball. Now. Not at the end of the season. Tonight's plea would make ten thousand and one attempts to reach and save him before it was too late.

However, this time she would also continue to make her appeal to someone else as well. This time, as she had done many times over the last year, she would also call Hugh Wilson.

No one other than Wilson knew that Cottage Park's number one proponent for firing and kicking the old men off their beloved baseball team was none other than the wife of the coach. She loved her husband dearly, but she knew the old men would never leave the team willingly. She persuaded Wilson to adopt her only hope, her best-made plan. He agreed to bring in a younger man to replace her husband—or at least work alongside him in his final season of coaching.

Once again, she surreptitiously called Wilson at home and began to delineate how that plan could and must work in order to make both of their lives easier and happier.

— CHAPTER ELEVEN —

Countdown to the Finals: 37 Days to Go

WHEN THE TELEPHONE RANG, EGG KNEW it was three o'clock in the afternoon. He made no attempt to answer it. It was Father Ryan calling—an agreed-upon wake-up call to rouse Egg from his nap. After three rings, Ryan hung up.

Egg straightened up slowly from his La-Z-Boy recliner, then rose to his feet. He looked outside his kitchen window at the tin thermometer. The temperature read ninety-three degrees. Egg headed for the garage, where T. J. was busy working. So far, he had painted over the words *Die, the,* and the letters *Ameri.*

"I'm glad I'm not paying you by the hour," Egg said. "If I'd been doing this job myself, I'd have painted the whole garage by now."

T. J. stood back and looked at his brushstrokes, smooth and even, as Egg had demanded. When he was done, the garage would look better than ever. Maybe he could work on getting faster. But in Cottage Park, where time often slowed to a dead stop, who cared about speed?

T. J. squinted sweat from his eyes and looked at Egg. Egg was back to his old self—full-blown cranky.

"What's biting your butt?"

"Emmetsburg," Egg said. "We've got a doubleheader. We're leaving in twenty minutes. Get ready."

Over twenty-four hours, T. J.'s attendance at a Holy Trinity baseball game had gone from anticipated to mandatory. Overnight, T. J. had become a vital cog in the Holy Trinity baseball machine.

"What are you worried about now? I thought you said you had the best team in the state."

T. J. fit the lid onto the paint can, then took it into the garage to pound it down with a hammer. Egg followed behind to put things in order. T. J.

waited for Egg to step back outside, then he used both hands to pull down the garage door.

"You said you'd win all your games this year," T. J. continued.

"We do have the best team," Egg said sternly. "But nothing is ever automatic. Emmetsburg is good too. They've got big, strong football players over there. They could beat us tonight, and—poof—there goes our undefeated season. It's been a while since we've gone through a season undefeated. That's important to us."

A few minutes later, Ryan drove up into Egg's driveway. Murphy was seated in the passenger seat. Egg and T. J. made their way to the back.

Ryan was leading a caravan of nine cars out of Cottage Park south on Highway 169. It would be a fifty-mile trek to Emmetsburg. Players drove many of the other cars, filled with friends and family members. Younger players were chauffeured by their parents.

In response to the energy crisis, the speed limit on interstate highways in Iowa and all across the country had recently been lowered from seventy-five to fifty-five miles per hour. The new speed limit was extremely unpopular with high school students who had received their licenses in the higher speed era. Before, they had always driven at least five miles above the speed limit—and often times much faster.

Now Ryan was barely moving at all, poking along at fifty to fifty-five miles per hour. Nearly everyone who followed dutifully behind him—especially the high school seniors behind the wheel—believed they could get out of their cars and run faster than Ryan was crawling along. Following the speed limit was driving those teenagers crazy, as was the route Ryan had chosen. They all knew an alternative blacktop route that could easily shave fifteen to twenty minutes off their time, even if they were poking along at or slightly below the new speed limit.

Had Ryan known that his careful, law-abiding behavior was creating so much consternation, he probably would have slowed down even more.

No one was more consternated, however, than T. J., who watched with growing dismay as Ryan drove his car directly down the middle of southbound 169. Over the years, T. J. had developed a lackadaisical attitude about his own mortality. But now at the mercy of the elderly driver who cruised unconsciously in an ultra game of highway chicken, he trembled with fear for his life. Fortunately, no northbound cars had approached them.

T. J. glanced at his fellow passengers. They seemed either oblivious to or unconcerned by Ryan's driving. In fact, as soon as the quartet had taken to the highway Egg had taken on the tone of a tour guide, educating T. J. of important regional information he thought would help the young man understand his family and his fellow community members from Cottage Park. To this point, almost all of Egg's travelogue had centered around accidents of one kind or another, mostly automobile. The subjects of these stories often ended up losing everything from limb to life.

As they passed over railroad tracks in Burt, Ryan slowed—without even a cue—as Egg somberly pointed out the crossing lights that had been erected after a freight train hit and killed an entire Holy Trinity family of six at that very spot.

And then in the far distance, T. J. could make out a car approaching. He waited expectantly for Ryan to maneuver the car to his proper side of the road. When the car did not move an inch, T. J. tapped Egg on the knee.

Egg did not appreciate the interruption. "What?" he said with a scowl.

T. J. pointed at the car now getting closer. Egg stared at T. J., not even turning his head in the direction of T. J.'s finger.

T. J. knew that if he took the time to explain his concern to Egg and then have that concern relayed to Ryan, his body would be compacted into the physical consistency of a very large can of stewed tomatoes. Instead, he immediately leaned forward in his seat and raised his voice without shouting.

"Father, you're driving on the wrong side of the road. We're going to get hit!"

Even with the car seconds away, Ryan didn't move the car into the proper lane.

Out of instinct, T. J. flung himself back into the seat, covered his face, and cried out, "Sweet Jesus! Please!"

Had he not been preparing for the crash and his death, T. J. would have experienced what few in Cottage Park had ever seen: the trifecta actually laughing at the same time. Really laughing. Even Egg's dark stony visage had cracked, revealing eyes that sparkled in merriment. The moment was fleeting, though. Before T. J. opened his eyes again, they immediately returned to normal as Ryan slowly veered his car over to the right to avoid a collision—and the northbound car hugged the edge of its own lane as extra insurance.

After T. J. heard the oncoming car pass, the first thing that he did was frantically fumble for his seat belt to lock himself in place, should Ryan not correct his driving technique. He was now the only person in the car to be belted in.

"You're not serious," Egg said matter-of factly. "Are you? This is how we drive around here. That way, you don't end up in the ditch."

"Yes, you're perfectly safe," Ryan offered from the driver's seat. "I've never been in a serious accident in my whole life."

T. J. shook his head. "Can't you drive on the right side of the road and still keep out of the ditch like everyone else?" T. J. looked out the back window. Everyone else in their caravan was driving in the proper fashion.

"We know what we're doing," Egg said. "And the next time you're begging for your life, I advise you to go directly to God the Father. Your Jesus fellow needs to get a haircut and shave."

"He's right," Ryan added. "What are you, some kind of Protestant?"

T. J. sat back in his seat and surveyed the highway in front of them. What he was, was grateful to be alive. However, Ryan had already steered his car back into the middle of road. T. J. had to choose from the impossible: He could fling himself from the moving car into the very ditch Ryan was working so diligently to avoid. Or he could continue on down the road, putting his life into the hands of old men who had no interest in accommodating what he perceived to be a safer strategy for the journey. In desperation, T. J. gave his trust and his life over to the old men—but he still flinched each time a car met them on the highway.

Nonplussed, Egg continued right on with his stories. He had at least one for each tiny town they passed through. Farther down the road, Egg announced the halfway point of the journey: the town of Algona, the county seat of Kossuth County, the largest county in terms of size of all of Iowa's ninety-nine counties. Algona was the big city in Kossuth County with over 5,500 residents. Despite the population difference, Holy Trinity had dominated Algona's Catholic and public school baseball teams for decades. Holy Trinity had lost to an Algona team twice in fifty years. The three old men could describe in great detail those two losses, which they believed were not really losses, but flukes.

There was more. Before Ryan turned west on Highway 18, Egg motioned farther down the road on Highway 169, pointing toward the hospital where residents of Cottage Park sometimes visited. West of Algona were signs for Whittemore—Murphy had a younger sister who lived there. And then there was West Bend, the home of the Grotto of the Redemption. Egg promised T. J. that the Grotto of the Redemption was one of the most spectacular Catholic holy places in the world, built by a priest in gratitude for surviving a critical case of pneumonia.

Down the highway was a sign for Rodman, where Egg had once labored somewhat unsuccessfully as a farmer.

"I made twenty-five cents a day spreading manure in 1920," Egg said with wonder. "Gosh, now we give a kid that amount when he returns a foul ball to us during a baseball game!"

Egg continued as tour guide, and Ryan and Murphy interjected from time to time. T. J. noted that while some stories were baseball boasts and personal directory updates, they always seemed to return to death, accidents and injuries, and depressing economic times.

Ryan slowed his car as they came around the curve into Cylinder, Ryan's birthplace. Ryan pointed at the single gas station on the highway.

His family's neighbors had once operated it. He lamented how now it was run by a man who owned a chain of gas-station-slash-grocery-marts across Iowa. He didn't even live in Cylinder. The three old men groused that consolidation and absentee ownership seemed to be the common thread destroying the schools, businesses, farms, and even churches in northwestern Iowa. At least you could still buy a gallon of gas and a gallon of milk in the small town. More and more Iowa towns could not make that claim. They had no easy solution to solve the quandary.

Throughout Egg's entire presentation, all T. J. truly noticed were miles and miles of corn and soybean fields periodically punctuated by tiny towns of tired, worn-out businesses. It all looked exactly the same to him. Everywhere Ryan's car took them was shrouded in quiet and solitude, not unlike a cemetery.

Finally, to the great relief of the cars behind him, Ryan arrived in Emmetsburg. Egg explained that they would be playing the public high school team. Emmetsburg Catholic High School had closed six years earlier in 1968, due to a shortage of teaching sisters. The three old men judged a town by the strength and magnitude of its Catholic church and school. Catholic school closures, even in strongholds such as Irish Catholic

Emmetsburg, gave the men a previously unthinkable sinking suspicion that even their powerful Catholic Church empire was beginning to crumble around them.

Ryan maneuvered down Emmetsburg's main street. The town was proud that it didn't have one stoplight. The main drag was slightly more active than that of the other towns.

Ryan slowed his car when he spotted the baseball field. He came to a stop on the grass along the right field fence.

"Glory be to God," Ryan said in thanksgiving for a safe passage.

"Amen," Murphy and Egg answered in unison.

"We'll say a rosary on the way home," Egg said to T. J. as they exited the car. "Father—or any of us, for that matter—aren't particularly adept at night driving anymore. Do you have your license yet?"

T. J. shook his head no. *That's one more thing I'll have to do to help these old guys*, he thought to himself. For the first time in several years, he offered his own simple and silent prayer that a meteorite would plunk him prior to the rosary-and-driving odyssey that awaited him later that night.

The rest of the caravan filed in line neatly behind Ryan. The passengers burst out of the cars to stretch and commiserate about their vapid journey. It was as if they had arrived from a two-month voyage from Ireland to Quebec in a coffin ship full of disease, with sharks circling the ship for the frequent bodies thrown overboard—the kind of story Egg told about his grandfather's immigrant voyage.

At the end of the procession was McKenna's pickup. The freshmen ballplayers took the bat and ball bags from McKenna's truck bed and followed Murphy, Egg, and Ryan onto the field. The varsity players stayed behind, congregating in or around the truck. McKenna ran speakers from the cab to the back of his truck and turned the music on to Three Dog Night. His mother had filled a picnic basket with enough sandwiches and pop for everyone on the team.

One player did not partake in the pregame meal. When Jack saw his brother drift away from the team and head toward the fence along the field, he grabbed a sandwich and a pop and followed him. Jeff stopped by the fence and looked out at the Emmetsburg players warming up on the field.

"Here you go," Jack said, offering the food to Jeff. "Eat."

"No thanks," Jeff said.

Jack forced the food at his brother, who deflected it back. After receiving a semi-mean look, Jeff reluctantly took the sandwich and nibbled on it.

"The last time I ate before a game, I got really sick. Anyway, I heard it's best to play on an empty stomach. I like being hungry. It psyches me up."

"As I've been trying to tell you," Jack said, "everything you think you know about baseball is completely wrong. If you don't eat, all you'll do is psych yourself right into a psych unit. From now on, whenever you have any thoughts about baseball, do the complete opposite." Jack headed back toward the dugout but then quickly turned around. "And we've got to get your mind off the game and into the gutter, like everyone else on this team. You need a girlfriend."

"You find me someone like Sarah," Jeff said, "and I'll take you up on it."

"You're right about Sarah," Jack said. "She is great. And it so happens, she's available. In case you haven't heard, we broke up."

Jeff hadn't heard. He tried not to show his surprise nor his disappointment. But he didn't know whether that surprise and disappointment stemmed from the fact that his brother had broken up with the best girlfriend he'd ever had, or from the fact that Jack hadn't even bothered to share this important information with his own brother.

"Just because I dated Sarah shouldn't stop you, though," Jack said. "You should ask her out."

Jeff took another bite of the sandwich and shook his head.

"I'm serious. And just because you're a freshman doesn't mean you shouldn't ask out a girl who's two or three years older. I'll bet you'd be surprised how much an older woman would be interested in you—and how much it would really get you to relax during the game."

"I'm always trying to get better," Jeff said, completely missing his brother's sexual insinuation. "I'm saying the Jesus prayer, and that's helping some."

Jack looked scornfully.

"Deep breathing," Jeff continued. "I think 'Jesus' when I breathe in. Then when I breathe out, I think, 'my Lord and my God.' It's an old meditation some of the saints did that helped them through tough times."

Jack had heard enough. He grabbed his brother and put him in an awkward headlock.

"Remember what I told you: No damn thinking. React." He muscled Jeff back toward McKenna's truck. "Now let's try this again." He let up on the headlock, then tapped his brother on the head. "Let everything in that brain of yours out. And from now on, if some new idea pops up in you, do the opposite."

Jack finally got a look of approval from Jeff. He smiled back.

"And I know you're still hungry. Rule number one: eat when you're hungry."

Holy Trinity won the opening game, which pit the schools' junior varsity teams against each other. Like their varsity brethren, the JV players were raised not to fear anyone on a baseball field. That included their older teammates. They believed they could step right in at any varsity position and be as good as or better than the player they replaced.

The varsity squads squared off next in the second game of the double-header. The score was one to nothing Holy Trinity when Jeff came up to bat in the third inning.

Murphy's words floated through his head: *When the count is zero and two, you can't sit there like a bump on a log. You have to go after the ball.* Murphy had said that many times and was even signaling this again when the Emmetsburg pitcher released a curveball that headed directly for Jeff's belt buckle.

Jeff prepared to swing his bat. But as the pitcher released the ball, he stepped out of the way, out of the batter's box. The ball swiveled and slowly sailed over the middle of the plate for strike three.

A thousand shouts and cries whistled through the ear holes of his batting helmet. Jeff ignored them. It wasn't until he took his helmet off that he distinctly heard his brother's voice yelling that the catcher had dropped the ball, turning it from strike three to a passed ball.

"Run!" Jack yelled.

Jeff dropped his bat and burst toward first, stretching his legs as far and as fast as he had ever stretched them. He was one stride from plopping his foot onto the middle of the base when he saw the first baseman reach down and receive a throw from the catcher. He was out.

"Out!" the umpire yelled a second later, repeating the obvious loudly and emphatically to everyone in the ballpark.

The call echoed as Jeff slowed his pace running down the right field line. He finally turned, head down and embarrassed, and slinked back across the field to the dugout. He cost them the third out of the inning. He feared he would hear that "Out!" for the rest of his life. He was definitely out—out of sync, talent, and courage.

Jack was waiting at the dugout with Jeff's glove. "Slow down," he said in a relaxed voice. "What's the hurry? Come on—catch your breath."

He took off Jeff's helmet and tossed it Frisbee style into the dugout. Then he handed Jeff his glove and laughed.

"You're fast. People better watch out if we ever do get you on base."

It'll never happen, Jeff thought to himself as Jack departed for left field. *I'm a loser.* He pounded his head with a closed fist. *Stupid freshman mistake.*

Then he stopped with a sudden realization. He looked back over his shoulder at Jack in left field. Two times in one day, his older brother had shown him attention—something he hadn't received since he was a little boy.

Jeff slowly jogged out to third. For the first time that season, he stopped the interior dialogue with himself.

By the top of the fifth, Holy Trinity held a two-to-nothing lead. With two outs, Spider darted off second, daring the pitcher or the catcher to throw the ball over to second and pick him off. Neither tried.

"Come on, baby!" Mrs. McKenna yelled as loud as she could as her son stepped to the plate.

Her cheer awoke fans from both teams. The Emmetsburg fans turned and peered to see who was making such noise. Once they saw and recognized Mrs. McKenna, they felt inclined to cheer silently or even out loud with her. After all, what damage could one more hit or even one run do in light of the support this mother and son deserved?

McKenna had figured out this pitcher. Already he had sliced two hits deep into left field for a single and a double. After he received the hit away signal from Murphy, McKenna set himself in at the plate.

The pitcher faked a throw to second, and Spider dived back to the bag. The pitcher brought the ball to his glove and took a long look at Spider. Then he went into his windup and release.

From the velocity of the movement, McKenna expected a fastball. He gripped his bat, flexed his arms and legs, and prepared to swing as fast as he could. He gave his full concentration to the baseball as it propelled from the pitcher's fingertips and zoomed at him inside, right at his chin.

McKenna waited until the last possible moment, then turned, ducked, and fell to the ground in an attempt to avoid the hit. In his retreat, however, the ball still struck him in the back of his helmet.

In the instant of the impact, his helmet flew back several feet, almost to the backstop, where it spun and wobbled before dropping to the dirt. The baseball ricocheted and rolled back toward the pitching mound. And McKenna slumped to the ground, his eyes closed. One hand gripped the bat tightly; the other hand clawed a fistful of dirt.

Mrs. McKenna screamed. She jumped down the bleachers to the fence, gripping it. Anthony's mother, following close behind, held and comforted her.

Ryan was the first person to reach McKenna. He knelt and began to query him about the pain while gently feeling for a lump along his temples and scalp.

McKenna took deep breaths from his nose. After a moment, he blinked his eyes and sat up.

"I guess I'm okay," he said softly to Ryan. "Just mad."

Ryan quickly stood and turned to Mrs. McKenna. "He's fine. He's catching his breath." Ryan then turned back to McKenna. "Thank you, God. Thank you."

McKenna surrendered the bat to Ryan, who turned and tossed it to the Holy Trinity dugout. Ryan then helped McKenna to his feet and assisted him down the line to first base.

Murphy headed straight for the umpire.

"Now, Coach," the umpire said. He took a step back and held up two hands. "I know what you'll say. Believe me, I'll take care of this."

"We don't want a brawl out here," Murphy said, his face flushing. "But if there's any more funny stuff"—the umpire tried to interrupt, unsuccessfully—"we'll have a heck of a time trying to keep Moriarty from retaliating—especially when they hit a kid like Marty McKenna."

"If this Emmetsburg kid throws anything close to a brushback," the umpire said, "I'll throw him right out. But the same goes for your big redhead."

Murphy looked at Ryan at first base, then at McKenna, who waved his hat to signal he was okay. Murphy returned to the third-base coach's box.

The umpire called Orlowski to the plate.

"Go ahead and hit me," Orlowski said to the catcher. "I won't go after your pitcher. I'll come right back at you."

Orlowski flexed into position, saw the sign from Murphy, then watched the first pitch sail directly across the plate for a strike.

Spider and McKenna both sprang from their bases at the same time. In a double steal, they slid successfully into second and third base, respectively.

It caught the Emmetsburg players completely by surprise. It served as a reminder that Holy Trinity really was supposed to win this game, as they always did. Somehow the breaks always fell to Cottage Park. It had plagued them all their athletic lives, whenever playing against a Cottage Park baseball team.

The Holy Trinity players could not contain their amusement at the double steal. Their raucous laughter was also an outlet for their contempt of the Emmetsburg pitcher's beaning McKenna.

Orlowski ended up walking to first to load the bases. Anthony was up next.

Mr. Civilla moved from his seat in the bleachers and stood directly behind his son at home plate.

"Make him respect you, Anthony," he yelled. "You're the man up there!"

Anthony received the take sign from Murphy, stepped into the batter's box, and prepared himself for the first pitch. It was a ball.

Holy Trinity players and fans smelled blood, and they knew whose blood it would be. Their cries started the moment the pitcher began his windup, and they continued as Anthony stepped into the pitch and swung his bat smoothly.

Everyone but Mr. Civilla watched the ball fly over the left field fence for a grand slam. Mr. Civilla never took his eyes from his son until he crossed home plate, where he was joyfully mobbed by his teammates.

Holy Trinity scored one other run that inning. Emmetsburg failed to score during the entire game, losing by a score of seven to zero. Holy Trinity remained undefeated.

"How many pitches did Moriarity throw tonight?" Egg asked T. J. as the players gathered to celebrate in the dugout.

T. J. glanced down at his scorekeeping guide, "Eighty-three," he answered confidently.

Egg was proud. His plan was working perfectly.

— CHAPTER TWELVE —

Countdown to the Finals: 33 Days to Go

ANY OTHER FATHER WOULD HAVE BEEN PROUD of his child for such an achievement. Each year, across all of Iowa, fifty-two young men and fifty-two young women were chosen to be the "Prep of the Week" in the *Peach* section of the *Des Moines Register*. "Prep of the Week" recognized outstanding high school performances with a story and picture of each athlete. This week, Pat Moriarity was "Prep of the Week."

All over the state, Iowans were waking up to Moriarity's photo—his broad face covered with brown splotches of freckles; his thick, bushy red hair parted at the side; and his huge, toothy grin. Those Iowans were laughing.

"Typical farm kid," they thought or said as they showed the picture to others.

But Moriarity wasn't a farm kid, and he wasn't typical by any definition. Nor was his father.

Bill Moriarity also came across the picture of his son at breakfast. It was six thirty in the morning. Only his wife joined him. Standing by the oven, she busily scrambled eggs and fried bacon in the same pan. Their six children, including Pat, were still asleep.

Far from laughing, Mr. Moriarity looked into his son's eyes there on the page and saw, in many respects, himself. Mr. Moriarity had also loved baseball and was a pitcher. Like his son, he practiced or played whenever he could, usually with his older brother, until that brother graduated from high school and began working.

After that, Mr. Moriarity played baseball with anyone in town. Constantly. He played long and devotedly because he believed his efforts would pay off with a trip to the big leagues. He also played because he genuinely loved the game.

As he grew bigger and stronger, he learned he could overpower smaller players. He became the mainstay on both the fall- and spring-championship Holy Trinity teams and the American Legion team. After graduating, he rose far—all the way to the top of the Detroit Tigers minor league farm organization.

But then the cumulative effects of wear and tear on his throwing arm ended his career. Now, even circling his arm in a basic throwing motion brought intense pain.

He could feel a twinge of that pain as he lifted the paper up and away from his eyes so he could focus on the article. Pat deserved the honor. Over four games, he had struck out twenty-five batters and thrown a one-, a three-, a five-, and a seven-hitter. All the games had been shutouts. Also during that time, he had made no fielding errors and was batting .316.

Mr. Moriarity looked once more into his son's eyes in the picture. Baseball now saddened Mr. Moriarity. He hadn't attended a full game, watched one on TV, or even read about a game since his injury twenty years earlier. He had practically shut baseball out of his life, even in a baseball town and having a baseball son. The same son he worried most about.

His son could not think a single thought or utter a single word unless it were connected to baseball in some way. Mr. Moriarity knew all boys go through a phase where they become fixated on a dream. With Pat, though, it was not a phase but a lifelong obsession.

When Pat was in fifth grade, his teacher asked the senior Moriarity to come in and observe his son in the classroom. There Mr. Moriarity saw for himself the blank expression, the faraway eyes. Pat was not a stupid child, the nun assured him. He could read and write. He was just preoccupied. And Pat was always forthright about his preoccupation. Baseball.

The more Mr. Moriarity worked to draw his son away from the sport, the more his son fixated on it. Mr. Moriarity did everything in his power to dissuade Pat from any thoughts of the big leagues, to introduce cold reality into Pat's fantasy world of life beyond Cottage Park. But now it seemed Pat was also obsessed with proving his father wrong—with proving he *was* good enough to play in the pros. Both were strong willed, but Pat proved to be the stronger of the two.

Eventually, the senior Moriarity gave up. Not on Pat, but on any notion of trying to inject sense into Pat about baseball. The side effect of giving up on that conversation, however, was that he did give up on his son. The two barely spoke to each other. Now, with the notoriety of the *Peach* acclaim, Pat's resolve was bound to intensify.

Mr. Moriarity groaned and muscled himself up from the table.

"What?" his wife, Julie, said.

"I truly give up," Mr. Moriarity said.

He handed her the sports page and watched her look until she found the article and picture. Before a discussion could begin, he grabbed his sack lunch and split early for work.

Declining enrollment forced public schools in northwestern Iowa—and in small communities all across the United States—to consolidate. Two, three, and four communities pooled their resources and efforts to provide their children with the best possible education. But these communities often had different temperaments, religions, and ancestries. Historically, they regarded each other as rivals. So, combining efforts, even for something as important as children's education, can be onerous when it involves a dreaded enemy.

Try as they might, folks in the consolidated school district of Cherry Grove–Earle were finding it problematic to come together. This was most obvious in the bleachers of Cottage Park Memorial Field when the team played Holy Trinity. Residents of Cherry Grove, with their mostly Dutch ancestry, sat opposite residents of Earle, with their mostly German ancestry.

As Moriarity struck out the fifth batter, one of the fans from Earle turned to another. "We haven't even made contact with the ball tonight," he said. "We're lucky we're only getting beat four to nothing."

His friend responded, "Yeah, well, look at who Coach is playing. The whole starting nine is from Cherry Grove. So is the coach. You think that's a coincidence?" He laughed, then got serious again. "He's got to give our boys a chance."

However, even if the Earle players had gotten a chance to bat, it would have made little difference that game. Moriarity was neither giving nor taking chances. He wasn't in the mood. His brain was split between the game and his anger.

Before Moriarity had taken off from home, all his father had said was, "Time for a haircut. You look like a circus clown." That was it.

Moriarity received the signal from Powers, then wound up and threw the requested fastball. The batter hit a weak grounder back to the mound. Moriarity picked up the ball and stared at the batter as he plodded down to first base.

His father had made no mention of his award as the "Prep of the Week." No "Way to go, Son. Keep up the good work in tonight's game." Nothing.

The ambling batter looked back at Moriarity with disbelief. Why hadn't he thrown him out? Now the batter thought he might be close enough to beat the throw. He kicked it into a higher gear.

Pat saw the determination in the runner's face, yet he continued to dwell on his encounter with his father. Tomorrow, his father would probably say even less words to him.

The umpire watched Moriarity hold the ball in grandstand fashion. He ached to call the approaching runner safe. Even if the runner were a little late, he'd still call him safe. That would surely teach this young pitcher a lesson.

But then Moriarity rifled the ball over. Its pop in the first baseman's glove was still a gasp ahead of the foot that stretched and thudded into the bag. The umpire had no choice but to call him out.

Murphy was mad, as usual, at his pitcher. He glared at him as the team entered the dugout. When Egg read the lineup, Murphy drifted over with Moriarity's warm-up jacket and draped it over him.

Moriarity dropped out of the left shoulder so only his right shoulder was covered. His jaw clenched. His eyes stared out at the opposition.

Murphy remembered something Egg had once told him years ago. As a young man, Egg had a job maintaining the railbed for the railroad. He learned there are two types of steel: hard and soft. The rail was hard. The spikes that held it in place were soft. You could drive a soft spike by hitting it with the hard steel of a spike hammer. But hit the spike hammer on the hard steel of the rail, and one or both of your eyes could be blinded with a sheared steel splinter.

"People are like steel," Egg used to say. "You have to determine if they're hard or soft—and you have to answer the same question about yourself."

The young pitcher was hard steel at least for today, so the old coach would have to become soft. He sat down next to Moriarity.

"You're throwing well tonight. How do you feel?"

Moriarity responded with a nod.

"Have I ever told you how important it is to take care of your hands?"

Moriarity held up his right hand and pointed to his nails. "You mean squaring off my nails so I can throw a knuckleball?"

"No," Murphy said sharply. He took a deep breath. "You don't need to throw a knuckleball."

He held Moriarity's hand in his so the palm faced upward. Murphy traced the palm lines with his fingers, then felt between and around Moriarity's fingers.

"A blister is a pitcher's worst enemy. I could tell you stories for the rest of the night about pitchers who fooled around and got a blister, then didn't take care of it. Those things get infected."

Murphy winced, and he was happy to see Moriarity do the same.

"But your hands look good." Murphy raised his hands from Moriarity's. "Katherine visited all the neighbors and collected your 'Prep of the Week' story. Why don't you come over tomorrow and get them? It'll give Katherine a chance to check up on you."

Moriarity nodded.

"If you can keep your head in the game out there, you could be 'Prep of the Week' next week too."

Moriarity quickly brightened. "Has anyone ever made it two weeks in a row?" he asked earnestly.

"No," Murphy said, shaking his head. He stood and clapped his hands. "But that doesn't mean it can't happen." He patted Moriarity on the back and moved on toward third base. "We need some runs. The race isn't over until we cross the line. And right now, we're a long ways away."

The game ended with a five-to-nothing win. Hours later, the bottles of beer were open and flowing in Orlowski's Ford Fairlane as it scooted across the gravel path to the quarries. Grass and brush scratched the floor of his car. It made so much noise that it drowned out the music from the radio, which blinked on and off each time the car dropped into a pothole. Beer spilled out over Orlowski's uniform and onto his seat upholstery. Each time the car hit a bump, his passengers—Michelle, Spider, and Margaret—were thrown into one another. They laughed louder and longer.

Orlowski parked at the base of the jetty, put his head back against the seat, closed his eyes, and listened to the laughter around him. The world seemed to spin. He held onto his steering wheel to ground himself.

Spider and Margaret crawled out from the back and grabbed the sole survivors of the case of beer. They followed Michelle and Orlowski, who traipsed in a zigzag pattern out onto the jetty.

A nearly full moon poured creamy light over them and the waters lapping up along the shore. Ten thousand stars lit the darkness, not unlike the morning dew that tipped the grass at Memorial Field. There was enough of a breeze off the lake to chill the young people. They drew their partners closer for warmth.

Orlowski spotted an open beer bottle in the path and stopped to pick it up. He shook it upside down, then frowned when nothing came out.

"Hey," he said, "if we were all stuck out here, and this bottle was our only communication with the world, what would you write on it?"

"Directions for others to find us," Spider said.

Everyone considered this possibility, then Orlowski reared the bottle back and set to throw it out into the water.

"Wait," Spider said. "Maybe we don't get found. Maybe we've got everything we could possibly need on this little jetty. More people might mess things up."

He gently kissed Margaret's cheek. Using the darkness and his body as a cover, he brought his hand up from her waist to trace the outline of her right breast. She leaned away. His fingers continued across her breast, finding and awakening her nipple. This time, she turned away.

"If what you've got on the island is that good," Margaret said, "it will survive when civilization beats a path to your door."

"I'm with you, Margaret," Orlowski said. He brought the bottle back and yelled, "Here we are, world! Come and get us!"

He threw the bottle out far into the night. Its splash wrinkled the moonlight on the water.

The group hiked out farther on the jetty and set up a fire. The conversation—as it had often been of late, especially at the quarries—was one of reminiscing. The stories recaptured their youth. Some recalled events in Cottage Park from when they were five and six years old. Their recollections were somewhat dulled by the beer that had saturated their senses. There was also a joint passed from hand to mouth to the next hand in a circle. Its Ouija effect allowed the young people to see and feel whatever they chose to see and feel.

Spider did not share the marijuana experience. He didn't wish to further alienate Margaret. When a second joint was lit and passed around, Margaret handed it to the next person, then got up and walked from the group. She was heading to the car. Spider jumped to his feet to follow her.

At the same time, Orlowski stood on unsure legs and strayed over to the rust-colored rock that eventually jutted into a twenty-five-foot sheer cliff. He tried to keep himself upright, but suddenly he toppled over and fell down with his face hanging over the cliff.

Spider saw the commotion and scrambled after him. He leaped across the grass and gravel to grab him by the ankles. While Michelle stretched out over Orlowski's back, Margaret came running back and held down his knees.

Orlowski looked down the rock to the waters that slapped against it, twirled, and retreated before the next wave hit again. He tried to follow the water until his own eyes swam and he became dizzy. When he burped, his friends laughed. But when he heaved gas and vomit over the cliff, Spider and Margaret backed away. Michelle stayed to stroke his forehead.

When he could breathe again, he rolled over on his back, closed his eyes and moaned.

"Even the moon is dancing," he said.

Margaret continued her brisk march back toward Orlowski's car, ignoring Spider's pleas to stop. Out of breath, he caught up with her, but even then she refused to stop. He finally reached out and held her.

"Let go of me!" Margaret said. She flexed, made fists, and swung free. "I've had enough of this life."

She took a few quick steps, then reached down and picked up a handful of gravel. She shook the gravel at Spider and threw it out into the water.

"I'm sick of the booze and the dope, and sick of people who act like dopes." She looked up into the stars. "I used to like coming out here because it was different. Do you remember?"

He nodded.

"Then what happened?" Now her words were less threatening, more pleading. "More and more, this place reminds me of what I came out here to get away from . . . Cottage Park."

"Maybe that's what happens when you get older," Spider said. "Maybe you learn that there are no treehouses where you can hide away. It's all one world."

Spider reached for Margaret, but she blocked him away.

"Come on," he said. "Baseball's almost done. We got fifty-six days before we can leave this place. Let's put up with it like we always have."

Margaret pounded a fist between her breasts. "I'm a young woman. I'm ready to do something with my life—right now. I don't mind working for it. I'm going to leave this place in better shape than it is now."

"The world doesn't change overnight," Spider said.

No, but it *can* change," Margaret said. She pointed back in the direction of Orlowski and Michelle. "That's not change. That doesn't even make an effort to change. They don't think of it." Margaret turned to the water and folded her arms. "I don't have all the answers, but I know I have one of them. People at least have to try to make things better. I need someone who'll work with me to do that."

"That's where I come in," Spider said. He moved close to Margaret.

"Maybe," Margaret said. "If you can see me for more than someplace to stick your wiener."

She turned back and saw the anger on Spider's face.

"I know," she said. "That night was wonderful. I know it feels good. But there's more to me than that. I'm not one without the other."

Spider was tired and angry. Both were born of frustration. For the last week, every day, all day, he'd reenacted that night, this place, when they were one. He dreamed and schemed to be with her again. And now so close, she was farther away than ever. Very little of what she said made sense to him. If she were right, he didn't care. He would gladly be wrong to be with her.

And so he looked at her. Of all the emotions that surged through him at that moment, he listened to and acknowledged the quietest one, the one that made the least sense to him, and the one that made the most sense to Margaret at that late hour.

"Let's go help with Orlowski," he said wearily.

Together, with his arm around her, they headed back to do just that.

At the same time the two couples had driven off toward the quarries after the game, Anthony had gotten in the car to drive home with his father.

"So you beat up on Cherry Grove–Earle tonight," Mr. Civilla said. "Big deal. That doesn't mean anything to me."

Anthony watched the houses and streets of Cottage Park pass across the windshield. There was nothing for him to say to his father. He knew how his father would reply. He had heard the arguments over and over again for the last two months. He had responded to them and in his mind defeated them. Still, his father persisted. Anthony had grown tired of trying to explain anything to his father anymore.

"You're too soft," his father continued. "My God, I can't believe I raised a boy who could be so soft about things. Don't you ever get mad at anything?"

He waited for an answer.

"I asked you a question."

Anthony sighed and looked out the window.

"That's what I thought," Mr. Civilla said. "You don't even have enough guff to answer me. You don't care. You're afraid of me, aren't you?"

Anthony shook his head.

"Then what? Why won't you speak to me?"

Mr. Civilla stopped the car outside the detached garage. Anthony opened the door, jumped out, and headed toward the house. Mr. Civilla drove the car inside, then followed his son.

"It's either hate or pity," he yelled. "And I won't be pitied!"

Anthony stopped in the kitchen to make himself a snack. If he didn't engage with his father, maybe he would go away.

"You pity me, don't you?" Mr. Civilla said, shaking his fist. "You feel sorry for your old man, working in a little hardware store that's going out of business."

Anthony stared at the cheeses, crackers, chips, and dip spread across the table in front of him. He had been hearing these words more frequently in the last few months—the closer he got to leaving for college. The more his father ranted on in this fashion, the more Anthony's disgust did turn to pity.

Mr. Civilla stopped only when Anthony's mother emerged from her bedroom to the kitchen and stood at the table next to Anthony. Dressed in her robe, she rubbed sleep from her eyes.

"Anthony is a good boy," she said, looking at her husband. "Why do you have to go through this every time there's a baseball game?"

"He's old enough to be a man," Mr. Civilla said. "But he's afraid. I don't want to see our son get intimidated by anyone."

Anthony's mother shook her head in disagreement.

Mr. Civilla continued. "You watch what happens when he leaves Cottage Park to go to the Finals or when he goes away to college. You wait and see." He threw his hands in the air and let them fall. "I've had enough. I don't need this." He got up from the table and stalked into the bedroom.

At the same time, Anthony poked away his food and got up from the table too.

"No," his mother said. She held him gently by the arm. "You're hungry. You haven't eaten since this afternoon. I'm worried about you not eating. Eat something."

Anthony slouched down next to his mother and looked downward. "I can't eat, Mom. I've lost my appetite."

She opened the bag of potato chips and the container of dip for him, then headed to the fridge to gather ingredients for a sandwich.

"Your father does love you," she said as she buttered bread. "You don't understand the way he shows it."

"Do you?" Anthony said. He broke a chip and ground it into powder.

"No. But then, I don't know that much about baseball. Your father feels very strongly about this matter. It's very important to him."

"He's crazy about me to 'be tough' and throw at someone during a game," Anthony said. "But I might be a lawyer someday. If I bean some kid, I could maim him—or kill him. I could never get into law school with something like that on my record."

"Your father believes he can help you," Mrs. Civilla said. "He thinks the boys on the other team might hurt you if you don't strike first."

She placed the sandwich before her son, then watched as he reluctantly accepted it and began to eat.

"I don't know . . . can you hit a boy with a ball without hurting him?" she offered. "Isn't there something you can do to make him happy?"

Anthony shook his head. "He's counting on blood." He rolled his eyes and let out a sad sigh. "Baseball. What a fun game."

"It's never been a *game*," Mrs. Civilla said. "Not in this town. Still, your father never put your older brothers through this. There must be some reason why he's focusing on you. Maybe it's because you're our youngest and you're leaving home soon. I'll help you with him, at least as much as I can."

She stood, leaned to kiss her son, then returned to bed.

— CHAPTER THIRTEEN —

Countdown to the Finals: 32 Days to Go

I T WAS MONDAY MORNING. HUGH WILSON SAT in his office at Holy Trinity High School and counted the money from the previous day's bingo and meat raffle activities. There was $550, plus $150 from concessions. It was not enough money. Over the last several months, there'd been a steadily decreasing trend, with less and less money from bingo. This was the smallest amount yet.

Across his desk were scattered bills. Wilson could meet the barest requests—fuel, energy, light, salaries, and necessary repairs. Yet he knew each teacher in every classroom needed new textbooks—except the few who had brought their own textbooks and materials. The others had used the same old copies for years. And on top of everything else, literally, the school needed a new roof. They'd been putting off the expense for years. "You're beyond the nickel-and-dime stage," the roofing contractor had stressed. "Each time it rains, you risk the possibility of major structural damage." It was almost too much for Wilson to bear.

Being principal often put him in an unpopular position. He found some solace, however, in the belief that very few could have managed so well with so little for so long. But all of that was changing now. Wilson knew for sure and so clearly that Holy Trinity was slowly dying, as was the parish, Cottage Park, even northwest Iowa.

Years ago, he had actually enjoyed the challenges of managing the Holy Trinity K–12 school system on a shoestring budget. He was young then and confident that this was a temporary position en route to a higher-paid position at a public school.

Then his own kids came along. His family grew accustomed to Cottage Park. That and he hadn't kept up with his professional education. Most

candidates for public school administrative positions had or were working toward their superintendent licensure, or they'd honed and developed
unique expertise in special education or middle school administration.
Wilson's opportunities for advancement at other school districts waned
over the years, and his energy followed. Unless he somehow received a
generous offer elsewhere, or unless Holy Trinity should close, Wilson
would stay in Cottage Park until his own children moved away to college.

That was his reality. But in Wilson's wildest fantasies, he had a time
machine. He would simply dial back to a previous era, when farmers had
large families and Holy Trinity was staffed almost entirely by nuns and
priests. Through the sacrifice offered by those nuns and priests, children
received a free education from oftentimes extraordinarily trained religious staff. They asked for little or nothing except to serve the families and
students.

But that pleasant journey in his time machine always ended in the
nightmare of the present: the relentless waves of children who graduated
from Holy Trinity and moved on, far away from the town's increasing challenges, leaving behind their parents and grandparents, who merely grew
older and older. Like Wilson, those elderly residents were desperate to
look back at better times, when they were happy and leading productive
lives. The only time they looked ahead, to the future, was to await their
upcoming journey to heaven.

And so Wilson's time machine always crashed, ripping him from the
security and glory of the past and forcing him to face the grim calculus of
the present and future:

Solve for the equation:

*Fewer children + paid staff (with salary expectations based
on public schools') + an evaporating economic base = What
day of school closure?*

Here Wilson sat at forty-four years old—the prime of his life. He had three
young children and a homemaker wife. His family, the school, the town,
even the crazy old coaches who fought him bitterly at every turn—all were
dependent on him. But Wilson was dependent on a future that inevitably

needed to be outside Cottage Park. This meant adjusting his slide rule for the somber terms of variables and constants:

Wilson's future livelihood = Wilson's reputation as an effective leader at Holy Trinity

Holy Trinity = baseball

Baseball = 3x, whereby x = three old men

The old men had been at Holy Trinity forever. In addition to baseball, they volunteered at the school every single day, weekends included. They never seemed to tire or even consider giving up. Whatever the young people needed—not wanted—the old men found a way to give it to them. In the event that a teacher was absent, one of the men was always nearby to perform as a substitute. During the noon hour, the three men sacrificed their lunch to be on the playground or in the gym, teaching baseball or basketball fundamental skills. (With basketball merely being a way to keep the boys in shape over the winter months to resume playing baseball again in the spring.)

They knew the name of every boy and nearly every girl, knew their dads and moms, most likely knew their grandparents, and oftentimes knew their great-grandparents—on all sides of their families. They used this familial knowledge to become honorary patriarchs themselves, playing their own roles in the boys' upbringing. The boys knew these father figures, trusted them, and could depend on them to always, *always*, be there—barking, scowling, glaring, and complaining—until the boys achieved greatness.

In most cases, the boys never appreciated the greatness they had achieved, let alone the coaches' guidance, until they had their own boys. Instead, most boys couldn't get past the memories of that nonstop harping and those sour faces. But the boys would often break down and eventually come to love the old men, as captives often break down and eventually come to love their kidnappers. It didn't hurt that the old men frequently spoiled the boys with candy.

Wilson could not deny that the old men knew the very souls of these boys. In fact, each of them had received the sacrament of baptism from Ryan in the first three months of their lives.

As with all sacraments, Ryan hurried through the process. As he anointed each boy with blessed oils and poured holy water over his head, he said, "I baptize you in the name of the Father, and the Son, and the Holy Ghost." (Through force of habit, Ryan continued to use *Ghost* instead of the church's evolution to *Spirit*.) He provided little or no explanation of how the child's soul was now free from original sin, a sin that passed down from generation to generation.

Any explanation and dialogue between priest and family was reserved for after the ceremony. That was when Ryan filled the absence of original sin with the presence of baseball—the Championship Baseball. Brand-new, each Championship Baseball was dated and signed with the boy's name. On the other side of the ball, Ryan would write, "Holy Trinity Will Win the Finals." There was no mention of or connection to baptism.

Ryan would instruct the father to put the ball between the boy's hands before the family returned home. Ryan would also explain that the ball was to be rolled back and forth from father to son, over and over again, as soon as possible, and as much as possible.

Families were grateful for Ryan's rite of initiation. They religiously followed his advice about the father-son game of catch—with one exception. The Championship Ball was never put in play. Instead, each family would place it prominently on a dresser or mantel, like the Eucharistic adoration, where it would oversee, define, and guide the boy through infancy, childhood, and manhood.

And Wilson knew that was merely the beginning. Ryan, Murphy, and Egg had developed a baseball instruction program from kindergarten through the eighth grade. Throughout the summer, from graduation day until the Finals, the old men gathered young people together each day from 10:00 a.m. to 2:00 p.m. to practice fundamentals. On Saturdays, they would compete against other small town teams.

In kindergarten, boys and girls played kickball together. They learned the concept of bases and even something as exacting as tagging up after a fly ball was caught. In first grade, though, boys were separated from the girls. Intensity increased, as did expectations, from year to year until the boys reached the high-pressure, show-time level of high school.

As they grew and matured, the constant of baseball never changed in the boys' lives. When they weren't practicing with the old men or playing competitively, they were playing pickup games around their neighborhood, playing catch (usually with their fathers), throwing tennis balls against garage doors, or swinging bats five hundred times a day.

Wilson had witnessed how baseball consumed boys' lives with his own sons, Dan in the fifth grade and Jim in the eighth grade. Dan seemed so restless. Wilson had chided him countless times about listening, yet the boy made the same mistakes over and over again. Jim was moody. He resisted direction and resented any authority his father offered. Both boys, however, worked for the old men without any question. They learned and followed fundamentals, the steady sequence of tasks and skills the old men taught them.

There in his office, Wilson shook his head. He did not dislike the old men. However, it did not bother him that people, including the old men, thought he disliked them. He allowed the appearance of antagonism because someone needed to balance their power.

And while Wilson may have not disliked the old men, he did not trust them, especially as official representatives of Holy Trinity. Once they stepped on a baseball field, they were liable to say or do anything. Wilson knew this recklessness made them so popular in Cottage Park and all over Iowa. Who wouldn't root for a team coached by cantankerous men old enough to be your grandfathers or even great-grandfathers?

On the other hand, he was certain that other people in Cottage Park— parents of ballplayers and on some occasions maybe even ballplayers them- selves—would love to see them leave. But Wilson had no illusions that the old men would voluntarily step down this season or ever. Why would they? It was their life.

No. He'd have to move the old men along and out of his way. It was time. The petition attempt failed. But he was confident in his new strategy. He couldn't help but smile as he looked down at the resume on his desk. It was quite likely the future of Holy Trinity baseball. In a short while, the applicant would arrive for his interview, and Wilson's plan would be well on its way.

And, of course, Wilson had a powerful ally. She was the one person who had always understood and shared Wilson's desire to remove the old men from the baseball team. That one person would endorse his plan and promise her full energy in its implementation.

Wilson pondered his plan for a while, then reached for the phone and dialed Katherine, with whom he shared the common goal of moving the coaches on and out to pasture. She was his strongest ally and confidante during this process of hiring a new coach. It was time to update her on his progress. He had a few minutes before the next applicant arrived.

Of the three teaching vacancies at Holy Trinity, Wilson had almost miraculously filled two. Qualified math teachers were a colossal challenge to land at any high school in Iowa, especially at an out-of-the-way small town Catholic school with a meager pay scale.

Then Wilson discovered that a recent Cottage Park marriage had brought a candidate with all the necessary credentials to the community. He immediately drove to their house in the country. Once there, Wilson explained the position and negotiated a signing of the contract right there at the same meeting. He felt good about this new teacher. She was young and wedded to a farmer, which meant she was wedded to the farm and the area. Her husband's solid income meant she would accept her salary schedule with little complaining. Her sole limitation: she was not a Catholic.

But that would be balanced as a result of the second position Wilson had filled. Qualified high school teachers in general were difficult to locate. Wilson had searched everywhere, including the motherhouse of the Sisters of the Presentation in Dubuque. Three Presentation sisters still taught in Cottage Park. Years before, there had been at least one Presentation sister for each grade. But it had been three years since a new sister had come to Cottage Park.

Then Wilson received an inquiry from an older sister who was returning to Cottage Park to care for an ailing aunt. He called the sister and hired her right over the phone. Sisters could sometimes be persnickety—especially an older, opinionated sister. But her teaching qualifications—and her low salary—would more than likely make up for any obstinacy on her part.

The third teaching vacancy, for seventh and eighth grade language arts, had yet to be filled. Wilson believed this position could be filled by nearly any of the nine applicants who responded to the advertisement in the *Des Moines Register*. Though the ad hadn't mentioned the added responsibility of coaching, this was the most important position to fill, with the greatest risk of failure. Wilson could expect to receive as much criticism, or more, for selecting the wrong applicant than for allowing the old men to stick around.

Five of the nine applicants were women. Their resumes were dropped from consideration immediately upon their arrival.

The remaining four applicants were all recent college graduates. Their licensures were in art, social studies, music, and language arts. Under Catholic school requirements, however, any one of them could fill the position.

Wilson first contacted the language arts teacher by phone. This young man wanted nothing to do with the position once he learned about the added duty of coaching—especially baseball, a sport he had never played.

Wilson interviewed the other three applicants in person. The first, with licensure in social studies, erred by not only asking the salary but also by asking how the payments were made. He was officially dismissed from consideration when he refused on principle to complete the five-question essay test Wilson had created to aid the interviewing process.

The next applicant, a music teacher, was not Catholic and had misspelled two words on the essay test. Wilson was not eager to have another music teacher on the staff. They seemed to come and go with regularity. However, Wilson thanked the applicant and promised to keep his resume for consideration.

And now Wilson looked over the essay test he had given the final applicant, a teacher with an art background and two years of substitute-teaching experience in Des Moines. A quick review showed that all words were spelled correctly. The punctuation also seemed in order.

Wilson stood and opened his office door. Sitting in the chair underneath the Infant Jesus of Prague statue—a spot usually reserved for a troublemaking student—was Don Cooper.

Cooper looked up from an aged *Reader's Digest* and smiled, showing uneven, pointed teeth set behind the dark stubble, even at this early hour, of a five-o'clock shadow. Cooper had a rapidly receding hairline that crept high and back over his forehead. Spindles of fine brown hair had been combed down with the hopes of covering this area, though they did not do so.

Cooper sat with legs crossed. Leg hair flashed between brown corduroy pants and blue woolen socks, all too short. His brown loafers were worn but clean and polished. Cooper straightened his blue woolen tie against the collar of his white polyester dress shirt.

He buttoned the top button of his brown tweed sports jacket when Wilson invited him into his office. Then he unbuttoned his jacket as he took his seat before Wilson's desk. Cooper started to cross one leg over the other but thought better and placed both feet firmly on the floor. He stretched his tie and adjusted it again.

"Honestly, I'm not used to this feeling around my neck," Cooper said, pulling at the shirt collar. "Subbing in Des Moines, I got in the habit of wearing clip-ons." He laughed. "Less chance of strangulation if some kid decides to play hangman." Cooper held up his tie like a noose.

Wilson nodded, then looked at Cooper's resume. "Dowling High School, Creighton University . . . I'm impressed. And I like your definition of the ideal student," Wilson said, referring to question number one of the essay test. He skimmed through the paragraph for key words and phrases to quote. "'Eager to learn, high energy, independent, and disciplined.' Discipline is important at Holy Trinity, especially in those formative junior high years."

As Wilson compared Cooper's resume to his test booklet, Cooper's hand once again strayed to his tie.

"In question two," Wilson continued, "you state that your vast experience as a substitute teacher in Des Moines has prepared you for our position at Holy Trinity. But I see your degree at Creighton reflects only a secondary education licensure in art. Care to explain?"

"When you substitute, you can pretty much go anywhere," Cooper said. "Most of my calls were for junior high language arts positions. It's a high-illness occupation." Cooper laughed, then quickly mimicked Wilson's seriousness. "I often took over for two or three days for some teachers. Up to a month or more for others." Cooper drummed fingers on his knees, something he would continue throughout the rest of the interview. "I was, for the most part, by myself in each setting. Because of that, I think I've learned how to teach this subject matter."

Wilson looked over the essay and focused on Cooper's answer to the final question. "You say here that you chose Holy Trinity because you're looking for a small Catholic high school with a family-centered value system." Wilson looked up at Cooper, who seemed almost childlike in his anticipation. "I believe you've come to the right place."

"Good," Cooper said. He clapped his hands against his knees, then took a deep breath and smiled.

"What about Cottage Park?" Wilson said. "Are you ready for small-town life?"

"I'm really excited to start," Cooper said.

Wilson looked at Wilson's resume. "You'll have to start at the first step of our salary schedule. I can't give you any teaching experience for the substitute teaching."

Cooper nodded.

"And how do you like baseball? Remember, this position includes coaching our baseball team."

Cooper gave a causal shrug for what he assumed was a casual question. "It's a good game," Cooper said. "I played at Creighton—softball. You know, intramurals. Same thing, really."

Wilson knew it wasn't the same thing. "We have a good team here," he said. "You probably noticed that we won our game last night. We'll probably win tomorrow and Friday night as well. In fact, I have little doubt that we'll be playing in Des Moines at the end of July in the Finals." Then Wilson drilled down to the bottom line. "Do you think you can step in and take over this job?"

"Yes," Cooper said.

The quickness and assuredness of his words, despite the obvious falsity, surprised even Cooper. He needed this job and would do almost anything, including coaching a sport of which he had little knowledge or interest.

"Yes, I'm ready to go on this," Cooper affirmed.

"That's the right attitude," Wilson said.

As desperate as Cooper was for a job, Wilson was every bit as desperate to hire a baseball coach—and the sooner the better. He came around his desk and shook Cooper's hand.

"Congratulations, Coach."

"Is that it?" Cooper said.

Wilson nodded. "Of course, I'll have to have all this approved by the school board." He winked and smiled. "But they respect my authority. I'll need you to start preparing for us. I think we'll introduce you in time for the Finals in Des Moines."

Cooper swallowed, nodded, and blushed.

Wilson continued sternly, "Coaching the baseball team is one of the bottom-line requirements of this job. If pay is an issue, we can work something out for your time. You simply have to be there for the Finals."

Cooper began to protest, but Wilson interrupted him. "Coach, I wouldn't ask you unless I really needed you there on the bench for Holy Trinity right away. We have an unusual situation this summer. Three old men have been coaching our team for decades. They started long before I came to town, so you might say they were grandfathered into their positions. Like everyone else in town, I've let them get away with more than I should have. They've promised that this summer will be their last. What they don't know, and what we don't have to tell them, is that from this point on, I give you my full authority to manage the Holy Trinity baseball team in the best way you see fit."

As Cooper swallowed uneasily, Wilson paused and reflected.

"It might be rather sticky," Wilson admitted. "They'll insist on making all the decisions. And that's all right with me, as long as you agree with them. Someone needs to be on the bench that I can trust in case they try to pull something. These guys are desperate. They're capable of saying or doing anything possible to win. If they do get out of control, you take over the reins immediately." Wilson shook his head slowly. "They'll try to keep you out of the dugout, but you'll have to finagle yourself onto the bench with them, as you did to get this job with me."

Wilson opened his office door, directing a dazed Cooper to exit into the dark hallway that led to the front doors of Holy Trinity High School.

"You've got to get on that bench," Wilson called out. "You're our last hope." Wilson pointed a finger at Cooper. "And it will look good for you too. This year, we might win the whole thing."

— CHAPTER FOURTEEN —

Countdown to the Finals: 25 Days to Go

"**N**O WAY, MOM!" T. J. SAID. "I'LL NEVER PUT THAT THING even near my body!"

The "thing" in question was a decades-old Holy Trinity baseball uniform. Murphy had given it to T. J. to wear to all the games. But first, T. J. was to wear it that morning in the Fourth of July parade. He and the rest of the team would be riding on Cottage Park's only firetruck.

The uniform had wreaked of mothballs, and T. J. had refused to wear it until the smell had been completely eliminated. His mother had washed it over and over again using different detergents, but to no avail. Then she concocted a mixture of vinegar, baking soda, and milk and let the uniform marinate in the solution overnight. This morning, she had washed it again. Finally, there was no hint of mothballs. But now there was a faint odor of skunk.

"I am not wearing it, I said!" T. J. repeated. His voice grew louder.

His mother responded by collapsing into a heap on the living room couch and weeping. T. J. remained frozen for a while but then came over to console her.

"I'll explain to Egg how I can't wear this uniform," he said. "We'll work something out. I don't need to ride in the parade. I'm not really even on the team, anyway."

"I'm sorry," his mother said through her tears. "None of this is your fault. It's those old men. Coach Murphy told me this was some kind of special uniform that meant a lot to everyone. I know how much baseball means to them. It's their whole life." She sat up and blew her nose. "And it's your grandparents too. They're coming into town to see you in the parade. It'll mean so much to them as well."

"Damn, Mom!" T. J. whined. "Why did you have to tell Grandma and Grandpa about the parade? Now I *have* to wear this stupid thing and be in this stupid parade!" He sighed angrily. "When do I ever get to do something for me?"

T. J. was trapped . . . again. He cursed himself for ever thinking that vandalizing Egg's garage would free him from Cottage Park. Since that time, he'd been under a cloak of imprisonment, forced to do everything for others. It terrified him to think he might live his entire life as some kind of voice-activated robot.

T. J. picked up the shirt, pants, and stirrup leggings and marched into the bathroom. He laid the entire uniform across the sink. He reached for a large aluminum can of Dial Very Dry Anti-Perspirant. He shook the can, took a very deep breath, plugged his nose, then sprayed the uniform back and forth for a full minute. When he believed his lungs would explode, he grabbed the uniform and ran outside onto the front lawn. He gratefully breathed fresh air back into those starved and empty lungs. While he gulped in sweet oxygen, he waved the damp—and in some places drenched—uniform like a flag of surrender until the deodorant had dissipated.

Now he had to place the collection of foul and toxic smells over his body. He barely stepped from his bedroom before crying out that the itchy woolen fabric was eating up his skin. He shed the decades-old uniform where he stood and waited for his mother to locate long underwear and a light sweatshirt. With the undergarments in place, he put the uniform back on. It still itched, but his mom gushed with pride and thanksgiving. She placed his Holy Trinity cap snug over his head as if she were dropping a cherry on a perfect ice cream sundae.

"Be sure to wave to your grandparents!" she said as he headed out the door.

Now T. J. was running late to meet Egg—though you certainly couldn't say he was actually running or making any kind of hurried movement. He was in no mood to move any faster than the very intentional leisurely stroll he had adopted.

T. J. hadn't proceeded far when a new smell filtered through the uniform. Perhaps as a result of having dressed like an Eskimo on a hot, humid July day in Iowa, his perspiration had reawakened long-calcified scratch-and-sniff colonies in the wool. They emanated the stench of rotten eggs. Twice along his route to Egg's, T. J. bent over and gagged. He was certain that at any time he might begin to actually vomit.

For his part, Egg also had a don't-mess-with-me-I'm-already-having-a-bad-day attitude. He had ordered T. J. to arrive at his house no later than 8:30 a.m. Now sixty minutes later, he was still waiting under the flagpole he had erected after his son Denny had lost his life in the Vietnam War. The flag lay motionless atop the pole. It was made of cotton and not intended to be flown outside in Iowa's unforgiving heat nor its bone-shattering cold. Nevertheless, Egg had decided that this flag would be a working flag, flying twenty-hour hours a day every day of the year. A spotlight illuminated it at night. The flag was to be taken down before a storm and only one other time: on this very day for the Fourth of July parade.

Then Egg spotted T. J. He drew in a breath, letting it fill his chest before releasing it. His face was firm.

T. J. noted Egg's reaction yet still was in no hurry as he casually approached.

"Get over here!" Egg finally barked.

"I'm sorry," T. J. said as he neared the flagpole. "I'm sorry I never seem to do anything to make you happy!" The expression started with a sulking tone but ended with anger.

Egg ignored T. J.'s response and loosened the halyard from its moorings, slowly and solemnly lowering the flag. Halfway down, T. J. interrupted the process.

"If we're running so late, why do we have to mess around with this flag?"

Egg stopped and tied the flag back down again at half-staff. He reached into his back pocket and resurrected his long-buried billfold held together by a doubled-over red rubber band. The billfold was stuffed with newspaper clippings, poems Egg had written, interesting puzzles, word games, inspirational stories, fifteen dollars cash, and about twenty laminated funeral cards. Egg slid out one of the funeral cards and handed it to T. J.

"This is my youngest child," Egg said. "We called him Denny."

T. J. examined the card. On one side was the Blessed Virgin Mary standing atop a cloud surrounded by roses, dressed in a flowing white gown and blue robe. A halo surrounded her head. Outside the halo floated a larger crown of twelve stars. Gentle rays of light shone downward from her fingertips.

On the other side was a formal portrait of a soldier in a full army uniform and beret. A private first class insignia was pinned to the lapel surrounding a black tie. Underneath the picture were the words:

In Loving Remembrance of
PVT 1/c Joseph Dennis Gallivan
Born at Cottage Park, Iowa
March 19, 1940
Killed in action in Khe Sanh, South Vietnam
November 1, 1967

Memorare

Remember, O most gracious Virgin Mary, that never was it known that anyone who fled to thy protection, implored thy help, or sought thine intercession was left unaided. Inspired with this confidence, I fly to thee, O Virgin of virgins, my Mother; to thee do I come; before thee I stand, sinful and sorrowful. O Mother of the Word Incarnate, despise not my petitions, but in thy mercy hear and answer me.

"I get it," T. J. said quietly. "I'm sorry."

Egg nodded to indicate T. J. should keep the card. T. J. slid it into his pocket as Egg returned his attention to the halyard, lowering it until he could release the eyelets from their snap hooks.

"Hold this," Egg said, carefully presenting T. J. the corner section of the stars. "Be very careful. This flag has never touched the ground."

Egg then slipped his hands along the flag until he had reached the end and stretched it tightly. He folded the flag in half lengthwise.

"I'll make twelve more folds," Egg said. He brought the striped corner of the folded edge to the open edge and inched toward T. J.

"First we give thanks for life."

Egg then turned the outer point inward, parallel with the open edge, to form a second triangle.

"Then we remember our belief in eternal life."

Egg folded the flag a third time.

"We remember my brave son, Denny Gallivan."

The fourth time Egg folded the flag, he announced, "Because we believe in God, we turn to her at all times."

After Egg's fifth fold, he said, "We honor the United States of America. It may be imperfect, but our love for her must always be perfect."

Egg shook and straightened the flag and folded again. With his right hand over his heart, he said, "The sixth fold is where our hearts speak and we pledge our hearts and our allegiance to our country." Egg lifted one hand from the flag and used it to invite T. J. to join him in the Pledge of Allegiance.

Afterward, Egg made a seventh fold. "This honors our armed forces and their battle to keep us free."

Egg folded again. "The eighth fold is a tribute to the one who gave us life, our mother." And folded again. "The ninth fold is a tribute to womanhood. I've told you my theory on women," Egg said. "I believe God is a woman."

T. J. nodded earnestly.

Egg continued as if he were saying these words for the first time. "I believe women are superior creatures to men in every way—physically, mentally, spiritually. Women live for others. They're constantly thinking of others." Egg lifted his hand from the flag and pointed to his brain. "Because we as men aren't capable of thinking that way, we need to trust women and follow their every wish and direction. You got that?"

Of course, this was not the first time Egg had said these words. T. J. had signed off on this lecture at least twice before. He nodded and quickly responded.

"Yes, I do understand. I know I won't be happy or successful until I submit myself to the will and the needs of women. I am not worthy," T. J. added with sarcasm Egg would not detect.

Egg's eyes lit up appreciatively. "You get it. That's good!"

Egg returned to the flag. "The tenth fold is a tribute to the father who has given his sons and daughters for our country."

Egg folded again. "The eleventh fold remembers our Jewish heritage— King David, King Solomon, Abraham and his children. Some people believe the Irish are one of the lost tribes of Israel. I'm one of them. Be good to the Jews."

Egg made one final fold, tucking it tightly with the stars visible on the top. The folded flag was now a perfect triangle.

"In the twelfth fold, we remember the concept of the Trinity—three in one," Egg said, pointing to each side of the flag. "God the Mother, the Son, and Holy Ghost. In God we trust."

Egg held the perfectly folded flag as a priest holding the Eucharist in Mass.

"This is my son," Egg said, nodding to the flag. "And this is my son," he said, pointing to T. J.'s uniform. He stepped behind T. J. and reverently traced the red silken Number 29. "We gave you Denny's old uniform. You have to always remember that whenever you put it on."

T. J dropped his eyes. It all made sense now. Now he understood Egg's reaction when he first saw the uniform. *He wasn't mad at me. He was proud of me*, T. J. thought.

T. J. also knew that his hope of replacing the uniform with one less smelly would never happen. It couldn't happen. Denny Gallivan had come back to life, in a way. This was a hallowed, beatified uniform. Any other boy from Cottage Park would have cheerfully and proudly tolerated the putrid smell for the opportunity to be somehow associated with the town's biggest hero—ten times more popular than Danny Stinson. T. J. would have to suck it up and wear the uniform and put up with its foul odors and scratchy fabric forever.

T. J. followed Egg's lead as they departed from under the empty flagpole and began their journey downtown. They travelled together in silence for nearly a block when Sheriff Huffman's car raced up on them, lights flashing. Sheriff Huffman slowed down alongside them and rolled down his window.

"You two realize, don't you, that it's five minutes after ten o'clock? The whole town is up there. They said we can't start the parade until you get there. Hop in!"

It was true. People were waiting on the pair. Everyone already knew about the return of Denny Gallivan's baseball uniform and to whom it had been bestowed. Sheriff Huffman drove Egg and T. J. to the starting point of the parade route—the parking lot of Schneider's Farm Implement, Inc.

Egg stepped from the car and stood alongside his friend Francis McCarthy, a ninety-year-old World War I veteran. Both men had fought in France. Both glanced at each other with appreciation that they had lived for another Fourth of July parade. At one time, two dozen World War I veterans had proudly marched in the parade. Now it was down to Egg and McCarthy.

And at this time in their lives, each man would have been happy to join their deceased comrades and allow the other to march alone in next year's parade.

McCarthy was Cottage Park's sole remaining barber. He also cut his own hair, which was full and white and combed straight back in a pompadour perpetually held in place with Brylcreem. It was a toned-down version of the hairstyle Elvis Presley had worn at the height of his popularity, which by no coincidence was also the height of McCarthy's professional career.

McCarthy had an especially severe affliction of resting tremors. Both of his hands flailed violently out of control, up and down from breastbone to belly button, and back and forth from rib cage to rib cage. The tremors attacked him only when his hands were at rest. As a result, those hands were constantly put to work at home and at his shop: cutting a head of hair, applying a straight-edge razor to give a man a premium old-fashioned shaving experience, or simply gripping and balancing the flagpole that rested in the carrying belt he wore that day over his short-sleeved red, white, and blue button-down shirt.

At any other time, McCarthy would have razzed his younger friend for his tardiness. And Egg would have meekly accepted the good-natured ribbing with a promise that he wouldn't make that mistake again. But today was different. Today Egg carried the memory of his child and the backbreaking grief of having buried him. McCarthy waited for Egg to get settled.

"I'm marching with the veterans," Egg told T. J. "You head back to the firetruck—it's at the end of the parade. Got it?"

T. J. nodded, and Egg, in turn nodded to McCarthy. The barber then raised a trembling hand to signal for Sheriff Huffman to proceed.

Slowly Sheriff Huffman led the procession of twenty-three floats representing what still stood of Cottage Park's business community: the drive-in, funeral home, pharmacy, grain elevator, bank, café, auto repair shop, used-car dealership, and seed-and-feed store. The service professions were also represented by a lawyer, accountant, plumber, electrician, and carpenter. Three convertibles (donated by the aforementioned used-car dealership) carried Cottage Park's dignitaries, including the mayor, the 1974 Pork Queen, and the Mother of the Year. All nineteen members of the Holy Trinity marching band were present, outfitted in uniforms purchased in 1963: black pants with white stripes running the length of both sides, white shoes, and stovepipe shako headdresses adorned with an ornamental plate of a regal raptor. They had already begun to play their medley of the greatest hits of Herb Alpert and the Tijuana Brass.

Next came the veterans. Immediately behind Egg and McCarthy were the World War II veterans, a group of twelve men slightly less somber and fervent. Four Korean War veterans followed the contingent from World War II.

Murphy was amongst the twelve from World War II. Like Egg and McCarthy, he had also served in France, but at a different time—from 1944 through 1946. Murphy created the Holy Trinity baseball program in 1929 and immediately amassed victories and championships until he enlisted in the army. During his tour, Egg and Ryan coached the team. Egg and Murphy had never spoken about their respective times in France. In particular, Murphy had seen some ghastly things there. Whenever questioned about his service in France, Murphy pretended not to hear or outright ignored the query.

The last of the veterans were those thirteen men who had served in Vietnam. They were anything but solemn. They laughed and called out to friends and family along the parade route, some of whom were actually fellow Vietnam veterans who had chosen not to participate in the procession. The contingent occasionally swooped directly into the crowd and spotlighted a reluctant or shy fellow veteran. Sometimes they were successful pulling that individual into their group to join them in the parade. For those in which they were unsuccessful they settled on an agreement to have a beer at the Lipstick afterward.

McCarthy and Egg weren't surprised that the younger men were laughing and horsing around during the parade. Since they had returned from Vietnam, everything seemed to be a joke to them. They seemed to take very little seriously. Their hair was long and uncombed. They wore beards and mustaches. Both McCarthy and Egg equated the appearance with dirt, filth, Communism, and homosexuality. Egg's effort to counsel the young men was to encourage them to visit McCarthy's shop, called forever the Modern Barber Shop since opening when McCarthy returned home from World War I, where he promised them a free deluxe shave and haircut. The old men believed that if they could clean up the younger vets, surely the rest of their behavior would also improve.

The last float in the procession was actually the Cottage Park firetruck. T. J.'s fellow teammates had already boarded it and filled the inside, with an overflow of players crouched across the top. Several bedsheets had been fastened together to cover both sides of the truck. Spray-painted on both sides were the words: *Halfway there! UNDEFEATED: 17–0!*

But T. J. would not get to ride on the firetruck that day. In fact, he wouldn't make it any farther back than the group of Vietnam vets. At the first sight of T. J. in his uniform, the Vietnam vets called out and huddled around him like a team around their quarterback. While Sheriff Huffman and the other vets marched on, the rest of the parade stopped right there behind the Vietnam vets in front of the abandoned and shuttered Five Star Theatre.

At first the vets didn't say anything. Denny had been their older brothers' age. Whoever said that history is always written by the winners had never visited Cottage Park or ever met Denny Gallivan, who frequently lost in athletic events before finally losing his life in Vietnam.

It seemed Denny could never catch a break. He was a decent athlete. Not as big and strong as Egg's other children, but he enjoyed playing basketball and baseball and never shied away from the challenge of a big game. In the diocesan basketball championship his senior year, he had a chance to win the game at the free throw line with two seconds to go against Early Sacred Heart. His first shot hit the back of the rim and bounced right back to him. No problem. He'd make the necessary adjustment. He'd done this at least a million times on the hoop hanging from the garage at home. He'd give his second shot more arc and exaggerate his follow-through.

He made his adjustments perfectly, but to the exact same result as the first shot. The ball bounced back directly into his hands, over and above the flat-footed Early defenders, who never expected such a trajectory.

With less than a second to go, he shot from the exact same spot, the free throw line. This time it was a jump shot.

He'd never missed three consecutive shots from the free throw line in his entire life. But he did in Sioux City that night in 1958 in front of a packed gymnasium and seemingly all his friends and family from Cottage Park. Holy Trinity lost the game but never that memory. The story was still frequently told in honor of Denny Gallivan, the tenacious young man who could never win.

Denny had a similar experience in the baseball Finals that same year. Holy Trinity had gone ahead two to one in the tenth inning. They had two outs and two strikes on a terrified batter from Burlington. Holy Trinity was one strike away from their first summer Finals championship when the batter somehow reached his bat out and fortuitously tapped the ball to the shallow gap between center and right. Runners on second and third were already racing from their bases.

Out in right, Denny knew he had to catch the ball or the season would end with yet another second-place finish. Running as fast as he could, he dived and scooped the ball an inch before it hit the ground. It was a fantastic feat—an impossible catch to be praised for all time.

Unfortunately, he hit the ground flat on his stomach, which knocked the air out of him. The impact bounced the ball from his glove and onto his back. As he tumbled, he also flipped over, sending the ball flittering back up into the air again. This time he reached for it with his left hand. The ball brushed off his fingertips, away from his grasp and onto the ground for good. Holy Trinity had lost the Finals . . . again.

After the missed free throws and the dropped ball, Murphy explained to an inconsolable Denny that pure, simple, and hideous fate had reared its ugly head. There was no other explanation. They were meant to be.

"Maybe someday," Murphy said consolingly, "when our lives have ended, we'll be granted the insight as to how and why these events happened to you."

Denny may have discovered that reason in Vietnam. He had narrowly missed being drafted, so friends and family were aghast when he enlisted in the army. Like everything else he had done in his life, he enlisted for one reason, which he could explain in two words: "It's time."

Denny was twenty-five years old, which made him a little bit older than the rest of his squad members. They called him everything but his real name. At first they called him Iowa, pronounced "I-owe-*uuuuuuh*," with caveman emphasis on the *uh* sound. They also called him Stank for the malodor that lingered behind after he visited the latrine. Some called him Methane Man for his abilities to belch and pass gas, sometimes at the same time. Upon rare request and in the open rice fields of Vietnam, Denny could recite nearly nine letters of the alphabet while belching, all to the accompaniment of passing gas that sounded like a riff from B. B. King's electric guitar, Lucille. He could perform these feats regardless of what or when he had eaten.

But his most popular moniker was Potato Head. "That's *Mr.* Potato Head to you," Denny would reply in feigned admonishment. At one time, such derision would have shattered him. Ever since he could remember, Denny knew he didn't look like anyone else. His mother said she could very clearly see a variety of traits from the Irish generations that made up his family tree: the Farrell bushy unibrow, the McCafferty rounded ears, and the McCoy chalky complexion. He also had Egg's hawklike nose. But Rose was always stumped when asked to explain the slightly protruding eyeballs neither she nor Egg had ever seen at family reunions or in ancient family photographs. That was Denny's unique feature, which he owed to no one. Like it or not, the platypus face of unrelated features really did most closely resemble that of Mr. Potato Head.

Denny was quite different from his fighting peers in Vietnam, especially when it came to illicit drug use. But the biggest difference was that he was not afraid of death. Denny routinely volunteered for the most dangerous assignments. So much so that his sergeant would initially wave him off, only to eventually relent under Denny's persistence. This steadfast nonchalance about death had a calming effect on his fellow soldiers. Denny promised they'd have the same unyielding courage and peace of mind if they'd simply follow his lead—join the Catholic Church, wear its spiritual armor, participate in the sacraments, and recite the right devotions. They readily agreed to go through the motions, even if they did not believe in all the precepts.

Through letters, Ryan coached Denny in how to baptize, offer Communion, and confirm the soldiers. Ryan even sent a large box of rosaries, medals, and scapulars, which were promptly draped around the necks of soldiers. Ryan and all of Cottage Park prayed for Denny and his squad and platoon, attended vigils, and offered special devotional Masses.

Denny offered a safe return home for all who followed his faith prescription. His prophecy rang true for everyone in this radical offshoot of Catholicism—everyone but Denny himself.

The last place anyone in Cottage Park had seen the Number 29 uniform was over Denny's closed casket on display in Holy Trinity Church, the only place in Cottage Park big enough to hold the portion of hundreds of well-wishers who had come from all over Iowa to pay their respects. Every Catholic high school in northwest Iowa and nearly all the public schools on Holy Trinity's sports schedule—from Adair-Casey to Woodward-Granger—sent a representative to the funeral.

Each represented community brought a baseball cap. Some schools brought several and placed them in a pile alongside the flowers next to the coffin. Each cap had been signed with the Number 29. The message on those caps was meant to communicate that Denny was bigger than Holy Trinity and even bigger than Cottage Park. He was an Iowa boy. All of Iowa was grief stricken.

On the day of the funeral, a bitterly cold day in mid-November, there wasn't enough room in Holy Trinity Church for all of those who had come to help the Gallivans carry their grief. So they lined the streets downtown and south to Resurrection Cemetery—nearly the same route as the parade. The gifted baseball caps were distributed to the mourners, who lowered them over their hearts as the hearse passed by to lay Denny to rest.

Denny used to tell his platoon mates that Cottage Park was pure heaven, that he was the luckiest man in the world because he would eventually make it back to his hometown one way or another, dead or alive. He would never lose, either way, as long as he returned home.

So at least once a year afterward, one or more of Denny's fellow platoon mates had shown up in Cottage Park, always in the summer, to see if the town was really as incredible as Denny had promised. The vets came to see this Promised Land. They stood out like rare diversified gems, offering the residents of Cottage Park their first introduction to African Americans, American Indians, and Latinos. Most of these guests to Cottage Park were from the South. Denny's fellow soldiers hadn't lived in such an idyllic hometown or experienced such an idyllic childhood.

Those soldiers arrived unannounced, often by hitchhiking. They found their way to Denny's home from the memory of Denny's painstaking descriptions. Once they met Egg and Rose, the vets didn't need to be told where they would be sleeping. They already knew Denny's room was at the top of the steps and to the right. There Denny's Championship Baseball shined like a beacon. They immediately autographed it. Now they too were a part of the grand Holy Trinity baseball tradition.

They also signed and dated the right inside bottom of the top dresser drawer—the spot Egg had been repairing when he stumbled upon a "safety," or condom, Denny had been saving for the right occasion. That was one of their favorite stories.

Egg had raced over to Holy Trinity, pulling Denny from class and out into the parking lot.

"Put up your dukes," he ordered his son. "You think you're a man? Let's see you fight like one."

The fight ended quickly with Egg blasting and knocking Denny to the ground in one punch. In the fight, Denny suffered nothing worse than bruised pride.

A fate worse than the knockdown was that Denny never found himself in any situation where he might have even considered using the condom. Denny was the rare soldier in Vietnam who told stories about the times he failed, lost a fight, or had a girl lose interest in him. Perhaps that was why his stories were so popular, why soldiers clung to them, rehashed to relive them, and chose to hear them over the many less-humorous memories other soldiers had to tell.

After getting situated in Denny's bedroom, the vets would race off to the Lipstick to tell and hopefully hear a story about Denny that they hadn't heard yet. Later that night, they would stop over at the elevator, where Denny and his friends drove Egg's car up onto the tracks, let air out of the tires, set the car in neutral, and coasted across the Iowa countryside under the sole light of the moon and stars.

Then the vets would make a visit to Holy Trinity Church, which Ryan kept open all night. It was said there were no atheists in the foxholes and battlefields in Vietnam. The same could be said about those who visited Holy Trinity Church. Cynical vets—whose minds were under the influence of Denny's favorite beer, Budweiser, and also clouded by marijuana, mescaline, and heroin—immediately transitioned from a drug-induced haze to a spiritual mysticism once they entered the church worthy to be called God's home.

Inside the huge wooden door entering the church, vets would bless themselves in holy water from marble fonts. Denny had taught them to do that while stating, "Wash away all my sins, O Lord."

Next they would proceed through the nave of the church: their footsteps breaking the pure and heavy stillness that hung like a shawl over them. On either side, they solemnly proceeded between dark-polished oaken pews—more like boats that could weather ocean waves. Flanking these pews were painstakingly detailed and brightly colored stained-glass windows dedicated to saints and biblical scenes. The windows were grouped in pairs, with a smaller window extending from the floor to eye level followed by a much larger window extending nearly to the point where the wall met the graceful arch of the ceiling. Each window was labelled with the name of a Cottage Park family whose grandparents or great-grandparents had financed its cost nearly sixty years earlier. Many of the same families now financed the growing expenses of Holy Trinity High School and supported their sons on the baseball team.

The vets stopped their procession as they arrived at the front of the church, where an elaborately carved Communion rail stopped them from proceeding any farther. There they would sit in the front pew and gaze at the flickering votive candles beneath the statue of the Blessed Virgin or gaze around at the fourteen Stations of Cross reliefs that strained to free themselves from agony.

The vets would sit in solitude and devotion amidst the statues of the Holy Family and the stained-glass saints that seemed to shimmer and breathe. In the serenity of that moment, the vets became one with time. The path to heaven was illuminated in the candlelight and moonlight streaming through the saints. The vets were moved to continue on that path—the path that led them home.

No matter what time the vets returned home, night or morning, Rose awaited them with grilled cheese sandwiches and tomato soup, along with Denny's staple item: a bottle of Pepto Bismol.

The vets had been coming every year since Denny's death. But this summer, no one had come.

Standing there around T. J., holding up the entire parade, Cottage Park's Vietnam vets speculated that the uniform—and T. J. himself—were some kind of gift from God to settle their frayed nerves. That uniform was the subject of intense local lore. Some had speculated that Egg had buried it with Denny. Others had said he had burned it to ashes, then spread the ashes across Memorial Field.

To see the uniform again was a source of pride, awe, and some humor. It was an enthusiastic premonition that something good would come from its return to battle. Perhaps Denny had come back to right a whole world of past wrongs, including finally winning the Finals.

With this promise, the vets were suddenly spurred on, resuming their march to the cheers of the crowd. Denny's legacy took root in T. J.'s mind as he marched along Main Street with the vets and waved to everyone who had come out for the parade, especially his mother and grandparents. The patriotic people of Cottage Park were willing and happy to afford T. J. hero status that day—and forever, for that matter. If the Body and Blood of Jesus were truly present in the Holy Eucharist, it was not a stretch to believe Denny was back and in and around the boy who wore his uniform in the formation with the Vietnam vets.

The parade came to an end in the parking lot of Memorial Field. The firetruck was the last to arrive, and T. J.'s teammates were able to see him for the first time that day. They mobbed him, removing his cap, tussling his hair, or slapping him on the back.

From his vantage point, Egg could see that his continually evolving plan of saving T. J. was coming along fine. Only Egg, Ryan, and Murphy could fully understand and appreciate the magnitude of Egg's gesture of gifting T. J. with Denny's uniform. Egg had successfully executed a very public branding of the highest standard.

All of Cottage Park now knew T. J. as someone important to Egg. Someone associated with the legendary Denny Gallivan. Someone who played an important role on the Holy Trinity baseball team. And most importantly someone who would live up to high expectations—someone who could do no wrong. Egg had created a self-fulfilling prophecy that would change T. J.'s life forever.

After today, T. J. would always carry Cottage Park with him, whether he wanted to or not. Wherever he journeyed, for the rest of his life, T. J. would get a call or an unannounced visit from a fellow resident of Cottage Park to share stories about life back home—and in doing so, keep T. J. in line with the rest of Cottage Park.

If he could have, Egg would have reached his right hand over his own left shoulder and given himself a massive pat on the back, similar to the pats T. J. was now receiving from his teammates. While Egg's family had written him off as a doddering and decrepit old man, he had in fact executed a master stroke of winning over T. J.

At the end of the parade, illegal but popular fireworks were set off. Groups of children would burst and scatter away, moving as quickly as the bottle rockets that chased them.

Now, Egg thought to himself, *let's get this kid cleaned up and playing baseball. And let's win those Finals.*

— CHAPTER FIFTEEN —

Countdown to the Finals: 23 Days to Go

O N THE SATURDAY MORNING FOLLOWING Holy Trinity's victory over Mason City, Egg headed out his front door and discovered T. J. seated underneath the maple tree. T. J. was dotting his left elbow with a wet finger.

"What's with the elbow?" Egg asked.

T. J. grimaced. "I got stung by a bee. It hurts."

Egg took a look at the sting. He reached out to probe the source of pain, but T. J. tucked the arm away.

"Come on," Egg said, motioning T. J. to follow to the house. "It's starting to swell. Let's put some ice on it."

Inside, T. J. recuperated at the table while Egg broke ice cubes from a freezer tray. Egg wrapped the cubes in paper towels and applied the pack to T. J.'s arm.

"I might not be able to work today with this," T. J. said. He winced and raised his elbow to remind Egg of his wound.

The two sat in silence for a few minutes while the ice did its trick. After a while, T. J.'s eyes wandered to a gray baseball sitting in the sunlight on a ledge above the sink. Egg had found the ball near the railroad tracks, scrubbed it clean, and dried it on the counter.

Setting the ice aside, T. J. got up, grabbed the ball, and sat back down. He massaged the ball between the tabletop and his palm, then stopped and looked into it as if it were a crystal ball. He studied the ball as he lifted it up to the sunlight. After a moment, he tossed it gently in his hand.

"It's as heavy as a rock. How do you catch it without getting hurt?"

"Well, the best way is to wear a baseball glove," Egg said.

T. J. pondered that possibility. "It still must hurt, even with a glove."

Egg stood and directed T. J. to follow him again. "Let's find out. I've got gloves in the garage."

Soon, Egg had T. J. positioned in the front yard with a glove. Egg tossed the ball. T. J. held up his glove to receive Egg's throw, but the ball dropped between the glove and his ear, bouncing and rolling behind him. T. J. lugged himself after the ball.

He positioned himself again. Breathing heavily and sweating through his T-shirt, T. J. awkwardly brought the ball back and threw it in Egg's direction. Egg lifted his glove, then turned to retrieve the ball that had sailed over and beyond his reach. But T. J. sped past Egg, picked up his own overthrow, and jogged it back to Egg.

Egg held the ball before T. J. "You throw a baseball like this."

He twisted the ball on its side until the seams made a *C* formation. He surrounded those seams with his index and middle fingers like fangs, then rested the ball against his thumb.

"This is called a four-seam grip," Egg said. "It will give you the most control."

T. J. took a closer look, then nodded as if he had known this all along. He turned and started jogging back to his position.

"Stop—right there," Egg said, motioning T. J. to stand closer than before.

"Come on," T. J. said. "This is kid stuff. Nobody played catch like this at practice."

"Let's do a few throws from there until your eye learns to follow the ball," Egg said. "It's one of the most important lessons."

He gently underhanded the ball to T. J., who caught it and threw it back. After several catches, T. J. began to edge backward and Egg lobbed more formidable pitches. As T. J. caught those throws, he began to imitate the casual throws and catches he had seen the Holy Trinity players make.

"It doesn't hurt," Egg said. "Does it?"

T. J. smiled and shook his head. But it did hurt. At times, the ball pounded into an area of the old glove where the padding had worn thin. It stung with a sharp pain. And soon his fingers began to swell and throb.

Egg threw a grounder. When T. J. stooped over to catch it, the ball hopped and banged off his knee. His smile disappeared.

"Good," Egg said with a nod.

Rubbing his knee, T. J. looked up in surprise.

"Some boys play ball all their lives and never learn to stop a ball like that."

The smile returned. As they continued out there in the front yard, T. J.'s pain gave way to the promise of giving and taking each throw, the security of the ball returning to his glove. Despite the pain—and the dropped balls—T. J. persevered.

After several minutes, Egg purposely threw the ball at T. J.'s feet to see if he could scoop it up. He did. After several more pickups, even these throws became routine.

"Ready for a pop-up?" Egg said.

T. J. nodded.

Egg looked up at a sober and lonely turquoise vault containing the sun, moon, stars, planets, and now a freshly tossed rotating baseball. T. J.'s head snapped back. He took a few steps forward, noticed he had gone too far, then took a quick step backward. But his legs buckled under the momentum of the shifting weight. First he collapsed on his backside. Then momentum and gravity stretched him flat out, his back against the ground. The ball thudded into the lawn a few feet from where he lay.

T. J. picked up the ball, then stood and knocked dirt from his pants. He threw the ball back to Egg.

"Again," Egg urged. "This time, follow the ball more closely."

When Egg threw the ball again even higher, T. J. froze, following the gray globe until he lost it as it crossed into the path of the sun. Still, he guessed where he should position himself beneath its descent. He raised his glove to make the catch—then covered his face and turned away in terror. The ball flattened the grass where his feet had stood a moment before.

"All right," Egg said, giving a wrap-up signal. "Let's go do some painting."

T. J. motioned him back. "Come on. One more," he pleaded. He pounded his fist into his glove. "We've got time."

"I've run my course for today," Egg said. "We'll play again tomorrow."

"But I can do it. I'll catch the next one."

T. J. waited until he had Egg's attention, then he flipped the ball high in the air, carefully positioned, and caught it.

"I told you," he said, showing Egg the ball in the glove.

He threw another pop fly and caught it. He threw the ball several more times. In each effort, he was determined to throw the ball higher than before. His gray T-shirt blackened with sweat.

Egg took his glove and headed for the garage. When he returned he tossed a tennis ball at T. J.

"Practice with this until we can play catch again," Egg said. "But keep the glove and baseball too."

T. J. collapsed on the ground, spread eagle. He then lumbered up, picked at his soaked shirt, fanned himself, and panted for air.

"I'll practice," he said.

He raised his elbow so Egg could inspect the bee sting. Egg took a quick look and dismissed the swelling welt around the stinger. Egg reached down to help T. J. to his feet.

"Let's finish this garage," Egg said.

On that same Saturday morning, McKenna sat in a pew at Holy Trinity Church. He watched the light come on and seep under the closed confessional door. That meant the person inside had finished confessing and raised from the kneeler, triggering the light. After a few moments, McKenna could hear the occupant fumble with the door handle it until it turned. An ancient woman, Mary Agnes Connelly, bent and determined, emerged. She shuffled from the carpet of the confessional to the tile of the church floor. She continued to a pew behind McKenna, where she knelt, straight and devout, then blessed herself and began her penance.

McKenna glanced at her. She nodded for him to proceed to the confessional from which she had exited. Both doors of the confessional now emptied light into the church, welcoming penitents with the privacy of darkness. McKenna looked at his watch. He had been in the church for an hour—an hour of unanswered, frustrated commune. Each attempt at examining his conscience was interrupted by anger, bitter and consuming. That too was a sin, McKenna thought. There were only fifteen minutes before the end of Ryan's 10:00 a.m. to noon Saturday confessional shift.

McKenna rose from his pew, genuflected, then proceeded to the confessional door. At the same time, Ryan exited the confessional, almost bumping into McKenna.

"Pardon me," Ryan said, looking up at McKenna and then immediately looking down and away. He backed into the stall again. "I thought everybody had gone home," he said, closing the door behind himself.

McKenna opened the door of the penitent's side. Above the plastic screen that separated him from Ryan was a crucifix holding the battered, twisted figure of Christ. He closed the door behind him and knelt before the crucifix, blinded by the darkness.

Ryan slid back the plastic screen of the window between them, whispered a brief benediction, and waited for McKenna to begin.

"Bless me, Father, for I have sinned," McKenna began. "It has been since last Easter that I made my last confession, and these are my sins." He took a breath. "I've thought about the things I've done since that time, and it all boils down to pretty much one thing: I can't get over what happened to my dad. I barely think of anything else. I just want to punch someone, sometimes anyone and everyone." McKenna thought for a moment. "I guess that's my biggest sin."

McKenna watched Ryan's hands through the screen as they locked together in a ball.

"I'm sorry for these and all my sins, especially for being so mad at everyone."

Ryan sighed. "That is a very honest confession," he said. "Why did you come to confession at this time?"

"Because," McKenna said, "I know what I'm feeling and thinking is wrong. I have to forget this stuff and get on with my life. Maybe confession will help me do that."

"I suppose it might," Ryan said. "You have every right to be angry. That's a normal stage in the grief process. I know you said you're mad at the rest of us. But you may be the maddest at God."

McKenna nodded. "Revenge," he said. "I want to see God suffer and die."

"Do you think that would balance the scales?" Ryan asked. "Would you feel better? More satisfied?"

"Yes," McKenna said. "I know it sounds funny, Father, but it's true. Seeing God suffer in my mind would make up for what we've been through from Dad's death."

"One of the truths of our faith is the belief in a very personal God," Ryan said, "not a God who sits up in the clouds or on the sun. Our God is right here with us now, beside us, inside us. God loves you. His only Son teaches us that simple fact. God is hurting with you too, Marty."

"I knew you'd say all that," McKenna said. "I've heard it all before. It still doesn't change the way I feel."

"I'm asking you to see a God in sorrow with you. Your father and our Heavenly Father grieve with you at this very moment."

"I still want revenge," McKenna said.

"Then make it positive," Ryan said. "Turn to heaven and keep praying for guidance. And turn to those around you, especially those you love. You're carrying a tremendous weight by yourself. Share it. Few answers to the human dilemma are found in isolation."

McKenna nodded.

"Death is a reality," Ryan said. "We all have to die. It's one more step in the cycle that begins and ends with God. For the purpose of your confession, I might suggest that you're angry not so much at your father's death but at its time and circumstances. If your father had been one hundred twenty years old, and you were at his bedside with your children and grandchildren to see him off to heaven, would you be as angry as you are now?" Ryan continued, "With your father at that age, you might even consider his death a blessing. I'm getting to that age myself. If you ask someone my age, they'll tell you they wouldn't choose to live forever, even under the best of circumstances. There is in all of us the expectations of the joys of heaven. Your father now shares those joys with God."

"But why my dad?" McKenna said. "Why now?"

"That's a mystery," Ryan said. "I have my own answer, though perhaps it's too simple: without the good and bad in life, there would be no free will. Every time we encounter hardship, we have the opportunity to walk away or answer with mercy. When we answer with mercy, we glorify God. What more can we ask?"

After several seconds, McKenna said wearily, "I don't know."

"God reveals himself to those who make an effort to know him," Ryan said. "So let's not let the sun go down on your anger. We may not reach that goal by tonight, but we can certainly get a start at it." Air rumbled into Ryan's lungs as he inhaled, then it whistled a few moments later as he exhaled through his nose. "Anything else you must confess?"

McKenna answered no, then received his penance, which was ten Hail Marys. He began to recite an Act of Contrition while Ryan absolved his sins.

Mr. Civilla stood in the early-evening shadows that spread over his garden. He had dark bushy hair, even now in his late fifties. His skin was the color of toast, dark and seemingly charred. Stubble seemed to darken his face no matter how often he shaved. He stooped over the spread of strawberry vines and uprooted tiny, infant weeds. Occasionally he spotted a strawberry beyond ripe, almost beginning to wither. He popped this aged fruit into his mouth, stem and all, chewing slowly before spitting the stem back into the vines and resuming his search for weeds.

Anthony, the youngest of his children and the only one still living at home, called out the back door. "Orlowski is on his way over to pick me up," Anthony said. "We're going out tonight."

"Come help me in the garden until then," Mr. Civilla said, plucking another weed.

"But he'll be here any minute."

"Orlowski knows his way back here," Mr. Civilla said, motioning his son to join him.

With a quiet sigh, Anthony unbuttoned his shirt and draped it over the wire cages that straightened the yellow-blossomed tomato plants. Anthony positioned himself in an area of the garden opposite his father. He began lifting the leaves and vines, finding no weeds.

"You're moving too fast," Mr. Civilla said, pulling another weed, not looking up. "Anticipate a weed. They're here. If you pull them out when they're small, you won't have big problems later."

Anthony slowed and found his first weed. He studied it, then tore it out and tossed it into the pile his father had started.

Mr. Civilla sliced a grub between his fingernails. "Don't you have practice tomorrow?"

Anthony nodded.

Mr. Civilla said. "You boys are good enough that you shouldn't have any close games. But I'm afraid you will have close games and probably get beat."

"We'll do our best," Anthony said. "That's all that we can do."

"There's a difference between doing your best and being the best," Mr. Civilla said. "I expect you to be the best."

He thought about telling his father that he too expected to be the best and that he was good enough to be the best by doing it his way, not his father's way. But then he reconsidered. He and his father had discussed this before. In each case, his father hadn't listened. He wasn't listening now.

"You've always had brothers who looked out for you," Mr. Civilla continued. "You never had to fight, so now you don't know how. But you have to learn now because it doesn't get any easier when you get older. No one in this world gives you anything. You've got to fight for it and take it."

Mr. Civilla noticed Orlowski appear around the side of the house and approach the garden. He nodded at Orlowski, then stopped back over to pick more weeds.

"I'll be back by midnight," Anthony said.

He grabbed his shirt and broad-jumped over the strawberry vines, landing on the lawn near Orlowski. As he departed from his father, he muttered, "I can't take him anymore." He passed Orlowski, who stood there in the same spot on the lawn.

Mr. Civilla watched his son for a moment, then stooped over again to resume picking weeds.

Orlowski called out, "See ya, Mr. Civilla."

When there was no reaction from Mr. Civilla, Orlowski turned and hustled to catch up with Anthony.

Orlowski got into the car behind the wheel. Anthony leaned back in the passenger's seat, eyes closed. Orlowski slid a Cat Stevens 8-track tape into his car stereo and turned the music down low enough so he could question his friend.

"The old at it again?"

That evening, while his brother joined Orlowski, Anthony, and others at the quarries to drink beer and dive from the cliff, Jeff dropped quarters in the coin box that regulated the batting machine in the cage next to the miniature golf course. There were two machines—one for slow pitches and the other for fast. Jeff positioned himself before the fast-pitch machine.

He stepped up to the plate and watched the first pitch sail by high and outside. The second pitch was also not over the plate. But the following pitches were perfect strikes. Jeff swung at each, missing most and fouling a few behind him. Once, when he did connect with the ball, the vibration of the bat against the ball stung his hands and wrists.

He tried one new bat after another, experimenting with a variety of lengths and weights. But no matter which one he used, he couldn't get it around in time to hit the ball.

He knew the reason, but not the answer, for his problem: he was afraid of the ball. Afraid of getting hit. He tried every time to correct himself, but he was still stepping out of the batter's box. Every effort to step into the pitch ended in uncertain, shuffling feet.

After several frustrated attempts, he squared around at the plate, planted his feet, and bunted the ball, first right back at the batting machine, then down the first and third-base lines.

As the sun set before him, big lights framed in tin bonnets turned on, attracting clouds of gnats, mosquitoes, and dull yellow moths. After his series of successful bunts, Jeff returned to his hitting stance. Once again, he locked his feet to keep from stepping away from the pitches, but he couldn't help himself. His swings failed to connect. He forced himself to keep swinging, though, and his swings became more strained and out of control. The dimpled, weathered gray rubber balls had been forged into cannonballs through years of constant hammering. They hit the steel chain-link fence behind him and rolled back down the runway that led to the conveyer belt feeding the batting machine.

Dented tin signs labeled Single, Double, Triple, and Home Run hung around and over the wire-mesh fence protecting the batting machine. Jeff envisioned himself hitting the ball over every sign, but he never did. Instead, he looked at the swelling swamp of baseballs at his feet and kicked at them.

Jeff could see the attendant pacing around, closing down the miniature golf course. Soon he would be over to close down the batting cages.

Jeff hurriedly dropped in another dollar's worth of quarters, returned to the batter's box, and resumed flailing at each pitch. After several more misses, he stretched his bat over the plate and waited. As the ball hit the bat, Jeff approximated the velocity of the pitch by the force of the collision.

He thought about pain and fear—and the real possibility that being hit by a pitch might cure him of his fear. He reminded himself that some professional baseball players actually stood out over the plate and made themselves a target so they could get on base.

As he continued to bunt the ball to the ground, he imagined the pain of taking one of those balls into his rib cage or back. Perhaps he would absorb the pain and move beyond it so he could actually stand in box, strike back, and attack a pitch. Or maybe the ball would crash into his skull and leave him blind or deaf or in a coma for the rest of his life. Fear of the known prevailed over fear of the unknown.

Jeff took a deep breath and pounded his batting helmet firmly down. After watching two more pitches race by, he took another deep breath and stepped out over the plate, ready to receive the ball directly into his back.

The machine's steel arm cranked and flung the next pitch toward Jeff. His heart pounded as the ball sped closer. Then at the last moment, he tried to dodge the impact—unsuccessfully. The ball caught his left shoulder blade like a bullet. The pain was overwhelming. For a moment, Jeff thought he might faint.

As the pitching arm reached back to throw another ball, Jeff shrieked and jerked away. He angrily kicked at the ball that had hit him, but he missed. He watched it roll back to the machine.

Trembling, he stepped out of the batter's box. The machine continued to crank and hurl balls across the plate and into the fence. One hit the steel pipe that supported the fence, then ricocheted directly at him. He dodged that ball, dropped his bat, and began to retreat from the cage.

He opened the door wide and took long running strides away from the clatter and bright lights of the cage to the crumbling, powdery blacktop that would lead him home.

After a brief but liberating jaunt, he slowed to a cooldown jog shortly before turning onto the street where he lived. Gingerly, he angled from the T-shirt from his back and noticed blood pricks dotting his skin, rapidly turning beet red and dull blue. It still hurt.

His experiment had failed. Now, more than ever, he was afraid of the ball and still without a clue as to how to get over that fear.

Later that night, Moriarity spread out on his bed in his boxer shorts, adjusted his night-light, and read another page of his favorite book, *Pitching Power and Presence*. He studied the filmlike pictures that showed the finger positions and wrist movement to throw a forkball. He would teach himself the pitch that night and add it to his bag of tricks.

But first he must take time to indulge himself in his annual Independence Day ceremony of autographing his Championship Baseball. This year he had been too preoccupied with the baseball season on the actual holiday to look back at his accomplishments in the first half of the season as well as to review his goals for the second half. He had participated in this ritual every year around July 4 since he learned to write his name with proficiency in fourth grade.

Now, two days later, he would make the time—he wouldn't know where he was going in life unless he reminded himself where he had been. As always, the introspective look at the first half of the season was short and concise. In his mind, he was the best pitcher his age in the state of Iowa—perhaps in the Midwest—as evidenced by his record of strikeouts and Holy Trinity's undefeated record. He'd met or exceeded all his personal goals. Now he needed to keep up the good work—and, of course, win the Finals.

This annual ritual also served as a self-imposed reminder that he was not long for Cottage Park. His time was coming. In a little over a year, he would be leaving for the big leagues for good. If and when he should return to Cottage Park, he would give autographs to everyone. Then he'd rightfully thank the people upon whose shoulders he had stood: mostly Murphy but also Powers, Egg, and Ryan. That was it—those four people.

Moriarity flipped his Championship Ball up into the air and watched it spin all his autographs over the years. He caught the ball in his left hand, pretending it had been tossed to him from a young fan. He took his black Bic pen and in a smooth, uninterrupted motion wrote the name Pat Moriarity, crossing over at the *t* in Pat to make one strong line. He stopped to admire his quick handiwork, then dived back into bed to continue reading his book.

Moriarity studied the finger placement diagrams and gripped his Championship Baseball in the correct fashion. Now he propped up in bed, brought his arm back, then in slow motion brought it forward, copying the motion exactly as it was pictured and described, including the follow-through. He repeated the motion dozens of times, watching from different angles with the help of his dresser mirror.

He imagined himself on the pitching mound, eyeball to eyeball, staring a batter down. No one blinked. Moriarity also saw Powers crouch over and flash four fingers, their new signal for a forkball.

There in his room, Moriarity nodded, brought his arm back and then quickly forward, releasing the ball at the apex of the cycle. He watched for the ball to drop, but its trajectory terminated as it pounded against the top drawer of the dresser. The sound boomed like a gunshot, then it repeated when the ball bounced onto the wooden floor.

In the next room, Moriarity's little sister began to cry. Older sisters tried in vain to quiet her and in their efforts began to fight among themselves. Moriarity's younger brother screamed for quiet. His other brother knocked on the bedroom wall adjoining his sisters' room as well as Moriarity's.

Moriarity felt the floor shake as downstairs his father pounded across the floor from his bedroom to the bottom of the staircase. He heard his mother's admonition to her husband to be patient.

"What the hell is going on up there?" his father yelled up the stairs.

Everything was perfectly quiet and still until Moriarity's little sister toddled to her door.

"Patrick is throwing his baseball again." She caught her breath and resumed crying.

"Pat!" his father yelled. "Open your door and get out here!"

Moriarity brushed his hair back and picked up the baseball. He stepped out in the doorway and looked down at his father, also in boxer shorts. Despite his height, Moriarity was a full inch shorter and still a skinny colt compared to his father's bulk. He enjoyed the superior angle, therefore, and the distance that the staircase would afford him for this scolding.

"It slipped," Moriarity finally said.

"Nothing slipped," replied the elder Moriarity. "You threw the ball. You've woken everyone now. Probably the whole neighborhood as well. I'm looking over that dresser tomorrow. If there's even a scratch on it, you'll pay for it."

Pat nodded. It was the same dresser his father had used for similar baseball exercises when growing up. Both Moriaritys knew this, and both maintained the proper behavior for their roles.

"We've got Mass tomorrow morning. For once I'd like to be on time." The elder Moriarity began to turn away to leave.

Moriarity called out. "You coming to my next game?"

"Not if I can't get any sleep tonight," his father said. "I told you I'd come to a couple of your games this summer. If I can get the time off from work, I'll come. Now get back into bed—and no more baseball." Then he stomped away.

Moriarity returned to his bedroom and closed the door behind him. He lay back down. With the baseball still in his hand, he picked up another book, this one fiction, entitled *Sandlot to Star*. He read the first few pages, then skipped through most of the other pages until the main character was pitching for the National League in the All-Star Game. He fell asleep with the book wrapped around his face.

— CHAPTER SIXTEEN —

Countdown to the Finals: 22 Days to Go

O N SUNDAY AFTERNOON, AFTER ATTENDING MASS and watching their own team practice, it was time for the old men to watch their other team, the St. Louis Cardinals, play the Cincinnati Reds. It was a key game for the Cardinals and their fans—as were all Cardinals' games.

Three of the Cardinals' biggest fans were seated at a kitchen table some distance away from the action in Cincinnati. There in Egg's home, they "watched" the game by listening to the action via Egg's vintage solid-walnut console stereo, a piece of furniture that could have easily passed for a coffin. In fact, Egg had often joked that if you removed the phonograph player and the Eddy Arnold albums, and if you bolted steel bars onto the side for carrying and lowering him into his grave, he would be perfectly happy resting for eternity in such an enclosure.

The old men were interested in today's game, but their gathering had another purpose as well. They had also met to plan for the Finals, now twenty-two days away, starting on July 29. The old men disliked such planning, preferring to devote their energies to their players on the field. But this year, more than any other, there was no disguising the fact that they had an extremely good team. They would definitely go to Des Moines. And over the years, they had learned that if they themselves didn't plan every detail of their trip and stay in Des Moines, someone else would do it for them, do it wrong, and worst of all spend a fortune doing it.

The Finals—a three-game single-elimination series leading to a championship game—was spread out over four days, Wednesday through Saturday. In past years, the Holy Trinity team had stayed overnight in Des Moines when the game schedule was tight. When the schedule allowed, the team had made the two-and-a-half-hour drive back and forth for each of the three games.

This year, the old men decided they would do a little of both. They would come home after Wednesday's game, drive back for Friday's game, then stay overnight in Des Moines for Saturday's championship game at 3:00 p.m.

Staying in Des Moines required something the old men were perpetually short of—money. They owned their own homes (except for Ryan), cars, and a few life insurance policies but had little cash on hand. Egg's cash holdings—again, which would now be distributed directly to his grandchildren— was less than $7,000. Murphy and Ryan had even less financial reserves.

Nevertheless, their thoughts were not on their own meager resources. They had to finagle the very best "good-guy discounts" for a bus, hotel, and meals so the cost wouldn't be an issue for their players, particularly McKenna.

Other (mostly younger) coaches across Iowa and their powerful booster club backers ensured the most comfortable transportation, the best accommodations, and the most nutritious food for their players. In contrast, the old men's driving principle was, first and foremost, not paying one penny more than absolutely necessary. If they could have stayed with gypsies for free in their trailers and popup tents in the Sec Taylor Stadium parking lot, they would have gratefully accepted that arrangement.

Egg began the planning session by reporting an update on his nearly yearlong effort to secure free rooms at Drake University, a mere three- and-a-half miles from the stadium. Egg had persistently argued to administrators at the elite learning institution that this would be a wonderful public relations move—students from Holy Trinity were certain to enroll at Drake once they were introduced to the campus in this fashion. He had been passed across several exasperated administrators in several different departments. They never said no but also refused to say yes.

Eventually, Egg resorted to complaining bitterly about his long-distance phone bill and the toll this experience was having on his eighty-five- year-old emotional and physical health. Out of guilt, the university agreed to give them an entire floor in their oldest dormitory. The rooms would not be furnished, which meant everyone would have to bring a sleeping bag. And a fan, as the dormitory had no air conditioning.

The rooms would be free, but on one condition: Egg was to find a different place to house the Holy Trinity team in the future. (However, Egg's experience was that large institutions in Des Moines had short memories, even if he signed a document with that agreement delineated in detail.)

Ryan had similar good luck. A priest friend had told him about a good Catholic man who owned a McDonald's near the Drake campus. After hearing Ryan's tale of despairing times at Holy Trinity and Cottage Park, the man agreed to feed the team and coaches the entire time they were in Des Moines. He'd also provide coolers of ice-cold orange drink for each game. Everything, the food and drinks, would be entirely free.

But Ryan didn't tell Egg and Murphy this detail. That was because Ryan instantly yet graciously refused the generous offer. He explained to the owner that while the people of Cottage Park may have been facing many toils and challenges, they were still proud and didn't expect charity. All they were after was the best possible deal. The owner kindly asked Ryan what amount the team could comfortably pay. Ryan said $150 seemed fair.

"Deal!" the patient owner had replied cheerfully.

So Ryan shared only the good news that he had arranged for food and drinks for a bargain deal of $150. He also relayed the owner's closing invitation: "When you win the Finals, you can all come back for a big supper, and I'll take care of the bill!"

The old men agreed they absolutely must win the Finals to take advantage of that free meal, if for no other reason.

After that discussion, it was Murphy's turn to explain the situation with the team's sole mode of transportation: the Holy Trinity school bus. It was a dilapidated old collection of rusty nuts and bolts held together in many places with duct tape and burning lots of oil. Even the old men knew it wasn't in any shape to make the trips back and forth between Cottage Park and Des Moines. At least not safely.

Murphy, who would double as the bus driver, had received an estimate from an auto repairman in Cottage Park. The mechanic had agreed to do the labor for free and find the lowest priced parts. Regardless, the bus needed a major overhaul: wheel work, brakes, shock absorbers, a complete tune-up, and on and on. The total cost would run hundreds of dollars.

Technically, maintenance of the bus was the school's responsibility— meaning that of the school principal, their common and dreaded enemy, Wilson. But as soon as Murphy finished his update about the maintenance costs, Egg spoke up.

"I got this one," he said. "I have no problem at all paying for everyone to be safe."

"How about I throw in half?" Ryan said.

"Or how about thirds?" Murphy said. "It's the best money we've ever spent if we don't have to mess around with Wilson. Let's not ask him for a single thing. I'll schedule the work for this week."

Murphy looked at his watch. It was time to strategize about baseball; namely, the opposing teams they would have to beat to get to Des Moines to make the Finals. Iowa had divided the state tournament into separate classes for large and small schools. With an enrollment of 109 students, Holy Trinity qualified to participate in the smaller-school class, yet they opted to play up in the larger-school class. They would face schools fifteen to twenty times larger in terms of enrollment, facilities, and resources.

The old men reasoned that Holy Trinity could and should beat any high school team, anywhere, at any time, regardless of size. The town had regularly done so long before the two-class system had been created. American Legion teams from Cottage Park routinely crushed big city teams in tournaments across the United States.

That Sunday's *Des Moines Register* listed the top-ten poll of Iowa's best high school baseball teams. Murphy focused on each team one by one. He began with a discussion of Estherville and the notable teams they had beaten and been beaten by to achieve their tenth-rated ranking. In their discussion of each school, the men commented on the coach and his style and the overall strength and weaknesses of the school program. Sometimes they even discussed the history of the surrounding community and how it had shaped the program. Very often, the old men repeated the same comments from program to program, but they didn't seem to notice or care.

Gradually the men moved up school by school. There were two undefeated teams in the state. One was their own second-ranked Cottage Park Holy Trinity. The other was top-ranked Davenport East.

Star pitcher Jordan Houston led Davenport East. Everyone across Iowa was aware of Houston, a talented basketball recruit who had been suspended from the state basketball championship. He had publicly vowed to avenge that loss in his life by winning the baseball Finals.

At last, Murphy focused their attention on Holy Trinity. There would be games, often doubleheaders, every day of the week except Wednesday and Sunday. Murphy listed the scheduled opponents for the upcoming week. They discussed the local opponents in very much the same way as they had discussed the ranked schools, but with one exception. Murphy had a large black notebook filled with detailed scouting reports of each opponent. Some programs were feared. Others had no chance at defeating Holy Trinity, something the men knew in their hearts but never acknowledged out loud.

"Now let's take a look at our team," Murphy said.

The trio had an understanding: any compliments bandied amongst themselves regarding their players would never be uttered anywhere else in public. It was imperative that the players never glean any indication of how highly the old men regarded them.

"Father, how do you think our infield is shaping up? In particular, what do you think about third base?"

"Jeff Burnette?" Ryan asked. "He's trying. He's always the first to show up and the last to leave."

Murphy looked at Ryan carefully. "But you're still not sure," Murphy said. "God knows I've made my mistakes. It's against my better judgment and tradition, but I have a good feeling about this kid. I think we should keep working with him. He'll come around. He'll be worth it."

Murphy suddenly checked his watch again, opened his portable pillbox, and swallowed a red pill with ice water.

"We've never played a freshman before," he said, setting the glass down. "Never had to. But this kid is the future. He's big. His teachers tell me he's straight A. On top of everything else, he listens. And most importantly, he'll be around for three more years after we're gone."

"He'll know the system," Egg said. "And he'll be a champion. That sort of thing is bound to rub off on the other boys."

"Even on the mistake Wilson will hire to take our place," Murphy said. "This is the kid who'll carry on the tradition for us. So let's stick with him and hope he comes around." Murphy looked at Egg next. "How do you like our outfield?"

Egg started to speak but was interrupted by a loud thumping from outside against the wall. The other men looked up in surprise, but he shrugged it off.

"It's T. J. throwing a ball off the wall," he explained.

"How's he doing repainting your garage?" Murphy asked.

The thumping continued as T. J. threw the tennis ball up against the wall, then shifted his feet, as Egg had shown him, to track the ball and catch it.

"We still paint from time to time," Egg said. "I'd say we'll finish up in a day or two. Now he comes over here every day to play baseball."

Murphy nodded and continued. "Okay, let's break down our catching. I like Powers. He seems to be figuring out Moriarity and getting him to respond the right way. As good as we are, we're going only as far as Moriarity takes us." Murphy adjusted his glasses. "Though I'll have motion sickness until we get there." He gently clapped. "Let's wrap it up. Any other items to discuss?"

His coaches shook their heads, so Murphy began to collect the notebooks and newspaper clippings. Then he got up and moved to the window to look outside at T. J.

In one quick movement, T. J. caught the ball one-handed and tossed it back up against the wall, over and over again. He had removed his shirt, something he never would have done a few months earlier. Fiery-pink skin covered his arms up to where his T-shirt sleeves had extended, then gave way to milky-white upper arms and chest. Rolls of loose flesh bounced and shook from the momentum. But he was losing weight and gaining muscle. He was confident he would be proud of his physique at some time in the near future.

Egg and Ryan joined Murphy at the window.

"He'd rather play catch, but he wears me out too fast," Egg said.

"Let's put this kid on the team," Murphy said. "I mean, really let him get in and play."

"Maybe," Egg said. "But he just started playing."

He quickly flinched as T. J. threw the tennis ball right at the window. T. J. laughed and loped over to pick up the ball.

"For now," Egg continued, "maybe it's best if he keeps the scorebook. If we get a big lead, maybe we could put him out in right field."

Egg pointed to the scuff mark on the window and yelled to T. J, "You're cleaning this up!" He lowered his voice and spoke to the other men again. "He's a big kid. I don't let him get away with anything."

Outside, T. J. picked up the ball and faked a throw back at the window. Now the other old men flinched. T. J. laughed, returned to his position, and resumed throwing the ball back on the wall.

"You know, I have something I'd like to try out with our T. J.," Ryan said.

— CHAPTER SEVENTEEN —

Countdown to the Finals: 13 Days to Go

T. J. made two more long, even brush strokes across the garage, then stepped back to admire his work.

"Done," he said.

He studied Egg, who emerged from the garage holding a cane pole with fishing line and a bobber attached to its end. He set it on the driveway.

"Going fishing?" T. J. asked.

Egg looked up. To his surprise, T. J.'s work really was done. The last of the graffiti was now gone. The entire garage had been painted, and it looked beautiful. The workmanship was excellent. The boy had made excellent progress and deserved a reward.

"Yes, *we're* going fishing," Egg said. "Put everything away and get ready to go. I'll be back in a minute."

Egg returned inside to call Ryan and Murphy. The plan was still on. He then swept his kitchen floor and washed his dishes. Satisfied with his work, he carefully navigated the wooden steps to his basement. In a dusty corner, he sorted through several old fishing rods until he found two he liked. Then he picked out a steel tackle box and began to sort through, fix, and polish leaders, hooks, sinkers, and lures. When the entire collection was ready, he gathered all the tackle and equipment and returned outside to monitor T. J.'s progress.

"I've never been fishing," T. J. said from his favorite seat—under the maple tree in the front yard.

"Then today's your lucky day," Egg said, "because I know where the fish are and how to catch them."

At that moment, Ryan and Murphy drove up in the driveway.

"Let's go," Egg said.

T. J. put the fishing gear, including the cane pole, in the trunk of Ryan's car. It hung out long after the trunk, like a straight tail, low to the ground.

As T. J. reached for the handle of the rear passenger door, Murphy suddenly got out of the front seat, brushed past T. J., and climbed in back. Simultaneously, Egg joined Murphy on the other side of the back seat.

With a shrug, T. J. took a step toward the front passenger seat, but Ryan had slid across the bench seat and was now riding shotgun. There was one open seat for T. J.—behind the steering wheel. Ryan pointed for T. J. to sit there.

T. J. stood stiff and frozen. He didn't know what to say and couldn't have spoken if he tried.

"Come on," Ryan said from inside the car. "You're such a good driver. Let's see how you do."

T. J. nervously protested and stammered, shaking his head no. He could have stolen a car and driven that just fine. But the thought of three old men impatiently gesturing for him to take control of the big Cadillac was immobilizing. There was no way he would ever take responsibility for the lives of Cottage Park's three most important members. Never. Not to mention, he had no idea of how to maneuver the big car, which seemed the size of a school bus.

"I can't. I'm serious," T. J. said. "I don't have my license. I've never really driven anything in my whole life. I'd get you guys in trouble or wreck your car."

Ryan laughed. "You're in Cottage Park. You won't get in trouble. Besides, this is an automatic. It drives itself. You can't break it. It's indestructible."

T. J.'s mind raced with more excuses. He considered the possibility of turning and running from the old men.

Then he heard Egg's griping voice from the back: "I told you he'd be afraid. Let me drive and show him how it's done."

The nagging voice and the thought of being in a vehicle driven by Egg emboldened T. J. to step quickly into the car and adjust the mirrors as if he had been driving all his life. T. J. buckled the seat belt—which had never been used before—and put the car in reverse. Without T. J. even having his foot on the gas, the car automatically moved backward. T. J. slammed on the brake, causing the old men to lurch violently forward.

Ryan righted himself back in the seat. "Power brakes," he said patiently.

T. J. checked the mirrors again. He hadn't run over anyone or crashed into a car . . . yet. He eased off the brake. Again, the car slowly retreated out of the driveway and onto Elm Street, where he straightened the steering wheel.

The three old men and T. J. all gave the two-fingered "farmer's wave" to Aunt B. From behind her living room window, she returned the greeting by dramatically clapping her hands together in applause. T. J. then set the Deville from reverse to drive, and the car led them down the street.

T. J. could not believe the immensity of the vehicle he barely commandeered down the quiet street. Before he moved to Cottage Park, he had never summoned God and requested assistance for anything. But since being here, he had prayed twice. He initially prayed for his life on his maiden voyage with the old men in this same car. And now, he begged God for intercession to keep all living souls (bikers, pedestrians, and, God forbid, oncoming traffic) as far away as possible from the massive vehicle.

The car nearly drove itself along desolate blacktop highways and gravel roads to their first destination, the nearby Union Slough. Northwest of Cottage Park, the 3,300-acre Union Slough wildlife refuge was one of the premier areas in the Midwest for observing hundreds of species of birds that inhabited or traveled through the marsh and upland habitat. A bird-watcher, Ryan had been alerted that a bald eagle had settled in the area and was selecting a site for a nest. Ryan desperately sought to see the majestic bird. But even more, he wished for T. J. to see it.

Ryan carried a pair of binoculars in the car at all times. As they approached the first expanse of water at the slough, he grabbed the binoculars from underneath his seat. He directed T. J. to pull the car to the side of the road.

Once they were outside the car, Ryan stopped and gently grasped the lanky green shafts of grass. T. J. and the others listened as Ryan explained that they were touring a prairie of native tallgrasses and flowers that had survived for many centuries. It was an ideal habitat for birds and, as Ryan added wistfully, "the mighty buffalo."

T. J. noted that Ryan's syntax changed as the winds blew across the marsh and filtered through the tallgrass prairie. He began to speak passionately about this area, using long, eloquent expressions to describe its history, its threats, and the solutions to preserve it. His face, usually florid like a Christmas bulb, assumed the honeyed coloration of the surrounding landscape. As Ryan introduced him to the land, T. J. could see that this—not the confines of Holy Trinity Church—was where Ryan found happiness and reward in life.

"Spiderwort," Ryan said.

He pointed to an elegant long-stemmed plant blossoming with purple flowers and yellow stamen. Bees swarmed each plant. Ryan carefully reached in and plucked the blossoms of a stem. He plunked one into his mouth and handed the other to T. J.

"Eat it," Ryan said. "These blossoms live for one day. And only for the morning. But a new one will take its place tomorrow. I wanted you to see them before they die."

T. J. made note of Ryan's use of the personal pronoun *I*. It was not common for the old men to speak of themselves directly, especially with an emotion of affection. He felt the need to reciprocate Ryan's enthusiasm.

"It tastes like lettuce," T. J. said, chewing heartily.

Ryan nodded in agreement.

Next Ryan gently cupped a taller-stemmed flower as if he were framing a cute baby.

"Purple coneflower," Ryan said.

T. J. was aware that Ryan was exclusively speaking to him now.

"You take this if you get bit by a snake or if you have a headache. Works for about anything that ails you."

Ryan toured along and pointed out several taller, longer leafed plants.

"Goldenrods," he said. "We'll have to come back out here after they bloom. They help predict what kind of winter we'll have. This whole place lights up bright yellow!"

They continued on.

"Black-eyed Susans." Ryan waved his hand over bouquets of yellow and gold flowers.

Suddenly Ryan stopped his discourse to proudly point. First, it was to a flock of white long-billed birds.

"Pelicans!" he excitedly announced.

He handed the binoculars to T. J. Ryan then pointed farther away to a pair of graceful white birds floating upon the water.

"Trumpeter swans!" he said in wonder. "A few years ago they were nearly extinct."

Ryan next directed T. J. to a string of trees along the edge of the marsh.

"See if you can spot our bald eagle."

T. J. scanned the area in vain for the eagle. He saw lots of other birds, however, mostly ducks, gulls, and geese. Yellow-winged blackbirds zoomed through the tallgrasses around them. American goldfinches shot past them like bullets before perching on tallgrass that slowly lowered to allow them a view of the human quartet.

Perhaps because Egg was the tallest member of the group, or perhaps because he had merely wandered too close to a nesting site, a furious red-winged blackbird dive-bombed at Egg repeatedly, narrowly missing the top of his head each time.

"I'm ready to go," Egg said, high-stepping his way back to the car.

Ryan bowed as if to apologize to Brother Bird, then he rounded up Murphy and T. J. to return to the car.

With one last look over the prairie, he announced, "Prairie needs a disturbance to thrive. That's why buffalo were so necessary here. They dug things up, which allowed new growth. That's why they set all this ablaze from time to time. Change is good for the prairie."

Safely inside the car, each of the men offered T. J. varying directions to their next destination, the McKenna farm. T. J. decided to follow Murphy's lead. It was a wise choice. Had he listened to either of the other two, they may not have ever reached the McKenna farm that day.

As T. J. drove the car off the dusty gravel road and onto the pristine white-rock driveway leading to the McKenna home, Ryan reminded all that they mustn't leave the car until Sissy, the German shepherd, was firmly under the grasp of one of the McKennas. Sure enough, as Ryan predicted, Sissy came bounding at the car, barking furiously, before it even stopped.

McKenna quickly called the dog off, and T. J. and the old men exited the car to remove their fishing gear from the trunk. The McKenna farm bordered the Union Slough. Now they would go on foot to their final desti-nation: the old men's favorite fishing spot, where the Buffalo Creek fed into the East Fork Des Moines River.

"She's a good watchdog," McKenna said, stroking the dog as he leaned into her and gave her a loving hug. "Last night, she got hold of a huge raccoon and shook him until she broke its neck." He scratched the top of her head. "We'll let her lead us to our fishing spot today in case we need her."

The dog led them a quarter mile along a path behind the McKenna home. As they all made their way behind the guide dog, T. J. wondered what other animal they might come across that would necessitate the services of the all-powerful German shepherd. Though she didn't need to protect them, Sissy did rouse a rooster pheasant, which burst from the tallgrass like an arrow before settling down again about seventy-five yards away.

Ryan stopped to introduce T. J. to milkweed plants, carefully turning over their rough green leaves to look for monarch butterfly larvae. He then excitedly pointed to a mature monarch farther away, bouncing bright orange up and down on its way south. Ryan explained that his favorite butterflies were the red admirals that flittered and shimmered in the sunlight from their perch atop the tall green grasses that gently waved back and forth. Ryan held his arms up and out like a scarecrow, hoping one might descend on him. After a moment, he continued on.

He next approached the water, where he showed T. J. the neon-green-and-brown-spotted leopard frogs that frantically sprang away in all directions on either side of them.

Once they reached the water's edge of the East Fork Des Moines River, the old men and McKenna moved in unison to prepare their fishing site. McKenna rolled out chunks of a fallen tree and fashioned them into crude chairs. Murphy gathered brush from along the banks and drove the branches into the ground as supports for the poles to lean on. Ryan prepared a hole, where the Folger's coffee can of night crawlers was placed. He covered the hole with branches to ensure it would remain cool. Egg showed T. J. a stainless-steel fish stringer and directed him where to place it in the river in preparation for the fish soon to be caught.

"The fish will be waiting right there, where the Buffalo Creek enters the river," Ryan explained to T. J., pointing across the river from them. "We'll catch catfish and striped bass—perhaps bluegill."

When Egg saw that the encampment was ready for fishing, he called T. J. over and showed him one of two ways to bait a hook with a night crawler. In this first lesson, he wrapped the worm around the hook, piercing it at each end.

Egg then took T. J. to the edge of the river and showed him how to cast the line far out into the water. He handed the rod and reel to T. J., who tried as best he could to follow Egg's directions. He cast the hook and sinker approximately five feet into the shoreline in front of them. His second cast was about twenty-five feet farther, into the water. Egg took the rod back before T. J. could try again.

"Come on—one more time," T. J. begged. "I think I'm getting it."

"No—it'll scare the fish away if you keep casting over and over. Plus, you lost your bait."

This time, Egg baited T. J.'s hook in the second fashion, by running the hook directly into and through the entire worm. Again he handed the rod and reel to T. J. He nodded appreciatively when T. J. deftly cast the line a few feet beyond the midway point of the river.

T. J. perched alongside the others and mimicked their behavior. They watched the river lazily flow by, occasionally looking to the tip of their fishing rods for the telltale sign of a fish's interest in a hook. T. J. was uncomfortable with the silence that resulted from gazing into the mesmerizing water, with its occasional swirls but otherwise disciplined flow on course to move out and away from Cottage Park to Des Moines. Even Ryan showed no interest in breaking the group's unspoken vow of silence. Sissy put her head down and between her paws as if she knew this were her opportunity to take a break from a busy day.

After what seemed like eternity—but in reality might have been thirty minutes—T. J. finally spoke.

"Do you think I should check my line?" he asked Egg.

Egg glanced at T. J. from the corner of his eye and shook his head. If Egg were to teach anything about Cottage Park to the boy, it would best be taught along this slow-moving river. It was a lesson in knowing your place and limitations in relationship to your surroundings, a lesson of being with friends, and a lesson of waiting and observing for the right time to act. Egg was concerned that so many people, mostly young people, always had to be *doing something.* Case in point, T. J. seemed to be squirming within himself like a snake shedding his skin.

"You'll scare the fish," Egg said. "Be patient."

Again there was silence. Another thirty minutes of T. J.'s life flowed out and away. Like the water flowing by in the river, those minutes were something he would never get back.

T. J. could take no more. He stood. Sissy moved toward him, also sensing a need for adventure. She nuzzled him excitedly.

"Can we check out the action upstream?" T. J. asked McKenna.

Over the years, McKenna had successfully tuned into the old men's nonverbal thoughts. He didn't have the same unsettled stirrings as T. J., but he stood and brushed himself off. The trio of two young men and a dog began to march along the riverbank upstream and around the bend.

McKenna reached down and picked up a toad. He handed it to T. J.

"Cool frog," T. J. said.

McKenna patiently shook his head, explaining the difference between a frog and toad. Later, he pointed out the water beetles that skated across the smooth surface of water behind a branch that had wedged along the bank. Further on, he showed T. J. a painted turtle sunning himself on a log that had also lodged itself in a crick of the river.

The lesson on amphibian life was interrupted by Sissy's angry barking. She circled and occasionally pawed away at a large hole in the embankment. Quickly, McKenna pulled her away.

"Run!" he said to both Sissy and T. J. as he darted away from the hole.

He spoke again after they were a good distance away.

"I'm pretty certain that was a badger hole," he said. "That would have been a horrible fight. Even Sissy would have had a nasty time with a badger."

They roamed nearly back to the slough, where the water slowed and swelled to the size of a small lake or pond. Again, Sissy galloped ahead and barked excitedly, this time not as much out of anger but more out of curiosity.

T. J. and McKenna raced up to see her encircling a terrified garter snake. McKenna met the snake head on, crouching low, flicking his hand out, and grabbing the snake behind the head. He held the wriggling creature, about two feet in length, up and above Sissy, who continued to bark.

"Holy shit!" T. J. screamed, quickly retreating away. "I'm scared to death of snakes!"

"Come on," McKenna said, now cradling the snake lovingly. "Has anyone ever told you you're a little dramatic?"

"Not about snakes," T. J. said.

McKenna shushed Sissy and stepped toward T. J.

"Feel her," McKenna said.

T. J. poked her with his finger, then retreated again.

"Take her and hold her," McKenna ordered.

This time, T. J. stepped forward and reached his hand around the snake, feeling her cool, supple scales. He lifted the snake and lowered his face to look at her close up.

Once convinced of T. J.'s conversion, McKenna said, "You head back with Sissy so I can let the snake go."

T. J. called for Sissy, and the two scampered back toward the fishing encampment. McKenna caught up to them a short time later.

When Sissy led T. J. and McKenna back to the fishing spot, the old men were silent. The young men mistakenly believed silence had prevailed the entire time they were gone. In fact, the old men had gabbed together nearly the entire time, first about the weather, then about McKenna, T. J., baseball in general, and the Finals. They clammed up when they heard the boys returning.

Having worked out his pent-up energy, T. J. was now prepared to sit and relax in his makeshift tree chair. Seeing no fish on the stringer, he was also prepared to offer some opinions on the subject of fishing.

"Egg," T. J. said, "are you sure we're supposed to just sit here like this? On television, the guys I see fishing are always reeling in or casting out. Aren't you supposed to sucker the fish into thinking something is alive and trying to get away from them?" He itched between Sissy's ears as she plopped her head in his lap.

Egg grimaced.

"We have visitors," Ryan said dramatically, pointing to a pair of large birds that soared directly above them.

"Vultures?" T. J. asked.

"Red-tailed hawks," Ryan answered. "Emissaries from heaven. The Santee Dakota who used to live around this area held them in special reverence. Their feathers were treasured." He pointed again to the birds that hung nearly motionless, suspended above them. "All that red means they are sacred birds. They carry our strongest wishes and petitions, the ones directly from our heart back to heaven." Ryan made a fist and tapped his heart his three times.

"We had a pair with a nest in the lights over center field years ago," Murphy said. "I'm not sure they ever helped us win any games."

"We never asked them for help," Ryan said. "We expect to win baseball games. Anyway, I don't think we should pass up this auspicious opportunity—from the Latin *auspicium*, the practice of seeing birds as omens and divining the future from their presence and movement. The high priests in ancient Rome guided public policy by such a sighting of sacred birds. I say this portends well for us all, for whatever we request. But we have to ask in order to receive." Ryan studied McKenna. "You ready to go first?"

McKenna quickly reflected over the myriad of problems and worries involved in maintaining, let alone managing, his family's farm. But his real wish was that the red-tailed hawks could return his father to him. He wished his father could face down the problems that were stacking up, showing no signs of going away, perhaps even growing more menacing as he killed time here fishing with the old men—something his mother had forced him to do.

He looked at T. J. and the old men. They were waiting. He needed to say something.

"I guess," McKenna said without any emotion, "I would ask for what my dad always begged for: one more crop. Though I might be greedy and ask for two."

The group nodded appreciatively. Ryan looked at T. J. to continue the sacred wish list.

T. J. needed no time to reflect. His wish was simple: to catch a fish, or at least to have someone in the group catch a fish. He now suspected that the old men had concocted the whole fishing trip on his behalf. For that, he was grateful. This day, like many of the other days he experienced in Cottage Park, had been one of the best of his life. All he hoped in return was to see them rewarded for their effort.

However, instead of voicing those thoughts, he answered Ryan with his own question.

"What would *you* wish for Father?" T. J. asked.

Ryan looked at Egg and Murphy and replied immediately. "Our wishes are all one and the same: to win the Finals."

"Then that's my wish too," T. J. said.

He gently lifted Sissy from his lap, stood, and raised his hands upward to the red-tailed hawks in supplication.

"Please, holy birds, as you return to heaven, take our requests with you . . . especially to win the Finals!" he said as loud as he could without shouting.

T. J. sat back down again and called Sissy to him. He petted her and carefully picked cockleburs from her fur.

After several more minutes, Egg announced it was time to leave. He was angry. He had brought his own children out here for many years and had never before been skunked. Now, when he intended to show T. J. a good time, there was nothing.

"Reel your line in slowly," Egg said, still mustering dwindling hope for a memorable fishing experience. "We might drag the worm across ol' whisker face and have him take a bite."

Now T. J. could practice the reeling techniques he had seen on television fishing shows. He reeled in for two seconds, jerked the rod, hesitated, then waved the rod and reel back and forth like a sorcerer. The others had already reeled their lines in, removed the remaining worms from their hooks, and secured their hooks in their rod eyelets. They watched in amusement as T. J. next waved the reel like a maestro.

Suddenly the tip of T. J.'s pole sprung forward. Then the whole rod bent over as if it might snap.

"You got a snag," Egg said. "Don't reel in—you'll break the line."

He reached out over the end of the rod and grabbed a fistful of line. He slowly brought it toward him, expecting to also pull along the branch or clump of whatever the hook had snagged. But Egg was shocked when the presumed clump of whatever tugged back—forcefully.

"He's got a big one!" Egg said, his voice raising. "I knew it!"

T. J. was suddenly surrounded. Egg was directly in front of him; Ryan and Murphy on either side. Immediately behind him, Sissy barked anxiously, periodically jumping up and pounding her paws on his back to get his attention. McKenna jumped down the three-foot embankment to a sliver of a sandbar. He quickly kicked off his shoes and socks and peeled off his long-sleeved shirt. He carefully waded into the river up to his knees and fashioned the shirt into a net to scoop up the big fish, if T. J. could get it in that close.

Everyone in the fishing party offered encouragement and or advice. But T. J. focused on listening to and acting on Egg's commands.

"Reel your slack," Egg said.

Slowly the pole arced forward again, then nearly jerked out of T. J.'s hands into the water. The fish rapidly zigzagged up and then down the river. McKenna followed the line as best as he could, preparing to dive into the water, if necessary, to wrestle the fish up onto the bank.

T. J. eased his pole back. "Am I doing it right?" The moment there was slack in the line, he immediately reeled it in.

"You're doing fine," Egg said.

In that moment, there were many stories Egg longed to tell about similar fish he and his sons had caught from this very spot over the years. But they had lost big fish as well. Egg forced himself to focus on the battle at hand.

"Firm but gentle with the line. Keep enough pressure to work him. He'll eventually tire. We'll wait all night if we need to."

"It's huge!" T. J. said, out of breath and never taking his eyes from the swirling activity in the water beneath him. His arms were beginning to weaken from the strain of the struggle. He'd seen deep-sea fishermen—again, on television—have similar battles with marlin.

The fish allowed itself to be reeled to the top of the water, a few inches out of reach of McKenna's shirt net, before shaking its head and submerging again.

"One more time," Egg said, now sounding like a midwife urging a mother-to-be to make one more valiant push. "You can do this."

T. J. again brought his reel back and immediately reeled in the slack. The fish appeared once more, this time still and not moving.

McKenna pounced at it, wrapping his shirt around the fish and lunging up and out of the water. He swung the makeshift fishnet into the midst of the group. The shirt opened up wide to reveal a huge carp gulping breaths of air.

A carp. Abject despair plainly registered on the faces of McKenna and the old men. But T. J. didn't notice.

"I did it!" T. J. said proudly. "That's my first! What is it? A bass or something?"

"You played him perfectly," Egg said. "And it is a huge fish. Got to be at least twenty pounds. But it's a dirty carp," Egg said disappointedly.

Egg pinched open the lips on the fish and in one quick movement dislodged the hook. He cleaned the hook and secured it, then he took the rod from T. J. and reeled in the slack until the rod was taut like a bow.

The fish took a deep breath. Its gills opened and closed. Thick darkgreen scales covered the fish from its yellow lips to a wide yellow fanned tail. The fish stood over knee length to Egg and was as wide as a football. It began to flop. Egg's feet, suddenly like a soccer player's, kept it from escaping.

"Crappy carp," Egg said disappointedly. "Can't eat a carp—too bony." He shook his head.

"We can still take it home, can't we?" T. J. asked.

"We'll come back out here again sometime and catch you a real fish," Egg said. "I promise."

Egg collected the fishing equipment, then turned and followed the others on the trail back to the car.

T. J. lingered by the carp. The fish opened and closed its gills, swallowing and seemingly gasping for air. After a few moments, the gills opened and stayed that way, closing when T. J. touched them.

"It's dying," T. J. called out.

"Not right away," Egg called back. "It takes about a week to kill a carp. Even if you bury it in the sand."

T. J. looked up and around for some sort of sign from the red-tailed hawks. They were gone.

T. J. backed away to rejoin Egg and the others. It seemed that the carp's left eye focused and actually followed him. T. J. took three steps, then returned to the fish, nudging it with his cane pole. It slithered in its own slimy juice to the edge of the embankment, where T. J. further prodded it off. It flopped onto the shoreline below.

Sensing the nearby water, the fish wiggled again until it reached the water. It lay motionless there, letting the water caress over it then coast it upside down downstream. After a moment, it kicked once again and disappeared below the broken sunlight rippling across the surface of the river.

— CHAPTER EIGHTEEN —

Countdown to the Finals: 11 Days to Go

WHEN HE WOKE UP THAT MORNING, Spider first called Margaret, but she was already out detasseling corn. At three o'clock that afternoon, she still hadn't returned his call. When he called her home again, he learned her older sister was back in Cottage Park for a visit, and Margaret was now babysitting her young nephew and newborn niece.

Spider rode his bike to Margaret's home. He was dressed in his full baseball uniform, already prepared for the game later that afternoon. When no one answered his knock at the front door, he strayed around to the backyard, where he found Margaret with two children dressed only in their diapers. In the shade of one of the oldest oak trees in Cottage Park, the trio played in a large tractor tire filled with sand.

At the sight of Spider, the two-year-old boy crawled away from Margaret, grabbed a tin cup, and began pounding it against the rubber tire. He offered the cup to Spider, then smiled when Spider took it and pretended to drink from it. Margaret held the sleeping newborn baby girl in her arms. The baby's skin was pale white against Margaret's suntanned-brown skin. Curly blonde hair laced the baby's scalp.

Spider sat down on the rim of the tire next to Margaret. "Didn't you get my messages?" he said softly.

"I didn't have time to call," Margaret said.

"I've got to get to the game tonight early," Spider said. "It's our last game. I absolutely cannot be late today. The old guys go completely nuts this time of year before the Finals."

"Go ahead," Margaret said. "Play your game. I'm not stopping you. But I won't be able to come to your game tonight."

"Come on, Margaret," Spider said. "You never miss a game. What's going on?"

"I'm thinking," she said. "I need some time to myself. Plus, I can always use the babysitting money."

The two-year-old boy brought a handful of sand to his mouth. Spider lunged to block the hand away. He wiped the boy's hand clean, then used a finger to scrape sand from the boy's tongue. The boy gagged. In fright and anger, the boy clamped his teeth on the tip of Spider's finger.

"Christ!" Spider yelled.

Now the little boy was even more frightened. He wailed loudly, raced over to Margaret's lap, and buried his face into Margaret's free arm. Disturbed, the newborn shook and also began to cry. Margaret stuck the tip of her little finger in the newborn's mouth, and the baby quieted quickly.

Spider examined his index finger. Beet-red blood formed a ring around the teeth marks. "I guess none of your family likes me," Spider said.

Margaret rocked the newborn in her arm for a few moments until she settled back to sleep. "You're too rough with kids," she said.

"Yeah, well, I would have been swatted if I'd ever put sand in my mouth," Spider said. "Especially if I'd tried to bite the finger off of someone trying to help me."

"He's a baby—he didn't know any better," Margaret said. "I think you're still a baby."

"I am not," Spider said.

"You're afraid to make a decision," Margaret said. "You put things off until it's too late. I won't let that happen to us."

"If things are right between us, we'll see it in time," Spider said.

"I don't have any more time," Margaret said. "I need to know now." With a plastic scoop, she traced a line in the sand. She breathed out a long, slow sigh. "I'm pregnant."

Spider closed his eyes and leaned back on the rim of the tire. He inhaled an equally long, slow breath and held it. He opened his eyes and focused his gaze on the little boy, who was kicking his heel into the sand. Spider slowly exhaled.

"When? How long?"

"Doctor Andersen told me yesterday," Margaret said. "I knew before that. I wasn't feeling that well. I'm sorry I don't have good news for you, Spider, but the world isn't always full of good news. We have to deal with this now."

Spider closed his eyes again and bowed his head. "I don't know what to do." After a few moments he opened his eyes and said bitterly, "Thanks for bringing me to this sweet spot in my life."

"What's that supposed to mean?" Margaret said in disbelief.

Spider knew exactly what it meant. In Cottage Park, the Holy Family of Mary, Joseph, and Jesus was worshipped as the perfect family. None of the members of that perfect family ever had sex—not once—in their entire lives. For everyone else, children happened by chance once a couple married. Children were the result of the sacrament of matrimony, not of sex. Margaret's announcement would now out him as someone who had done something no one else had ever done before in Cottage Park (or at least no one who had continued to maintain residence there): he had sex outside the sacrament of matrimony. Soon everyone would know of his lust and play out in their imaginations his one single lapse, which would result in Cottage Park's newest resident in approximately nine months.

"I mean," Spider said, "I'm doomed. I'm damned."

Spider imagined a life of work ahead of him, a life of generating money for someone else—Margaret and his child. He thought he had escaped Cottage Park and was free to have some fun in college. But all his hopes and dreams had ended now.

"My life is over," he said.

Spider ground a tall plastic glass into the sand and carefully shimmied the cup up and off, revealing a smooth tower. A moment later, the still-angry two-year-old dashed over and defiantly smashed it to the ground.

The thought of how the pregnancy had already impacted and would continue to impact Margaret's life never entered Spider's mind—at least not that day. He simply had no point of reference for it. Unbeknownst to him and others, unwed mothers had always been whisked away from Cottage Park and sent to a home in Sioux City until their babies were born or wedding arrangements were finalized.

Spider collected a handful of sand and let it dribble through his fist as if his hand were an hourglass. "How much time do we have?"

"I've got more time than you think," Margaret said. "I won't start showing for at least a couple more months. By then, we'll be off to school. If we act right away, we can work this thing out so nobody knows anything."

Spider looked confused.

"I mean get married," she explained. "It won't be the first time it's happened in Cottage Park. People already figure we'll get married anyway."

"Wait—don't we have any other options?" Spider asked.

"Yeah," Margaret said. "Somebody else can marry me and father this kid." She gently patted her stomach. "I know I could never give my baby up for adoption."

"That's not what I meant," Spider said. "I meant . . . I don't know . . . maybe there are other options out there. Something we haven't thought of. We go to Des Moines next week. Let's wait and see if we can get some help there."

Even as he spoke them, Spider knew these were empty words. He knew there were absolutely no other options—none they would ever consider, at least. There were two options, and two options only: he could either marry Margaret and raise this child with her, or he could leave Cottage Park forever. Still, he floated this fantasy of other options in faraway places in hopes that it might buy him more time to experience his own youth, which was now rapidly dissolving into memory.

"Oh, please," Margaret said. "There's no help for us." She shook her head as she stroked the hair of the baby in her arms, now resting again. "You have until the end of the Finals. I know you won't be able to think about anything else until then, anyway. But one way or the other, after the Finals, I have to go my way and you can go yours."

It was Spider's turn to kick his heel into the sand. "God, what lousy timing!"

Spider looked up in the stratosphere for some indication of the sun's passing toward dusk and the inevitable passing of time, then back at Margaret. He winced.

"I guess I'm scared, Margaret. I really am still a kid myself . . . I'm not ready to be a dad."

He began to back away. Then with his right hand, he reached out and circled her womb, moist and warm. He took a deep breath, stood, and stooped to kiss Margaret's forehead.

"I've got to catch my ride to the game," Spider said.

As he walked away, he tasted the salt of Margaret's sweat on his lips.

Katherine peeled a card from the deck and placed it at the top of a row of cards, completing a line of solitaire. She drew the next card and scanned the rows of previously played cards. Unable to play the card, she set it back in the deck. With a sigh, she took a long look at the clock radio at the other end of the table, then she played the next card.

For the next two hours that evening, she played several more games. Occasionally, she'd break away from the games to call three of her four children living in other cities across Iowa. As she began another game, her husband entered from the kitchen door, plodded in, and dropped down at the table beside her.

Murphy blew out a long breath and said, "I'm home." He shook his head. "What a night."

Katherine stood, kissed her husband on the top of his head, then stepped over to the refrigerator to prepare him a sandwich. "What kept you?"

"We played Carroll Kuemper, and they gave us a more difficult time than we expected. They put a lot of men on base, and their pitcher stalled on every pitch. They tried all their usual tricks. Their batters wouldn't get in the batter's box, and when they finally did, they'd call time out and step out. You know . . . trying to upset Moriarity or make him balk."

"Well, you're home now, and that's all that matters," Katherine said.

"We won," Murphy said. "Junior varsity game too. Our varsity finished at thirty-four and zero for the season. That's our ninth undefeated summer season."

Katherine brought a turkey sandwich, potato chips, and a glass of milk to her husband. She positioned herself across from him at the table to watch him eat. A moment later, she got up again to spread a napkin over his lap.

"Those kids on the junior varsity will be strong in a few years," Murphy said. "They've got all the makings."

"And you'll be able to say you planted the seeds," Katherine said.

"I wish you could have seen Moriarity tonight," Murphy said. "I thought they might get his goat and he'd throw a bad game, but he kept on top of it. I was proud of that kid. He's so up and down, but I think he's coming along. If I could only get him to be consistent."

Katherine picked up her cards, shuffled them, and began another game of solitaire. "Now that the regular season is over, when will you be finished with all this baseball?"

"Soon," Murphy said. "The first round of sectionals starts on Monday. If we lose that day, I'll be officially retired."

"Officially?" Katherine repeated, not looking up from the cards she laid down quickly in neat rows.

"Officially, unofficially, everything," Murphy said. "Whatever you call it, I'll be through. But if we win on Monday and keep on winning, then about two weeks from tomorrow we'll return from Des Moines with the state championship trophy," Murphy said dreamily. "That's how I'll go out."

"A lot can happen in two weeks, Al," Katherine said. She frowned. "I'm afraid something will happen."

"I couldn't be better," Murphy said, lying. "I feel great—haven't felt this good in years. I won't give out."

"Hugh Wilson called here tonight to visit with you," Katherine replied, wise to his fib. But she herself was also lying about the nature of Wilson's call.

"He didn't call for me," Murphy said, equally wise. "He has a baseball schedule. He knew I wouldn't be here. He called for you."

"Well, we had a good conversation," Katherine said. "He has a thankless job to try making everyone around here happy."

"And . . .?" Murphy cast an impatient stare at his wife.

"And he thinks you three should have some help during the tournament," she said. "It makes sense to me—with the stress and the heat. He's hired a nice young man who will do a great job as the new coach. I think it's a wonderful idea—and very fair—to let him get started down in Des Moines. Let's let somebody else worry about the Finals."

"You don't understand," Murphy said. "I don't think you'll ever get it."

"It's almost over now," Katherine said. "Wilson really does want to help. So do I. Can't you let us help you this one time?"

Murphy looked at his wife. "He'll help me into an early grave."

"He's trying to do the opposite," Katherine said. "If you'd listen to him. As I said, he hired a nice young man to replace you—a good Catholic boy from Des Moines who'll teach in the eighth grade. Hugh told me his name . . ." She put two fingers to her lips and thought for a moment. "It was a name I didn't know, and now I don't recall it. I'm sure there will be a story about him somewhere or other in the paper once the word gets out."

"Unbelievable," Murphy said, shaking his head. "And right before the Finals. Wilson's definitely diabolical. I give him credit." Murphy slid his plate away virtually untouched. "Does this new guy know anything about baseball?"

"He played in college," Katherine said. "I think Hugh said Creighton."

"If he did, then I'll have heard of him." Murphy stood, sighed, and looked toward the living room. "Maybe I can still catch some of the Cardinals game. It's a late game. They're playing on the West Coast." He took a step, then stopped and waved his hands in disgust. "I've got two weeks of baseball to play in my life. I won't take any chances now with distractions like Wilson and his new coach."

"I'm the one who's taking chances!" Katherine said. She brought her hands to her neck. "Every time I send you off to a baseball game, I'm worried I'll get a phone call from the hospital." Katherine took a breath, then spoke more softly. "Al, please—you're an old man. You're not as strong as you used to be. You know that. You're not strong enough to coach those boys anymore. And Ryan and Egg are no better. The bunch of you should come to your senses and leave baseball to someone else."

Murphy bristled. "We haven't had any problems all year."

"It's the postseason now. It's like a whole different season itself," Katherine said. "You've been telling me that for years. There's more pressure with all the time and energy you put into the Finals."

"I'll pace myself."

"You'll forget," she said. "When you three start playing baseball, that's all you think about. And there isn't one of you who knows or cares enough to choose your safety over winning some game. Your lives are at stake!"

Katherine looked down at the table and her playing cards. After a moment, she gathered them, then began to shuffle them. There were several moments of silence until she set down the cards and looked back at her husband.

"I can't lose you over something as silly as a baseball game."

"It's so much more than a game," he said. "Look at me. Look at Cottage Park. Other than family, baseball is the most important thing in our lives. Would you ask a doctor to quit in the middle of an operation? Or turn over his responsibilities to someone who'd never held a scalpel?"

"All Hugh asks is to put the new coach on the bench with you," Katherine said.

"If that were true," Murphy said, "or if he were truly concerned about our health, I'd give in. But he's worried about image. Holy Trinity is the only team in this state that has a priest, a retired businessman, and someone like me for coaches. We're all old. We aren't fashionable—but a younger man is, even if he botches things up."

"You don't listen," Katherine said. "Even to me. Hugh was right—you three are desperate."

"He's the one who's desperate," Murphy said. "He'll sabotage us yet. Then he'll be happy. He's trying to play you and me against each other."

Murphy brought the fingertips of each hand to his temples, then lowered them to the table. He knew this was one of those times when he had to say or do something dramatic to win over his wife, to connect with her. It was like the times the doctors had wheeled him in for surgery with no guarantee he would be wheeled out alive.

"I listen to you, Katherine. And I do," he stammered, "love you. But this time, there's nothing I can do. I won't insult my coaches. And I won't jeopardize our chances in the Finals."

Murphy sulked away to the living room. A moment later, he was situated in front of the stereo, following the action and drama of his second-favorite team as they battled the Dodgers in Los Angeles.

Katherine tapped the cards against the table and shook her head in resignation. These next two weeks could not pass fast enough for her liking. In all honesty, she couldn't care less who won the silly Finals. She wanted her husband alive and well and done with the entire mess.

After a few moments of staring at the deck of cards, she slowly rocked herself up from her chair. She collected Murphy's plate of food and his drink and carried them out to him.

Standing before him, she spoke once more, firmly resolved and determined to bring closure.

"After the Finals," she said, "we're done with baseball."

Murphy turned away from the broadcast and nodded—as he habitually did, regardless of what Katherine said or did.

Once she had situated Murphy and he began to eat, Katherine backed away from him. She headed to the bedroom, where she closed the door to quiet the sounds of the game.

— CHAPTER NINETEEN —

Countdown to the Finals: 6 Days to Go

J EFF LOOKED AT THE CLOCK. It was 4:52 a.m. Time to get started with his day. He'd been waiting in bed long enough.

Ever since baseball season started, Jeff had not been sleeping well at night. He was rarely sleeping at all—more like resting for hours, eyes closed, motionless, as if he'd been buried alive. Jack's steady breathing in the bed across the room reminded Jeff that he was not alone.

Jack and his sleep-craved peers could sleep nearly unconsciously until noon or 1:00 p.m. every day if they were allowed. But Jeff had to force himself to stay in bed every morning until no sooner than 4:30 a.m. and no later than 5:00 a.m. Any time within that specified range, he would dress in his shorts and gear and don actual running shoes: lightweight, form-fitted, with waffle soles. Jeff's green-and-gold shoes were like no other pair in Cottage Park. Most of his peers wore Converse Chuck Taylor All-Stars in black or white, low-top—except for Moriarity, who preferred the high-top version.

Then whether by fading moonlight or emerging sunshine, he would set off on a run across Cottage Park and beyond. Depending on the day, he'd run to the quarry or the slough or even to nearby towns such as Seneca, Swea City, Ledyard, and Lakota. Running alongside Highway 169 north, the route from Cottage Park to Lakota and back was a little over twenty-six miles, slightly over the official distance of a marathon. He had run that marathon twice already: once in June and then a week ago in mid-July. On the second run, he shaved thirty minutes off his initial time, finishing in three hours and thirty minutes. He was certain he'd easily best that time when he'd run the marathon again in August.

The accomplishment of completing a marathon as a soon-to-be sophomore was Jeff's personal secret. So were his everyday run-ins with wildlife, including deer, skunks, opossums, foxes, coyotes, owls, and raccoons—lots of raccoons. The animals were so surprised to see someone running out in the country at that time of day that they didn't turn and flee. Rather, they froze to watch him as he passed by.

Jeff felt increasingly comfortable and relaxed during these morning runs. He noticed that the more he trained and disciplined himself, the more energy he accumulated to go even farther and faster. So as his training intensified, he was even less inclined to need or expect a good night's sleep.

During his daily runs, Jeff forced himself to avoid fretting about baseball. Instead, he focused on his newfound confidence to establish a goal and work to achieve it. More and more, he was running all the time. Jeff understood that to continue this lifestyle, he must eventually run away as far as possible from baseball and eventually Cottage Park. Baseball had become a sliver in his foot that hurt whenever he moved. No one would help him pull out that sliver. He had to do it himself. So his number one goal was to be done with baseball—to have the sport completely out of his life.

Every morning as he raced along his ever-increasing routes, he role-played every possible permutation of the conversation he would soon have with Murphy about leaving the team. He would never use the word *quitting*. His emphasis would be that he needed space in his life for the sport in which he showed real promise, the sport that brought him such peace and joy. Running. He even planned to tell Murphy that he might get a college scholarship if he pursued running exclusively. After hours of rehearsal, he'd planned his exit strategy in such a way that any rational human being— even Murphy—simply couldn't argue against it.

Jeff's run that particular morning had taken him nearly ten miles straight west on a desolate stretch of blacktop, then he turned to make the trek back home. Along the way, his wildlife companions were the crows, blackbirds, sparrows, and wrens dotting the telephone poles and wires. He interpreted their chirps and calls as a chorus of support for his plan. The chirping increased in volume as the sun first showed its face, a tiny drop of blood on the horizon that lit the horizon and clouds in soft swirls of cotton-candy pinks and blues. It prompted Jeff to fully commit to his decision to approach Murphy after the Finals. He would recite the words he had painstakingly assembled to give him the freedom to move on and away from a life of fear to one of enriching self-discovery.

Having made these decisions and knowing now there was an end in sight, Jeff felt he could gut it out until the Finals ended. Life would soon get much better for him. This was a new day, a day of promise and hope.

As he turned off the blacktop onto his own street, he accelerated his pace, sprinting the last half-mile as fast as he could. Sweat slid along shiny arm hair, then flew off and splattered onto the concrete. It dripped off his hair onto his face, onto his soaked shirt and shorts, and down his long legs to his athletic socks.

He quietly entered his house, opened the refrigerator, and poured himself a glass of orange juice. He leaned his back against the refrigerator, then slid down its length until he collapsed on the cool linoleum floor.

"Is that you, Jeffrey?" his mother called out from upstairs. "Don't come in my living room after you've been running."

From the tone of her voice, Jeff could picture the face she was making.

"Go take a shower first, then I'll fix you breakfast," she said.

Jeff skipped up the flight of stairs to his bedroom, two steps at a time. The last four steps, he hopscotched one leg at a time.

Jack was already up, sorting clothing from drawers into grocery sacks placed throughout the room. The AM radio station from Omaha was playing "The Locomotion" by Grand Funk Railroad.

"Running again?" Jack said, not turning away from his task at hand.

He knew his brother had been running. That was all Jeff did. However, asking the question was easier than expressing a morning greeting.

Jeff nodded, then peeled off his shirt, sat on his bed, and kicked off his shoes.

"I'm surprised you're up already," Jeff said.

"Time's run away from me," Jack said. "So it's time to go." He waved his arm across the collection of clothing laid out on his bed. "You can have any of this junk. Otherwise, I'm dumping the rest in the Goodwill box."

Jeff looked at the collection grouped in piles. "You're giving away everything you own?"

"Just about," Jack said, emptying a drawer and moving to the next one. "I'll be leaving with the shirt on my back and whatever I can fit in my duffel bag and suitcase. Anything more than that would slow me down."

Jeff picked out a handful of worn athletic socks and stuffed them in his drawer. "Have you picked a time yet when you're leaving?"

"Right after the last game," Jack said. "Whenever that is. If we make it to Des Moines, all the better. It's three hours closer to where I'm trying to go."

"Which is?"

"South," Jack said. He stopped dropping clothing into the sack and turned to his brother. "Tulsa first, for sure. I'll try to find some work there. If things don't work out, I'll keep moving south. New Orleans maybe."

"Mom and Dad think you're crazy," Jeff said.

"I probably am," Jack said. "I'm so ready to blow out of this town."

"They think you'll forget about us."

Jack shook his head. "I won't forget. I'll call from time to time." Jack picked up an old compass, jiggled it to check directions, then slid it in his pocket.

"I think you owe people, at least Mom and Dad, that simple respect."

"I think the only person I owe is myself," Jack said. "I've put in my time here. In no more than six days, I'm free to start living for myself. I'm doing what I have to do."

"When will you ever come home?" Jeff asked.

"I don't know. A while back, I would have said, 'Never.' Now I'm telling people, 'Maybe never.' I won't travel any longer than it takes to answer my questions about what the rest of the world looks like. But the question I ask you is, when will *you* come to my new home?"

Jeff shrugged his shoulders.

"How about we make a bet?" Jack said. "I bet you'll come visit me before I ever come back here."

Jack thrust his hand out for Jeff. Though Jeff agreed with his brother, he couldn't remember if or when he had ever shaken hands with him before, so he reached out and accepted the bet.

"Well, that's all a ways off yet," Jack continued. "For now, we have to finish up here—and that means baseball practice in an hour."

Moriarity pitched his first perfect game, and nearly everyone on the team hit the ball as Holy Trinity advanced in the state tournament. The Finals experience would be upon them soon.

A light practice was held on Thursday morning in preparation for the game on Friday evening in Fort Dodge. Concerned about the effect of the sweltering heat, the coaches relaxed in the safety of the shade in the Holy Trinity dugout. They watched the players, one by one, arrive for practice, find a partner, and play catch. Even T. J. joined them, as he had begun playing catch with the team before each practice and game.

After twenty minutes, Murphy called the team to the dugout to go over the scouting report for Holy Trinity's next opponent, Sioux City Heelan. Holy Trinity had already played and defeated Heelan during the season. It was Murphy's intention to remind his team how they had accomplished this feat. They would review the opponent's strengths as well as weaknesses, especially their erratic pitching.

For instance, Murphy advised batters to take the first pitch and continue waiting until there was a called strike. The Heelan catcher would also be targeted. Murphy alerted runners that once they reached first base, they should be prepared to steal second base at the earliest opportunity. Also, Heelan's pitchers did not know how to hold a runner on first base. By the time the catcher received the ball, an alert runner could steal third base or even home plate.

No one questioned Murphy's instructions, so he next directed his starting lineup to take position on the field for what he called gamers, or game situations to test his players' knowledge of position and strategy. Murphy lined up the reserves behind home to run the bases after Egg hit the ball to designated fielders.

Jeff charged at and snagged Egg's first hit, a slow grounder, then he threw a straight shot to first for the out.

Egg popped up the next hit high over second base. Orlowski dropped his shades and called out for the ball, but then lost it in the backdrop of a white sun. As the ball sped downward, Orlowski yelled for help and covered himself. Anthony took three quick steps and reached over his friend to catch the ball. Orlowski brought his arms down from over his head, and Anthony gave him the ball.

Egg dropped the bat at the plate. "Are you thinking about baseball or your girlfriend?" Egg barked out to Orlowski.

"Baseball," Orlowski replied. "Hit me another one, Egg."

He motioned for a pop-up, but Egg shook his head. Instead, Egg attempted to hit the ball over Orlowski to center field, but the ball squibbed off the tip of his bat and skidded to Moriarity. The English on the ball was so severe that when Moriarity reached down to pick up the ball, it skipped away to the side. The reserve was able to reach and round first base.

Egg bunted the next ball between third and the pitching mound. Powers yelled that the play was at first. Moriarity scooped up the ball and threw the runner out at first while the previous runner advanced to second base.

"One out," Murphy said to Powers.

In turn, Powers whistled sharply, held up an index finger, and also shouted, "One out!"

Egg stepped out of the batter's box and looked over the players in the field, all crouched and poised to move with the ball. Egg stepped back in the box and batted the ball between first and second.

Each Holy Trinity player shifted to a new position: Jeff dropped back to cover third. Jack backed up Jeff in the event of an errant throw. Spider did the same for Anthony, who moved to second. McKenna sped toward the ball as Orlowski took several steps toward first.

However, first baseman Stephen Schmitt beat everyone to the ball. He quickly underhanded it to Moriarity, who had run over from the pitching mound. Moriarity jabbed his right foot into the base a split second before the runner did the same.

Both players looked to Egg to make the call. Egg motioned that the runner was safe.

Moriarity clenched the ball in his right hand, then pounded his glove hand against his leg. "You're *crazy!*" He jumped into the air to punctuate his words.

Murphy took a few steps in Moriarity's direction and pointed to the runner on third. "Don't stop the game to bellyache! You've got another runner who'll score."

Moriarity quickly looked over at third and faked a throw. Then he appealed to Murphy with his arms held as if in surrender. "But we got him out, Coach."

"Maybe you did," Murphy said. "But your umpire saw it differently. Sometimes they make mistakes. We live in an imperfect world."

Moriarity grumbled, flipped the ball to Murphy, then stomped back to the mound.

Murphy held one finger above his head to indicate there was still one out. The infielders rotated and relayed Murphy's message to the outfielders, who confirmed and returned the signal.

Egg next hit long and high into right field. McKenna turned and rushed several steps back, then straightened and searched for the streaming white meteorite that would show itself as it seared across the sapphire sky. He calculated he was four to five feet from the wall behind him, yet he seemed to feel the wall around him, pressing and restricting. The wall could punish. Each step backward would be a compromise between calculation and instinct.

The sunlight burned, blinding him until he shielded his eyes with his glove. He saw the ball float, then drop at him straight and fast. He followed the ball's path, watching its spinning colors mesh to gray. As the ball neared, he identified the direction of the spin. In the final seconds, he even separated the stitching pattern from the rest of the ball's skin.

McKenna locked his legs into position and received the ball deep into his glove. The force of the impact thrust the glove down to his free hand, which snatched the ball. McKenna's legs shuffled his entire body forward as he launched the ball fast and straight back at the sun.

The ball shot past the first relay man, Orlowski in shallow right. Stephen poised himself to cut off the throw midway between first and home.

"No!" Powers yelled.

Immediately, Stephen withdrew his glove, allowing the ball to continue to the plate. It had all the velocity and precision of a Moriarity fastball. Deeper in sound—almost as loud as a rifle shot—the ball sunk into the thick padding of the catcher's mitt.

Powers turned to the runner, who stood frozen and exposed between third and home. Powers raced at him, and the runner offered his back for the easy putout.

Powers held the ball high and out toward right field as if to offer praise to McKenna. The other teammates offered fist pounds and gestures of praise.

McKenna took his place back in right field as practice resumed. He continued to follow the flight of each ball. He positioned himself correctly in each situation. But his mind raced backward and forward and far away from right field.

He first felt tears in his throat. Then he smelled those tears. And then he tasted them. As the tears released, he saw a blurred infield and the movement of players. His tears mingled with sweat and flowed the length of his face before dripping off his cheeks and falling to the grass.

McKenna wiped his face with his glove. Very much against his will, his tears continued. His shoulders shook, and his breathing stuttered. He turned toward the outfield fence, crouched down, and blew his nose onto the field.

These tears, he knew, would not stop. He did not wish to be trapped in such a state in front of everyone, but leaving the field in this condition would draw even more attention to him.

McKenna took a deep breath. In as steady a voice as he could muster, he shouted out, "Hey, Orlowski—can you ask Father Ryan to come out here for a second?"

Orlowski relayed McKenna's request. Ryan was startled. He hiked outside the first-base line to right field in a confused state.

McKenna edged over until he straddled the foul line. He turned his back to the team and waited for Ryan. Cupping his right elbow in his glove, and his left elbow in his throwing hand, he held and rocked himself, humming as children sometimes do when they cry. His nose dripped. He coughed, then huffed air back into his lungs. His chest jerked as he swallowed the air.

Nearly out of breath himself, Ryan slowed before peering around McKenna's shoulder—suspecting, but still surprised, to witness the grief. By reflex, Ryan produced an ever-ready handkerchief from his pocket and placed it into McKenna's hand.

"Oh," Ryan said awkwardly. He patted McKenna on the back as a father might pat his baby to sleep.

McKenna stuttered broken words that Ryan instinctively understood.

"I know," Ryan said. He stopped the patting and now put his arm around McKenna.

McKenna blew his nose in the handkerchief, wadded it, then rubbed it over long strings of tears. He kicked at the ground until he uprooted a small piece of sod. He ground the handkerchief into the dirt, then dabbed it under his eyes.

He looked at Ryan. "If anyone asks . . ." His lips quivered. He took a slow, deep breath and tried to steady himself. "Tell them I was putting pitch under my eyes."

Ryan nodded.

McKenna took another deep breath. "I got blindsided. I couldn't stop it."

McKenna waved the handkerchief in farewell to Ryan, jammed it in his pocket, and returned to his place in right field.

— CHAPTER TWENTY —

Countdown to the Finals: 3 Days to Go

Holy Trinity advanced to the Finals by winning their game on Friday night against Spencer. Murphy made Saturday a day of rest. Practice was scheduled for Sunday afternoon and then again on Monday and Tuesday mornings. The team would drive down to Des Moines in their refurbished school bus on Wednesday morning for their first game of the Finals later that night.

Murphy asked for the community to join the team at a special Mass on Sunday morning. Nearly everyone was present: nearly every player, every coach, every parent, and every fan. Holy Trinity Church was full.

However, churchgoers would have graciously and happily slid over to make room for one more—the scorekeeper, Number 29, T. J. Moments before Mass began, Egg turned from his pew in the front of the church and searched the rest of the church for T. J. All morning, he had been searching for him so much, there was a crick in his neck. Still there was no sign of T. J.

Egg suspected he knew why T. J. hadn't chosen to participate in the Eucharistic sacrifice, a sacrament of the church that binds its members under the penalty of grave sin. And it had nothing to do with T. J.'s belief that the Catholic Church was filled with hypocrites.

Overhead ceiling fans and tall steel-cage-enclosed fans at all the entrances blew warm, heavy air across the church. The air carried the cries of babies attempting to be muffled by mothers who plugged pacifiers into their mouths, then tucked them to their bouncing shoulders with one arm and slowly fanned their own faces with devotional missals. Despite the mothers' best efforts, sweat dripped down their faces and onto their clothing, which they peeled away before it could paste to their skin.

To compete with the babies and the heat, Father Ryan boomed out his greeting and began the liturgy. The babies seemed to hush for a time. But then one cried a few minutes later, triggering another round of cries in unison across the church.

The Holy Trinity team congregated in the first two rows with Egg, Murphy, and the half dozen elderly women who came early and stayed late for every Mass. These women led the congregation in standing and sitting for each service.

Each player on the team dressed alike, in button-down white shirts, mostly short sleeved, with ties and dark pants. All except Moriarity had fresh haircuts courtesy of Francis McCarthy, who had cut the team's hair the day before. And courtesy of Egg, who had financed the operation.

Murphy and Katherine sat in the front pew, and Egg sat at the opposite end of the third pew. Egg followed the Mass with the aid of a thick black missal he always kept in that pew. It was stuffed with holy cards he had collected from funerals, often duplicates of the collection in his billfold. After glancing at several of the cards, he turned to the section at the back of the missal with offerings for specific occasions. He finished one such entreaty, the Act of Hope, in the time it took the congregation to situate themselves after the Gospel and before the homily.

Ryan used his handkerchief to wipe the sweat along the top of his brow, then his entire face. He looked out over those present—never looking at any one person, his eyes always moving, usually skimming across the tops of his parishioners' heads. He cleared his throat, gripped the stand with both hands, and spoke into the microphone.

"When I first came to Cottage Park out of the seminary, the monsignor here at the time would say I was greener than the corn. He claimed he heard me say "Gosh!" every time he passed by my confessional.

"I'm not sure I was really that surprised when I listened to those confessions. But I was surprised then and now by the friendliness and caring I've seen in this community. We know our neighbors. We help them when they need a hand. In the dead of winter, if your car doesn't start, you know the next person will stop and help you out. If you're sick, you know someone will come over to give you medicine, food, and, most important, time and attention. It seems someone is always there for us.

"That spirit is even more evident on the good baseball teams I've had the opportunity to work with over the years. Our Holy Trinity team here today, like the Holy Trinity teams of the past, is an excellent example of community spirit. The players believe in their coaches and in one another. And they believe in their school and Cottage Park.

"Of course we have difficulties and we make mistakes. But when that happens, we're not alone. There's a whole team with and behind us. That's important to remember as we honor this team, what they've done, and what they're about to do. In so doing, we honor ourselves—and our God. When we do this, we really cannot lose, regardless of the outcome of the game.

"This team is undefeated." Then Ryan lifted his arms out to the entire congregation. "We are all undefeated. Each and every one of us are champions. Don't ever let anyone tell you we aren't."

Ryan looked down at the book of liturgical readings. "Today's Gospel reading is simple." He discovered reading glasses from somewhere in his vestments, placed them on his face, and adjusted them to focus. "Come to me, all you who are weary and find life burdensome, and I will refresh you. Take my yoke upon your shoulders and learn from me, for I am gentle and humble of heart. Your souls will find rest, for my yoke is easy and my burden light."

Ryan closed the book, removed his glasses, and looked back out over the crowd. "God is greater than any problems we have. He is here. He is with us. He will help us."

Like a light breeze, Ryan's words floated through the church, touching each person. His message filled hearts and souls with confidence and hope. Everyone believed that God really was there with them that day, on their side. And not merely a God who would stand and watch passively from the bleachers. This was a God who would actively help them triumph in the Finals.

Ryan had always told them they should pray in communion, in large numbers, unceasingly flooding heaven. He told them to believe that God, similar to a politician, counted votes and petitions. God would eventually fill the pothole in the street if enough people persistently and pervasively cried out for the hole to be filled.

So the Holy Trinity parish had faithfully complied with Ryan's counsel to petition God not only that Sunday but every day for years and decades. No parish had worked as fervently in offering their own prayers to God— even imploring deceased loved ones now in heaven to take up the cause, using their direct connections to powerful saints and God.

No people could possibly be more deserving to have their single most important petition considered and requested. Surely this God could not turn his back on them once again at the Finals.

So as Ryan called out "The Lord be with you" to conclude the Mass, the parishioners responded "And also with you" while already experiencing the ecstasy of God's greatness—and already visualizing the state championship trophy in the display case outside the Holy Trinity gymnasium.

"Bow your heads and pray for God's blessing," Ryan said.

There was silence as everyone, including Ryan, bowed and prayed.

"May almighty God bless you," Ryan said, slowly making the sign of the cross as he continued, "the Father, and the Son, and the Holy Ghost."

The congregants responded, "Amen."

"The Mass is ended," Ryan said. "Go in peace."

Out of the hundreds of parishioners leaving the church that Sunday, at least one did not leave in peace. Egg was beside himself with worry. T. J. should have been at every Sunday Mass, but especially that one. He needed to be worshipping in unison with his team and Holy Trinity and the whole town—for Holy Trinity to win the Finals. The fact that T. J. didn't even care to show up for the team Mass, that he might not care enough to beg for God's intercession during the Holy Trinity crusade, gave Egg nightmarish distress. Perhaps God would put his energies on some other team during the four-day tournament.

Egg took off directly out of church and right by the groups of friends and families making brunch plans. He had never been to T. J.'s home—not inside it, anyway. He knew where it was, however. It wasn't far from his own home. After journeying the six blocks to the green Victorian two-story home with the wraparound front porch, Egg proceeded up the wooden steps and knocked on the screen door.

Mrs. Jones answered the door and welcomed Egg inside to sit down. Egg sunk into a couch while Mrs. Jones made her way to T. J.'s room to announce his visitor. A moment later, she returned.

"Can I get you something to drink? Coca-Cola? Water? Coffee?"

"Yes. I'll have a . . ." Egg forgot the name of the soft drink she had mentioned. "I'll have the one you said—brown liquid, bubbles . . ."

"Coca-Cola?"

"That's it!" Egg said, grateful his memory lapse had ended. "I feel like a Coca-Cola."

Egg was happily drinking the real thing when T. J. plopped himself down at the other end of the couch. A Holy Trinity baseball cap was pulled down over his head. Mrs. Jones also brought her son a Coca-Cola. Like Egg, he took a long drink.

Egg decided to get directly to the point.

"I just came from Mass," Egg said. "Everyone was looking for you. You're a part of our team. And now more than ever before, we need you. We need your total involvement if we're to win the Finals."

T. J. let out an irritated groan. "Look at me!" he said, yanking off the cap and pointing at a new, much shorter hairstyle. "I told you about my hair and how important it is to me. Now I'm the laughingstock of this stupid little town."

He shook his head back and forth. Where hair used to wave lazily back and forth, short hair now stood straight and motionless. The ponytail T. J. had cultivated for two years was gone, exposing a white neck.

"You said I would get my hair cut, not cut *off*."

So Egg's suspicion had been right—the haircut was why T. J. hadn't shown up for Mass. But while Egg had understood that much, he truly did not understand T. J.'s despair. Egg believed all men should have short, neat haircuts and be clean-shaven. He could understand no other viewpoint.

He looked at Mrs. Jones, then at T. J.'s haircut, which had, in fact, dramatically shortened and thinned his hair. He noticed T. J.'s forehead, ears, and neck for the first time. He really was a good-looking young man. No one would even recognize him as the same young man Egg first met. Thank God. His plan to save T. J. and make sure he became an outstanding young man was nearly complete.

"From what I can see," Egg said, "you got a great haircut. That's the best I've seen you look."

"Yeah, right," T. J. said with disdain. He rifled his hand through his hair, which fell neatly back into place. "Now I look like a jock. Your barber friend hacked me up like he does everybody else around here."

"You got a good-looking haircut," Egg repeated. He turned to address Mrs. Jones. "McCarthy's a real professional. He's been my barber for sixty years. None better."

"I look like an old man," T. J. said. "I spent twenty minutes telling him exactly how to cut my hair. He stood there and acted like he was listening to me. But then he blundered ahead and cut it his way."

"I guess I should have told you he's deaf," Egg said earnestly. "If you have to tell him something important, you should write it down for him to see."

"I'll be sure to remember that for next time," T. J. said sarcastically. "Seriously, though, I'm never going back there. That guy's a hundred and ten years old."

"No," Egg said. "I don't believe he's that old yet. And he's still the best at what he does, as far as I'm concerned. And he asks a very reasonable price. Name me one other business that still charges the same that they did twenty years ago."

"I really should have known better," T. J. said. "I knew something was horribly wrong because all of a sudden my hair was flying all over the place." T. J. looked at Egg with exasperation. "There were piles all over me and on the floor. I didn't know how bad it was until he brought out that little hand mirror at the end."

T. J. grabbed his hair with both hands and tried to pull it out.

"The funny thing is, your barber buddy was so damn proud of what he had done. He had such a big smile on his face. I couldn't go off on him," T. J. said, shaking his head sadly. "He was so pleased with himself."

It was true. The moment McCarthy had set down his scissors, his arms flailed out of control with resting tremors until he gripped and steadied the hand mirror for T. J. He proudly circled T. J. for the best views, occasionally stopping to point out features of the new style. The old-timers who loafed in McCarthy's shop looked up from their aging *Sports Afield* magazines and complimented McCarthy for his barbering artistry.

So when McCarthy asked T. J. how he liked his new look, all T. J. could do was muster up the standard two-word Cottage Park response: "It's fine."

He then came home and barricaded himself in his room for the next hour, slugging his pillow and mattress until his arms flailed out of control, like McCarthy's.

There was his dilemma: Should he have to sacrifice the things that mattered most to him—in this case, his precious hair—for all these old people in Cottage Park? It seemed all the things he hated and rebelled against mattered the most to them. And he kept meeting more and more old people in Cottage Park. They popped up everywhere, like a whack-a-mole game, all persistently and insistently demanding he change who he was and who he would become.

"Mom, how do you like the haircut?" Egg asked.

Mrs. Jones gave a thumbs up, then added quickly, "But I know T. J. feels pretty bad. He says he won't leave the house again until his hair grows back."

"Your mom is happy," Egg said to T. J. "That makes me happy. You should be happy. From now on, you have to get a haircut every month. That's a wonderful way to make us all happy."

Egg nodded but T. J. grimaced.

"Now then," Egg said, his face turning solemn, "I have something very important I need to explain to you: I need you to come back to church with me as soon as possible to make sure we win the Finals."

"Oh my God," T. J. said in mock horror. "Did you hear a single word I've said?"

The answer was no, as evidenced by Egg's immediate and urgent response: "You have to come to church. You must. Some of us have spent our whole lives and have dedicated everything we have to baseball and winning these three games. You must understand that this means every-thing to me and to everyone else in Cottage Park."

"Mom!" T. J. cried. There was nothing mock about the horror his face now communicated. "This is like a cult!"

Egg stared at T. J., unwittingly looking like the glassy-eyed, obsessively crazed devotee T. J. accused him of being.

"I am asking you," Egg continued fervently, "this one last time to—"

But T. J. interrupted Egg. "It's not 'this one last time.' Every day you ask me to do something for you this one last time. I trust you and do it for you. But then the next day, we start all over again. I'm sick of doing favors for everyone in this town."

In anticipation, T. J. mimicked the old man's voice and said, "T. J., this will be the one last time that I ask you . . ."

Egg was startled yet relieved that T. J. had guessed his very words. So he picked up where T. J.'s right-on impersonation had stopped.

". . . To come back to Holy Trinity Church and pray for victory. It's so important to the team and the town. Please. Right here in front of your mom, I'm telling you this *will* be the last time I'll ask you for anything."

Egg could see T. J. wasn't budging, so he took a deep, dramatic breath.

"The Finals are over on Saturday, and that's it for this old man." He took a long drink of his Coca-Cola. "I'm done with baseball after the Finals.

I could pretty easily be dead a week from now. How do you think that would make you feel?"

Egg paused and studied T. J.'s reaction. The last line was a winner.

"So let's get a move on," Egg said. "We need to get back to church to at least say a rosary or something. At the most it might take about twenty minutes of your time today."

T. J. sighed as he looked at his mother. She nodded.

"I can drive you two back to church," Mrs. Jones said.

"Then it's a deal," Egg said, clapping his hands and standing up from the couch. "I'll even take you two out for lunch at the Morning Sun afterward," Egg said.

As the three made their way outside to the car, Egg quickly added to T. J., "Part of the deal for the free breakfast is that you come back to Sunday Mass at least until I die." With that, Egg ducked into the car.

"Mom!" T. J. cried out again.

But T. J.'s mother had also already gotten into the car. When T. J. climbed inside, Egg continued to beseech him.

"Come on," Egg said. "I'll be eighty-five in March. I'll be dead and gone soon enough."

T. J. shook his head in disagreement. It was more likely that the old man would in fact kick dirt on T. J.'s coffin someday. He undoubtedly would be one of those people who could and would live forever, if for no other reason than to make T. J.'s life so wretched.

As they drove to the church, T. J. thought about Egg's insistence that he join Cottage Park in prayer. It wasn't such an unreasonable request. It wasn't like he never prayed. T. J. had asked for God's help twice in the last few weeks. In both cases, he came out of harrowing circumstances with a happy ending—that is, his continued life on earth. And he certainly wouldn't like to be remembered as the one kiss of death that derailed Cottage Park's quest for glory.

Besides, what harm could come from divine intervention in a successful conclusion to the Finals? What if God really answered his prayer?

— CHAPTER TWENTY-ONE —

Countdown to the Finals: 2 Days to Go

MONDAY MORNING AFTER PRACTICE, the old men treated T. J. to lunch at the Lipstick. They slid into the booth just as the church bells rang at noon to signify the Angelus and the beginning of lunch hour.

O'Connor would ultimately present the quartet with the bar's specialty, cheeseburger baskets with french fries, which the old men called potatoes. But the entire transaction was actually a detailed and painstakingly orchestrated negotiation.

It began with O'Connor presenting the menu and announcing that day's special—meat loaf with mash potatoes and green beans for $5.25. Next, the old men studied the menu as if they hadn't seen it before, even though they had pored over it once or twice a week for several years. They were hoping in vain that by some miracle one or more items had come down in price, making them cheaper than the least expensive entrée, the cheeseburger basket at $3.75. Getting the best deal meant everything.

Like every other merchant in town, O'Connor wished the old men would allow him to treat them at no cost. But he knew they'd be offended. Rather, he had to patiently answer their questions about the other items on the menu. Today, the old men were interested in the roast beef sandwich, the chicken tenderloin, and even the shrimp and steak tips combo, all completely out of their price range—luxury delicacies they believed they could never afford and didn't deserve.

But also like every other merchant in town, O'Connor had limited time to devote to this chase-and-hunt game. The old men were now approaching the five-minute mark. Other customers were waiting.

"How does the cheeseburger special look to you today?" O'Connor asked, as always. "I think I could throw in free Cokes."

O'Connor waited for the old men to make the next step; otherwise, the entire process would break down and restart again. He'd learned that the hard way.

"And what about some ice cream?" Egg asked. "Maybe a couple of scoops?"

Again, O'Connor waited. He had to pretend he was embarrassed he hadn't thought of the same thing.

"Makes sense to me," he said. "Sure."

Egg smiled. "Then I think we'll all have the cheeseburger special. With the drinks and ice cream thrown in." He handed O'Connor the menus. "And put the boy's meal on my bill."

O'Connor had barely walked away when the old men turned their focus on T. J. and their next negotiation.

"We have a job for you," Egg said. "Mowing and cleanup at the cemetery, plus running errands for us." Then Egg slipped and revealed the rationale for the open position. "We have to start pacing ourselves for the Finals."

The open admission was unheard of—never uttered before in public. The old men never spoke of how their advancing age and or declining health affected their lives. They never admitted their need to conserve their energy and invest that savings in good health. But today, this outward acknowledgement may have seeped from Egg because all three of the old men had come to trust T. J. and see him perhaps as one of them.

T. J. had been in Cottage Park long enough to know this was a special honor. He nodded and agreed to whatever it was the old men had just assigned him.

He completely gave up trying to say no to any of the old people in Cottage Park. Like everyone else in town, he was now doing his part, meeting his obligation to give the old men what they wanted and needed. Even in his frozen, present-tense stage of youth, T. J. suspected that at some time in the future, he would like to say he had done all he could to help the old men achieve their ultimate goal in life: winning the Finals.

That and he loved driving Ryan's car.

During their meal, the old men elaborated there was much to do before Wednesday's initial game of the Finals in Des Moines. They had a campaign of sorts planned at various stops around town. They explained that they would need T. J.'s assistance at every step along the way. If the men could remain healthy, then they sincerely believed that this year, like every year, would be the year they would finally win the Finals.

The town fire siren sounded at 1:00 p.m., ending the lunch hour. It was time to get to work.

The first stop on their campaign was Sunset Estates nursing home.

"Pull into that spot," Ryan said to T. J., pointing to an open parking space almost directly in front of the front door.

T. J. sucked in and held his breath until he angled and maneuvered the big Cadillac between two cars. Ryan motioned for T. J. to pull a lever that opened the trunk. When the trunk flipped open, Ryan ordered T. J. to retrieve a box and a grocery sack and follow the old men inside.

T. J. had never been inside a nursing home. His first reaction was, *Soap.* He smelled it everywhere: on walls, on the floor, even on people.

"Over here, boys," a woman called out to the quartet, curling her index finger over and over in a motion that expected obedience.

It was obvious that she had been expecting these visitors. She had articulated the word *boys* in such a way that it could not be confused as a term of endearment. She had chosen that exact word for its literal definition of a male child lacking in maturity and judgement.

The woman sat by herself at a round table. But in the lobby were a dozen other residents—nearly half the population of Sunset Estates. They grouped there every day, most of the day, waiting for someone or something to arrive. With a little prompting from staff, the residents recognized the coaches and delighted in seeing the young person accompanying them. They commented about their visitors in voices loud enough that even the visitors could clearly hear their every word.

They loved T. J.'s haircut. It was perfect. It was like their hairstyle when they were his age—and like their current style, for that matter. So different from the mops most young men wore across their heads nowadays, making them look like sheepdogs—or worse, young women. T. J. had never heard people discuss him in terms of being so handsome.

Using her eyes and the finger that still hooked and reeled the quartet, the woman sat them around her at her table. She was ninety-six-year-old Mary Agnes Connelly. She had been at Sunset Estates for a little over a year, having been placed there by her children when their father, a banker and the wealthiest person in Cottage Park, passed away.

In the days and weeks following their father's funeral, her loving children faced a predicament: how to care for their remaining parent. It was a predicament the children of elderly Cottage Park residents found themselves in all-too frequently. In this case, Mary Agnes was forced to choose between two options: One, she could move far away, often outside of Iowa, into the loving home of any one of her seven well-to-do children, all with children of their own. Or two, she could move right down the street to Sunset Estates. Mary Agnes chose the latter. She stayed behind in Cottage Park—or from her perspective, her children moved on to more exciting lives.

Her children, guilt ridden, informed the administration at Sunset Estates that their mother was to be allowed to do whatever she wanted and to be given whatever she needed toward that end. Money was not a factor. That was business as usual for Mary Agnes, who had pretty much gotten whatever she asked for all her life.

One of the things she requested was to bring her new friends from Sunset Estates along with her to events such as bingo night at the Lipstick, Sunday Mass at Holy Trinity, coffee and cookies at the Morning Sun, candy runs at Orlowski's Family Grocery, ice cream cones at Schmitt's Dairy Creme, and of course all the Holy Trinity baseball home games, to which she still wore a bright-red vinyl jacket declaring that she had been the designated medic since her own boys had played for the old men decades earlier.

While the other Sunset Estates residents exuded a pallor of gray and ivory, this woman displayed rich, full, professionally colored red hair cut short in a fashionable style. She wore a neon jungle-floral-patterned muumuu.

Without looking at him, Mary Agnes reached her hand out to T. J. She held his hand tightly and would continue to hold it with urgency, as if she had something unbelievably important to say to him, but first he must wait while she addressed equally important matters with the coaches.

At the moment, her entire attention was on Egg. She slid a brand-new black polo short-sleeve knit shirt across the table to him. She was as serious as a panther.

"You need to go try this on," Mary Agnes said sternly, her voice low and booming. Her fellow residents, even those with very poor hearing, could plainly hear her. "It's a baseball coach's shirt. You have to wear it when you go to Des Moines."

Egg looked warily at the shirt as he unfolded it. He liked his own shirts, specifically the red-plaid short-sleeved collared shirt he wore nearly every day. But Mary Agnes was correct. This was a baseball coach's shirt. It said so in white stitching over the right breast: "Coach Gallivan, Holy Trinity Baseball."

Mary Agnes took an almost perverse delight in watching Egg look at the shirt as he tried thinking of a reason why he couldn't or shouldn't wear it to the Finals. Finally, in solemn and meek desperation, Egg spoke quietly.

"I don't need—"

"Egg. Look at me," Mary Agnes interrupted.

Egg knew he couldn't withstand her long, fixed stare. So he continued to look at the shirt, as if his whole world of comfort and familiarity had collapsed into its knit pattern.

"Look . . . at . . . me," Mary Agnes said again louder, slower, and more deliberately.

There was a long pause. She was prepared to wait as long as it took. Time was on her side. Though she still hadn't looked at T. J., she pumped his hand a few times to remind him that he hadn't been forgotten and that she would get to him in a moment.

When Egg finally did look up, Mary Agnes lifted the palm of her free hand as if she were offering Egg a gift.

"I've already paid for that shirt and two others like it. You'll wear a clean shirt for each game. Now go along with Coach Murphy to my room and get into that shirt and the pair of pants I also bought for you. They're lying on the bed. Then march right back out here and show me how nice you look."

Murphy slowly stood from his chair and stepped behind Egg. He knew how useless it was to exert any energy toward changing Mary Agnes's mind. He gently patted Egg on the shoulder to remind him of this very fact. The two hit the road for Mary Agnes's room to prepare Egg for his runway show.

"And throw his old clothing in my hamper," Mary Agnes called out to Murphy. "I'll have it cleaned by the next time you boys are back here."

Now Mary Agnes turned her full attention to Ryan, whom she had loyally supported for over fifty years at Holy Trinity.

"What did you bring me?" she asked.

However, she knew exactly what Ryan had brought her—at their last meeting a week ago, she had written down a detailed list. The expectation was that Ryan, like everyone else in Cottage Park, would meet or exceed her request.

"Everything you asked for," Ryan said. "And a few other things I thought you should have."

Ryan slid the box from the trunk across the table, then stood alongside her. He removed the items one at a time and explained their features and value like a salesman.

"You asked for more hosts," Ryan said. "Here's two packages with one thousand each. Unconsecrated."

Ryan had always stopped by Sunset Estates at least once a week to deliver Communion to its Catholic residents. After a while, Mary Agnes demanded more hosts so she could give out daily Communion to the residence's Catholics. Mary Agnes had been a devotee of daily Mass for decades, so Ryan thought it a fair enough request. Plus, he knew she simply wouldn't take no for an answer. He was in essence making her an extraordinary minister, a layperson approved to distribute the Eucharist.

And extraordinary she was. Then two months ago, she started her own daily prayer service, modeled very closely after the Mass, for all of the residents. Residents and even staff met there in the lobby approximately forty minutes before supper. Mary Agnes followed the general order of the Mass, complete with a homily in which she practiced the Socratic method of asking questions to those in attendance. Sometimes the questions stemmed from her own bewilderment about the Liturgy of the Word and its meaning. Very often, the group started a discussion. They'd come to a consensus about the readings and how they could incorporate the newfound lessons into their current lives of hardship.

It didn't take long for residents and staff to look forward to the daily gathering. All were participating, Catholics and non-Catholics, the latter who often had better training in scriptural translation.

And so it made perfect sense to Mary Agnes that all should be able to receive Communion—the non-Catholic residents as well as their family members who had stopped by to visit. Mary Agnes even gave Communion to two staff members who attended Mass every Sunday at Holy Trinity but were prohibited from receiving the Eucharist: a man suspected to be involved in a gay relationship, and a divorced woman. Mary Agnes made this decision because the two staff members represented Jesus exceptionally well every day without fail. They patiently directed residents with slipping memory functioning and cleaned up after those who had accidents and incontinence.

Ryan himself had always been uncomfortable withholding the Eucharist from anyone invited to Mass. Ryan believed the Catholic Church could and should learn a lesson from the gracious manner in which Cottage Park families greeted guests to their homes. Food and drink were always shared with guests, who were referred to as "company." No one was more of a recipient of that hospitality than Ryan.

And in particular, that graciousness was most often and best offered by the women of Cottage Park. They had, in effect, mothered him for generations. How could it be so wrong, then, to have women provide the same love and care in the administration of the sacraments?

Besides, what harm could Mary Agnes's inclusive ministry do at Sunset Estates? How could anyone ever find out about her unique trailblazing ministry tucked away in a little nursing home in Cottage Park? Again, couldn't this be seen as a decidedly *extraordinary* ministry according to definition, though not according to church law?

While the prayer service was wildly popular with everyone at Sunset Estates, it earned a completely different sentiment from the bishop when he received a lengthy letter from a Lutheran family member of one of the residents. In her letter, the family member was quite enthusiastic. She complimented the bishop on his progressive thinking and encouraged him to replicate Mary Agnes's spiritual innovation, as it was an excellent model for promoting and accelerating Christian unity.

Hearing about the ecumenical heroics of Mary Agnes Connelly was the last straw. For several years, the bishop had heard stories about Mary Agnes and received countless letters directly from her. She often demanded, not asked, that the bishop would speak out on social justice issues and a more expansive role for women in the church. Sometimes her incessant beseeching was simply for him to come out to visit Cottage Park.

After being harangued and intimidated long enough by Mary Agnes, the bishop decided on a different tact. Although it was in direct contradiction of Jesus's parable of the persistent widow who nags a judge until he does justice for her, the bishop chose to ignore her. Eventually he avoided Cottage Park altogether. He would not look the other way, however, with a matter as severe as the misadministration of holy sacraments.

The moment he finished reading the letter, the same bishop ordered Ryan to a disciplinary meeting at 9:00 a.m. the next day. The three-hour drive to Sioux City meant Ryan would miss leading daily Mass. When Ryan voiced this concern, the bishop's secretary, a fellow priest, announced, "That should be the very least of your worries at this point."

At the meeting, the same secretary took dictation of the litany of Ryan's grave offenses, enumerated in rapid-fire succession by a seething bishop. The offenses included, but were not limited to, Ryan's support of practices that promoted general confusion regarding the following:

1. The sacrament of the Eucharist: "This is the real presence of Jesus, for God's sake!" the bishop cried out.

2. The sacrament of Holy Orders: "You've been ordained to bring the sacraments to your parishioners," the bishop continued. "We don't go for that nonsense about the people taking over this sacred responsibility— especially a daffy ninety-six-year-old woman!"

To Ryan's great relief, the bishop hadn't yet heard anything about Mary Agnes's practice (with Ryan's coaching) regarding the Anointing of the Sick.

"What were you possibly thinking?" the bishop asked as he ended his scolding. He threw up his hands in disgust and answered himself before Ryan could speak. "The answer is, you weren't thinking. You were *drinking*. Admit it. You're a boozer. And a loser."

The bishop angrily waved Ryan to the door. If he didn't stop at that point, he might say even more hurtful things.

"That's all, Father."

Ryan nodded and promptly exited the office. He hadn't said a word throughout the twenty-minute rant.

As he made his way back to his car, he pondered whether he could have uttered a single truthful word in his defense, had he been given the chance. There was no defense. Mary Agnes had, in effect, wore him down.

He gave her everything she needed in her quest to make the church responsive and relevant.

In the final analysis, Ryan was one man giving his all to do a good job. There needed to be fifty or one hundred more priests like him, even in (especially in) a community like Cottage Park, whose needs were many and everywhere. All their lives, Mary Agnes and her feminine peers had magnificently addressed the physical needs of their families and the community. The plain truth was that women really were in charge of families in Cottage Park. So it made common sense to Ryan that they could and should also address the spiritual needs of their families and community.

Ryan understood that the bishop had a job to do too. It was the bishop's responsibility to ensure that sacraments were administered in proper fashion. In addition, it was his responsibility to ensure that any individual delegated to administer those sacraments was also teaching the truth. A truth already revealed to and known by priests—not based on the whims of folks sitting around at a nursing home in Cottage Park for Mary Agnes's prayer service.

Most importantly, the bishop was indeed correct that Ryan was a boozer. No one, particularly Ryan himself, could ever deny that simple truth. As if to acknowledge and prove that truth, Ryan immediately drove to a nearby city park and guzzled directly from the plus-sized bottle of vodka in his backseat. He sucked from that jug of vodka like a backwoods hillbilly moonshiner until his hands stopped shaking and he could relax again.

But of all the bishop's accusations and hurtful words, the biggest assault, the harshest insult that stung the most, was that he was a loser. Ryan was so enraged because it may have been a reference to Cottage Park, particularly to Holy Trinity, which inexplicably lost the Finals each year. The school was often ridiculed as the state's most dependable losers.

Flawed as he was, neither Ryan nor his parishioners nor the townspeople were anything but winners in his determined yet now dizzied eyes.

He would show the bishop who was the loser.

Thus, Ryan stood right by Mary Agnes there in the Sunset Estates lobby as he continued to show her the items from the box: a cruet of holy chrism, a gold chalice, and finally a black satin stole, which he placed over her shoulders.

For the first time, Mary Agnes released her hold of T. J. so she could help Ryan adjust the vestment. She felt the white embroidered crosses and lowered her fingers further until she lost them in the white sash. She turned and modeled the stole to her fellow residents.

"If I'm already set to burn in hell for eternity," he said, "I guess I might as well go all the way."

"Go right ahead," Mary Agnes said. "I'm pretty certain I'll be there too to greet you."

Ryan solemnly placed his hands over Mary Agnes's head and announced the very words spoken to him at his ordination: "May the Lord who has given you the will to do these things give you the grace and the power to perform them."

"Amen," Mary Agnes responded.

Both Ryan and Mary Agnes looked at T. J. until he also said amen and blessed himself.

Everything in Ryan's priestly life told him that what he had done was gravely wrong. Yet a persistent rebellious voice—which he believed to be God, his conscience, or a harmony of both—also told him that the spiritual needs of those at Sunset Estates could best be met in this fashion. Since the beginning, this had been an extraordinary situation. God certainly gave Mary Agnes the will. Ryan merely gave her the grace and the power to go with it.

The Catholic Church had always held to the primacy of conscience, meaning that individuals must follow their consciences, even when it pushes back or lays out flat church doctrine. Granted, the bishop would never accept this line of reasoning. Ryan would surely deal with that confrontation at a later time. For now, Mary Agnes was happy and so was he.

"Keep up the good works," Ryan told her. "And don't let anyone try to intimidate or stop you. The bishop will try—"

Mary Agnes immediately cut short Ryan's warning with a dismissive backhand and a roll of her eyes.

"I can only hope I'm known by my enemies," she said. "And I'm proud to say that nitwit is my biggest one. If he ever shows his face anywhere near Cottage Park, I swear I'll give him a good kick in the bee-hind."

Ryan knew he had chosen a worthy successor, one he could be remembered by.

"Congratulations," he said. "Welcome to the priesthood. And now if you'll excuse me, I need to go say hello to a few people."

"Those are good boys," Mary Agnes said as she watched Ryan leave for the bedridden residents.

She held her hand up and out for T. J. to take it again. He did. Slowly she turned in her seat until she was giving him her full attention.

"I'm Mary Agnes Connolly," she formally introduced herself.

She held out her right hand to shake his. She now held both of his hands.

"I'm a Mulroney," T. J. answered.

By now, he was very familiar with Cottage Park's "last name first" convention whenever a youth was introduced to an elder. Because there were no Joneses in Cottage Park, T. J. identified himself with his mother's maiden name, as the Mulroneys were well known. If prompted, the next step in the introduction convention was to name his mother, her parents, and even her grandparents. In this case, though, Mary Agnes's primary business was knowing the business of all Cottage Park families, so that would be unnecessary.

"I know you," Mary Agnes said. "And I know all about you."

Now she would begin to lecture about her favorite subject: herself. This included her views on philosophy, theology, and current events in Cottage Park. She leaned forward so close that T. J. could smell the coffee on her breath and see tiny cookie crumbs around the edge of her lips.

"I'm ready to die, and I could go at any moment, so listen up." Seeing no reaction from T. J., she continued. "At your age, you never think about death. When you get to be ninety-six, you never stop thinking about death. I've lived my life. I'm ready for God to take me." Again, Mary Agnes studied T. J.'s face for a reaction and saw none.

As it turned out, the old men had taught him well over the summer. He had become adept at masking his reactions when conversing with the elderly in Cottage Park. He simply nodded empathetically to their daily news: meals, sickness, deaths, and updates on family.

While he played along, he focused on Mary Agnes's hand, light and airy, with skin as soft as the satin stole still draped around her shoulders. He felt no bones, no muscle. He held the hand for a moment, until the woman lowered it to her lap.

"I need to tell you the most interesting story," Mary Agnes said. She tightened her hold again until she gripped his hands. "When my husband died last year, I had a sundial especially made for my family. It sits exactly between our two graves. You'll see it when you go out to the cemetery today."

T. J. didn't know for sure he would be working at the cemetery, but Mary Agnes seemed to know with certainty.

"But that's not the interesting part. What's interesting is that the whole top of the sundial is covered with the names of my family: my husband and I, our children, our grandchildren, and nine great-grandchildren. All day long, the sun will shine on my family. And when the gnomon—that's the triangular blade—casts its shadow on a name, you should say a Hail Mary for that particular person. I even have the Hail Mary spelled out on the marker so people won't have the excuse that they don't know the words. You do know the Hail Mary, don't you?"

T. J. nodded with confidence—and with desperate hope that Mary Agnes wouldn't ask him to prove his declaration. She sensed his dishonesty, eyed him disparagingly, but continued regardless.

"You know, for thousands of years we measured time by numbers. I think we really need to measure time by our children—how they come to life, grow up, and move away." Mary Agnes sighed and took a deep breath. "Time is a gasp of breath that passes in and out of us, then passes right by us like the sun. There's not much we can do to stop it."

She paused a moment, then gave his hand another squeeze and brought him very close to her. He could see clearly into her mouth where several teeth were black with deep cavities.

"You make sure to always keep the area around that sundial clean and well kept. That's extremely important to me."

T. J. once again nodded. Again, he felt one of Cottage Park's ancient citizens placing a millstone around his neck that would grind him down—as well as ground him in this community forever. She hadn't bought his nod and was waiting for a stronger affirmation of his commitment to her life after death.

"I'll take good care of the sundial," T. J. said sincerely. "I promise." Then to quickly cover himself if she should someday come back as a ghost, he quickly added, "For as long as I live in Cottage Park."

Though she didn't smile, the tone of her voice lightened. "See? Isn't that the most interesting story you've ever heard?"

Mary Agnes didn't wait for an answer. She continued.

"That's why your friends here have such an unimaginable time giving up their baseball," Mary Agnes said, nodding her head to the places where Murphy, Egg, and Ryan had been a few minutes earlier. "Their baseball team never changes, at least not the positions. They always have someone to step in and fill a spot. And once the game starts, all time stops. There is no clock. If it has to, a game can go on forever. That's what those three are trying do—play this game forever."

Mary Agnes released her grip on T. J. after seeing Egg and Murphy approach. Egg was finally dressed in the new shirt and pants. She clapped enthusiastically and cheered, then asked those around her in the lobby to do the same.

"Well, everything fits," Egg said glumly. He carried two other new shirts and pairs of pants.

"And you're so good-looking," Mary Agnes said happily. "Turn around and let me see the back."

As Egg promenaded back and forth at Mary Agnes's request, she oohed and aahed with excitement.

"Now take a bow," she ordered.

Without thinking, Egg complied.

Mary Agnes beamed. "I think you boys look good enough to win your Finals this year!"

The quartet eventually said their farewells to the residents at Sunset Estates. T. J. maneuvered the car from the parking lot out to the blacktop road that led to the cemetery.

The men were completely silent, as they always were after their weekly session with Mary Agnes. The woman so completely confounded them that they now sat back and luxuriated in blessed silence, giving complete autonomy to the fourteen-year-old driver.

T. J. was the first and only person to see a freight train racing toward the unmarked crossing ahead. He carefully stopped the car several feet from the crossing, then shifted into park. The wheels of the freight clicked out a lively cadence over the rail joints. It was a long train.

"Go ahead and turn off the engine," Ryan instructed.

With the silence broken, Ryan had an opening to get down to business—the business of getting T. J. back to church.

"I see your mother every Sunday at Mass," Ryan said. "Is there a reason you're not coming with her?"

"I used to go," T. J. said. "Egg's making me start back up again."

T. J. then mumbled something the others couldn't quite hear—something about how happy he was to be making everyone else happy.

"Excellent," Ryan said. He glanced in the rearview mirror at Murphy and Egg. "Well, I guess we earned our angel wings today."

The trio waited another minute before the caboose passed by. Egg and Ryan simultaneously gave the okay to precede across the tracks. T. J. waited a few more moments until he was sure the clicking and the rumbling were memories, then started the car and wobbled over the tracks to the other side.

Egg reminded him to turn onto the gravel road that led up a small wooded hill, the highest point in Kossuth County. Then they drove through a silver cast-iron gateway announcing "Resurrection."

Before them were leveled rows of tombstones, most glossy, polished marble. There were also rust- and charcoal-colored stones with squat, flat faces engraved with the family names of Cottage Park. As T. J. drove farther down the path—which consisted of two crushed-rock tracks separated by brown grass—some of the grass and weeds brushed against the bottom of the car.

There were more tombstones. A few, once tall and white, now leaned one way or another as if they might topple to the ground. Dry green moss grew like sores and bruises over some of the tombstones. On closer inspection, some tombstone's dates could be read—or at least felt. Some of the names had entirely worn away, forgotten forever unless Ryan retrieved the ancient cemetery directory.

Ryan directed T. J. to drive off the path onto the grass, then behind a row of pine trees that caught and whispered the wind. T. J. parked the car there.

Inside the shed was a riding lawn mower. Ryan started it up and backed it out.

"You ever driven one of these?" Ryan yelled at T. J. over the sound of the motor.

T. J. shook his head.

"It's simple," Ryan said.

He got up and motioned for T. J. to take the wheel. Ryan pointed to the shifting gear.

"Go ahead and set it into drive. Now slowly press down on the accelerator."

T. J. put his foot down, and the mower lurched straight toward a headstone before T. J. steered it away and remembered to take his foot off of the pedal.

"You've got it," Ryan said. "Keep going now."

T. J. smiled, waved, and drove the mower away from the old men. Both Ryan and Egg followed behind for a few steps until they felt T. J. had mastered control. Finally, they stopped and watched T. J. maneuver around each tombstone.

Egg discovered a needy tombstone and used his pocketknife to slice long green vines from its body. He then scraped the knife against the dull surface to remove more dirt and moss.

Ryan returned to the shed, which also housed a push mower, for the spaces between stones that were too narrow for the larger mower to pass through. Despite several attempts, he wasn't able to pull its starter rope forcefully enough. Feeling a stinging sensation in his chest, he decided it was better to leave the gas-choked air of the shed for the grass-scented air outside.

"Let T. J. start that mower," Egg said, not looking up from the tombstone. "At our age, we're asking for a stroke or heart attack doing this stuff."

Ryan loosened his shirt from his pants and fanned the shirt against his chest, slowing the perspiration. Two butterflies—one white, the other yellow—jittered over a dandelion that had turned to puff.

"Somebody has to start it," Ryan said. He picked the dandelion out by the roots.

"T. J. is good enough for now," Egg said. "The work is good for him."

Egg closed his pocketknife and put it in his pocket. He then straightened his legs, pushing the rest of his body up his legs and hips until he stood straight.

"Let's go see Rose."

Ryan followed Egg across the plots and green aisles, their steps flushing out brown moths and grasshoppers with black-caped wings. They flittered and raced for new cover.

One tall polished marble stone was engraved with the name Rose Gallivan. Underneath her name were her dates of birth and death. Alongside her name was Egg's name spelled in full. Under that, was his date of birth, a dash, then smooth marble waiting to be engraved.

Both men knelt, blessed themselves, and bowed in prayer. The riding lawnmower droned at the other end of the cemetery. Closer to them, a crow screamed an angry but toothless warning to two smaller birds that ushered it from their territory. Both men blessed themselves again and stood.

"I've got one more thing to do, then I'll be okay to join her—then they can put a date on the end of that dash," Egg said.

He turned away, waving for T. J. to come over and see his name engraved in the tombstone.

— CHAPTER TWENTY-TWO —

Day 1 of the Finals

S TILL IN HIS BATHROBE, MURPHY TURNED UP the volume on his kitchen clock radio to hear the weather forecast. It was six o'clock in the morning—still ninety minutes from when he would meet Egg and Ryan at Mass.

Murphy hunched over a glass of water and two pills Katherine had set in front of him for his heart condition. He had slept fitfully, often getting out of bed to shoo away bad memories and gloomy omens of the Finals, which would begin at 5:00 p.m.

For the first time that summer, Murphy concluded that Wilson had been correct all along and so had Katherine—he was too old to be coaching this team. He now fully agreed with Katherine that he indeed was a silly old man playing a boys' game. What had he been thinking? Why did he think the results of this trip to the Finals would be any different from the past trips? And what good did these stupid pills do, anyway?

When Katherine stood up to return to their bedroom and turn off their alarm clock, Murphy darted to the back door with the pills. He checked to make sure Katherine could not see him as he stepped outside, wound up in the same fashion he had taught Moriarity over the years, and threw the pills across the yard. They landed on his garage roof and rolled into the gutter.

He returned to his spot at the table and drained the entire glass of water as Katherine returned. She praised him for taking his pills and hydrating for the day ahead.

As he wiped a napkin over his mouth, he listened intently to the radio.

"Increasing chance of precipitation beginning later tonight," he said, mimicking the announcer from WHO Radio in Des Moines. He stretched his hands out as if to beg. "What does that mean? That forecast doesn't tell me anything. I need to know exactly where and when it will rain."

"It means you have to be prepared for rain," Katherine said. "Take your extra jacket in case you get chilled." Katherine cleared the last of the dishes from the table, then rejoined Murphy. "How long will it take you to get to Des Moines?"

"Two and a half hours," Murphy said. "Iowa City West has about half that far to drive. Heck, they might have stayed the night in Des Moines. Maybe we should have done the same."

"Well, it's not worth getting upset over now," Katherine said. "There isn't one thing you can do about it." She patted his hand. "Or the umpiring."

"I hope they're not from Des Moines," Murphy said. "I don't trust those guys."

"You always believe everyone is out to get you."

"I dread leaving anything to chance or to hometown umps. I've seen too much, coaching as long as I have. If we're not ahead by the fifth inning, and it starts sprinkling . . ."

"Then he can call the game, and they don't have to make it up," Katherine finished.

"Which is fair with me," Murphy said. "But if West is ahead and it's sprinkling, they can connive an umpire into calling it a downpour. I've seen umpires buckle under—especially if they're homers. That way, they can get rid of the little Catholic school from the little town with the crazy old coaches." Murphy scratched his nose. "We've been in a drought for the last month. Why rain tonight?" He sighed. "Sometimes I think if I bought a pumpkin farm they'd cancel Halloween."

"If it's going to rain," Katherine said, "you'll have to make sure you get an early lead."

"I always teach that," Murphy said. "But it takes time to loosen up after a long bus ride. That's part of the politics too—us having to travel so far. They seem to get us about any way possible."

Murphy made his way from the kitchen. A few minutes later, he came out dressed in his Holy Trinity uniform.

"Where's my coat?" Murphy said curtly.

Katherine shuffled over to the closet and slipped two coats from their hangers.

"You shouldn't leave this early," Katherine said anxiously. "Mass doesn't start for at least another hour."

She stared at her husband. He was in one of his moods, moods that were especially prevalent before big games. This was a particularly bad mood. There would be no convincing him of anything at this point.

She helped him into the first jacket, a black Holy Trinity windbreaker and even snapped the buttons together for him. At the door, she handed him the second jacket, heavy and woolen. She kissed him and held his hands.

"One more thing, Al . . . the young man who's coaching next year might be at this game."

"And?" Murphy said with growing exasperation.

"Why don't you let him help you out?" Katherine said. "Do it for me. I'm sure he could help."

Murphy stepped outside and looked back through the screen door. "I told Wilson," he said, "and now I'll tell you: that would be a slap in the faces of my coaches. What's worse, he might ruin everything we've planned."

Katherine opened the door. "You always told me you wouldn't be a selfish old man and muddle up everything for whoever came after you."

Murphy waved her off and began to move away to the door. "That's next year," he growled. "I have to finish this season my way."

He stopped and looked back at his wife. He saw the hurt on her face.

"I'll think about it. But not until we win this game tonight—*if* we win. Thinking ahead like that is the surest way to lose."

Katherine called out that she loved him. Murphy responded by waving good-bye and grumbling something about loving her as he turned and walked away.

Katherine watched Murphy make his way down the street toward Holy Trinity Church. She was sure he wouldn't return home until much later that night, but still, she locked the door. She never locked the door, not in Cottage Park. But she had never hidden anything of this importance from her husband before. She couldn't risk his surprise reentry.

Katherine's heart raced as she knelt down at a kitchen cupboard. If Murphy had been listening, even a block away, he might have heard the clanging of pots and pans. She reached for the item she had hidden there the day before and now longed to read in great detail. It was the "Special

Finals Baseball Edition" of the *Cottage Park Chronicle*. With newspaper in hand, she slowly leaned and maneuvered herself against the cabinets until she stood back up. She took her seat at the kitchen table.

Mr. Burnette, circulation manager, had given Wilson several early copies of the paper. Wilson then surreptitiously contacted Katherine and made arrangements for her to pick up her copy by checking her mailbox at a designated time. At this moment, Katherine was one of three people with knowledge of the edition.

But soon, the cat and the newspaper would be out of the bag. The newspaper would be delivered to each and every home in Cottage Park— even to those with no subscription and those delinquent on their current subscription. This edition was of critical importance to every resident of Cottage Park. And as a newspaper was delivered to the grateful hands of each adult resident of Cottage Park, special instructions were painstakingly imparted: *do not share any of this content with the old men.* They were already grouchy, and this tribute might send them over the edge.

For once, Mr. Burnette had actually made a generous profit on his work. The advertising revenue generated for this Finals edition was greater than the revenue from any previous issue of the *Chronicle*. And he knew the edition would bring the community, with its emigrants and wayfarers, together, like the previous special edition covering damage from a tornado that swept through town fifteen years earlier.

Katherine spread the newspaper out in front of her. The front-page banner read: *Good Luck, Holy Trinity, at the 1974 Finals!* Underneath the headline was the same horrid picture that graced the posters downtown. The coaches and players looked so serious. Not one smile or even a hint of enjoyment. She asked herself the question that always came to mind whenever she looked at a Holy Trinity baseball team photograph: How could anyone on that team be having any fun?

The front page also featured tournament brackets and a full schedule with scores from their undefeated season. A large sidebar entitled "Season Scorecard" displayed batting averages, home runs, runs batted in, stolen bases, pitching wins, and earned run averages.

Katherine turned next to a two-page spread with player photos and names. Mr. Burnette had been forced, as he had every year, to use the boys' school photos. The old men refused to allow individual photographs of players in their Holy Trinity uniforms. That violated the old men's strict creed of baseball being a team sport. Any singling out of players in any shape or form could bring ruin to this time-honored philosophy. Likewise, there were no individual photographs of the coaches, who would have been perfectly content to coach anonymously and have their personal information managed in a witness-protection program. T. J. too was missing out on a photo. He too would be perfectly happy with this omission.

Pages four and five showcased a collage of action photos from the summer season. Each player had been captured in some exciting way: tagging a player in a rundown, beating out a throw to first, sliding in to home, or preparing to swing at a ball. There were also pictures of the fans and players' families cheering in the stands or selling Holy Trinity T-shirts, sweatshirts, hats, and stocking caps.

Arranged around the photos was a baseball adaptation of Aunt B's popular "Blotter." It stated that the nine starters had each been arrested for a baseball-related offense: stealing home plate, beating out a throw, hitting and running, taking a pitch, littering the field, and so on.

Katherine knew the three old men would be disgusted by the showy tribute. She could hear them: in no way should a team receive adulation, unless they won the Finals. And even then, stick to the facts—no gooey sentimental stuff.

Pages six and seven provided stories and pictures of Cottage Park championship baseball teams from both Holy Trinity and the American Legion. The photos dated to 1936, one year after the old men joined the baseball program. All the photos shared the same common composition: the old men, grim faced, overseeing equally joyless players surrounding a large trophy.

There were so many spring and fall championships and near-summer championships. So many player awards, not to mention two players from Cottage Park who had gone on to play in the big leagues. It was easy to forget that Cottage Park was another small Iowa town of over seven hundred residents.

Yet Katherine noted that the overall tenor of the spread was not pride and joy. Regrettably, it had the somber aura of an obituary. The photos showed the faces of once-youthful players now dead or, like their coaches, slowly dying one way or another.

And then Katherine turned to pages eight and nine. For the coaches, this spread would have made them even more acrimonious than had the spreads that came before it. It wasn't acrimony but an entirely different wave of emotion that overtook Katherine that morning. There before her was a marquee headline stretching across the top of both pages: *Good-bye, Coaches! Thanks for the Memories . . .*

The personal and professional lives of the three old men were laid out in pictures. It started, of course, when they began working with each other shortly after the Depression and then created the Holy Trinity baseball program. Their stories were told almost entirely through their devotion to their God, their devotion to their families (First Communion, Confirmation, and weddings served as Ryan's "family" photos), and finally their devotion to their Holy Trinity School, especially the baseball team.

After nearly an hour of poring through the articles and pictures, Katherine reached the back page. It was divided into three sections: a thank-you to the local merchants who had funded the special edition, a story and picture welcoming new head coach Don Cooper, and finally a large picture of the Sioux City Diocese bishop, outfitted in a summertime Mass cassock with cincture, biretta, and a pom. Under the photo, it stated: *The Most Reverend Gerald Schramn congratulates Father John Ryan for over five decades of service to Holy Trinity Parish and Cottage Park. I wish you continued success in your new assignment at Sheltering Arms Catholic Retirement Community in Sioux City, beginning August 24.*

Any and every part of the special edition would have upset the old men, but this very last picture of the bishop would have unhinged them, particularly Egg. Unbeknownst to Egg or anyone else in Cottage Park, the bishop had more than suggested that Ryan move to a Catholic retirement community in Sioux City. Ryan had been ordered to move and ordered to communicate with his parishioners about the move, which was scheduled for the last week in August. Ryan intended to share the news as soon as the Finals ended. The bishop, on the other hand, demanded the information be posted immediately. Wilson had informed him that the "Special Finals Baseball Edition" would be an ideal manner to reach everyone in Cottage Park at the same time.

Though it was not stated there in the paper, Katherine had heard from Wilson that when Ryan retired there would be no replacement for him.

Holy Trinity would be consolidated, with coverage from a priest (another man near retirement age) currently assigned to another local church.

Life without Ryan . . . Or for that matter, life without any of the old men . . . Katherine mulled over those ominous scenarios and considered all the ramifications it would have on Holy Trinity and Cottage Park. For some time, the possibilities had been playing out in the back of her mind. But with the bishop's official announcement of Ryan's departure, those thoughts now raced to the forefront, obscuring nearly all other rationales and considerations. The upcoming reality was extremely worrisome.

However, she reminded herself, Ryan and the other old men were still alive at the moment—though precariously, which was even more worrisome.

As usual, she would break down that worry all day long by offering up to God the following: prayer, menial tasks like cleaning around the house, and a shopping visit to Orlowski's Family Grocery. On Wednesdays between 7:00 and 9:30 a.m., coffee, donut holes, and conversation were free for patrons over seventy. In addition to life-sustaining conversation with her friends, she would also pick up a roast, carrots, and potatoes to prepare a late-night meal for the triumphant return of her husband.

Moriarity was also up earlier than usual that day. He was the newspaper deliverer for the *Chronicle* and planned to deliver his 168 papers before the bus departed for Des Moines. Besides, rain was coming. The farmers were calling it a billion-dollar rain because it was coming at the right time for the corn and soybeans. The rain would ensure another successful money-making crop.

Moriarity was up and ready to go when the papers were dropped off at his house along with a stern admonition from Mr. Burnette, the circulation manager, that the old men were not to see any article in this "Special Finals Baseball Edition" until *after* the Finals.

At the end of his route, Moriarity had an additional five papers, which he stuck into his duffel bag. Once the team was en route on the 157-mile-long bus ride to Des Moines, he snuck the paper out for discrete reading.

Normally averse to the written word, Moriarity could not divert his eyes or attention from this special edition. He had never seen anything like it. There before him were his heroes and many he hadn't been aware were heroes: grandfathers, fathers (his dad in particular), professional ball players, neighbors. Even Mr. Burnette. Almost all the men of Cottage Park stared back at him from pictures of glory and achievement.

Those stares were filled with sober expectations for those who would wear the Holy Trinity baseball uniform after them. It was a blunt message and very to the point: in Cottage Park, you win. You have to win the last game, because that's the game you'll remember, the game you'll take home, the game you'll live with for the rest of your life. That message was frozen now and forever in the stern expressions of each team picture.

Moriarity shared his copy with Powers, his seat mate. The other four papers had been distributed to eager teammates assembling in the back of the bus, where the seniors ruled. There they unfolded and turned pages with the same care and awe as if they were studying a very rare copy of *Playboy* that had been smuggled into Cottage Park.

The faded-yellow Holy Trinity school bus traveled 169 South toward Des Moines, passing through towns with baseball teams that Holy Trinity had defeated this summer: Algona, Humboldt, Fort Dodge. Then they headed east on Highway 20 through Webster City.

East of Webster City, on the ramp leading to Interstate 35, the breakdown started. It wasn't the bus that the old men had proactively refurbished to avoid such a calamity. It was Murphy. With him right there behind the wheel, another spell was coming on.

Murphy slowly angled the bus off the road until all but the left front tire remained on the ramp. When the bus came to a complete stop, Murphy slammed the gear into park, yanked the lever that opened the bus door, and slouched over with his head bowed nearly all the way to his knees.

The seniors had vacated their seats and gathered with the old men and T. J. in the very front of the bus. They watched for the other old men to do something.

Egg and Ryan were doing something. They were waiting. They had become accustomed to Murphy's spells, which they referred to as "catching his breath."

However, after a few minutes of silence and unrequited anticipation, even Ryan became concerned. Standing at the front of the bus alongside Murphy, who still slumped over with head bowed low, Ryan cleared his throat to make an announcement.

"We're taking a brief break," Ryan said. "This is a great time to use the facilities." Ryan pointed to the nearby cornfield beyond the gentle ditch. "I shouldn't have to remind you to pee on the ground and not the corn."

With that, Ryan waved the team off the bus and toward the cornfield. Everyone cleared the bus, including Ryan and Egg, who never made it anywhere near the cornfield, choosing instead to water the left rear tire.

The coaches and players came back feeling more relaxed, rejuvenated, and ready to continue the last leg of their journey. Everyone except Murphy, who remained doubled over the steering wheel. He eventually sat himself up straight but still hadn't said anything to anyone. After using the long flat mirror above his dashboard to count off everyone, he slowly closed the door, restarted the bus, shifted into drive, and barreled down the ramp onto I-35 South to Des Moines.

As long as the boys had known Murphy, he had never looked well. He never had any kind of healthy color or exhibited any kind of energy that indicated good health. But now, the five seniors hunched forward in their seats to study the pallid, frail man whose hands barely grasped the steering wheel. Now they yearned for Murphy to be as he had been before—or at least to be a version of himself where his life wasn't seeping away right before their eyes.

Still the bus traveled on at a steady fifty-five miles per hour, occasionally veering too far left into the passing lane, sometimes veering too far right onto the gravel shoulder. Sometimes Murphy's head bobbed, then he'd catch himself immediately. Sometimes he'd crank open his window and let life-giving oxygen either awaken or resuscitate him.

The closer the bus got to Des Moines, the more erratic Murphy's driving became and the more certain the seniors were that they would never reach their destination, at least not with Murphy behind the wheel.

In addition to baseball, the old men had taught the seniors the art of communicating without saying a single word. For the past hour, while watching Murphy, they had also been watching each other. From Spider to McKenna to Jack to Anthony to Orlowski, they communicated disquieting thoughts instantaneously—thoughts they never could have verbalized, not even with the assistance of alcohol or marijuana at the quarry. These thoughts translated into messages of doubt, fear, and eventually certainty that Murphy was dying before their very eyes. And every bit as vexing, they knew that Egg and Ryan would not be of any help.

For the first time in their lives, they had to be responsible for the old men. And if they didn't take that responsibility soon, Murphy would take them along on his journey to death or at least a long stay in a hospital.

With nods, the seniors communicated that it was time to act. Each would have a role. They made their way up front.

Orlowski stood and took two steps over to Murphy. He genuflected to begin the bloodless revolution.

"Coach," Orlowski said.

Murphy didn't respond, seemingly in a self-imposed cruise control destined to reach Sec Taylor Stadium no matter what.

Orlowski gently nudged Murphy. "Coach, pull over up there—at the exit."

Though he didn't say anything, Murphy did comply. He maneuvered the bus onto the ramp, stopping midway before reaching the road that led to Ankeny, about fifteen miles north of Des Moines.

Murphy set the bus in park, turned off the ignition, and reached to open the bus door. The handle slipped from his fingers. The door partially opened, then immediately snapped shut. He reached back for the emergency signal but instead slumped over the wheel and stayed there as if hung on a rack.

Orlowski gently helped Murphy off the steering wheel and into his arms and Anthony's, who then shuffled him into the front row seat. Immediately, Spider leaned forward and held Murphy upright, with his back against the window.

Jack raced to the back of the bus, ordering all to open their windows and be still. He motioned for Powers to step up next. The team had afforded him physician's status because he had passed both a CPR and an American Red Cross lifeguard training class.

Powers raced to the front of the bus and nearly sprang onto Murphy, kneeling before him. Placing two fingers on Murphy's wrist, Powers searched in vain for the artery and then a pulse. He asked Egg to silently count off thirty seconds on his watch. Over and over again he repeated the request, and Egg dutifully complied.

No one liked the look on Powers's face. He was not finding any pulse, and when he finally did, it was fast and irregular. He was even more concerned that Murphy's fingers were cold. Shortly before his great-grandmother had died, he had held her hand. Her fingers were also cold—an indicator that the heart was not pumping blood out to the extremities.

From this boiled-down checkup, Powers could be certain of one thing: his patient needed medical attention—real medical attention—urgently. But he knew Murphy well enough to not dare suggest it.

Sensing desperation in the boys around him, and believing for the first time in a long time that that desperation was warranted, Murphy prepared himself to speak what might have been his last words.

"Get Moriarity up here!" he cried out.

Powers held a water bottle to Murphy, who placed his lips on the extension tube and Powers squeezed water into his mouth, and Murphy gulped it down. In an instant, Moriarity appeared, his face frozen with worry.

Seeing his pitcher, catcher, and both assistant coaches surrounding him, Murphy spoke boldly, jabbing a finger at Moriarity for emphasis.

"I've got you for sixteen innings for the Finals. I figure we'll throw you five of those innings tonight—if we're lucky and can play that long. My arthritis is acting up so bad, I know rain is coming." Murphy stopped and groaned as he inhaled. "If we win tonight, we'll throw Anthony on Friday and have you again for the Final."

Still detailing the strategy for winning the Finals to Moriarity, his eyes focused powerfully for the first time that day as he moved on to the game plan for that night.

"Listen carefully. You have to move the game along tonight. Only strikes. Three up and three down. And no thirty seconds to shake Powers off between pitches. Our opponent tonight is not Iowa City West but Mother Nature. We have to get to the fifth inning before she arrives. She's coming fast. We have to be faster."

"I promise," Moriarity said. "I won't let you down," he added confidently as the pitcher with the most potential in Iowa high school baseball—and knowing it. "But Coach, we have to get you to a hospital now."

"We're not wasting time at a hospital!" Murphy hissed.

He looked at his watch. It had stopped at noon.

"Goddamn time!" he roared.

He unhooked the watch and flailed it across the leather cushion of the seat rail in front of them. It cracked the face rather than shattered it as he had hoped, so he stopped after two swings.

"What time do you have?" he asked Egg.

"Ten after four," Egg said.

Moriarity snatched Murphy's watch before the old man could resume beating it. Moriarity wound its stem several times, then set the watch to the correct time and handed it back to Murphy. Murphy looked at it and fastened it with the face pointing down on his left wrist, as he always wore it. He studied the watch. Now it seemed the second hand spun faster than usual.

"We've got to get to Sec Taylor and fast," Murphy said.

Although severely compromised, he was still crafty enough to realize that he had to redirect everyone's attention, or they would continue with their hospital hysteria.

"They'll forfeit us out of the Finals if we're even a minute late after 5:00. Don't any of you doubt it for a second."

Murphy was also aware enough to recognize that he could not drive the bus to Sec Taylor Stadium or home later that night. God forbid, maybe he'd never get behind the wheel for the rest of his life.

"Father, would you please drive us the rest of the way into Des Moines?"

Ryan immediately stood up, but stopped in his tracks at the sound of involuntary and frantic groans.

The boys knew that even Murphy—who lay dying, propped up by Spider—could deliver them more safely and on time than Ryan. Worse, Ryan's slow-poke road-hog driving style would create the biggest traffic jam Des Moines had ever seen and embarrass Cottage Park forever.

"I could drive," McKenna said, speaking up for the first time that afternoon. "I just got my commercial license," he continued, lying, "so I can drive a school bus in the fall."

Seeing doubt in Ryan's eyes and knowing the team was counting on him, McKenna added six words he knew would sway Ryan: "My family needs the extra money."

Ryan still didn't quite believe McKenna. He would surely ask him to examine his conscience for this falsehood next time McKenna appeared in his confessional. And he still didn't understand the commotion when he tried to get behind the steering wheel.

But whatever the boys had planned would have to do. Ryan's primary responsibility now was to prepare Murphy for a good death, a holy death, by administering the sacrament of the sick.

"Go ahead," Ryan said to McKenna.

The boy raised his hands for everyone to sit down and be still again. It was unusual for McKenna to speak at all, let alone make a public presentation. His teammates listened carefully.

"Please sit down and be quiet," McKenna said devoutly. "Father Ryan will be administering last rites. I ask that you use this time to pray for the full return of Coach Murphy's health today and throughout the Finals."

"Amen," several of the players responded sporadically.

McKenna situated himself in the driver's seat. He checked all the mirrors, clicked his seat belt, set the bus into drive, and drove up and over the road leading to Ankeny. He noticed, but did not follow, the sign pointing to the Iowa Medical Clinic less than two miles away. Soon he successfully merged the bus back onto I-35 South.

Egg had bit his tongue long enough. Once the bus was speeding down the interstate, he decided to vent a summer's worth of rage against Moriarity and his stupid hair. Moriarity was the only player who hadn't been victimized by McCarthy.

"You listen to me, Moriarity—"

However, Ryan cut him off as soon as he heard those words. "Please— let's have a moment of silence and respect for the sacrament."

Saving Murphy's soul and perhaps even his life would require complete reverence from all on the bus. They would be pleading—demanding—that God give Murphy the strength to continue to lead Holy Trinity through their trials and tribulations and any other agony in the garden they might experience in Des Moines.

Ryan tried his best to remember words and phrases from the ancient sacrament, which traced its roots to the time when Jesus sent his disciples to preach, cast out devils, and anoint those who were sick.

As Ryan began, Murphy received what he needed more than anything to heal: the grace of sleep.

— CHAPTER TWENTY-THREE —

Day 1 of the Finals

As Murphy had predicted, the game was called because of
rain after five innings. Holy Trinity had secured the lead in time,
earning the win. And Moriarity had pitched exactly as Murphy had
hoped—one strike after another, barely even stopping to catch his breath.

It was still raining heavily when the Holy Trinity bus returned to
Cottage Park three hours later, at nearly 11:00 p.m. McKenna didn't mind
driving the slippery, sometimes blinding route back home. He welcomed
the rain. It ended the heat and humidity that had clung to Cottage Park for
the last three weeks. More importantly, each drop of rain meant money
and prosperity for farmers like himself and those who supported the farmers. In Cottage Park, that was nearly everyone.

Headlights blinked and car horns sounded as the bus turned into the
Holy Trinity parking lot. Inside the bus, the players stood and cheered. A
few waved out open windows through the rain.

Murphy stood up, turned around, and motioned for his players to settle back down. The players immediately slapped the windows shut and took
their seats.

"Practice tomorrow at three," Murphy said. "If it's too wet, we'll use
the gym."

He was back to his old self—all business. The victory over Iowa City West
had miraculously, or at least temporarily, cured his multitude of ailments.

"You all need to get some sleep, so go straight home and get to bed."

The players cheered again. Murphy, Ryan, Egg, and T. J. congratulated
each player as the team filed off the bus.

Orlowski and Anthony were the first to exit. In front of blinking headlights and honking horns, they each stabbed fingers into the rain to indicate

who was the number-one team in Iowa. Then they quickly sidestepped and jumped across puddles on their way to Orlowski's car.

Suddenly a car abruptly stopped in front of them, scorching them in light and frightening them with one sharp blast of its horn. Anthony used his hand like a visor to see through the light.

"My dad," Anthony said grimly.

His father, alone in the car, rolled down the window.

"I thought I told you Orlowski would give me a ride home tonight," Anthony said.

"No." His voice was cold. "Not tonight." Mr. Civilla rolled up the window and waited.

"I'll see you tomorrow at practice," Anthony told Orlowski as he got into the car.

The coaches and T. J. waited in Ryan's car and watched as the players headed to their own cars or matched up with their rides. Jeff gave the coaches a light wave as he got into Jack's car and Moriarity clambered into the back seat.

When the parking lot was completely empty ten minutes later, the Deville drove out and down the street. Nearly a block away from the parking lot, Murphy was the first to see his star pitcher on the side of the road. Moriarity stood with his arms out and cupped upward, his glove between tight knees, his head back, and his mouth wide open.

"Stop the car," Murphy said.

As Ryan steered over near Moriarity, Murphy rolled down his window.

"What in God's name are you doing out here?" Murphy barked.

Moriarity dropped his palms and rubbed them across his uniform. "Catching rain, Coach."

"Honest to God!" Murphy snarled between gritted teeth. Then, more loudly: "Get over here and get in the car!" He shook his head and rubbed his eyes in exasperation.

Ryan turned to T. J. "That's how you catch a cold," he said.

"And how you catch hell," Egg said.

Sensing another verbal and perhaps even physical attack, Moriarity edged around the car, using T. J. as a buffer between him and Egg. T. J. scooted across the seat as far as he could go, pressing into Egg, as Moriarity angled his long legs inside the car.

Ryan drove off, splashing water along the bottom and up the sides of his car. They drove in silence until Murphy turned around and looked at Moriarity.

"I thought you went with the Burnettes," Murphy said.

"Yeah," Moriarity said. "But I asked them to pull over and let me out. I had to feel the rain tonight. It's a magic night. I want it to last forever."

Moriarity huffed a fog canvas on the car window and happily drew a smiley face with his pointer finger that perfectly matched his current emotion.

In the Civilla family car, no words were spoken. The silence was broken by windshield wipers whining and slapping across the glass. When the car stopped in front of the garage, Anthony got out, lifted the door, and watched his father steer into the garage. At the door to the house, both men hesitated until Anthony reached around his father and held the door for him. He followed his father into the kitchen.

Anthony hadn't eaten anything since breakfast; he was famished. He first grabbed a tall glass and filled it with milk. He gulped half its contents, then refilled the glass. With the refrigerator door open, he next filled his arms with ketchup, mustard, relish, mayonnaise, cold cuts, lettuce, and green onions. He set it all on the table, then returned to the cupboard to grab a loaf of bread.

Mr. Civilla crept down the hall to close the door to the bedroom where his wife lay sleeping.

When Anthony turned around, swinging the bread at his side like a billy club, his father was blocking the path to the table.

Anthony stopped and tried to step around him, but Mr. Civilla held his arm out and forced it against his son's chest.

Anthony stepped back. He couldn't continue to the table to prepare his meal. Even a retreating exit to his bedroom had now been blocked off. His options were to stand his ground or to step toward the back door—to leave the house.

He quickly recounted the number of days (three) and even the hours (seventy-two) until his baseball life would be over. Surely he could placate his father one more time.

"Dad, come on. We won tonight. We'll win Friday. We'll win it all on Saturday. I promise you."

"I carried you from the time you were a baby," Mr. Civilla said. "I know you. You're weak. You'll get beat in Des Moines. Every year, you kids get beat down there."

Mr. Civilla's manner was deliberate and crisp. He had obviously rehearsed this presentation a number of times. His body was flexed and his fists were clenched as he spoke.

"I've told you over and over what you have to do down there. You've got to make them respect you. You've got to make them fear you. But you never listen."

"I *do* listen," Anthony said. "Teams do respect me—for my talent and my dedication. I can't make people respect me your way. I could kill someone if I threw the ball or hit them the way you expect me to."

"Yeah, well, it's too late for any of that now. All you had to do was prove yourself one time. Every one of my boys did what I told them, and they turned out good. Every one listened—but you."

"I'm not like them," Anthony said.

He reflected on his older brothers. Each had responded to his father's demands in different ways: one quit baseball, another physically fought his father, and one was famous for spiking or barreling over opponents on hard slides. All were now long gone from Cottage Park.

"I can do things they couldn't. I'm fast. I jump over people. I step aside. I go around. What's the difference? The job gets done, and we win."

"The difference is, you're not in the driver's seat," his father said. He pointed his finger, then jabbed it into Anthony's chest, pushing him backward. "Dammit!" Mr. Civilla said through tight lips. "Don't you ever step around anyone. You make them step around you."

"Ask me anything else, Dad," Anthony said. "Please don't ask me to hurt people."

"You *have* to," his father said. "I'll *make* you."

He inched against his son.

"Hit me."

Anthony immediately stepped back and away from his father toward the back door. "No," he said, shaking his head. "No."

"Come on. Take a swing at me." He slapped his son's shoulder. "Show me you're a man. Show me what you're made of."

Anthony kept his eyes to his father's eyes as he took a step back. He reached and felt for the door knob.

"You're a worm!" Mr. Civilla whispered loudly.

Suddenly, Mr. Civilla brought his right fist back then forward in a powerful swing.

Anthony ducked. The blow cuffed the back of his head—as did the next three swings from the left and right.

Anthony straightened himself and held his tongue behind his lips, which he pursed like a mouth guard. His eyes never strayed from his father's. His entire body was poised to dodge the blows. Anthony did not feel pain, only the dissipation of the fear of this summer-long drama with his father. Now whatever was about to happen would play out. It would soon be over and done.

"Then at least take it like a man," Mr. Civilla said as he closed his fists.

He delivered a left into Anthony's stomach and followed it with a dis-abling right that connected below his rib cage. The latter blow had surprisingly knocked the wind out of Anthony.

Anthony dropped to his knees, wrapping his arms around his father to catch himself during his collapse. All the while, he gasped in an effort to force air into his lungs.

Mr. Civilla grabbed his son by the scalp and swung him back and forth like a bell. Anthony flailed at the arm that gripped his hair. But his father blocked him and quickly swung a right against his son's left cheekbone. Anthony reached up to cover his eye. His father brought the same fist crashing into the other cheek.

Now Anthony covered his face with both hands. With each blow, and still unable to catch a breath, he was suddenly growing tired. When his father released the grip on his scalp, Anthony fell back, propped up by his ankles.

Mr. Civilla looked down at him. "Fight!" he roared.

He slapped Anthony once, twice, and again. Anthony fell back over his heels, arms listless by his sides, head toppled onto the linoleum.

Thin black lines separated swollen cheeks from swollen eyelids. Thick, heavy blood dripped from his nose. Anthony gasped and tongued the darker—almost black—blood beading from his torn lips. More blood replaced it.

He curled to circle himself, nestling his arms between his legs. He felt a prick of pain in his ribs as his father kicked him to roll him over. Anthony's hair smudged into the pool of blood beneath him.

"Worm!" Mr. Civilla screamed.

His father yelled his loudest, shrieking for him to get up. The words blurred and eventually drifted farther and farther away. The balloon circles that floated through Anthony's mind popped to darkness. He finally rested in quiet. He was no longer hungry but now ready to sleep—there on the floor in his blood.

At last the bedroom door opened. Anthony's mother had heard the argument and even the scuffles. Father and son had argued before and had resolved their differences with little or no injury. She thought this situation would be no different.

And so she screamed, then fell to her knees and cradled her son's head. The rest of his body slumped over her lap. Bunching the sleeve of her bathrobe, she clotted the cuts across his face. Her tears mixed with his blood.

Standing behind her, her husband had not moved since she entered the room. His eyes, originally locked in fury, grew ever more distant.

"You're a monster!" she screamed. "Call an ambulance!"

Mr. Civilla blinked his eyes and looked around the room. The phone was on the table. He stepped over his son's body to the phone. Blood tracked on the floor behind him.

He drooped down and closed his eyes. Then he blinked and cleared away the food his son had set out, some of which had tipped over and spilled onto the floor.

Mr. Civilla looked at his son, then the phone. He picked up the receiver and tried to place his finger in the hole for zero. He tried again and again, but his finger was swollen and shaking.

Finally he fingered the rotary dial from zero all the way back to the metal stop. He let go, then watched and waited as the dial returned to its original position.

Before he even had the receiver fully to his ear, an operator came unto the phone and politely asked if he needed help.

⚾

Jack placed a chair to the bedroom window and looked out through the rain and darkness over Cottage Park. The streetlights had stopped working when the storm began. Now the only light outside was the occasional lightning strike that split and shivered across the darkness.

Jack's eyes strained to see even the objects on the lawn below. He settled instead on studying the designs the rain made on the window. He watched raindrops strike and clutch the glass before being struck by other drops and racing together to the ledge. Then the drops lost their identity and massed into a dark kaleidoscopic blur. As Jack leaned closer to the window, he eventually saw himself.

It was then he heard the siren—or thought he heard it. The wind often whistled and moaned against the window. Jack had heard sounds like sirens come from it before.

Jack raised the window and stuck his head outside into the wind and rain. Again, he heard what he thought was a siren.

Jeff awoke as the wind and rain blew into the room. He covered his chilled feet with blankets and angled up in bed. When his eyes cleared, he saw the shadow of his brother crouched at the window.

"What are you doing?" he called out to Jack.

"I heard something," Jack said. "I'm still trying to figure it out."

He put his ear to the open window, waited, but heard nothing. He closed the window and slid all the way to the floor with his back against the wall.

"On a night like tonight, if you sit still long enough, you may hear almost anything."

"Still can't sleep?" Jeff asked.

"I won't sleep," Jack said. "Tomorrow is my last real day in Cottage Park." He sighed wistfully. "You know, all this time I've been dreaming about leaving. Now that it's really time to go, I'm thinking I might actually miss this place."

"Then don't go," Jeff said. "Everybody wants you to stay. There's plenty of stuff you can do right here in town."

"Nah," Jack said. "I have to go. But it'll be harder than I ever thought. Now I wonder how long it'll be before I come back." He laughed. "If I have to sit under a bridge or in some dinky boarding house and look out at a rain like this, I might thumb it back here."

"You don't have to wait until it rains," Jeff said.

"Rain makes me think," Jack said. "Man, I'm starting to get homesick, and I'm not even gone yet." Jack tapped on the window as if it were an aquarium. "Maybe it's for the best. I remember Murphy saying once that it's okay if you get nervous before a game. It means you're honest and considering all your possibilities, like a soldier getting ready for battle."

"The old guys seem to relate everything to a fight or battle of some kind," Jeff said.

"Yeah," Jack said. "What about you? You still nervous about the Finals?"

"Yup," Jeff said with a shrug. He paused. "You ever get really scared? Like, you-can't-even-move scared?"

"Not playing baseball," Jack said. "Just the opposite. Once I step on the field, I'm ten feet tall and stronger and faster than anyone. I can take anyone, anytime. I've never had a doubt. And I've never had a doubt that my teammates will come through with their end. That's how we've all been raised. That's another thing I took for granted about baseball here at Cottage Park: you can count on people to get the job done right."

"And then there's someone like me . . ." Jeff said.

"Murphy has his reasons for putting you out there," Jack said. "Whatever they are, they're good enough for me. And that probably goes for everybody else too. You keep trying. I'm right behind you out there."

Jack stopped, stood back up, listened, then cracked open the window again. This time, a siren clearly pierced the rain. Its wail was sharp and frightening. Red warning lights waved above white headlights as an ambulance sped by their house. Both colors sparkled in the water covering the street.

"I'll bet he's lost," Jack said, his eyes full of concern. Still in his uniform, he quickly yanked off his socks. "That's the new guy from Algona. He doesn't know his way around town. And now some other poor guy is dying while he figures it out."

Barefoot, he leapt downstairs and out into the rain, chasing after the ambulance.

Jeff jumped from his bed and grabbed his jeans and a shirt. Already, from outside, he heard his brother's hoarse shouting.

Jeff stepped into the closest pair of shoes at the back door—his brother's. They didn't fit. He kicked them off and bolted barefoot out the door and down the street after his brother.

— CHAPTER TWENTY-FOUR —

Day 2 of the Finals

THE RAIN FELL THROUGH THE NIGHT. By morning, it drizzled, then sprinkled, then gradually gave way to a rising sun. When the children of Cottage Park awoke, the clouds had finished emptying themselves and disappeared. Now their parents were busy pumping pools of water from flooded basements into rivers that flowed along curbs to storm sewers.

McKenna's little brother stripped to his underwear and jumped into a ditch that had filled with water. He bobbed in the water, splashing it in all directions. Sissy barked playfully at the water that splashed her way. He teased her by splashing her until she backed farther away.

Then the boy suddenly imagined hundreds of underwater creatures waiting to bite or suck onto his legs. He ascended and escaped from the water, grabbing his clothes along the way, then chased Sissy back to the house.

On the west side of town, the East Fork Des Moines River had flooded its bank. It covered the street with a thin veneer, through which boys raced their bikes. Those boys with Stingrays wheelied through the water. A few jammed their brakes and cranked their handlebars to make fishtail motions.

Young girls rode their bicycles down the dry sides of streets in pairs, more interested in observing downed branches and damage to houses. They laughed about their own fright from the storm the night before, and occasionally they peeked at the daredevil boys maneuvering through the water around them.

Younger boys ventured the streets, plucking night crawlers and worms that had rolled over curbs. They dropped their finds into coffee cans. The boys would use the bait themselves or sell them at fifty cents per dozen.

When no more worms could be found, these boys packed mud and leaves into lumps the size of baseballs and lobbed them like hand grenades at trees and traffic signs.

While all of Cottage Park was either playing in the water or working to rid themselves of it, Murphy and Egg knelt in the Holy Trinity church until McKenna, the altar boy, snuffed out the candles to end their daily Mass. Then both men stood and bowed, shuffled from the pew, and reverently genuflected at the tabernacle. They proceeded up onto the altar to collect the water and wine cruets, cleansing bowl, and towels Ryan had used before the Offertory.

They carried everything back to the sacristy, where Ryan was unbuttoning his vestments. Murphy and Egg next helped Ryan from the vestments. He thanked them, then hung the vestments in a long wooden closet filled with other brightly decorated vestments.

"I've got some bad news today," Murphy said. "Jack Burnette called me before I came over this morning. Anthony Civilla had a disagreement with his father last night. His father beat him up pretty badly. Jack and his brother followed the ambulance, and they ended up driving Anthony's mother over to the hospital in Algona."

"Anthony wouldn't ever fight back," Ryan said. "Why can't that man accept his boys as they are? In spite of their dad, they've all turned out to be good boys." He shook his head. "Can Anthony still play for us?"

"Jack says Anthony looks worse than he really is," Murphy said, "He ended up with bad cuts that needed stitches, and his eyes are almost swollen shut. Some bruised ribs, but no broken bones. They've got him drugged up. He has to mend in the hospital for at least a couple of days." Murphy sighed. "He certainly won't play for us tomorrow. He might not even be back to play in the Final."

Murphy shook his head, overcome with sadness for Anthony and his team. Murphy and the other coaches were not surprised it had come to this. They knew—and disapproved of—the pressure Mr. Civilla put on all his sons. Anthony had done his best to defuse the inevitable. Now, in the midst of the Finals, it seemed hideous fate had once again robbed them of their best chance to win the championship.

"Civilla demands tough sons," Murphy said. "I wonder if he got his wish."

"It sounds like he's got a tough-*looking* son," Ryan said.

"We were pitching him tomorrow night." Egg shook his head and moaned. "It's always something around here."

⚾

Powers knocked on the door of Moriarity's house, waited for an answer, then knocked again. From inside, he heard *Captain Kangaroo*. He opened the door and yelled in, "Pat, we got practice!"

"Come on in," Moriarity answered from the television room. "I'm in here."

Powers entered the room. Two of Moriarity's younger brothers lay in front of the television watching *Captain Kangaroo*. Moriarity's five-year-old sister smiled at Powers and waved from a chair behind her brothers. Behind them all, Moriarity tossed three beanbags in the air and let two drop to the floor.

"Boy, am I a sucker," Moriarity said. "I paid four bucks for these things." He pointed to the bags on the floor, then to the illustration of a successful juggler in an open book on the floor. "And two more bucks for this stupid book."

Powers picked up the book: *You Can Juggle in Fifteen Minutes*. He skimmed through the pages. "Why do you want to juggle?"

"It's entertaining," Moriarity said. "I think people would enjoy watching me perform." Moriarity nodded in the direction of his brothers and sister. "These little critters will be at the Finals—my whole family. Dad's renting a room at a real nice place."

Moriarity dropped the bags and picked up the sports section of the *Des Moines Register*. He flipped it to Powers. On the front page was a headline, story, and picture of Don Cooper, the man named to replace Murphy as the new coach at Holy Trinity.

"Ugh," Powers said, dropping the newspaper onto a table.

"The new coach don't look baseball to me," Moriarity said. He then spoke somberly. "As cranky as Murphy can get, you have to admit the guy knows his baseball." Moriarity turned away from Powers and swallowed. "It won't be easy saying good-bye to that old bird."

Powers had voiced the very same concerns when he raised this issue with his grandfather a few weeks earlier. He had been surprised by his grandfather's reaction. His grandfather gently dismissed his concern with a reassuring nod. It was that reassuring nod so common to the elderly in Cottage Park, who often knew something about the future but didn't care to share every detail of what was to come. The best that Powers could get from his grandfather was the impression that the old men's retirement was somehow part of a carefully orchestrated plan.

"You don't need to worry about Coach Murphy or Father or Egg—or even your baseball team," his grandfather said.

When Powers asked him to elaborate, the old man merely stared back at him as if he knew a secret he couldn't share.

Powers, in turn, also decided not to share this secret, especially with Moriarity. For all anyone knew, Murphy may have created an elaborate ruse of retirement to get Moriarity to play up to his true potential. So Powers kept quiet, even though it meant watching his friend's visage shift from earnestness to the edge of sadness as he contemplated his coach's retirement.

"Come on," Powers finally said. "We don't have any more time to waste."

Like the sad clown at the circus, Moriarity loped to the television, turned it down, and waved good-bye to his siblings.

"Hey! Turn up the TV!" the brothers whined in anger.

Moriarity shrugged his shoulders, then he and Powers walked out of the house for practice.

Murphy checked his watch and looked out at his players sitting on the gymnasium floor at Holy Trinity. Practice would be inside rather than at Memorial Field. Though not obvious to the eye, the outfield was as waterlogged as a marsh. What was more obvious was the effect of the massive rainstorm around home plate. Water stood in puddles that nearly covered the lines of each batter's box.

Murphy cleared his throat to begin. "You've all heard the story by now about Anthony. All that matters is how it will affect this team. He definitely won't practice with us today, and he won't be coming with us tomorrow for the game. He might even miss the Final, if we make it that far." Murphy scanned all eyes in front of him. "That means we'll need someone to step up and take his place. This isn't the first time we've had to substitute in a pinch, and it won't be the last. Everyone here better be ready to step into that position.

"You people who are coming back next year need to use this as a reminder: next year, we won't have Anthony nor four other starting seniors as well. Somebody has to be ready to continue our tradition. You all need to start asking yourself, 'What will my legacy be at Holy Trinity?'"

Murphy paused to look out over his players, then out the gym doors to the parking lot.

"Our first game tomorrow is at five p.m. We'll leave here tomorrow at noon."

Murphy's eyes locked on Moriarity, who obviously had drifted off into a daydream. Most likely about the signing bonus for a top-ranked baseball player. The coach stepped over to his star pitcher and placed a hand on his shoulder.

"What time did I say?"

Moriarity looked around at his teammates as if he were in trouble. "Yes, Coach," he replied.

Murphy unlatched his wristwatch and handed it to Moriarity. "Put that on," he ordered.

Moriarity complied.

Then Murphy turned to Powers. "He needs to be here tomorrow at eleven thirty. And you need to be with him at all times while we're in Des Moines."

Powers nodded.

"All of you need to be in dress shirts and ties when we're in Des Moines," Murphy said. He paused for a moment to think. "And don't forget—you also need to bring a sleeping bag and a fan."

Murphy signaled to Egg, who handed him a collection of newspaper articles. Murphy leafed through them as he spoke.

"Let's move on to tomorrow's opponent, Cedar Rapids Kennedy High School. They're good." Murphy adjusted his glasses and began to read from a *Des Moines Register* article: "Cedar Rapids Kennedy has the biggest, strongest, and fastest baseball team in Iowa. Six of their nine starters have received Division I athletic scholarships in football, basketball, or baseball."

He sorted through a few articles and singled one out from the rest.

"Rumors of our demise have been greatly exaggerated by the *Fort Dodge Messenger*." Murphy found the section of the article Egg had underlined and began to read it out loud: "Look for Cottage Park Holy Trinity to bow out earlier than their usual Final swoon this year when they face Cedar Rapids Kennedy, one of the most talented groups of baseball players ever assembled on a high school baseball team."

Murphy then held up some scouting reports his coaching friends around the state had prepared for him. "I saved the best for last," he said. "Almost their whole team is on the football team too. They're big, strong, and fast. Physically, they will be the toughest ball club we've ever faced—in Holy Trinity history."

Murphy then dramatically charged over to a trash can and deposited the whole collection of articles and scouting reports. He came back and stared at each player before him.

"I'm telling you this now so you can prepare for the fight ahead. Don't be intimidated when you see these guys. They're huge. They're fast. They're strong. But we know our baseball here. If you play as we've taught you, we'll do fine."

Now it was Jeff's turn to drift off, though his mind's escape was not a daydream about signing bonuses. It was a nightmare about the men—not boys—on the Cedar Rapids Kennedy baseball team. Even before this upsetting news, Jeff had gotten almost no sleep the night before. For hours, he had tossed and turned and analyzed his playing ability over the course of the entire season.

The Finals played out in his head like a pinball game. And no matter how he lifted, shook, or jiggled the machine, he was unable to change the trajectory of the shiny steel ball that jostled back and forth between the levers. The ball always slipped past the levers and out of action.

Loser. He was a loser.

As his brother had predicted, Jeff's fear of baseball had not diminished over the course of the season. Instead, it had intensified. Worse, now he had lost hope that things would ever get any better. He was afraid for himself, and he was afraid for his team. He worried about his coaches, especially Murphy, who had seen something in Jeff that resembled talent and taken a chance on him.

Jeff visualized the first batter in the Cedar Rapids Kennedy lineup digging in at the plate, turning, staring, and even pointing his bat toward Jeff. He imagined the bat extending until it was inches from his face. Then, at Moriarity's first pitch, the batter squared up as if to bunt. Jeff rushed in. But at the last moment, the batter shifted back and swung away. The ball came toward Jeff too fast to catch, too fast to even get out of its way. Yet in every visualization, he was able to redirect his focus before the ball ever hit him.

If only the ball would hit him and hurt him enough that he would be unable to play. If only he could be free of baseball and its responsibilities and threats. If only he wouldn't be branded a quitter for the rest of his life. If only he could leave Cottage Park, whether they won or lost their last game, like Jack. If only he could have been in Murphy's shoes when he fell ill the day before and nearly died.

Murphy was addressing that very point when Jeff drifted back into reality. Murphy had promised his team that on the next day's bus ride, they could focus entirely on baseball and not his health.

"I'll take my heart pills," Murphy said. "I might even take a double dose. And we have a new driver." Murphy pointed to the back row, where McKenna sat with the other seniors. "Show them your license."

McKenna reached into his pocket and retrieved an Iowa commercial driver's license, something he had received earlier that morning. He waved it proudly to his teammates and coaches as they clapped and cheered.

Even Murphy was beginning to believe that perhaps the miracle of David and Goliath might play out once again at Sec Taylor Stadium as they faced Cedar Rapids Kennedy. But it would still be a battle. And it was Murphy's job to prepare his team for that battle. To begin doing that, he and his coaches would lead the team for the next two hours in the lost art of pepper.

Pepper was a pregame ritual where a batter tapped hits to four fielders until he missed or hit a pop-up. The boys on the team—including T. J.—separated into groups and began to play. Murphy, Egg, and Ryan watched, their tired hearts warming and beating in time with the steady pulse of bats connecting with softly tossed balls. To himself, each old man groused that many younger coaches had forgotten or didn't even know about pepper.

Not so these old men. They had played pepper when they themselves were growing up and learning the game of baseball. Pepper was so engrained that whenever the old men happened by a group of boys hanging out around town, they would stop and command them to start a game.

In their mind, pepper was the perfect chicken soup to cure whatever ailed a baseball player. Better yet, regular and devoted practice of pepper nurtured soft hands and taught players how to track the ball and ensure the meat of the bat met the ball.

Most importantly, the old men knew that pepper gave a ballplayer—even a struggling, doubtful player such as Jeff—the one thing no person and few or no drills could give him.

Confidence.

— CHAPTER TWENTY-FIVE —

Day 3 of the Finals

A T NOON ON FRIDAY, JEFF FOLLOWED MURPHY and was the first player onto the bus. He picked a seat in the middle, a few rows beyond the old men's conversation and far enough away from his teammates' chatter. No-man's-land. Then he created a buffer in the seats in front and beside him with his duffel bag and fan.

As his teammates filed by him to the back, he closed his eyes and hoped for sleep. Jeff's soon-to-be sophomore classmates settled quietly in the seats around him, respecting his effort to sleep. A few minutes later, the last of the players and coaches boarded the bus.

The very last was Jack, who lugged a huge green leather Samsonite suitcase in addition to his fan and sleeping bag. He transported the load as far as his brother, then swung everything onto the seat in front of him. He took his seat alongside Jeff, who had fallen asleep.

McKenna honked the horn three times. The bus jerked forward from the parking lot amongst the cheers and chants of over two hundred friends and family members who had come to see the team off to Des Moines. The players clicked down their windows and waved back to the crowd until McKenna yelled from up front.

"Hey! Until I see hands and arms back inside the bus, we're staying right here!"

Receiving instant and full passenger safety compliance, McKenna continued out of the parking lot.

The three old men simultaneously bowed their head and signed themselves in the name of the cross as the bus passed by Holy Trinity Church. Farther on, McKenna politely waved and honked at the residents who had come out of their homes to wave and cheer. The bus slowly navigated the streets leading downtown.

Murphy pointed farther ahead to Sheriff Roger Huffman's squad car waiting with its lights and siren on.

"He'll take us over to 169," Murphy said.

McKenna followed closely behind Sheriff Huffman in a very slow two-vehicle parade. They passed Orlowski's Family Grocery, the old Peterson's Shoe Store, and the vacant storefront that had been covered all season long with posters and banners tracking Holy Trinity's progress toward the Finals. Mr. Burnette had already changed the banner to read: Countdown to the Finals: Day 3 of the Finals.

With camera in hand, Mr. Burnette stepped out from his office at the *Chronicle*. Sheriff Huffman obliged by stopping the parade caravan directly on Main Street, allowing Mr. Burnette to take photographs of the bus from all angles. Mr. Burnette then boarded the bus and took several photos of the players, including Jack, who posed with his sleeping brother leaning up against him. Murphy cleared his throat to indicate that Mr. Burnette should finish up, which he did, then quickly exited the bus.

Sheriff Huffman continued on, then came to another stop in front of the also-vacant Five Star Theatre. The marquee lights had been turned on for the first time since anyone could remember. They blinked and raced around a hand-placed message in bold red letters: WIN THE LAST GAME.

Sheriff Huffman resumed the route out of town, driving by the Lipstick, where O'Connor and several elderly patrons had come out to pay homage to their team. O'Connor raised his large, solid fist in a pose similar to the Black Panther salute, lowering and pointing the fist at the bus all the way until it reached the stop sign at Highway 169.

There, Sheriff Huffman drove his car out onto the highway to stop traffic, but there was none. McKenna waved to thank Sheriff Huffman and safely drove the bus onto Highway 169 South toward Algona.

The players had gradually come to their feet throughout the parade, but they now took their seats. Except for one, who looked backward and strained to take in as much as he could of the panoramic view as the bus now drove faster and farther away from Cottage Park.

"I hope you guys don't mind," Jack said to the boys around him. "This is my last look at that little town." He glanced down at his brother soundly sleeping. "I don't know when I'll ever come back, so I've got to take all of this in."

He waved his hands forward as if he were surrounding himself with the sights and sounds of Cottage Park, even breathing it in, until his view was nothing but a solitary highway between fields of thick, brushy soybeans and tall, strong cornstalks seven feet high and bearing at least one large ear of corn and many times two. He sighed as they drove by the gravel road that led to the quarry.

"You're damn lucky to get out of here," one of Jeff's classmates said.

Jack shook his head. "That's what I thought," he said. "All my life I've been getting ready to run away from this town. Now I'll probably spend the rest of my life somehow running right back to it."

"What's your favorite memory about Cottage Park?" the same boy asked.

He waved his arms all around him. "This," Jack said. "This is how I'll remember Cottage Park. Wearing this uniform." He beat his heart. "Being treated like a hero as we passed through town." He sighed. "It's probably the last time in my whole life I'll be treated like a god."

Though his fellow seniors beckoned him to join them in his usual seat at the back of the bus, Jack declined their offer. Instead, he sat back down next to his sleeping brother.

At five o'clock that night, Holy Trinity would meet Cedar Rapids Kennedy in the first game of the tournament semifinal doubleheader at Sec Taylor Stadium, home of the Iowa Oaks Triple-A minor league team, a farm club for the Chicago White Sox. Number-one ranked Davenport East would play the nightcap at 7:30.

Moriarity hoped to be drafted by the St. Louis Cardinals so he and Danny Stinson might one day take the field together. But if not the Cardinals, the White Sox would be his next best choice. Then he would certainly spend some time living and playing here in Des Moines before being called up to the big leagues.

He was so ready for that future, but first, so ready for this next game to begin. Moriarity had absolutely no doubt that he could dominate this game, even if he were playing at first base. He couldn't wait for tonight to be over so he could mow down the batters on Saturday too.

In contrast to their last game against Iowa City West, Holy Trinity arrived at Sec Taylor Stadium long before the game began and long before Cedar Rapids Kennedy even arrived. The Holy Trinity players loosened up by playing catch, then Murphy broke them into groups of four and five to play pepper.

When Cedar Rapids Kennedy arrived at the stadium, Murphy immediately called his team into the dugout, allowing the opposition the opportunity to warm up. The other team played catch, then took infield practice. Holy Trinity would take to the field for practice afterward.

Jeff watched their opponents from the end of the bench. He was surrounded by teammates but very alone with his reoccurring fears. Those fears, formerly imagined, now dashed and jumped on the field before him. How in the world had it come to this point in his life, when he was playing a game he detested in a stadium where hundreds of people and all of Cottage Park would watch him flounder and bring down his team? How could he—or anyone on this team—possibly compete against boys so much bigger and stronger?

Cedar Rapids Kennedy was a relatively new school, started seven years earlier in 1967 due to the town's continuing population growth. As with every other new school Holy Trinity played, it seemed Kennedy's newness seeped down: the new school had a new baseball team with new coaches, new equipment, new uniforms, and new strategies for creating bigger, stronger, and faster athletes.

Every player took part in a year-round weight-training program monitored by the coaches from all the sports he played. Kennedy athletes also enjoyed camp experiences, where they received quality instruction, often from athletes who had played professionally.

The Kennedy booster club arranged for their team to stay at one of the nicest hotels in Des Moines. They didn't consider bargaining for a lower rate or, like Egg, no rate at all. The booster club parents, like the players' parents, were accomplished lawyers, doctors, accountants, and chief executive officers of successful companies.

The sport of baseball and this game particular were investments they had made in their children from an early age. These parents were not clutching Rosary beads and flooding heaven with hopes and intercessions, trying to lift themselves into a higher, very rare realm of mysticism. Rather, the Kennedy parents confidently expected their investment to prosper in exponential fruition, like the multitude of other investments they had wisely nurtured.

The first of five full school buses from Cottage Park arrived. The fans took position behind the Holy Trinity dugout and began to cheer their team. The players' families would arrive by car after the buses. So would Katherine, in a rare visit to one of her husband's games.

All Cottage Park businesses had closed that day at three o'clock, even the Lipstick. Nearly everyone who could drive or ride had made the trek to Des Moines. Only the very elderly who had stopped driving and weren't up for the long bus ride, the nursing home residents at Cottage Park Sunset Estates, and Sheriff Huffman would stay behind—but only because they assumed tonight's victory and were saving their energy to attend the championship game the next day.

Ryan untied his shoes, slipped them off, placed his stockings inside them, then hoofed the shoes underneath the dugout bench. Along with Egg and Murphy, they were mesmerized as they watched the opposition. Even with all their tournament experience—or perhaps because of it—the old men were especially tense and irritable. Anytime any player asked any question, they'd all answer immediately: "I don't know. Figure it out yourself!"

The old men took short, shallow breaths as one after another, the Kennedy players fielded the ball cleanly and made the final throws from the outfield to home and from the infield to first. The Kennedy coach hit a high pop-up back behind the plate, and the catcher caught it. Then the team finished and headed for their dugout. The field lay quiet and empty.

Inside their dugout, the Holy Trinity players dug their hands deep into their gloves, wriggling their fingers as far as possible into the soft leather. Then they smacked their closed fists into their gloves. Idle chatter faded until the team could hear the fidgeting and nervous discourse of the crowd.

Finally, Murphy signaled for his team to take the field for infield practice. All their anxieties burst into electrified pride as they rushed from the dugout. Their fans stood and cheered wildly, calling players out by name.

Confidence now replaced doubt. The Holy Trinity players now believed they could and would beat any team that stood in their way to the Final.

The Kennedy players were startled by the cheers—by the number of Cottage Park fans, their intensity, and the duration of their ovation. Those same players were somewhat in awe of the scrappy, little players before them, players who seemed like throwbacks of another era. They bombarded their coaches with questions: Were these guys some variation of the Amish they had seen south, near Kalona? And what was the deal with the priest not wearing shoes? What was that supposed to mean?

Still standing and cheering, the Cottage Park fans nearly drowned out Ryan's words as he held the baseball high in the air, pointed it to Jack, then hit a line drive. Jack caught it and fired it back to Powers at home. The fans cheered as Ryan next hit to Spider and McKenna. They sat down when Ryan began to fungo the ball to his infield.

From his seat high in the bleachers behind home plate, Don Cooper watched the team warm up. He waited until Murphy stood alone at the end of the dugout, then Cooper kissed his wife and two little boys.

"Wish me luck," he said. He shrugged in a "What the hell—I'll give it a try anyway" motion.

Cooper descended the bleachers and then through the gate until he stood alongside Murphy.

"Excuse me," he said.

Murphy frowned at whoever dared interrupt his observance of practice. When he turned, he recognized the smiling face of the new Holy Trinity baseball coach. Murphy had seen his picture in the previous morning's *Des Moines Register*.

"I'm Don Cooper," he said. "I'm the guy trying to fill your shoes next year."

Murphy nodded, then immediately turned back to his team on the field.

"You've got a great team," Cooper said.

Again, Murphy nodded without taking his eyes off the field.

"And they look like good kids too," Cooper continued.

"The best," Murphy said.

Cooper stood there expectantly. Murphy didn't know whether the young man was waiting to speak or waiting to be spoken to. Murphy didn't care either way.

Finally, Murphy glanced away from his team. "Look—I'm really busy with this game."

Cooper cleared his throat. "About that . . . I have some ideas and methods I'd like to share with you that should help us win these games. If you'll let me, I'd certainly like to help you out tonight, and if we win, again tomorrow in the Final."

Murphy slowly shook his head no. He started to speak with irritation, then quickly corrected himself, stopped, took a deep breath, then forced his words out through a clenched jaw.

"Thank you," Murphy said. "But we've done nothing but plan for these games since we arrived home with the runner-up trophy last year. It's too late to make changes to that plan."

"I'm sure I could help out in some way," Cooper persisted, his voice straining in desperation. "Would it hurt if I sat on the bench?"

"Actually, it would," Murphy said. "We don't need any more distractions."

Cooper took a step forward. "I know I could learn a lot from you," he said. "I promise I won't get in your way."

Murphy shook his head again and headed off to check on Moriarity at first base.

"Coach—wait," Cooper called after him, his arm raised.

Murphy spun around. "I've got a game to coach. Probably the biggest game of my life. So let's get on with it. What?"

Cooper brought his hands together in prayerful formation. He quickly bowed his head before Murphy, then pointed the imploring hands directly at him, gently bouncing them for emphasis.

"I'll be honest with you," Cooper began. "I know you don't want me here. Even I didn't want to come here tonight. I put this off as long as I could. I don't know a thing about baseball. I know I need a job. And this one happens to include coaching baseball at Holy Trinity. And I have to get myself on that bench tonight, or I won't keep this job." Cooper looked down at his feet and picked at the chain-link fence.

Murphy stared at Cooper, looked out at his team for a second, then turned back to Cooper. He let out a slow sigh. "Jobs are really that scarce to come by?"

"It's bleak," Cooper said. "I've been subbing for two years here in Des Moines. I don't think I worked more than ten days in May. I need a real job and real money. I also need to get my life started somewhere. Cottage Park seems like a good enough place—especially for my kids." He motioned to the bleachers behind him. "I've got my wife and boys back there."

"Did you ever even play baseball?"

Cooper shook his head. "No. But I did play intramural softball in college." As Murphy stared him down, Cooper continued sheepishly, "Well, slow-pitch. Usually with a keg in the dugout."

"I knew it!" Murphy said.

Wilson was so desperate to get rid of the old men that he had found some poor sap who needed a job so badly that he'd agree to coach baseball with zero knowledge of the game.

"So what in the world are you planning to do when it's time to actually coach in the fall?"

Cooper once again shrugged. "I haven't thought that far ahead."

"There's something you need to get straight right now," Murphy said. "You can't fool the people in Cottage Park when it comes to baseball. These folks will figure you out in a hurry. They don't care if you're a nice guy. If you don't know baseball, they'll strip the flesh right off your bones . . . while you're still alive. Except one guy," Murphy added. "Wilson sure thinks he's got a baseball coach."

He smiled wryly. Even Cooper nervously smiled.

Murphy reached out over the dugout, pinched some dirt, then tossed it into the air to judge the direction of the wind. There was none. The dirt settled right back to the ground.

Murphy looked at Cooper. "I know the story with Wilson. I know he wants you on the bench. And I know he'll make my life miserable until you are."

Cooper motioned back to the bleachers. "My family, Mr. Wilson—they all think I'll be on the bench with you tonight. I can't let them down. And I won't let you down either. I swear I won't open my mouth. Please let me sit on the bench."

"All right, then," Murphy said. "Under one condition: you keep your promise about not speaking. Not a single word!"

Cooper nodded and immediately headed into the dugout.

"Not so fast," Murphy said, waving Cooper to stand still. "I'm not done. I have another condition: next spring when these boys need a coach, and before anyone finds out about your baseball past or lack thereof, you agree to let us pick your assistant coach or coaches."

"You're on!" Cooper quickly and gratefully said with a smile.

"You can collect the paycheck," Murphy said. "It's not that much. But let us decide who does the real coaching."

"Fine with me," Cooper said.

He reached out to shake Murphy's hand, then started for the dugout again. Once he made it to that bench he'd begin to figure out what he had gotten himself into this time.

On the field, Ryan hit the last of the infield grounders, then popped up a foul ball for Powers to track down and catch. Ryan waved the players to the dugout, where Egg, Murphy, and now Cooper were there to meet them.

Cooper stood amongst the players and looked up at the stands. He waved first to his wife, then to Wilson, who smiled and gave him a thumbs up.

The players eyed Cooper. They too recognized him from the newspaper. Moriarity glanced at Powers, his eyes as full of dread as they had been the day before. Powers quickly looked away, lest his eyes speak to the nebulous secret he held.

It was a brief ceremony. Murphy introduced Cooper to the team as "The coach of the soon-to-be 1974 state baseball champions," the team clapped, then everyone took their seats in the dugout.

Egg commanded Cooper to sit next to T. J. "Here—help T. J. keep score during the game."

Cooper nodded in quick compliance, but T. J. shook his head in confusion.

"How?" he asked. He wasn't sure what type of help he would need—or could get—from Cooper.

Hearing the interrogative sentence, Egg immediately resorted to the usual reply: "I don't know. Figure it out yourself!"

Then Egg turned around to shout out the batting lineup. As Egg repeated their names once again, the first four batters sorted through batting helmets and bats until they found their right combination.

Jack would lead off. After several practice swings, he stepped into the batter's box, stared down the pitcher, cocked his bat, and waited for the first pitch of the game.

— CHAPTER TWENTY-SIX —

Day 3 of the Finals

O NE HUNDRED FORTY MILES FROM DES MOINES, in a hospital room in the neurology unit in Algona, Iowa, Anthony fine-tuned the radio dial until he came across O'Connor's recognizable voice. The bartender and owner of the Lipstick was also the team's play-by-play announcer.

When loud static drowned out O'Connor, Anthony slowly slid himself out of bed and turned off all the lights in his room. In near darkness, the static ended, and O'Connor boomed back throughout the room.

Anthony opened the shade. Late-afternoon light flooded into the room. On his way back to bed, he stopped into his bathroom and looked in the mirror again.

His left eye was still nearly swollen shut, with a straight and frozen crack that showed a sliver of a red eyeball. He could open and close his right eye, though the purplish-black swelling underneath it was every bit as pronounced as the bulge around his other eye. Black stitches weaved through the bushy black eyebrow over his right eye. More stitches festered from the lower corner of heavy, pouting lips.

Since arriving in the hospital Wednesday night, Anthony had been wearing a towel filled with ice cubes over his wounds. He checked the mirror every two hours to see if the swelling had subsided. It hadn't.

Anthony had played basketball and baseball all his life. Never had he missed a single game. Even when sick or mildly injured, he played on regardless. This was a miserable first in his life—a life he believed had come to an abrupt halt with baseball taken from him.

On Thursday, the doctor had informed Anthony that he had experienced a concussion. As a result, the doctor insisted he cease playing baseball until he completely healed—which could take weeks.

The normally polite and well-mannered Anthony was anything but when he heard the report. He angrily insisted he needed to be at practice that day, at the semifinal on Friday, and, most likely, at the Final on Saturday. The doctor, in turn, stressed that Anthony's playing days at Holy Trinity were over. At which point, Anthony countered that he was eighteen years old and would be leaving the hospital immediately.

Seeing Anthony's feet already out of bed and touching the floor, the doctor struck a final offer: if Anthony stayed in the hospital until Saturday morning, the doctor would discharge him with no stated recommendation that he not play in the Final. But until then, Anthony had to allow the staff to continue treating his concussion by limiting his physical movement and cognitive activity.

Anthony accepted the deal. The doctor's orders meant no reading and no watching television. But the doctor had never said anything about listening to the radio.

Now he lay in his hospital bed, his face once again swaddled in an icy towel, clenching fistfuls of bedsheets on each side of him as O'Connor explained the ongoing, unfolding drama at Sec Taylor Stadium. Anthony's brain was far from at rest. His doctor would have sustained a traumatic brain injury himself had he known how much cognitive function Anthony generated in listening to the broadcast.

Jack had been walked. Anthony did not take it as a good omen when neither Spider, McKenna, nor Orlowski was able to advance Jack. Before the station broke for commercials at the middle of the first inning, Anthony could detect someone shouting hoarsely from the dugout—probably Egg or Murphy asking whether these failed batters had ever seen a curve ball before.

O'Connor returned from break and introduced the top of the batting lineup for Kennedy. Anthony clearly envisioned Murphy studying notes on each batter, then signaling a pitch to Powers, who in turn relayed the pitch to Orlowski. Orlowski—not Anthony, who had been scheduled to pitch.

As O'Connor explained to the listeners, Orlowski was a solid pitcher. He simply threw the ball over the plate consistently, sometimes with speed, but mostly with good control and placement.

"Orlowski to start the game with a fastball low and outside that scratches the corner of the plate for a strike one," O'Connor said.

Anthony knew that Murphy expected the first pitch to be a strike. It was important for Orlowski to get his confidence early. Orlowski worked quickly. In contrast, Moriarity took the maximum time allowable, a full thirty seconds, between pitches. He mostly spent this time preening and attempting to negotiate with Powers about which pitch should be thrown.

O'Connor noted that at 225 pounds, Orlowski was the biggest player on the Holy Trinity roster, whereas nearly all the starting nine at Kennedy were at or above that weight. O'Connor also added that the Kennedy players' weight was made up entirely of muscle, not fat. His observation wasn't intended to insult Orlowski but to create a realistic visual for the folks listening at home.

What's the opposite of low and outside? Anthony thought as he tried to predict the next pitch. Murphy answered that question by calling for high and inside. Orlowski threw a fastball as directed. It was clearly a ball. It served its purpose, however, by making the batter shuffle backward to avoid being hit.

Anthony guessed correctly that Orlowski's next pitch would be knee-high across the center of the plate. The batter tapped a grounder to Orlowski, who tossed it to Moriarity for the first out. So far, the coaching trio's cat-and-mouse game was working.

Anthony thought about his replacement at short and Orlowski's at second, both juniors. He pictured them turning and signaling the first out to their outfielders.

Anthony heard footsteps enter his room and stop, then he heard the sound of someone sitting down and getting comfortable in the chairs. Whoever it was, was very quiet. Anthony waited until the next batter popped up to McKenna, then he loosened his towel to see who had come in. It was his parents. He shifted up and gathered a bathrobe around himself.

"We thought you might be sleeping," Mrs. Civilla said as Anthony emerged from his towel. "We didn't want to disturb you."

Anthony did not acknowledge his guests' presence nor their conversation. Neither of them. In the emergency room on Wednesday night, he had made something clear to his mother: he told her he might beat his father to death if he should ever see him again.

And now with his father a few feet away, Anthony raged at himself for how stupid he had been to passively absorb those violent blows. Had he stood up and blocked them—which he could have easily done—he would be pitching in the game rather than listening to it on the radio.

All his life, Anthony had envisioned his father large and menacing. Now as his father sat before him, Anthony thought him small and harmless. Pitiable.

Still, he would never again put himself in an opportunity where his father could hurt him. As proof, Anthony swung both legs over the side of his bed and prepared to stand. He would be ready this time to defend himself if his father should attack, which he might.

Anthony would never ever sidestep or dodge his father again.

Something happened in the game, something that had O'Connor obviously very excited. But as devoted as Anthony was to his teammates, and as important as this game was in the course of his life, all thought and interest for the events in Des Moines vanished now that he had seen his father.

Anthony's doctor would have been happy to know that his patient wasn't really thinking at all as he prepared to speak to his father. Anthony's mind was at complete rest. He would deliver his words not unlike someone unpacking boxes from a delivery truck: cool, calm, and dispassionate. He tempered the rage—quiet yet constantly striking, like the heat lightning that frequently lit up a hot, humid Iowa night—though it would cast fiery illumination on key words and phrases.

"Mom," Anthony began, "we spoke about what I would say—what I might do—in this situation. Didn't we." It was a statement.

"Yes," Mrs. Civilla said. "We did discuss that possibility."

Her hands shook nervously as they reached inside her purse. A moment later, the same nervous hands brought a tissue to her eyes and nose, then back to her lap. It had become a familiar routine over the last few days.

"But you can't put me in that position. You have to see your father. Your father is so sorry for what he did."

Mr. Civilla showed concern for his wife's struggle to speak. Yet in his father Anthony detected no remorse, no responsibility for the beating two days earlier.

"You need to apologize to him," Mrs. Civilla said, urging her husband to speak.

Anthony guessed the two had rehearsed this scene prior to coming over.

Mr. Civilla looked downward and sighed. "I'm very sorry you're missing that game," Mr. Civilla said, nodding toward the radio. "That was never my intention."

"What *was* your intention?" His voice was quiet, but rage welled up inside his throat. He focused on remaining on the bed and not lunging toward his father.

Mr. Civilla's eyes looked back from the floor to his son. "To make you care about something," Mr. Civilla said. "To care about something so much, you would be willing to stand up and fight for it. To give your life for it. To bury me if you had to. I told you all summer—the whole world must know what you care about. I thought it might be baseball."

"It *is* baseball," Anthony said. Then he immediately corrected himself. "No. It's not baseball. After tonight"—he paused as again O'Connor excitedly called out—"I might never play or watch a baseball game as long as I live."

Anthony slowed his speech, forming one word at a time, for emphasis.

"For me, what I care about is being with my friends, making those old men proud, and doing something for Cottage Park. That's what I'll fight for."

"And family," Mrs. Civilla quickly added, as if running after a child with the lunch box he nearly forgot on the kitchen counter. "You can't walk away from your father, your family."

"Mom," Anthony said, "family doesn't do this." He framed his face with his fingertips. "Family is trust. I have no trust in my family. Not him, anyway."

Anthony looked at his mother.

"Pick a time when I can come over and get my stuff. He can't be in the house when I'm there. I'm staying at Orlowski's until I go to Iowa City."

Anthony then looked down at his father with scorn.

"You're dead to me. Forever."

"*No!*" Mr. Civilla cried.

On Wednesday night, Mr. Civilla had been prepared to receive a beating from his son. He had even looked forward to it. That beating—even that death, should it have resulted—would have been his son's initiation into manhood.

But he was not prepared to be dismissed as casually as a hangnail by a son that he revered, to be buried *alive* by his own flesh and blood. Unable to think of one word that might prove his love and preserve his family, he again balled his fists to strike.

This time, Anthony was ready. He caught his father and placed him in a headlock. He lowered his father's head almost to the ground.

Mrs. Civilla shrieked and screamed. Her husband flailed his arms helplessly, cursing and spitting. In desperation, he grabbed at the radio cord. The radio hit the floor and shattered. Mr. Civilla whipped the cord at his son's legs.

Anthony coolly restrained his father. Occasionally he tightened the headlock enough to give his father a sensation that his scalp might separate from his skull.

Eventually, more out of fatigue than serious injury, the elder Civilla stopped fighting. He hung motionless.

The security guard, nurses, and doctor rushed in. The security guard spoke calmly to Anthony.

"Come on, kid," he said. "You can let go now."

Anthony did.

Mr. Civilla dropped to the ground on all fours.

Immediately, a nurse beckoned Anthony to follow her to a vacant room down the hall. A few moments later, she brought him his clothing.

"They're escorting your family out of the hospital," she explained. "For your safety and for the time being, please stay here."

He did. For approximately fifteen minutes, that is. That was long enough to shed his bathrobe and hospital gown and get into his T-shirt, jeans, and tennis shoes. Anthony then dashed down the hallway and escaped to the back staircase. He raced down the steps two and three at a time until he reached the exit to the back parking lot. Humid air greeted him.

Right there, like a river flowing southward, was Highway 169. He knew his parents were now driving in the opposite direction, north toward Cottage Park.

Anthony sprinted alongside the highway in the growing shadows of tree-lined sidewalks. Liberation morphed to exhilaration. For the first time in his life, he felt unburdened and free.

Like most people in Cottage Park, he typically never ran any farther than the ninety feet between bases. Now he felt he could race along 169 out of Algona and farther away from Cottage Park forever. The farther and the faster into his flight, the bigger and stronger he became. Stronger than any man or force. He was fully confident he could eat up the 140 miles to Des Moines in no time.

In the summer of 1974, there was no better place than Iowa to hitchhike, especially if someone recognized you, even with your blackened and swollen eyes. And especially if that someone once played baseball for Algona Garrigan against you and was listening to the game as he pulled over and told you to hop in. And it was best of all when that same someone was a resident assistant on his way back to Drake University in Des Moines.

"Hey, man—Holy Trinity is winning six to four," the driver immediately assured Anthony as they sped off down the highway.

Anthony was glad to hear it. O'Connor was expounding about Orlowski's pitching and the Holy Trinity defense, both of which had been exemplary, but he never once stopped to give out the score.

"How'd they score?" Anthony asked.

In between Orlowski's pitches, the driver explained how both teams had scored. He relayed every detail, almost as if he had studied for and anticipated a pop quiz before the teacher told her students to clear everything except their pencils.

"You guys always win everything," the driver said. "You didn't actually think you would lose this game, did you?"

Anthony didn't respond, for fear he would jinx the team one way or the other. But silently, he reflected upon the question.

The kids from Kennedy could lose this game, go back home, and have all forgotten in a few days. They had interesting, fulfilling lives. But the Holy Trinity players—their life was on the line. Orlowski's in particular.

For the rest of his life in Cottage Park—work, church, the Lipstick— Orlowski would be known and remembered for the last game he played in a Holy Trinity uniform. Even if he should leave Cottage Park, he could never look in a mirror again without his own reflection judging, demanding whether he had given his very all to win that game.

So, no—Anthony had never doubted for a moment that Holy Trinity would lose this game. He couldn't harbor doubt and still live with himself.

A paradoxical occurrence takes place when a driver picks up a hitchhiker. Though strangers, the riders must create an immediate and intense trust in order to journey together. Trust, of course, is the foundation of any caring relationship. Hence, intimacy then bursts forth immediately between people who may not even know each other's names.

Between commercial breaks, the normally reserved Anthony shared his entire life history. He unfolded it in reverse: The confrontation in the hospital. The nearly deadly assault Wednesday night. The threats throughout the summer. And finally the lifetime with a father who showed no love for his child nor anything in his life except what everybody in Cottage Park valued above all else—baseball.

The two drove the same route Murphy had taken the day of his episode behind the wheel: south on Highway 169 through Fort Dodge, then east on Highway 20 through Webster City. Each mile brought them closer to Des Moines yet farther away from Algona, where the radio tower stood.

Right where Murphy had weakened and all but died, the radio reception did the same. And so, like Murphy, the driver parked his vehicle off the ramp where Highway 20 meets Interstate 35 South.

"This is probably about as far as we can go without losing reception," the driver said. He didn't need to say more. Both young men understood they would stay there on the side of the ramp until the game ended.

Through the popping static, O'Connor sounded tense, then outright scared as he described Orlowski's pitches to the leadoff batter in the bottom of the seventh. Three pitches bounced before they hit the plate. The fourth wasn't anywhere near the strike zone. Ball four. Runner on first.

"Orlowski is spent," O'Connor said. "The catcher, Sean Powers, sees it. He has stepped outside the catcher's box. He's looking to the bench for some direction. He knows Orlowski is done." There was a tense pause. "But no signal from Murphy. Boy, it looks like Murphy will go the entire game with Orlowski. I don't know about this."

There hadn't been one shred of objectivity during O'Connor's two-hour broadcast. He had been all over the emotional map: at times assured and even cocky, sometimes whiny, teary, angry, jubilant, and now terribly anxious.

Anthony and the driver listened as O'Connor described the next batter confidently stepping up to the plate and swinging for the fences. He cracked the ball high and far over the left field fence, but foul.

"Orlowski is now aiming the ball, merely trying to get it over the plate!" O'Connor cried out.

Unbeknownst to the listeners, O'Connor dashed from the press box down to the seats directly behind home plate.

"Call time out!" his booming voice bellowed out to Powers.

Everyone heard it, from the listeners parked on the ramp to I-35 South to the players on the field.

Powers did as he was told.

"Now go over and talk to Coach Murphy!"

Powers seemed reluctant.

But O'Connor, the former catcher, was insistent. "Do it now!" he shouted.

There at Sec Taylor Stadium, Murphy suddenly sprung to his feet and made his way to the pitcher's mound. His body, at least, had responded to O'Connor's outburst. His brain, however, still needed a moment.

What had he been thinking? Orlowski was clearly struggling to get pitches over the plate. In all honesty, Murphy hadn't been thinking anything. Like everyone else, he'd been watching the game—even if it was the biggest game of his life.

By the time he reached the mound, Murphy was fully tuned back in as coach and tactician. He shook hands with Orlowski, thanked him, then directed him to take his usual position at second base. Stephen Schmitt moved from second to first.

And Murphy's prodigy—the project to which Murphy had dedicated the last twelve years of his life, for specifically this type of occasion—confidently cruised from first base to the mound and accepted the ball.

— CHAPTER TWENTY-SEVEN —

Day 3 of the Finals

"START OFF SLOW," MURPHY OFFERED CALMLY and reassuringly, still on the mound as Moriarity lobbed the ball to Powers. "That's good. Nice and slow."

The Kennedy batters chirped confidently about how this scrub would be easier to hit than the last pitcher.

Murphy chattered right over their noise. He offered soothing, confident words of praise: Moriarity was looking good. He had come into situations like this in the past and had always done well. He was a winner. He would win again.

When the umpire signaled that Moriarity had taken his limit of warm-up pitches, Powers and the rest of the infield trotted over to join the conversation on the mound. Murphy placed his arm around Powers and spoke in a loud whisper.

"What do I expect from you?" Murphy asked.

"The number-one sign," Powers said. "Nothing but fastballs."

"Don't forget to pitch out of your stretch," Murphy said, now focusing on Moriarity. "Look over there to first at least once, and hold that guy on. He's not going anywhere, but keep him honest. Remember, you already have one strike on this guy. The rest of you"—his eyes darted around the horn—"look for two. It's coming. Whether it's with this guy or the next, we'll get two." Murphy looked back at Moriarity once again. "Keep it low."

"Coach," Moriarity said. "Please. I got this." He smiled and winked at Murphy. "I gotcha."

Murphy stifled his inclination to scold Moriarity for his brazen cockiness. Instead, he directed his attention to the rest of his infield. They did not have the same confidence in their pitcher as their pitcher had in himself.

"We can do this," Murphy said.

Those were the final words spoken before the team broke from the huddle and returned to their positions. Murphy started back to the dugout, knowing those words were meant to build confidence—probably more for him than for his team. Especially Moriarity. To him, this batter was a simple formality that must be endured before he would go on to further glory in the Final.

No sooner than Murphy had entered the dugout, Moriarity slipped a chunk of Bazooka bubble gum into his mouth and began to chew. Had Murphy seen the gum, he would have demanded that Moriarity spit it out. Now Moriarity casually chewed the gum and even blew a tiny bubble, sucking it back in his mouth and popping it in silence. He basked in the glow of the stadium lights, which he believed were more like spotlights directed at him. The gum's flowery smell of vanilla filled his nostrils as he leaned over for the sign from Powers. He twisted and turned the ball behind him in his hand on his back. Eventually he gripped the seams for a fastball.

O'Connor had returned to the press box to resume broadcast of the game. Now radio listeners would be treated to yet another side of O'Connor: high anxiety.

"Moriarity pitching from the stretch. Takes a look over at first to hold the runner. Delivers his first pitch . . . strike two! Batter clearly taking on that pitch to see if Moriarity could groove one in there. He can. Moriarity up oh-and-two. Working quickly now. Checks his runner on first. Throws and delivers a fastball. Contact off the end of the bat. Powers tells Moriarity to go to second! He goes to Orlowski for one! Orlowski to Schmitt at first for . . . the double play! Two out!"

As was custom in Cottage Park, upon the last out of the game, the entire crowd stood in appreciation of their team. Especially in appreciation of their pitchers, who had again delivered victory. A victory the fans, like Moriarity, believed was a forgone conclusion even with one out remaining. Holy Trinity had never lost a game in this situation.

"Ho-lee Trin-i-tee," the crowd chanted, following it with the cadence of clapping hands and stomping feet: *clap, clap, clap-clap-clap.*

O'Connor had relaxed too, though he reminded listeners that the next batter was no slouch. He was Moriarity's height but much heavier—over

315 pounds. He had received a four-year scholarship to play on the offensive line for the Iowa Hawkeyes.

"Can you imagine," O'Connor asked his listening audience, "what Moriarity must be thinking at this very moment, as he battles the strongest athlete in the state of Iowa?"

Moriarity had, in fact, rehearsed a thousand times how he would answer this very question, should he be besieged by radio and television announcers after the game. What was he thinking as his bigger, stronger opponent squared away in the batter's box? Actually, he was thinking of a nature show, when he saw a huge Burmese python capture a similarly sized crocodile somewhere in the marshes of Southeast Asia.

Now pitching from a full windup, Moriarity reared back and threw with such ferocity that he grunted at the end. The ball seared into Powers's mitt for a called strike one. Moriarity clearly envisioned the snake coiling around the struggling crocodile, which still believed it might escape.

Moriarity wound up, firing his second pitch right down the middle but too fast for the batter to respond. The python squeezed tightly until the crocodile lost consciousness and then life. The crocodile now lay stretched out and lifeless in the python's coils.

With an oh-and-two count, Moriarity faced down Powers, who called for another fastball. Moriarity shook him off for a slider. Powers ignored the request and signaled again for the heat.

Moriarity then looked at the batter, the strongest high school athlete in Iowa. He was already defeated—and knew it. Again Moriarity blazed a high fastball right through the batter's feeble swing. Strike three.

Moriarity watched the batter drop his bat, buckle to the ground, and weep. What he really saw, however, far, far away in his mind, was much different: a python beginning to swallow a crocodile whole.

"That's the game," Anthony said to his driver. "We can go now. We're in the Final."

He motioned for the car to proceed to the interstate.

"I know where they are," Anthony said. His team was now undoubtedly feasting, courtesy of Ryan, at the low cost–no cost McDonald's on the Drake campus.

The driver got back on the freeway and drove straight to the restaurant. There was only one McDonald's on campus. He ate there all the time.

Sure enough, as they arrived, Anthony saw the place was filled with the Holy Trinity baseball team and their friends and families. There was also an overflow of people outside, milling around cars with familiar Kossuth County license plates. The scene was not unlike Schmitt's Dairy Creme in Cottage Park on any given summer Friday night after a baseball game.

Even though he had asked the driver to bring him here, Anthony suddenly sunk in his seat and raised his hand over his face. His mind frantically raced.

Growing up in Cottage Park, life had always been paint by number. Now an entire bucket of paint had been thrown on the canvas, and he needed to take his fingertips and make art out of the mess in front of the whole town. Cottage Park would be judging his weaknesses and imperfections, as it always had. Now more than ever, he was completely beaten down and alone: no family and no team to blend into and behind. For the first time in his life, he would show himself for who he really was, in all his emotionally painful and physically unsightly honesty.

As he prepared to make his grand appearance before the crowd, he silently mulled over questions he asked himself frequently about Cottage Park: *Who are they? What do I owe these people?* He then followed those questions with one last question he had rarely, if ever, asked himself before his father had forced him to address it: *Who am I?* Anthony was now rapidly gaining the answers.

The driver glanced at Anthony, still slouched. "You want me to come in there with you?"

Anthony shook his head. "No. But could you drive right up to the front door?"

As the driver complied to his request, Anthony knew he must act quickly and decisively. He must use all his ducking, dodging, and jumping abilities to redirect the old men and his teammates from any inkling that he might not be at full strength. He couldn't let them consider for a moment that he shouldn't play in the Final.

Anthony nodded to the driver, reminding himself of the hitchhiker's bond: in the hour and forty-five minutes they had been together, this person had been his best friend. But Anthony's real best friends were all in McDonald's.

Anthony blurted out a heartfelt "Thank you," then quickly opened the car door and bolted to the entrance. Before he opened that door, a plan crystalized in his mind. The plan would begin as do all plans about baseball in Cottage Park: with the old men.

Anthony marched in, scanning the eating area. He found the old men seated together in a booth near the front. His own friends, as he expected, were as far away as possible, in the back of the dining area.

Anthony bound over and stood before the old men. "I'm here," he said like a soldier reporting for duty.

The three men were excited to see him.

"You're back!" Murphy called out. Each of them angled out of booth to shake his hand. "I was afraid we might not see you again until after the Finals."

Anthony reached for Murphy's hand first and took it as a means to embrace him in a bear hug. He squeezed the frail Murphy enough to ease a little breath from Murphy's lungs.

He then whispered into Murphy's ear. "I might need you to help me straighten out a situation I might be in at the hospital."

Throughout this embrace, Murphy had held his arms out high and upward as if being held up by a robber. He would offer no resistance to nor acknowledgement of this act. Men did not hug other men in Cottage Park— or in any public places where Cottage Park residents gathered.

Anthony did the same for Ryan, though he was actually waiting for the hug and willing to reciprocate it. It felt good to hug these men, who must have hugged him at some point in his childhood. Having buried his father alive a few hours earlier, it especially felt good to be embraced by Ryan, the other father he had known all his life.

And at last, there was Egg, who knew what was coming. He nodded his greeting, then quickly turned his back and scurried to angle back into the booth. Thus, he intended to avoid any kind of physical contact altogether.

Anthony intercepted him, however, taking his right arm and sweeping it behind Egg's knees. He then used Egg's own falling momentum to swoop him back into his left arm. He now cradled Egg completely off the ground and in his arms.

Anthony was surprised at how light Egg was—or how strong he had become. He pumped Egg up to get a better grip and felt Egg's hands wrap around the back of his neck to brace and support himself. The pair looked like a groom carrying his bride over the threshold.

Anthony looked into Egg's eyes, expecting either to see amusement or rage and fury. What he actually did see, though, were the bright, lively eyes of a little boy in a face-cracking smile. Perhaps he even heard a quiet giggle. Anthony read into those eyes that the little boy was having fun.

So he twirled Egg around once, twice, three times—all the while watching his eyes and seeing them shake as he grinned. Anthony then helped Egg on his feet and led him with the only dance he knew, a waltz he and everyone else at Holy Trinity had learned in the dreaded ballroom dancing section of fifth grade phy ed.

A crowd had originally gathered in awe to watch Anthony hug Murphy and Ryan. Those two men now joined the spectators and watched in amazement (and relief that they hadn't been selected for the dance).

Anthony led Egg around McDonald's in a perfect waltz. One, two, three, back and forth, dipping Egg down low and lifting him back up again. The two waltzed by teammates, parents, groups of school children, alumni who had come from all over the Midwest to watch the games, and regular Cottage Park folks who had come to Des Moines to see their favorite baseball team. Around and around the two danced—twirling, gliding, and dipping. Little children followed them, and others crowded in so close that they often slowed or stopped Anthony.

No one cared about Anthony's battered face. No one cared about the raging gossip of if and when he would ever go back home to his parents. He now seemed happy. His happiness mattered most. That's all the people gathered at McDonald's that night really craved to see.

That and Egg's glee. This was a once-in-a-lifetime moment to see the cranky old man smiling, even laughing, his impeccably groomed white hair flying up and down like angel's wings.

Mr. Burnette, camera in hand, wisely knew to capture that vision for those back home who didn't have the benefit of witnessing the spectacle live. He asked the dancing duo to slow down long enough that he could get the perfect picture to accompany tonight's story he had written for the *Chronicle*.

All good times must come to an end, especially around the old men, who feared any kind of unrehearsed movement. On Anthony's second loop around McDonald's, Murphy ordered Anthony to place Egg back in the booth. He did, and Egg slid back into his seat, patting down his hair and collecting himself.

Murphy looked to check the time, then remembered his star pitcher was wearing his watch.

"What time is it, anyway?" he asked.

"Nearly ten," Ryan answered.

Now Murphy was irritated. He immediately called out for the team to board the bus as soon as possible.

Once again, time had slipped by and eluded him. Everyone should have been in bed and asleep at the dormitory no later than 10:00, including and especially himself. Plus, now he needed to find a phone to contact the Algona Hospital about Anthony and whatever situation he was in. He was exhausted, but it might be awhile before he could lay down to rest.

— CHAPTER TWENTY-EIGHT —

Live Finals Update Here: 2 Hours til Game Time

I T WAS SATURDAY, AUGUST 1,1974, AT ONE O'CLOCK P.M. The Final would start in two hours. Every resident of Cottage Park knew this time and date and had been counting down to the moment for the past year. Nearly every one of those residents were at or now making their way to the game.

Thin clouds hung like gauze over the sun in Des Moines. Occasionally, they would loosen and drape over Sec Taylor Stadium. The sun burned their skin; the humidity made it weep. Moisture brushed upon anyone who exerted themselves, even those who fanned themselves with expensive glossy state tournament booklets.

McKenna slowly maneuvered the Holy Trinity School bus across the expansive parking lot beginning to fill with cars. He parked in the designated area for busses. Once the bus came to a stop, he slid open the door for players to leave. During the ride, each player had positioned himself under a window, sucking in fresh air like minnows in a bucket. The players now stood, clacked their windows shut, grabbed their duffel bags, and prepared to leave the hotbox of a bus.

"Sit down!" Murphy ordered. The players complied, and Murphy stepped to the front of the bus to address his team.

His trademark Holy Trinity black vinyl windbreaker was buttoned up tightly right up and under his chin. All he needed was a towel over his head and tucked into his collar to complete the Dan Gable look. Gable was the famed wrestling star at Iowa State who trained intensely in a heated room under several layers of workout gear. Gable used the additional layers to better condition himself. Murphy used them to maintain a body temperature at which all his internal functions could operate with optimal efficiency. At least he hadn't also put on his woolen jacket—not yet.

At the same time the Davenport East luxury bus pulled up directly alongside Holy Trinity's. The Davenport East coach, a genuinely nice young man that the old men respected, bounded from his bus to the Holy Trinity bus. Coach Rasmussen—or Razz, as Jordan Houston had nicknamed him and now everyone called him—greeted each of the old men by name, shook their hands, and huddled around them.

"I want you to know—we're letting our bus run out here the entire game," Razz said. "It's *very* air conditioned, has a refrigerator with ice-cold sports drinks, a bathroom, the whole works. It's there for you too. Anytime you or your players need to catch your breath this afternoon, please take advantage of our bus." He smiled. "Let me know whatever you need today, and I'll take care of you."

"Thanks," Murphy said. The other old men nodded.

"Mind if I address your team here?" Razz asked.

Murphy gestured. "Go ahead."

Razz turned to the players now desperately wishing they hadn't shut the windows.

"Fellas, I'm Coach Rasmussen, the baseball coach at Davenport East. I want to congratulate you on your season. You've been magnificent. I want you to know that coaching today against Coach Murphy, Egg, and Father Ryan is the best thing that has ever happened in my coaching career. Like Coach Murphy, I also started the baseball program at my school, but that was only six years ago. What Coach Murphy has done and what you all have done for Cottage Park over these many years is nothing short of breathtaking. Our players are truly honored to be on the same field with you this afternoon. They know they'll have to play the game of their lives to make it even close. You should know that nearly everyone in the stands this afternoon will be rooting for you." Razz pointed to himself, then loudly whispered, "Even some of us in the other dugout!"

Razz raised his hands and clapped them, reaching out as if he were taking in the entire team. "If you ever need a place to stay in Davenport, look me up!"

On his way out of the bus, he again shook the old men's hands and wished them well.

Murphy resumed the stance he had taken before Razz had overtaken his stage. He scratched the back of his neck. He despised phony pep talks and personal stories that other coaches pulled from a hat and could quickly put away until the next time they needed to manipulate someone. What he was about to say would come from a place no one even knew existed in him.

For the most part, he had lived his entire life in Cottage Park and had worked with these boys since they were practically toddlers. They knew everything about him that they possibly could. He was plain old Murphy—but there was one exception. He had never told anyone about the trials and tribulations he faced as a soldier in France. Not his fellow veterans with whom he marched every Fourth of July. Not Katherine. Not Ryan or even Egg.

Murphy and his fellow soldiers were amongst the first wave to land at Omaha Beach during the D-Day invasion. Even in the fiercely blowing ocean winds, he smelled the exhaust of the other amphibious vehicles in front of him. It was not unlike the diesel exhaust of the luxury bus that began to permeate the Holy Trinity bus. That day, he also smelled the nervous exhaust of his fellow soldiers as they jostled about him. It was not unlike the exhaust of his Holy Trinity coaches and players as they fidgeted and shook nervousness from their arms and legs. Today, he smelled worry, doubt, fear, and even inexplicably death. Perhaps—probably, hopefully— only his own death. He was fully prepared to die now, as he had been on that beach so many years ago.

All of the sights and scents of an impending battle came rushing up today in the form of words. Murphy had no more control of those words today than he had had of the rations he had spewed over the side of the boat right before they landed.

They were not glorious words of inspiration, harkening pleasant images of God, country, and family. Rather, they formed a severe, eternal threat. He would now repeat the words his sergeant had yelled at him and his team of soldiers before they began their fight to take that beach. They were grim, ugly words spoken before the sergeant spectacularly sacrificed his life, which had likely saved Murphy's own life and allowed him to stand before these young men today.

"I am not going to stand up here," Murphy began, barely speaking above the rumble of the idling luxury bus, "and make some big speech and dedicate this game to someone. We've never done that at Holy Trinity. We've never had to." Murphy nodded back to Egg and Ryan. "We lead by our example, our actions, our day-to-day lives."

Because Murphy almost always kept at least one eye on Moriarity, he immediately noticed that something he had said had upset the young man. He was now insistently pointing to the front of the bus. At first, Murphy tried to ignore the distraction. Finally, he had to turn around to see what could have possibly unnerved his star pitcher. Seeing nothing out of the unusual he stopped his address and angrily confronted Moriarity.

"What in the Sam Hill are you pointing at?" Murphy barked.

"T. J.," Moriarity said. "We dedicated the game against Fonda OLGC to T. J."

Murphy looked bewildered.

"Old Ladies Gossip Club." Thinking the acronym was what had confused his coach, Moriarity used the derogatory moniker instead of the actual name of the school, Our Lady of Good Counsel.

"I know what OLGC stands for," Murphy snapped.

"Well, you said we've never dedicated a game to someone," Moriarity continued. "But actually, we dedicated the Fonda game to T. J., and we won."

Moriarity—like his teammates, like all in Cottage Park, especially the old men—were slaves to superstition. The fact that Murphy had been blatantly incorrect regarding the issue of dedications meant he now had to address it. The sooner the better to avoid a calamitous jinx.

"Then I think we need to dedicate this game as well to T. J.," Murphy said, "and to anyone else who has ever worn that uniform, especially Denny Gallivan."

Then to make up for his oversight, Murphy took one step back and placed a hand on T. J.'s shoulder. "You are responsible for holding onto the trophy after the game."

T. J. nodded proudly.

The entire team politely clapped. Murphy waited again for silence. He could now continue with his speech as planned.

"This is it for Egg, Father, and myself," Murphy said. "This is the day, this is why we've lived our lives—for this one day. We've been working for and waiting for this day for forty-five years. And here it is—our last game at Holy Trinity. There is no tomorrow, no next season. There's nothing for us other than this one day, this last game. We simply have to, we must, win this last game."

Murphy clenched a fist and pounded it into his heart three times. "I'm interested in one thing about this game . . . winning it. That means I'm *not* interested in whether you play like gentlemen, whether you model Jesus Christ on the field, or whether you 'come close' to beating a big public school from a big city. I'm not interested in any of that happy horseshit your mommies tell you every night before they tuck you in so you don't wet your bed."

Murphy began pacing up and down the aisle of the bus, staring down each player.

"I want everyone on this team to understand that I am only interested in winning. We must win. A win is all that counts. You cannot, you will not, lose this game. However, if something should happen whereby we do lose . . ."

Murphy let the words trail as he advanced to the front of the bus, then he raised his voice slowly and angrily as he spat each word from his mouth: "I swear to Christ, I will haunt you every last day you crawl across this miserable earth and in hellfire for eternity after your pitiful deaths. Do you all understand that?"

Murphy waited until each player meekly said yes out loud or nodded. Seeing that his team clearly understood his message, he had no other thoughts or words to express.

Murphy looked over to Egg. "You want to say anything? This is your last chance."

Egg shook his head.

Murphy looked at Ryan and offered the same invitation. Ryan popped up from his seat like a jack-in-the-box.

On the way over to the stadium, Murphy had ordered the bus to pull into McDonald's. Having had no breakfast, the players were starving. They believed they were now stopping in for lunch. Instead, they stopped only long enough to pick up two large coolers of free orange drink, then left immediately for the stadium. Ryan was eager to assure the team the coaches hadn't forgotten about their hunger.

"If," Ryan began, then immediately corrected himself, "*when* we win, we'll go back to McDonald's for a big all-you-can-eat buffet. They've never done anything like this for anyone," he added almost dreamily. "And it's all free."

Then he plopped down as quickly as he had stood up.

"Let's go then," Murphy simply said, his words devoid of any further emotion or elaboration.

He stepped off the bus to the entrance to the stadium. The other old men were right behind him. The trio was the first to feel the full force of the sultry heat that rose from the soft tar covering the parking lot. Ryan slowed at once.

Pumping his fist into the air, T. J. pressed on past Ryan and the other old men as he led the team into the ballpark.

Razz was a nice and, generally speaking, honest man. But he had told several bold-faced lies in his welcoming salute to the Holy Trinity team. He sincerely admired and respected the small-town team. Rather, the lies were about his own team.

Those lies were apparent as T. J. led Holy Trinity into their dugout. The Davenport East players smirked and rolled their eyes at the punks with their nearly mummified coaches. Actually, they were lower than punks. They were country punks. Hicks. Hayseeds.

We could definitely take these guys, the East players thought as they exchanged glances and knowing nods.

Before each game, every boys' team in Iowa—except Holy Trinity—sized up their opponents and asked themselves at least one, sometimes two, or even three questions from the tough-guy challenge:

1. Could we take these guys in a fight? (*If answer is no, proceed to question 2.*)
2. What if we were really mad? Then could we take them? (*If answer is no, proceed to question 3.*)
3. Could our toughest guy take their toughest guy?

Holy Trinity felt little need to speculate about their opponents in such ways. They believed they had been blessed with the divine right of kings. They didn't need to fight. To defeat anyone in their way, all they needed to do was practice and play baseball all the time and listen to the old men.

Up until this year, the players from Davenport East had never both-ered with the tough-guy challenge either. They were river rats. They grew up fishing, boating, swimming, and falling deeply in love with the beauty of the Mississippi River. It mesmerized them, sapped them of their drive and ambition, and sometimes lured them into disregarding its many dangers. Every river rat knew someone who had drowned in the river or had been paralyzed from a dive into shallow water on a sandbar.

Up until this year, they never would have looked down upon their coun-try cousins with such severity. Instead, they would have engaged in a debate about the best beer bash locale: a desolate river island or a remote quarry. They would have argued that their deep-fried onion rings, catfish, and cheese curds tasted better than Cottage Park's pork chops and mashed potatoes. And like their coach, they would have insisted that their opponents come and stay with them to see the beauty and wonder of the Mighty Miss for themselves.

But everything had changed this year. All season long, they loved to pose the tough-guy challenge before every game. They never had to ask beyond question 1.

Their confidence didn't stem from the fact that they had drubbed the best teams in eastern Iowa and western Illinois. Like Holy Trinity, they were undefeated, but against much better competition.

Rather, their newfound tough-guy confidence stemmed from the fact that should they have ever needed to address question 3 regarding whether their toughest guy could take their toughest guy, the answer always would have been yes. A resounding yes.

Their Jordan Houston could take anyone's toughest guy, and he inspired his teammates to be as tough and as fearless as him.

Houston had been born in Chicago and raised in the Cabrini-Green Homes for the first two years of his life. Though he had no memory of that time, he knew life there could not have been as pleasant as the hit televi-sion show *Good Times* depicted. *Good Times* didn't show a dad and then his family abandoning the mother of his son.

At two, Houston and his mother moved to her home back in East Saint Louis. But then his mother died, and he landed with his aunt. When his aunt died, he landed with his grandfather. Then when he died, Houston landed with his grandmother in Davenport. He lived like a migrant, shuf-fling through seasons of death.

When his grandmother died his junior year, Houston wondered where he would possibly go next. His probation officer, also a black man, answered that dilemma by accepting him into his own home, thus continuing his miraculous four-year enrollment at Davenport East.

No one in Davenport ever believed Houston was a mere five feet eight inches tall. He projected a much larger persona—a persona he had earned by challenging the toughest guy in any group until the opponent backed down. He was undefeated, whether as a Golden Gloves competitor, streetfighter, running back, or point guard.

Lacking a worthy opponent in any of these contests, Houston was forced to fight himself—and he always lost. He had been arrested for possession of a pistol, and he often battled teachers and administrators.

Houston's constant run-ins with educators forced Razz, also the school's dean of discipline, to address the entire faculty at a staff development session before Houston's junior year. His goal was to enlighten his colleagues about this young man and tap his enormous potential.

In truth, Houston was an asset, not a problem. Razz knew Houston could enhance instruction at Davenport East and make everyone's lives easier. Razz had a saying: As Jordan Houston goes, so do the other seventeen hundred students at Davenport East.

If he could have spoken freely, Razz would have told the staff about the intel he had received from the police. Over the summer, Houston had created La Familia, a United Nations–like umbrella organization that oversaw all the gangs in Davenport. Under Houston's direction, La Familia offered voice, protection, and even dispute mediation to the Vice Lords, Bloods, Crips, Gangster Disciples, and any other established gangs.

The police had told Razz that because of Houston, the gangs were no longer fighting amongst themselves. That meant no more fights in the classrooms and hallways at Davenport East. It should have been good news to share with the staff about Houston's character. But any mention of gangs terrified and upset the staff, so Razz stuck to his other talking points.

"Respect," the coach said. He then repeated himself: "Respect." He let the word trail slowly into silence. "Jordan Houston is the kid who wants to ride into your classroom on a white horse and save you, save everybody, and save the day. He can and will do it for you if you let him."

The teachers began gesturing wildly and conversing amongst themselves. The coach continued through the emerging chatter.

"He does *not* want you to know this, though, because it would completely blow his tough-guy cover. But that's a big front for a guy who really wants to be a hero."

Hands went up all over the auditorium with urgent pleas for counterargument.

"I promise that this kid will give you exactly what you give him. You give him respect, and he'll give it back to you tenfold. This is a kid like no other kid in this school or anywhere else. He will die for you."

He tried to move on again, but angry, loud, and clear statements erupted from the teachers.

"How, in a classroom of thirty students, can you have respect and special rules for one individual—who also happens to be a thug?"

"Is it fair to pamper a student in high school when the real world simply doesn't work that way?"

"Why are we always bending over backward for disruptive kids yet we do absolutely nothing for kids who behave themselves?"

The meeting ended not more than five minutes after it had started.

So for the next two years, the teachers chose to battle Houston, usually confronting him and singling him out even when other students were involved. It was easy to find him in the mix with any given incident at school. With his gift for diplomacy, Houston interjected himself into any situation he deemed unfair.

Just as Razz had foretold, Houston gave the teachers exactly what they gave him. In this case, though, it was disrespect. The result of these teacher-initiated battles was always the same: Houston would offer some variance of defiance with a strong curse word or two (though never spoken to the teacher's face), and the staff would counter with a one- to three-day suspension.

One of these battles and resulting suspensions came the day before the basketball state championship game. It was fateful timing, as Houston had somewhat surprisingly, given his lengthy suspension record from school, become the all-time scoring leader at Davenport East. It began with the basketball team, unsupervised in the lunchroom after the pep rally, being loud and unruly. A teacher told them to get a move on. When Houston moved on too slowly for her liking, she turned her sights on him. His reply was a muttered F-word. The school's reply was a three-day suspension.

"It's not my fault he'll miss the 'big game' tomorrow night," the teacher said with mock emphasis.

Razz probably could have been fired for insubordination, but he refused to process the suspension papers. Though he had never once uttered this expression while fighting for his country in Vietnam, he told his principal, "This is the hill I want to die on—there's no better place."

Nonetheless, the principal processed the suspension himself and hand-delivered it moments before Houston could ascend the steps of the luxury bus bound for the state championship game in Des Moines. The suspension banned him from school, which he couldn't care less about, but also from Veterans Memorial Auditorium. He couldn't even be in the building as a spectator.

The next night, Razz joined Houston and his guardian at their home to watch the game on television. As expected, his teammates failed miserably in defeat without him. The Happy Joe's pizza went untouched. Not even Razz, who loved cheese and had the high blood pressure to show it, could eat it.

Houston switched off the television, then spoke deliberately and vapidly, directly to the screen.

"We would have won that game," Houston said. "I would have made the all-tournament team."

The toughest guy in Davenport with the teddy bear face flicked away a tear that had slipped from his eye.

Razz yearned to tell Houston how much he admired his courage, honesty, loyalty, and how hopeful he was for his future. But right now, the silence was cleansing, like a stinging antiseptic.

Then Houston broke the silence and Razz's heart. "I quit. I quit it all, man."

"No," his guardian said. "I can certainly understand your hurt, but the condition of your parole was enrollment in high school. You quit now, you go right back to juvenile detention in Eldora." The guardian shook his head violently. "And if you get in trouble there, you're close enough to eighteen that they'll put you right down at Pen City in Fort Madison."

Houston turned from the blank television to his guardian.

"We've talked about this, you and I," said the parole officer. "You've got three months left in school. Finish up. Then you can choose wherever you want to go."

Houston liked the idea of the future: a brief one- or two-year stint on scholarship at a prestigious basketball junior college, followed by another scholarship to a powerhouse basketball university. However, a dreadful three months of kowtowing to the staff seemed like an impossible and wasted effort to cross that river to the promised land.

That was when Razz offered his own proposal to Houston—which, along with his marriage proposal, was one of the smartest proposals he had made in his whole life.

"Would you like to help me get our baseball team to the Finals this year?" Razz asked. "There's no question that we're going. We'll be really good this year, but I need someone to make these guys a little tougher mentally. As a group, they're weak. You know most of the guys. You can be my equipment manager or something."

The more the dean and coach listened to himself, the more his idea made sense to even him.

The more it seemed to make sense to Houston too. His eyes lit up. He half raised his hand to add something to this winning arrangement.

"Let me finish," Razz said, ready to seal the deal. "You get us to Des Moines and the Finals, and I swear you'll be front and center in every picture with the state championship trophy."

"Razz—" Houston interrupted.

"One more thing," Razz interrupted back. "You want to stick it to Davenport East? Guess what? So do I." Razz reached out and placed his hand on Houston's shoulder. "We'll to do it the Jewish way, though. They believe the best revenge is to live a good life."

As Razz took a deep breath, Houston raised his hand again.

"Can I pitch?" Houston asked.

The answer was yes. Unbeknownst to Razz or anyone in Davenport East, Houston could pitch. Very well, in fact. Rather than become the equipment manager, he became the best pitcher in Iowa that year not named Moriarity.

When Houston was a little boy in East Saint Louis, his grandfather had taught him how to pitch. His grandfather had been a very good pitcher in the Negro Leagues, playing against the legendary Satchel Paige.

His grandfather heaped volumes of disdain upon him laced with mild profanity. Houston suspected the constant verbal assault was intended to make him stronger.

His grandfather had a tender side, though. He doted affection on his grandson when he excelled on the mound and even more when his leadership played a role in a victory. There were no heartfelt moments after a loss. So Houston learned to win.

After his grandfather died and Houston moved once again, he found it easier to play basketball. Yet he still played baseball year-round in mind and memory, night and day. In these visions, he always won. He always pleased his grandfather. He always made him proud.

So when Razz put a baseball in his hands and told Houston to show his stuff, Houston was like a genie in a bottle set free. He could once again work his old-school Negro Leagues magic that other players and teams did not, could never, understand.

Houston was having the time of his life. And now here he was, watching puny Holy Trinity practice before the Final championship game. Without a doubt, he would soon be accepting the state championship trophy, and all of Iowa would be forced to watch him do so. More importantly to Houston, they would also be forced to watch his deceased grandfather come back to life in him to accept the same acclaim and trophy. Houston vowed that his own sullen face that glowered at anyone and everyone who crossed his path would explode in defiant laughter in each and every photograph at the celebration.

Razz had been honest when he said the majority of fans would be rooting for the small-town team. Everybody loved the underdog. But some of the fans weren't so much pro–Holy Trinity as they were anti–Davenport East. More specifically, they were anti–Houston. How dare he, they believed, make the bedeviling sport of baseball look too easy? How dare he not only brush up against the law but fall into its enforcement webbing? And how dare he so far scrape together the wherewithal to survive an impossible upbringing and still become a proud young African American man?

Razz wasn't particularly wrapped up in the need for Finals victories like his opposing coaches were. His focus had always been on a different kind of victory. Yet Razz wished to win the Final as much as he had ever set his sights on anything. Not for himself. Not for the team. But for Houston.

Houston sat next to Razz as Holy Trinity wrapped up their practice.

All around him, teammates jeered Holy Trinity. Even though Houston was the reason for that very attitude all season long, he didn't hold these opponents in disdain. Not this time. This pitiful group of country bumpkins posed no threat to him and his quest for state championship fame and glory.

"Their uniforms are fly," he told Razz after a few minutes of studying Holy Trinity. "I want me one of those throwbacks. That's the kind my grandpa used to wear."

As Houston watched his opponents, he found himself moved to sympathy for the first time that season. Red faced and angry, the old coaches harangued their players. The players, in turn, bore the wrath with the passive acceptance of youth that had been taught to respect their elders under any circumstance. The old men reminded Houston of the only man he had known in his family, his grandfather. Houston understood that the old coaches, like his grandfather, disguised their hopes, dreams, and even love in their unrelenting anger and disgust.

At any point in his life, Houston had never once felt the need to pose the tough-guy challenge. Rather, he always zeroed in on the most imposing figure in front of him. Today, that was Moriarity.

"That little boy is supposed to be the best pitcher in Iowa?" Houston asked in sheer disbelief. "Better than me?"

"I don't believe that," Razz said. But then he saw an opportunity to stoke Houston's competitive fire, so he added, "But a lot of folks out there do feel that way."

Houston humphed and shook his head caustically.

"We'll see about all that. Little boy is clownin' with his hat cocked GD," he said. "My pop's a GD," he added.

The observation amused the coach, that Houston could possibly believe that the homely red-haired kid with bad acne might be paying allegiance to the Gangster Disciples by cocking his baseball hat to the right.

Then Houston shrugged. "It will give me a little more motivation today."

Though he still saw Holy Trinity as no threat, he resolved to strike Moriarity with all he had, like lightning to a weathervane.

— CHAPTER TWENTY-NINE —

Live Finals Update Here: 40 Minutes til Game Time

HOUSTON HAD MISTAKENLY PEGGED MORIARITY as Holy Trinity's strongest and toughest guy, its leader. The more accurate target would have been Orlowski.

Inside the Holy Trinity dugout, Orlowski situated himself on the far end of the bench, farthest away from the coaches, off by himself. He opened a tube of eye black. He applied the black greasy mix in one wide band under each eye. He then began to apply it to each player on the team, including T. J.

Yes, it was to help reduce the glare of the sun. But more importantly, the makeup artistry was an attempt to better conceal the worst imaginable black-and-purple bulging circles around his best friend's eyes. Orlowski feared an umpire would visit the dugout at any time and inform the coaches that Anthony's physical condition precluded him from playing.

Orlowski roughly smeared eye black under each of his teammates' eyes. He explained that the Santee Sioux, who had fought for the land of Cottage Park, had applied similar war paint. Black symbolized strength and victory. Orlowski told each fellow warrior that in this battle, they must give everything. Death should not be feared.

Orlowski knew the old men had used ashes to decorate themselves in similar fashion when they played baseball. Orlowski summoned the solemnity of the ordained man at the other end of the bench, using this ritual to remind his teammates of the inevitability and the plain truth of death.

"Remember, man," Orlowski said, "thou art dust, and unto dust thou shalt return."

Davenport East finished their warmups early and returned to the shade of their dugout. Murphy took a few steps up and out of their own dugout and looked back at the crowd. From a glance, he could see that nearly almost everyone from Cottage Park had made the trip.

Only three residents stayed behind: Spider Schmitt's father, Sheriff Huffman, and Mrs. McCarthy. Mr. Schmitt was the volunteer fire department chief. He, like Sheriff Huffman, was unable to abandon his post, even for the biggest game in his family's and his town's history.

While the rest of the town eagerly awaited the start of the game, Mr. Schmitt and Sheriff Huffman wheeled out the fire department's roadside message board and faced it toward Highway 169. The board was usually reserved for announcing chili feeds, raffles, and open houses. Today, it would become a scoreboard. The duo used plastic red letters and numbers to update the game stats for the edification of visitors driving through Cottage Park. When they had finished, their scoreboard read:

LIVE FINALS UPDATE HERE: 40 MINUTES TIL GAME TIME

Mr. Schmitt drove the town's sole fire truck alongside the scoreboard. Sheriff Huffman anchored the other side of the scoreboard with his police car. Both men turned on the flashing lights of their respective vehicles, then stretched out on lawn chairs adjacent to the scoreboard. They tuned into the Algona radio station that would soon deliver O'Connor's play-by-play broadcast.

The third essential personnel who couldn't ever leave Cottage Park was also standing by her post. Hers was Holy Trinity Church. But Mrs. McCarthy was not in a good mood. All ninety years of her life, she had faithfully practiced her Catholic religion, worshipping God. As an adult, she had drawn believers and nonbelievers alike to this very church through the ringing of the church bells. All those years, she had never once asked God for anything in return—except for the good health of her children, grandchildren, and great-grandchildren.

Today, though, as she reclined in the front pew and stared at the life-sized crucifix, she was not asking God for a Finals victory for Holy Trinity.

She was demanding it. Like many of her same-aged peers, she was not afraid to speak her mind, even to the creator and ruler of the universe, who she knew would very soon determine her eternal fate.

If these boys don't win today—like Mary Agnes Connelly, Mrs. McCarthy saw very little differentiation between the coaches and the players and as such included the coaches in her use of the term "boys"—*the very first thing I'll do when I meet you is ask you why you dealt me such a lousy hand of cards all my life, after all the nice things I did for you.*

Mrs. McCarthy then respectfully thanked God ahead of time and predestined the victory by planning to ring the bells forty times—one for every victory in their undefeated season—at the start of the 3:00 p.m. game.

There at Sec Taylor Stadium, far away from Holy Trinity Church, Murphy continued his scan of the crowd and noted several familiar faces.

Aunt B was sitting by herself, recording the names of Cottage Park residents who had made the voyage to Des Moines. In her official capacity for the *Chronicle*, she was delighted that her press card had actually gained her free admittance. It saved her the eight-dollar ticket fee, which she equated to the cost of a Broadway show.

Each year, Mary Agnes Connelly attended one away game for Holy Trinity. She always reserved this occasion for the Final. She and four other residents of Sunset Estates positioned themselves immediately behind the bench, resting comfortably in the shade provided by three golf umbrellas so overwhelming that no one could sit behind them for the next two rows. Mary Agnes and the other seniors were full of hope and anticipation. Staff at Sunset Estates were always startled that signs of dementia seemed to disappear at Holy Trinity baseball games, especially the Final.

Most of the ballplayers' families had stayed overnight in Des Moines and arrived at the stadium early in order to save seats for their friends and other relatives. They spread long blankets over the hot wooden bleachers for comfort and to establish territorial rights.

Moriarity's family gathered in one such area—or at least his parents and baby sister did so. At her discretion, the baby shifted between parents, with the request always in the form of tears. Moriarity's other brothers and sisters tore up and down the aisles, chasing each other, fighting, falling, then crying. After several minutes of chasing, Moriarity's two younger brothers vanished from their parents' sight and began searching for lost items in the refuse under the bleachers.

Behind the Moriaritys sat the Burnettes. They chatted with McKenna's mother, whose children had also strayed from their area and now joined their friends.

The players' girlfriends grouped behind the parents. Segregated by class, the freshmen girls, excited and giddy, sat closest to the adults. Upperclassmen girls confused the freshmen's liveliness with obnoxiousness. They passed judgment even more so than the adults. They were unaware that they too grew more excited as the start of the game grew closer.

Graduated seniors such as Margaret were a few rows farther up. Over the last few days, Margaret had begun to experience the early signs of pregnancy. She was easily fatigued, she needed to use the restroom more frequently, and she had thrown up twice at the hotel the night before. She feared that her efforts to conceal her pregnancy would come undone, as was her makeup, in the harsh conditions of the stadium. Her swelling and aching breasts, the breasts she once admired as sexual and beautiful, now felt as though they were no longer hers. She gazed onto the field where Spider was stretching, alone. She too felt alone in carrying this baby and carrying the burden of its upbringing.

Junior high students stood on the top bleacher, looking tough with their backs to the field. They gazed out and over the walls of the ballpark to the capital city of Iowa, Des Moines.

Murphy's gaze stretched over to the bleachers behind home plate. They were the next to fill with Holy Trinity fans. These fans did not have immediate ties to the players. Their observations as well as their encouragement were less heated than the section behind the Holy Trinity dugout.

T. J.'s mother had first situated herself in this section but was unhappy with the view it afforded of her son. She soon moved to an open area behind the Davenport East dugout, where she had a clear view of him.

Due to their late arrival, a few other Holy Trinity fans were in this area as well. These fans restrained from cheering, in respect to the Davenport East player families sitting there.

T. J.'s mother wasn't concerned about cheering. She trained her binoculars on her son, studying his actions and reactions. T. J. seemed happy. She was jubilant.

Anthony's father was in this section as well—by choice. Anthony's mother, out of obligation as his wife, sat by his side. He had stood and cheered when Holy Trinity had first taken the field for warm-ups, and he planned to cheer throughout the game. Despite the Davenport East fans' intensity, they did little to discourage the dangerous-looking man sitting amongst them.

Murphy returned his scrutiny to the seats behind the dugout. This time, he noticed Cooper sitting with his wife and two small boys. The new coach was eyeing the old coach expectantly. As much as it pained him, Murphy gestured to Cooper in invitation. Cooper kissed his wife, high-fived his little boys, adjusted the shoulder strap on his satchel, and made his way down the aisle before hopping over the fence to join Murphy.

For the first time, Murphy pitied Cooper. The young man hadn't a clue what he had gotten himself into.

From the shade of the umbrella, Mary Agnes had never taken her eyes off Murphy as he scanned the crowd. She knew the sun's wearying effect on Murphy, and she had waited patiently long enough (about thirty seconds) for him to come to his senses on his own.

"Coach Murphy!" Mary Agnes barked out. "You can't be out here in the sun! You need to be back in that dugout!" She jabbed her finger toward the dugout.

Murphy ducked as if to escape the tongue-lashing, though it was futile. He waved to acknowledge her and immediately started back toward the dugout. As if guilty by association, Cooper sheepishly scooted in behind him.

"Help keep score with T. J., like you did yesterday. And remember, don't say a word!" Murphy gnarled, still recuperating from Mary Agnes Connelly's verbal whiplashing.

Cooper nodded in agreement and took his seat.

T. J. and Egg stood by the water fountain. "Drink," Egg ordered. "If you wait until you're thirsty, it might be too late. That's how you get dehydrated."

Egg stepped aside and T. J. bent over and took a long drink of water.

The public address system crackled as the announcer welcomed the fans and both schools to the championship game. The announcer stated the paid attendance for the game, and every one of the record-setting 5,314 fans in the audience cheered in unison.

"This is the largest crowd we've ever played for," Egg told T. J.

Razz was correct that the majority of the crowd, as much as 75 percent, was rooting for Holy Trinity. Many attendees had at one time lived in Cottage Park and used the game as an excuse for a reunion. Other Holy Trinity backers were from neighboring schools in the Cottage Park region or from schools of similar size. Some had come only to cheer for a Catholic school. Others who lived in and around Des Moines had come to watch the last game coached by these legendary old men who had developed the powerhouse tradition over the decades.

Davenport East was introduced first, starting with their reserves, mostly juniors and seniors. They took their places along the first-base line and faced their fans in the bleachers. Then the Davenport East starters were introduced by name and position.

When Jordan Houston was introduced, he sauntered onto the field with a white towel pulled down tightly over his head. He gripped the white cloth tightly between fingers of both hands. The towel isolated him from his teammates, who had been energetically connecting with each other by slapping, shaking, and smacking one another. Later, the towel would insulate him from the crowd that watched in dismay and then rage when he failed to remove it during the National Anthem.

The first Holy Trinity player to be introduced, a freshman reserve, quickly took his position closest to third base. He was too scared to look at anything but his shoes. The rest of the reserves were similarly shy or shell-shocked by the magnitude of the crowd and game.

The first starter to be introduced, Orlowski, was also the first Holy Trinity player to show any emotion. He pointed his index finger to the sky, then stabbed it defiantly (and uncharacteristically for someone from Cottage Park) to indicate that Holy Trinity, not Davenport East, was the number-one team in the state.

Orlowski continued to hold his hand high to meet Spider when he was introduced. Spider jumped up to slap it. Both shouted out to each other that this was their time. They had to win this game. No excuses.

They were much more subdued when Anthony was introduced, as was the entire assembly. Fans strained to study the bruises on Anthony's face, then they murmured their own speculative explanation for them.

Mr. Civilla cheered over the murmurs. "Anthony moves well," he said to his wife and anyone else interested.

His wife shook her head.

"I said he moved well," Mr. Civilla repeated to answer her doubts as much as his own.

Jack was the last starter to be introduced. Then T. J. was introduced as the scorekeeper and Egg and Ryan as assistant coaches.

In the final introduction, the announcer boomed, "The winningest high school baseball coach in the United States, coaching his last game at Holy Trinity—Coach Al Murphy!"

The standing ovation lasted a full ten seconds and did not diminish until Murphy respectfully tipped his hat and lifted it over the field.

After the national anthem, Murphy directed his starters to their positions. The rest of the players and coaches followed him to the bench.

Moriarity threw seven warm-ups, then signaled to Powers that he was ready for his last pitch.

"Coming down!" Powers yelled out.

Receiving the pitch, Powers launched up and rifled a throw over the mound to Anthony's ankle-high glove waiting at second. Anthony tagged the dirt for an imaginary out, then gloved the ball to Orlowski, who whipped it to Jeff at third. Jeff underhanded the ball to Moriarity.

The entire infield gathered to surround Moriarity. All raised their right arms, then reached out to lock hands in a teepee-like formation over the mound.

"Let's get this one for the olds on the bench," Orlowski said.

Each player affirmed this dedication in his own words. They held their hands together in silence for a moment before letting go and returning to their positions in the infield.

— CHAPTER THIRTY —

Live Finals Update Here: 1st Inning 0–0

THERE WAS NO DELAY TO THE SHOWDOWN between the state's two best pitchers. Houston was Davenport East's leadoff batter. Moriarity's first pitch to Houston was a called strike as Murphy had told him to throw—explosive and low at the knees.

Moriarity took a deep breath and glanced out over the crowd. He had not seen the scout from the White Sox, whom he had heard would be present.

Powers signaled for the next pitch, a fastball to the outside. Moriarity delivered, and Houston swung and missed.

Ahead with two strikes, Moriarity stared down Houston, who crouched over home plate as stiff as a statue. Again Powers signaled for a fastball; this time something high and inside.

Moriarity shook the signal off.

Powers tried again—another fastball, low and outside.

Moriarity nodded. He'd been holding out for a curve ball but begrudgingly threw what Murphy and Powers had ordered.

Houston started to bring his bat around, then tried to stop midswing. The result was a clumsy, listless swipe that earned him his third strike. Houston was furious. He had planned to jump on Moriarity right away. Mostly, he was furious at himself. He murmured curse words and derisively tossed his bat toward the dugout.

Moriarity interpreted the display as a sign of disrespect. With a three-pitch out, Moriarity didn't deserve to be grandstanded by the batter he struck out. Moriarity knew Houston was a pitcher, but he didn't know (or if he did, couldn't have cared less) that Houston was an extraordinary pitcher. The only extraordinary pitcher he was interested in was himself. At this moment, all that mattered was that he felt slighted by Houston's disrespect. He resolved to publicly humiliate Houston before this game had ended.

The first inning continued in a mostly uneventful manner with Moriarity throwing smoke that batters whiffed helplessly against. Cooper grew bored following the tedious scorekeeping, which he still didn't understand. He eventually drifted farther down and away from T. J. and Egg on the bench, where he could get a view of the entire team.

Cooper opened his satchel. He took out his notebook and pencil and prepared to indulge in his passion, drawing. He was particularly skilled at charcoal sketches. Maybe next year he could do personalized drawings, but not this year. Everyone seemed so uptight.

At the moment, his biggest concern was how to sketch the heat pressing on the stadium. He could almost see the heat in the air and how it dulled colors and shapes. Somehow the players seemed oblivious to the humidity and the pools of sweat soaking their uniforms. He turned and looked behind the dugout at the Holy Trinity fans waving programs across their faces. A nice subject for an impressionist piece. Young men had already shimmied off their T-shirts.

Cooper looked back in the dugout and focused on Ryan, who picked his black shirt from his chest and fingered sweat from around his Roman collar. Ryan stood to get a drink from the water fountain. He rinsed his wrists with the cool water, then dampened his handkerchief. Taking his seat again, he rested his head back against the screen and spread his handkerchief over his face.

Cooper liked the contrast of Ryan's black clothing with the white collar and handkerchief. It seemed to show both resistance to and resignation of the heat. He began to sketch Ryan, who held that pose until Moriarity retired the side and the Holy Trinity players on the field charged back into the dugout. Ryan set the handkerchief in his pocket, then set off barefoot for the first-base coach's box.

T. J. waited until everyone was in from the field before handing the scorebook over to Egg, who yelled out that inning's batting order: "Orlowski,

Anthony, Powers, Spider Schmitt, Moriarity, and Jeff Burnette." Egg repeated the first three batters, then angrily ordered, "Hit the damn ball!"

The Holy Trinity batters did hit Houston's pitching, but at the wrong time and to the wrong places. They loaded the bases in the second inning but never scored. Holy Trinity sent six batters to the plate in the third inning and had a runner on third in the fourth but still couldn't score. They had rarely failed in such situations. Players, coaches, and fans expected a run and were frustrated when one never came.

During that same time, Moriarity continued to throw his fastball by the Davenport East batters. A few made weak contact but were easily thrown out.

Facing Houston again in the top of the fourth, Moriarity was surprised when a jab bunt rolled between first and the pitching mound. He sprinted over to pick up the ball, but Stephen Schmitt reached it first. Moriarity continued by him, receiving Stephen's underhand throw and tagging first a moment before Houston did.

The umpire indicated out, but shouted, "Safe!"

Moriarity looked at the umpire to clarify the correct call.

"The runner is safe," the umpire said.

Holy Trinity fans were furious. Students and a few of the parents loudly questioned the umpire. Some booed.

Houston jumped toward second base and crouched low as if he would steal. "I'm on to you!" Houston yelled out to Moriarity.

Houston was the very worst nuisance that could have befallen Moriarity. Both players knew it.

"You heard me," Houston sneered. "You're a nutcase. What are you going to do about it?"

Moriarity pointed the ball at him. "You're going down!" he yelled back.

Houston's laughter and heckling continued, but Moriarity managed to focus on the batter, whom he struck out. He also struck out the next batter. The third batter grounded to Orlowski, who then tagged second base to end the scoring threat and Houston's threat to Moriarity's fragile mental state.

Moriarity pointed and laughed at Houston as he strode by him to the dugout.

Houston stopped and pointed right back at Moriarity. "You and me gonna box," Houston said. "I swear to God!"

Moriarity continued to laugh but picked up his pace and jogged to the dugout in time to hear T. J. read his name first in the batting order for the bottom of the fourth. Moriarity was the number eight batter in the lineup. Officially, that meant he was the second weakest batter in the lineup, but unofficially in that moment, he was the most confident.

Cooper watched Moriarity swing three bats lazily in the batter's circle. He saw Jeff, the team's ninth and worst hitter, edge toward the bat rack. He reluctantly moved to the on-deck circle when Moriarity left for the batter's box. Cooper started sketching Jeff. He always noticed a player whose actions spoke loudest, because they were often the quietest.

Cooper next glanced at McKenna, who wiped sweat from his forehead, careful not to smear the black tar stripes under his eyes. The stripes reminded Cooper of a soldier's stripes. Cooper studied the contrast between the black stripes and the pale patch of white skin across McKenna's forehead, perpetually shaded by a hat. The rest of McKenna's face was cinnamon brown. Patches of pink skin glowed along his neck.

Moriarity stepped up to the plate. Now it was payback time for Houston. Now he would really have some fun.

Houston threw his first pitch behind Moriarity. It was a slow lob. Still, a batter's first inclination is to step backward when he sees any kind of pitch thrown outside the strike zone. However, a batter's second inclination is to avoid being hit at all costs. Having already taken one step back but still seeing the ball making its way to his face, Moriarity collapsed to the ground a half second before the ball would have harmlessly kissed off his cheek. Ball one.

Moriarity stood back up, brushed dirt off his uniform, and squared himself again. Houston and his catcher agreed on the next pitch, a pitch Houston correctly guessed Moriarity would wait on. Houston delivered his own fastball, fat and juicy like a big meatball, belt high down the middle of the plate. Strike one.

Houston picked up a rosin bag and squeezed it. The powder usually blew off and away like dandelion puff, but this time its white powder flittered downward at his feet. At that very moment, he realized his pitching career was also slipping and falling back to earth. He would never pitch again after this game.

Houston stepped up to the pitching rubber and stared down Moriarity. He envied him and the senior year he would have after Houston was done. Baseball was so fun.

Houston then focused on his catcher and shook off each pitch until they agreed on a curve. But this would not be an ordinary curve ball. Houston released a slow curve, not much faster than the lob he had thrown earlier. To Moriarity, it looked again as if he would be hit. But Houston had violently snapped his wrist as his grandfather had shown him many years ago. This time, Moriarity hit the ground while the ball spun wickedly back into the strike zone and over the plate. Strike two.

Stepping off the mound with his back to Moriarity, Houston caught his teammates' attention. He was like a professional wrestler querying the crowd for their favorite hold to end the match. For Houston, it was the blooper ball. His teammates loved it. Some of them were smiling and laughing, trying to cover their faces with their gloves. Razz did not like the blooper ball, but he indulged Houston to throw it at least once a game. In playful defiance and to the delight of his teammates, Houston sometimes threw several consecutive blooper balls in games with a big lead.

Houston returned to the mound and stared down Moriarity again. He went into his regular windup, though when he released the ball, it went nearly straight up twenty-five feet into the air before it made a slow descent, like a hot air balloon. Houston reserved this pitch exclusively for anxious, highly excitable rubes. Moriarity was the perfect foil, shuffling his feet and swinging upward as furiously as he could, expecting to see the ball sail away for his first home run. Instead, it dropped like manna into the catcher's glove. Strike three. The ball made its way around the horn while a baffled and agitated Moriarity tried to understand what had happened.

Murphy knew exactly what had happened to the floundering and frustrated Moriarity. It was the same thing that had happened to his team, which was also floundering. Murphy could feel life being drawn out of his team—and life being drawn out of him. He was literally winded. Life was slipping away from him. He needed help.

As Jeff stepped up to bat, Murphy called for time out. He edged back to the dugout and called out Cooper's name. He discovered Cooper in somewhat of a trance, seemingly drifting away in the small circular motions of a drawing technique called scumbling, which had perfectly captured Ryan's socks and shoes under the bench. He set his artwork down and hurried to hear Murphy's concern.

"I need a little oxygen," Murphy said. "There's an ambulance in front of the ballpark. They'll send in someone with a tank. Go now and ask them for it." Seeing the alarm in Cooper's face, he said, "Don't worry. I've done this before. I think I had to do the same thing last year when we played here."

Cooper started to run from the dugout. Murphy turned and stopped him.

"No—don't hurry. You'll scare people," Murphy said. "And before you do anything, go up into the stands and tell my wife I'm all right."

Cooper nodded and now jogged from the dugout. He nearly got clipped by Jeff, who was warming up by swinging away in the batter's circle.

Jeff's swing at Cooper's head was the closest he had come to a hit in the Finals. When he returned after his second strikeout that afternoon, Jeff made his way to Murphy with the idea of asking to remove himself from the lineup. But then, a paramedic scooted across the field with an oxygen tank for Murphy who grabbed its mask, and gulped air deep into his lungs.

Ryan and Egg flanked Murphy on the bench.

"You all right?" Egg asked Murphy.

With the mask still pressed to his face, Murphy nodded. He then offered both men the oxygen. They declined, despite their discomfort and unspoken doubts about their own stamina to finish the game in the unrelenting heat. They believed Murphy needed the life-giving supplement much more.

Meanwhile, T. J. marked bold, black *K*s in the scorebook as the bottom of the Holy Trinity batting order struck out.

In the top of the fifth, the leadoff number seven batter hit a line drive that bounced at Jeff's feet. He scooped at it, then raised his glove, surprised to find the ball perched there like an ice cream cone. He threw to first base. The ball bounced into Stephen's stretching, sweeping glove for the first out.

"See that?" Murphy said. He brought the oxygen mask down over his chin so he could speak. "I knew Jeff would come through for us."

Murphy returned the oxygen mask over his face again and breathed deeply. His health and comfort seemed to mirror whatever good or bad things were happening to his team on the field.

The next batter bunted in front of the plate. Powers threw off his mask and waved Moriarity away. He swooped down and picked up the ball, then cocked it back to his ear and fired it to first for the second out.

Moriarity's first pitch to the third batter was a slider that floated rather than slid. The batter swung too fast, well before the ball had reached home plate. Moriarity followed up with two blazing fastballs, both strikes, to end the side. Neither team had yet scored.

In the bottom of the fifth, Spider led off with a hit down the third-base side, all the way out to left field. Ryan waved him on to second base, then immediately regretted the decision. But Spider was already on his way to second, so Ryan screamed out for him to slide. At the end of his head-first slide, Spider grabbed the base as the second baseman dropped his glove to Spider's waist.

The umpire signaled and shouted, "Out!"

Spider jumped to his feet. "You can't call that!" he said. "I slid underneath him." Spider used both hands to implore the umpire. "I was safe!"

The umpire turned to his position behind first base in shallow right field.

Spider waited a moment, then looked toward Murphy, who wiped sweat from his forehead with a white handkerchief. He showed no sign of protest. Spider reluctantly stepped off the bag, kicked it, then sulked from the field amidst booing from both sides.

The next batter, McKenna, swung mightily, missing the first two pitches. He watched the next two fastballs barely miss the outside corner, then watched a curve ball bounce at the plate. With a full count, he stepped from the box and looked at Murphy, who gave him the hit-away sign. McKenna set himself for the next pitch.

As the ball came toward the plate, McKenna began to swing, then checked himself and froze as the ball sailed away from the plate. Fully expecting a call of ball, he tossed his bat to the dugout and started off toward first base. The umpire saw it differently and signaled him out.

This time, Murphy trudged to the umpire and looked him in the eyes. "He's got to break his wrist to call him out," Murphy said evenly.

"He did, Coach," the umpire said deferentially. "I got a good look at it."

Murphy shook his head. He waved both arms for McKenna to go to the dugout.

In the dugout, Egg slapped his hands in anger. First the umps called Houston safe in the fourth, and now these two calls in the fifth.

He looked at T. J. "Those idiots do this to us every year! And then people wonder why we get beat when we come to Des Moines."

The next batter, Orlowski, hit the first pitch three hundred and forty feet to the left field wall. But it was high, so high, that the left fielder had all the time he needed to position himself, take in the ball, lean against the wall, and give thanksgiving the ball hadn't sailed a few feet further for a home run. The inning had ended.

Egg couldn't contain it any longer. He cupped his hands and yelled in the direction of the umpire at home plate. "What are you guys getting paid for? Wake up out there—call the game the right way!"

The umpire looked at the Holy Trinity dugout, trying to zero in on the source of the critical performance review.

"I said, wake up out there!" Egg yelled out again.

Ryan stood up from the bench in an attempt to block the umpire's view of Egg. It definitely wasn't a good sign that Egg was already so rattled here in the fifth with no score.

Egg was not a good captain; he would not go down with the potential sinking ship of another Finals loss. Rather, everyone knew he would deliberately escalate his behavior—beginning with belittling the umpires, then cursing them, and on and on—until he got himself thrown out of a game. At the championship game the year before, Egg had flung bats and balls onto the field. The year before that, he kicked dirt onto the umpire's shoes.

Granted, this arrangement seemed to work for everyone. Egg was able to save face—the face that always won. And in doing so, he gave Cottage Park fans—who knew an umpire never, ever deserved such treatment—a means to vent their rage and frustration through Egg. Watching Egg protest was easier than accepting the fact that the hardest working baseball team in America wasn't as good as their opponent that day. Egg's ritual at least reminded all that Holy Trinity would always be back next year with a vengeance.

Murphy also moved between Egg and the umpire. He clapped his hands to address his whole team. "We can hit this guy." Though physically weak, his voice rung with a tenor of angry frustration.

"Next time we'll get him," Ryan agreed.

Facing the bottom of the Davenport East lineup in the top of the sixth, Moriarity thought little of balls and strikes. He thought weaknesses and strengths.

The first boy who stood before him was unsure of himself. Moriarity stared as the batter shifted to find his position. Moriarity would not waste his time or arsenal with this helpless batter. He threw three quick strikes for the first out. The other two batters were a bit surer at the plate but slower of bat. They went back to the dugout as quickly as the first.

Anthony led off the bottom of the sixth with a soft line drive that landed outside the first baseman's glove in shallow right. Powers bunted down the first-base line, sacrificing himself to move Anthony into scoring position at second. Stephen then advanced Anthony to third with a line drive. It was long and foul, but the Davenport East right fielder caught it and threw it to first behind Anthony, who had slid safely at third.

The stadium announcer introduced Moriarity as the next batter. The announcement was exactly how Moriarity had heard it a thousand times in his dreams, when his team and all of Cottage Park needed his heroics to make the big play and save the day. He had hungered for this opportunity, and now it was laid before him. He crouched and filtered dirt through his fingers to dry the sweat, then wiped the dirt on his pants and stepped up to the plate.

Murphy signaled for Moriarity to swing away. But before Houston began his windup, Moriarity squared away to bunt, then pulled his bat away when the ball bounced into the dirt. Moriarity turned and watched the catcher kneel and block the ball down with his thigh. Moriarity signaled for Anthony to hold at third.

The catcher called time out and jogged out to the pitcher's mound. At the same time, Murphy took several steps toward Moriarity and called out, "Did you see my signal?"

Moriarity nodded. Of course he had seen the hit-away signal. He had just wanted to disrupt Houston's rhythm and fool the Davenport East infield. Moriarity took another practice swing.

This time, Murphy signaled for Moriarity to take Houston's next pitch. Moriarity did, watching it go by with the bat still on his shoulder for a called strike.

Moriarity then received the hit-away sign. He waited for the pitch, a fastball belt high. He swung with all his might. The ball cracked off the bat and flew right back at Houston, who blocked his face and knocked the ball down to the ground.

Anthony had already begun to slide into home plate. Now it was up to Moriarity to win the footrace to first. Moriarity swung the batter's helmet from his head and chopped his feet into the ground. He saw the anxiety on the first baseman's face and heard the cheers from the crowd.

Houston had turned completely around, his eyes frantically searching for the ball, his ears trying to isolate the frenzied screams of teammates racing over to direct him. Finally finding the ball, Houston pounced on it and fired it to first.

To the umpire, at least, the pop of the ball in the first baseman's glove sounded louder and earlier than the stomp of Moriarity's foot on the base. That ended the Holy Trinity threat in the bottom of the sixth inning.

— CHAPTER THIRTY-ONE —

Live Finals Update Here: 7th Inning 0–0

WITH THE SCORE STILL TIED AT ZERO, Moriarity stepped to the pitching rubber to begin the seventh and final inning. The first batter he would face was Davenport East's weakest hitter, followed by Houston and their best hitters.

Moriarity made short work of the first batter, who hit a weak pop fly ball to Orlowski for the first out. Moriarity hoped he would retire Houston as easily.

Houston took his sweet time situating at the plate. He held his hand back to the umpire to indicate he was not yet ready. He pressed both feet into the batter's box and eased up against the plate. When he lowered his right elbow to indicate he was ready to accept the first pitch, he also pointed the end of his bat at Moriarity as if he were preparing to joust.

No one had ever publicly challenged Moriarity like that before. Moriarity chose to brush him back. He began his windup and threw a fastball high and inside, two inches from Houston's face.

Houston turned and dropped to the ground. The bat, however, had still waved behind, nicking and fouling the ball back behind the plate for the first strike.

The umpire threw a new ball out to Moriarity. He turned away to the outfield and smiled. Unlike when Houston smiled at his outfield, Moriarity's smile generated a "Just throw the damn ball" sentiment. Moriarity returned to the mound and stared down Houston as he edged back to the plate.

Moriarity shook off Powers's next three calls for fastballs. Instead he threw another curve, a forkball, and a slider, each drew a call of ball. After a fastball for a strike, the umpire signaled a full count.

Moriarity's next pitch, also a fastball, hit the outside corner. It could have been called either way. The entire stadium held its breath until the umpire motioned for Houston to take first base.

Egg already knew how the call would be made. The outcome of this game had been decided behind the scenes here in Des Moines. Justice would not be delivered on this day.

"The fix is in!" Egg yelled out from the bench. When the umpire ignored him, Egg continued. "You've been doing this to us for years. We don't forget over here!"

Moriarity rolled his eyes and also cursed the bad call. He then glared over at Houston, who clapped his hands and smiled.

Moriarity now pitched from the stretch. The moment he began his motion, Houston jumped off toward second. Orlowski covered second, and the right-handed batter took advantage of the situation, driving the ball where Orlowski had previously been. It rolled beyond to McKenna in right field.

As McKenna returned the ball to the infield, Houston continued past second and stood up safely at third.

Murphy called time out and headed to the mound. Powers pulled off his mask at the plate and started out with him, but Murphy waved him back.

"No," Murphy said. "You know what to do."

At the mound, Murphy folded his arms, took a long breath, then let it out with a sigh. His eyes locked sternly on his pitcher.

"You were pitching a good game until you started to fool around with Houston. What's going on out here? Do I have to pull you from the game?"

"Come on, Coach," Moriarity said. "I'll get out of this. Don't give up on me."

Murphy continued to glare. "I'm not giving up on you. But I'm not giving in either. We didn't come this far to have you monkey around out here. I won't let you fiddle this game away."

Murphy started back to the dugout, stopping to point at Anthony. The shortstop ordered the infield to edge in closer to home to prevent the runner from scoring.

Moriarity looked over at first and then at third, where Houston danced off the bag.

"You're nothing. You're worthless!" Houston called out.

Moriarity ignored him and threw a fastball for a called strike.

Powers crouched over again and signaled a pitchout. Moriarity nodded and threw the ball high and outside, where Powers stood waiting. The runner on first raced toward second, but Powers fired the ball across the mound at Anthony, who caught it on the run, charged into the runner, knocked him down, and tagged him for the second out.

With the base runner sprawled on the ground between his legs, Anthony then pivoted to stare down Houston, who had come nearly half the distance to home. When Houston head-faked as if he might finish his journey, Anthony correctly called the bluff. He fired the ball to Jeff at third. Jeff swung down to tag Houston, narrowly missing him as he darted back to the base.

Anthony jogged back to his position at short. The Holy Trinity fans rewarded his play with loud cheers. But the collision had opened the stitches on Anthony's lower lip. Blood trickled down his face along with sweat.

Anthony could hear one voice booming out louder than the others—his father's. Ignoring the voice, he stuck the tip of his tongue over the broken stitches, hoping the wet pressure might restore the scab that had been broken.

Jeff walked across the field from third and tried to hand the ball to Moriarity, but Moriarity instead placed his glove over Jeff's hand.

"Keep it," Moriarity whispered. "I'll pretend to take it." Jeff objected, but Moriarity continued through gritted teeth, "Get back there and tag that guy as soon as he steps off the bag."

Moriarity then faked the ball to his glove and stepped back on the pitching rubber before Jeff could object again. Jeff hustled back to third base.

Moriarity looked down from the mound at Powers, who signaled for a fastball. Moriarity nodded and took a look at third. Houston stepped off the bag, took a large step toward home, and began to taunt Moriarity once again.

In a single quick motion, Jeff pulled the hidden ball from his glove and tagged Houston on the back.

Startled, Houston shoved Jeff back and out of the way and sprinted back to the bag. Jeff held the ball high in the air. Moriarity signaled the out from his position on the mound. The Holy Trinity fans cheered wildly.

The normally placid Razz burst from the dugout and nearly collided with the home plate umpire. He gesticulated to third and then to Moriarity.

"That's a balk!" Razz yelled frantically. "The pitcher can't be on the mound when they try the hidden-ball trick!"

The umpire nodded in enlightenment, as if he had forgotten this rule himself. He turned and waved Houston from third to home.

Murphy slumped back on the bench, took off his glasses, and rubbed his eyes. "He's right," Murphy said. "It's a balk. The runner advances to home. We probably just lost this game."

T. J. turned to Egg. "What do you mean, a balk?"

Egg didn't respond. He only stared as Houston jogged to home plate. Houston shook his fist at Moriarity and at the end of the short trip jumped both feet into the middle of the plate.

T. J. spoke as if he were having a bad dream. "Wait a minute. Hold on. This doesn't seem fair. He tagged him fair and square."

He looked at Ryan, who seemed resigned. Egg was definitely mad, but T. J. didn't know who or what was the object of his wrath—nor did he know why. Nevertheless, T. J. reflected Houston's advance from third to home in his scorebook. The score was now Davenport East one, Holy Trinity zero.

"I did not tell him to do that," Murphy called down from the bench to no one and everyone.

He coughed and cleared his throat. He ground the heels of his palms into his eyes over and over again.

"But I'm sure that's how I'll be remembered," he muttered, this time to himself.

All he could do was hope history would never link his conference on the mound to the disastrous trick play.

As he put his glasses back on, he spoke the biggest lie he had ever told himself or anyone else: "It's only a game."

As he regained his bearings and looked out onto the field again, Murphy realized the game had completely stopped. Moriarity had descended from the mound and was waiting for Murphy to say something.

If he had done the same while Jeff applied the tag a minute earlier, then the hidden-ball trick would have been perfectly okay. Jeff could have tagged the runner out, and Holy Trinity could be in their dugout, preparing to get the one run they would have needed to win this game. Now they needed one run to tie the game. And it was highly unlikely, given Houston's increasing strength, that they could even accomplish that feat.

Oblivious to the entire universe, Moriarity stood there, staring at Murphy. His hands were raised in innocence as if to say, What? Who? Me? He would have stood there forever, waiting for Murphy and only Murphy to clarify and hopefully validate that Houston's playful trot to home plate was all a misunderstanding.

But a second trip to the mound would automatically activate the umpire's substitution of a new pitcher. All Murphy could do was step outside the dugout and yell from there.

"He's right, Pat!" Murphy said, furious but too weary to show it.

He was even more upset with himself. Moriarity's mistake was not that he had misunderstood the hidden-ball trick. Rather, his grievous sin was not knowing his entire focus should have been on the next batter, whom he undoubtedly would have retired to end the inning. And for that, Murphy blamed himself. He had failed to get Moriarity to understand his own strength and power to dominate and control, especially in these sorts of situations.

Moriarity continued to stare at Murphy in bewilderment until Powers and then the umpire reminded him that he needed to resume pitching. He nodded, though he still didn't know exactly what he had done wrong.

Jeff threw the previously hidden ball to him. Moriarity covered his face with his glove and peeked between the glove fingers for the signal.

In the stands, Moriarity's mother also put her face into her hands. She slowly lowered her face to her lap.

"There's the big hot shot," Mr. Moriarity said, pointing out to the mound. He waited until she looked up at him, then he handed their baby boy to her. "I knew he'd pull something like that."

The elder Moriarity then stepped away from the bleacher seats, and headed up the aisle until departing the stadium.

Houston was mobbed in a celebration at home plate. On his way to the dugout, he continued to harass Moriarity. A few of the Davenport East fans laughed derisively from the bleachers.

Moriarity kicked away dirt in front of the pitching rubber. He looked to his right at Jeff, at Anthony, then at his outfielders, and finally at Orlowski. They were all still ready to play and win. They hadn't scolded him, even though his error had almost certainly jeopardized their chances of winning the game.

Moriarity took a deep breath and looked down at Powers. He couldn't see the sign. Moriarity realized that tears of sorrow and aggravation were welling in his eyes. They mixed with sweat and eye black.

As Murphy had taught him, he stepped off the rubber, took another deep breath, wiped his eyes into his shirtsleeve, then stepped back. Now the area surrounding home plate was a blur, but Moriarity began his windup anyway, knowing he could direct the pitch from memory.

He threw a fastball at the knees over the center of the plate for the first strike. Powers yelled out praise. Moriarity blinked his eyes for clarity, then braced for Powers' sharp throwback that often accompanied a first strike.

Moriarity stepped off the mound and reached for a rosin bag. He tossed it in his right hand several times. He dropped the bag to the ground and watched its dust blow down like a meteor shower.

His eyes cleared to the scene at home plate. He took another deep breath, then shook his shoulders back at complete rest.

He started his windup and let out a hoarse grunt as he released the ball—a ball as devastating as he had ever thrown. The batter had already stepped toward the dugout before the umpire called the third strike for the third out.

Murphy stood up from the bench and shook his head in disbelief. "Maybe our boy has learned how to pitch."

Tired players jogged from the field and gathered around Orlowski, in front of the dugout. Soon the players on the bench and T. J. came out to join them. Only Moriarity continued on his way by the huddle directly to the dugout.

"This is why we were born," Orlowski said. "To finish this thing once and for all and to win."

He grinned cockily, and the bench players joined in his brash confidence.

Orlowski continued. "It's all on us now. We can do this!"

And with that proclamation, he swaggered from the huddle toward the dugout. His teammates self-assuredly followed him.

From inside the dugout, Murphy clapped and greeted his players. "Need some hits out there!" he said. "It's time!"

Ryan stood to take his position at first but was blinded by a bright light, like a bolt of lightning only he saw. The force and intensity knocked him right down to the bench again.

Once as a young man early in his priesthood, he asked God that he be given advance notice of his death, even if for a few moments, to prepare himself for the afterlife.

God had now answered his prayer.

The blinding light triggered intense, disabling pain throughout his chest. Icy fingers seemed to scratch across his chest, then plunge in and rip his heart from his body. Suddenly he was very cold. As he stood again, he felt as if an entire house were pressing down on him. There was no possibility he would return to first base to resume his coaching responsibilities. Death was now impatiently awaiting him.

Ryan was neither afraid nor frantic to reach lifesaving measures. It was clearly his time to leave this earth. And this was as good a place as any from which to leave this world.

Ryan rapidly examined his conscience. He had drunk too much for too long—his entire adult life. Had he made reparation to others for his drinking? *Not necessary*, he thought to himself. Had he made reparation to himself? *Not possible*.

He quickly redirected his thoughts. *Need to go now. What do I need to accomplish before I leave here?* He had but a few moments to collect himself and move along—out of the dugout and away from the baseball field, where his death and the resulting commotion would be a sacrilege interrupting the sacred game he loved as much as his church.

First Ryan directed one of the benchwarmers to substitute as the first-base coach. Next he stepped his piggies into his stiff black wingtip shoes, shoelaces untied, leaving his socks where they lay. He then grabbed the mesh of the dugout screen like a cane and began making his way out of the dugout.

Because Egg was busy pacing angrily through the dugout, T. J. took it upon himself to call out the lineup: "Bottom of the seventh! Jeff Burnette, Jack Burnette, Spider Schmitt, and Marty McKenna on deck."

Moriarity sat down alongside Murphy, took off his glove, placed it over his face, closed his eyes, leaned back, and folded his hands. He looked as if he were trying to sleep.

But behind the glove and the closed eyes, Moriarity was actually trying to do anything but sleep. In his mind, his life was over, at least in Cottage Park. He could never return there. Moriarity now invited death to take him away from the stadium and from Cottage Park, so he would never again have the capability to mess up everyone's lives. He wondered, if he were to take his life, what method he would employ.

As Murphy looked down at Moriarity next to him, he began to feel the onset of another slow dance with the Grim Reaper. Today's episode couldn't possibly come at a worse time. He desperately sought to advise his batters one last time about how to approach Houston. Instead, he was rendered helpless.

Murphy strapped the oxygen mask back over his mouth. He too closed his eyes and leaned back against Moriarity to help him through yet another dalliance with death.

Jack found his brother sitting at the end of the bench with his head down, looking at the floor. He tapped him on the shoulder.

"What are you doing? You're up first."

"I knew it was too good to be true," Jeff said. "It was all Moriarity's idea. I tried to tell him it was a mistake, but he wouldn't listen to me. Now look at the mess we're in. That cost us the game."

"Forget it," Jack said.

"No," Jeff said. "I'm done. I'm taking myself out of the game. I'm done with baseball. I finally figured it out once I figured you out. You—you have to leave home and live for yourself. It's what you need to do. Me, I have to leave baseball."

"Hold on," Jack said. He placed an arm around his brother, then leaned in and half hugged him. "Baseball has to be a part of you—at least for one more bat. Then I don't care what you do."

"No," Jeff said. "Really, I've cost us another Final. I'm asking Coach Murphy to take me out of the game."

"He won't do it," Jack said, chuckling. "But you interrupting him now would definitely get him riled up again." Although Murphy was still nearly unconscious, slumped against Moriarity, Jack pointed to him in utter sincerity. "Swear to God, he'll jump right back up and hit you with an uppercut right here in front of everybody and tell you to be a man. That's how these old guys play the game."

Jeff slapped the back of both hands against his knees and looked desperately at Jack. "I can't hit the ball!" he whispered. "And I'm scared. Everyone in the stadium knows that." His voice changed from fear to anger. "All I ever do is strike out."

He stood from the bench and started toward Murphy. Jack pulled him back to the bench. He took both of his brother's wrists and held them.

"Listen," he said softly and reassuringly. "I haven't been the best big brother. But at least I try to be honest with you. And truth is, you can hit this guy," he said, motioning toward Houston. "Mom could hit this guy. He's done. He's all worn out. All he's throwing now is soft stuff. He's aiming fastballs right down the middle. Put the bat out there on the ball, run it out, get on base, and we'll take care of the rest."

"One last bat," Jeff said, nodding. "And then I'm done with this craziness forever." He took a deep breath. "I guess I can do that."

He stood up from his seat, and headed to the batter's circle with Jack right behind him. The boys carefully maneuvered themselves out of Egg's way on his angry tirade up and down the dugout.

Ryan was right behind Egg, his gait much slower and more deliberate. Ryan could see right where Egg was headed. Now would be the perfect cover for Ryan to slip away forever from the team and the town, silently and unobtrusively. But there were still a few matters he must address before leaving the team.

The first was to share a critical observation he had made over the course of the game. Ryan reached out and took McKenna's arm. It was as much to steady himself as to get the boy's attention.

McKenna, in turn, grabbed both of Ryan's arms to prevent him from falling. Ryan's ghostlike appearance frightened him.

"Father," McKenna said worriedly, "we should get you a doctor."

Ryan waved him off. "Listen," he said carefully. "Houston has been throwing the slow curve on his second pitch nearly every time." He dabbed the sweat across his face with his handkerchief. "Edge up in the batter's box without him knowing it, wait for it, then drive the ball to right field."

McKenna, like his teammates, had run out of answers on how to attack Houston. Being down by one in the bottom of the seventh, Ryan's tip made as much sense as anything else the team had tried.

"Thanks, Father," McKenna said. He patted Ryan's hand, cool and moist, making sure he didn't pull away too quickly. "But what about the doctor?"

Ryan tapped his heart as if to keep it running a little while longer. "No," Ryan said. "Your job now is to hit the ball." He clenched McKenna's hands. "I have to get to the bus and rest. I can make it." Ryan then let go of McKenna, turned from him, and continued to the exit. "I'll see you after the game," he lied as matter-of-factly as possible as he shuffled away.

As he came across the duo of Moriarity and Murphy at the end of the bench, Ryan unbuttoned his shirt collar, pulled out his Roman collar, and folded it into Murphy's hand. Ryan then took Murphy's hand and held it tightly as he silently recited a Hail Mary. Murphy never stirred. At the end of the prayer, Ryan squeezed Murphy's hand as vigorously as he could muster, as if he were somehow pumping a gas pedal to start a tired car engine. Whatever little life Ryan had remaining, he begged God to transfer it over to Murphy. Eyes still closed, Murphy grabbed the collar and held onto it for what seemed his life.

Ryan turned back and looked at the players on the bench one last time. He was certain he still had one more thing to do or say, but he simply couldn't remember what it was. He had to keep moving. With any luck, he would make it to the Holy Trinity bus with time to toast a life lived fairly well with a fresh bottle of Irish whisky that called from his duffel bag. Besides, if he needed to escape under the cover and commotion of an increasingly irate Egg, now was the time.

As Ryan started his way out of the dugout and into the seats, Egg bristled by him. Biting his lower lip and nodding to himself, Egg emerged halfway from the dugout to the umpire brushing dirt off home plate. Now was a good time for him to make his exit as well.

"Hey, ump!" Egg waited until the umpire looked over. "Thanks for giving the game away today!"

The umpire recognized the voice and started over to Egg.

And so it began. As Egg shouted more and more, a confluence of players gathered alongside him, trying their best to restrain him.

For his part, the umpire made his best effort to determine what had so upset the coach. He studied Egg lunging at him for God only knew what reason—and God only knew what the old man would do if he did break away from the players restraining him. The umpire felt pity more than anger, which intensified Egg's wrath.

"Sir," the umpire said in a patient voice, "we've had a great game here. Let's keep it that way. Come on—I want you to finish up with your team."

If the umpire had been a psychologist instead of a mortgage loan officer, he surely would have recognized the classic symptoms of a primitive separation anxiety. He would have understood that Egg's foul behavior was due to a perceived emotional abandonment of a primary bond. That is, he was upset because something very important in his life seemed to have been taken away from him.

A clinical psychologist would have noted: "Subject is hungry, angry, lonely, and tired. The loss of the baseball game—associative to loss of son, loss of face within the community, and loss of meaning in life—has triggered physical pain centers in the brain, causing a rapid transition from fight to flight."

Egg, of course, couldn't have cared less about a clinical diagnosis. He only wanted to throttle the umpire.

He pointed at the umpire. "You big coward!" Egg said. "You homers never give our kids a fair chance at winning down here. Our boys always have to play behind the eight ball."

The Holy Trinity players now swarmed around Egg, gently pulling him back toward the bench, reassuring him and the umpire that the other man was a really nice guy.

Cooper sat his drawing utensils and sketchpad down on the bench and squirmed uneasily. This was exactly the situation Wilson had predicted would happen. The old men would lose control, and Cooper, as the newly designated assistant coach—or head coach, as Wilson had already crowned him—would have to step up and restore calm. He looked at Murphy for any kind of direction or assistance. There was none. The old man was still seemingly asleep with the oxygen mask strapped on his face.

Cooper took a deep breath and stepped to the edge of the dugout. "Please, Mr. Egg," he said with all the bravado he could muster. "Come back and sit down!"

Egg snapped his head back at his "fellow coach." Now the focus of his rage zeroed in on Cooper, who quickly backed into the safety and silence of the dugout.

"You keep your mouth shut, Buster!" Egg bellowed at Cooper. "You get out of here! You're the one who's leaving. Not me!"

Egg headed off to throttle Cooper. Again, players stepped in front of Egg, assuring him that Cooper meant no ill will.

Regardless of who the old man wanted to throttle, it became clear to the umpire that there was nothing he could do to make Egg happy—short of changing the score to Holy Trinity's advantage. It was clearly time for Egg to leave so the game could proceed.

The umpire looked into the dugout one last time for some assistance or direction from Murphy, but he and Moriarity were still leaning against each other with eyes closed, completely checked out of the game. Despite the riotous scene a few feet away, Murphy still didn't move a muscle. He breathed in pure oxygen from the tank that rested in his lap.

"This is your last chance," the umpire told Egg. "Get back in the dugout and sit down and give these boys a good example, or I'll have to let you go."

"You can go to hell!" Egg said. "And you can go right now!"

"If that's how you want it," the umpire said matter-of-factly. "You're history." The umpire looked to the dugout again. "Sorry, Coach," he yelled to a still-unresponsive Murphy. "This guy has to go!"

The umpire then turned back to Egg, lowered his voice, and respectfully stated, "Listen, you can go now by yourself, or I can have a policeman escort you out. I hope you'll leave by yourself."

"I've had enough of this travesty!" Egg said. "I hate coming down here year after year with the same fixed ending. I'm going back to Cottage Park, and I'm never coming back!"

With that, Egg stormed off in the general direction of Ryan's exit.

"Come on, ump!" T. J. yelled from inside the dugout. Unlike Moriarity and Murphy down the bench from him, he was fully aware of the situation. "Be real! Give us a break, and cut him some slack!"

The umpire quickly turned and tracked the voice to T. J. "Careful, or you'll be leaving too," the umpire said, pointing directly at T. J. "Both you and the old man."

"Screw you!" T. J. replied. "And the slow boat you sailed in on."

With that, the umpire looked up to the bleachers and signaled for a police officer.

All around, Holy Trinity fans booed and stamped their feet on the aluminum flooring. From the broadcast booth, O'Connor vividly described Egg's theatrics for the listening audience, particularly Sheriff Huffman and Mr. Schmitt camped in front of the fire department back in Cottage Park. He compared Egg's dramatic farewell at Sec Taylor Stadium to "Handsome" Harley Race, a popular professional wrestler who often theatrically battled not only his opponent but the referee and even the fans who had come out to an event.

When the police officer made it down on the field, the umpire pointed to Egg. "He's out. And him," he added, pointing inside the dugout to T. J.

"But he's our scorekeeper!" several of the Holy Trinity players explained to the umpire.

"I don't care if he's Senator Harold Hughes," the umpire angrily responded. "He goes with the old man, and he goes now."

T. J. flipped the scorebook to a befuddled Cooper and marched out to stand next to Egg in solidarity. T. J.'s mother had been studying him during this near riot. She had hoped he could hold it together, but now she saw him slipping away. She could no longer contain her fear.

"Do exactly what the officer says!" Mrs. Jones called out to her son.

He'd progressed so far this summer. For the first time, Mrs. Jones could envision a future for T. J. that didn't include drugs and bad decisions. In this future, he had friends and purpose and potential. All that progress, however, would be in vain if he should now do something stupid, intentional or otherwise, to raise the ire of the policeman. Although standing up to defend his coach and friend was admirable in certain ways, it could land him back into the criminal justice system.

The officer motioned for Egg and T. J. to follow him off the field. At the gate leading to the seats he gently took Egg's arm. "Let me help you up these steps, sir."

Egg yanked his arm away and snarled. "I'll go on my own!"

As they proceeded together up the stadium steps toward the exit, Egg continued to berate the umpire and his integrity. Though the Davenport East fans couldn't hear all his remarks, they were irritated and bored with Egg's tirade. They booed him lustily.

Once Egg and T. J. were off the field, the umpire glared down the Holy Trinity players who had filled in where Egg and T. J. had once sat.

"One more word out of any of you," the umpire said, "and I'll throw you all out. Every single one of you! Game over!" He returned to his position behind the plate. "Now, batter up!" he bellowed.

As peace and quiet finally returned to the field and the stands Jeff took a breath. He waited as Murphy gingerly stepped from the dugout to the third-base coach's box. Murphy signaled that Jeff should take on the first pitch from Houston. Jeff then took to the plate in his own box where he situated himself into his batting stance.

Outside the stadium, the mild-mannered policeman ushered the contentious duo to the parking lot. The policeman had a very white, almost albino, complexion. Any type of prolonged exposure to the sun made him extremely uncomfortable, and now the sun beat down unmercifully. He stopped and let Egg and T. J. plod across the soft blacktop as they made their way to the bus.

"Well, I'm going back in there to finish up the game," the policeman called out to the two, though neither of whom acknowledged the policeman's invitation. "If you want to come back in for the awards ceremony, as long as the umpire is gone, I don't have any problem with that." The policeman waved and returned inside.

Egg wiped beads of sweat from his forehead. "At least we're not going to jail," he said. "I've ended up there a few times before."

"Me too," T. J. said. "And that ump's lucky he didn't grab you, because I would have hit him before you did."

"Thanks," Egg said, "but I can fight my own battles. Remember those punks we took care of from Schaller?"

Egg looked up at the bare sun, then pointed to the luxury bus idling in the distance.

"Let's get in some air conditioning," he said.

They had made their way around a few cars when suddenly T. J. cried out, "Father Ryan!"

Ryan was slumped over in the arms of Mr. Moriarty, who was trying to keep him from collapsing to the ground. Ryan's mouth was locked open. He was struggling, gasping to take each breath.

T. J. bolted ahead and tried to pull Ryan to his feet by his belt.

"No," Ryan said between heavy pants. "It's no use."

It was clear Ryan didn't have the strength—or the will—to stand, even if placed upon his feet. Still, T. J. held the belt as if it were a lifeline.

As Egg caught up to the parking lot pietà, Ryan slightly relaxed his panic-stricken face.

"Make sure he gets my car," Ryan told Egg, nodding to T. J. Then he turned to T. J. and nodded toward Egg. "You need to take care of him. Take him wherever he wants to go."

"I will," T. J. said, his voice breaking. Then he glanced at Egg, who looked as though nothing was out of the ordinary, so he also composed himself. "I promise."

But nothing at all was ordinary about Ryan's condition. Ryan began to lose consciousness.

"Egg!" T. J. cried out helplessly.

Mr. Moriarity tried to position himself to better support Ryan. "Go get that ambulance over there," he said to T. J.

Before T. J. jumped to his feet, he loosened his hold on the belt. Ryan sank farther into Mr. Moriarity's arms.

T. J. raced as fast as he could to the ambulance parked in front of the stadium. A moment later, the lights flashed as it followed T. J. back to the sight of the emergency. When it jerked to a stop, a paramedic rushed out.

Ryan was now holding Egg's hand. He was very quiet. The paramedic checked his vital signs and quickly returned to the ambulance. The driver had opened the latch to the back of the ambulance and slid out a stretcher.

Still holding Egg's hand, Ryan began to recite an Act of Contrition. Mr. Moriarity joined him. Before they could finish the prayer, Egg let go of Ryan to allow the men to position him on the stretcher, then glide him into the back of the ambulance.

From inside the stadium, a thunderous ovation shook the rafters. Fans kicked their feet against the flooring of the seats.

Mr. Moriarity and the medic helped Egg up into the back of the ambulance. For a moment, the dramatic sounds from the bleachers drew Egg's attention away. He glanced up at the stadium. Then he looked back down at Ryan on the stretcher. He took Ryan's hand again as the medic placed an oxygen mask around Ryan.

Before the ambulance hatch closed, Egg called out to T. J. and Mr. Moriarity. "Something good happened. You both need to get back in there. Wait until the game is over before you let Coach Murphy know about us."

T. J. nodded and waved. The hatch then closed. The siren began to wail, and the lights wobbled dizzily as the ambulance sped away through the parking lot.

Inside the ambulance now racing toward the hospital, Egg clenched Ryan's hand tightly. He captured a bead of sweat along Ryan's hairline, then traced a sign of the cross on Ryan's forehead. At the completion of the baptism, Egg clasped both of Ryan's hands and resumed the Act of Contrition. The paramedic prayed along as he steadily pressed the heel of his palm over Ryan's heart.

As the two men recited the closing words of the prayer, Ryan squeezed Egg's hand three times—a universal expression for the words *I love you*. Ryan then exhaled a breath that sounded like air being released from a tire. He never inhaled again.

— CHAPTER THIRTY-TWO —

Live Finals Update Here: 7th Inning 1–1

M R. MORIARITY LED T. J. BACK INTO THE STADIUM. Mr. Moriarity returned to his family near the field. T. J. stayed behind, at the top of the section where the most fervent Holy Trinity fans were sitting—or more correctly, standing and cheering wildly. He inconspicuously slid into a seat near the aisle.

He sat down and started to collect himself when an old woman motioned for him to come over and sit by her. Even amidst the intense emotion of the game, she stopped everyone and made them move over to make room for T. J.

T. J. recognized her as the woman from the Holy Trinity graduation ceremony nearly two months ago. She also recognized T. J. immediately, especially in Denny Gallivan's uniform.

"I told you that you would play baseball in Cottage Park!" she boasted.

As T. J. sat down, the woman pulled him close to speak excitedly into his ear.

"My grandson, Jeff Burnette, was the first boy to get on base this inning. He got hit by a pitch. Didn't seem to bother him at all," she said. "In fact, he flew down to first base like he was angry. We never see Jeff get mad about anything. Then his brother, Jack, hit the next pitch all the way to the fence. You should have seen Jeff run those bases. He scored all the way from first base! Now it's tied with Jack on second and no outs!"

The woman opened her right hand, where she'd been clutching a rosary clumped into a ball. She stretched the middle decade over to T. J. and insisted he follow along with her.

Over and over again, she prayed the Hail Mary out loud, as did those around her, everyone except T. J. He had not yet memorized the prayer, but he listened respectfully and prayed his own desperate plea for intervention on behalf of the team and Ryan, for whom he was also profoundly worried.

Spider stepped up to the plate. He let the first pitch go by for a called strike. Spider stepped out of the batter's box, studied Murphy's signals, then stepped back to face the pitcher. As the next pitch flew to the plate, Spider squared away and bunted down the first-base line.

For a moment, Houston and his first baseman were confused about who would gather the ball and make the throw to first. Finally, the pitcher grabbed the ball and in one motion lifted it to the second baseman, who had come over to cover first. There was now one out with the score tied.

Now on third, Jack clapped his hands above his head. As Houston eyed him, Jack began to lead off toward home. Behind him in the third-base coach's box, Murphy gave McKenna the hit-away signal.

McKenna stepped into the batter's box. He dug his back foot into the dirt until he felt comfortable. He then cocked his bat back and braced his entire body to pulverize the ball.

Houston wiped sweat off his forehead with the back of his glove. He studied McKenna, then looked over at third, where Jack had now increased his lead to two full strides away from the bag. He leaned forward as if he might bolt toward the plate at any moment.

Houston jerked his foot off the rubber and faked a throw. Jack dived back to third.

McKenna asked the umpire for a time out. McKenna stepped from the box and took a few casual swings before sauntering back into the batter's box and setting into his stance again.

Houston glanced quickly at Jack, then concentrated solely on his catcher. He reared back and threw a fastball high and inside for ball one.

The catcher fired the ball back to Houston and called out encouragement. Jack lifted his hands to the pitcher as if to help him, but clapped obnoxiously instead.

McKenna dug back in at the plate, then remembered his father's words about how to hold the bat loosely. His father had told him that the bat should almost slip out of his hands when he swung it. One time during batting practice, his father had actually encouraged him to let the bat fly loose as he swung. A few minutes later, his father had to duck to narrowly avoid being hit by a flying bat. McKenna had been so worried about almost hurting his father, but his father merely laughed.

Now as McKenna waited for Houston to look back from third, he loosened his fingers and tenderly grasped the handle of the bat. Then he remembered Ryan's observation that Houston's second pitch was always a curve.

McKenna nodded at Murphy's swing-away sign, leaned back, took a deep breath, then stepped as far up in the batter's box as possible. He waited patiently through all of Houston's skittish mannerisms meant to distract him from what he knew was about to come his way, a slow curve ball.

The first and second basemen had both moved up as close as they dared in order to make the play on Jack, should he decide to advance home. Houston went into his stretch. His arm rose backward, then forward.

McKenna's father had told him to try to read the name of the ball as it was thrown at him—to find the seams and look for how they were spinning. So as the ball flicked from Houston's hand, McKenna watched it bear down directly at him. He would not move, as he fully believed he would see the ball sail across the plate.

As it did, he heard his father and Ryan shout together, "Drive the ball!"

McKenna ferociously swung, hitting the ball an inch or so outside and behind the center of the plate. He followed through with his swing and watched a line drive sail over first base and directly down the first-base line. The umpire signaled fair.

McKenna tucked his chin, chopped his hands and feet, and drove his feet like pistons to first base, rounded it, then burst toward second, sliding into the bag and standing up safe.

When McKenna stood up to call time out and dust himself off, he realized that Houston and the Davenport East players were leaving the field. Jack had safely reached home.

With the score at two to one, the game was over.

Holy Trinity had won their first Iowa summer baseball championship. The jinx that had bedeviled Holy Trinity since 1929 was over.

"Thank God Almighty!" O'Connor yelled into the live radio broadcast microphone. Next he continued with a victory proclamation he had rehearsed over several years but never thought he would utter: "Pop all the champagne corks at the Lipstick! Holy Trinity is the state champ! Drinks are on me, everybody! We're coming home!"

A few teammates were throwing their hats into the air and screaming as they raced toward McKenna to celebrate. But another, larger group of teammates were racing toward Murphy who, like Ryan, had collapsed.

Murphy fell forward onto his knees, then onto all fours. He immediately passed out—or died. It was impossible to tell the difference. Moriarity caught Murphy's body before it hit the ground.

Murphy was truly dead. But he was also truly free—free of his broken lifeless body, and his spirit was now free to do whatever he pleased. His spirit, his being, his soul was drawn to leave his now-lifeless body.

The Holy Trinity team was screaming at each other in fright and most importantly screaming for someone to help them revive Murphy.

From the press box, O'Connor noticed the commotion and began to blubber. Murphy was dead. He was certain of that much.

He willed himself to explain the situation in a calm, reassuring manner that would not alarm his listeners, but it was of no use. The only words he could barely manage to express were to describe Mary Agnes Connelly making her way down to the dugout to take charge of the situation.

"Coach Murphy . . ." he sniffed. "Mary"—O'Connor wept heavily—"Agnes Connelly"—the sobs continued—"down."

And those were O'Connor's last words on radio. He wept profusely for another full minute on the air before the Algona radio station cut him off and broke in with an improvised start to their "Radio Rosary" program earlier than usual.

Back in Cottage Park, Mrs. McCarthy had intrinsically translated O'Connor's weeping. She knew it was Murphy. Even when the station switched away, she awaited the death notification, ready to properly honor his passing with the ringing of the bells.

However, neither of the men at the fire station were overly alarmed at O'Connor's broadcast. They knew he was an emotional man who frequently wept after big games, whether Holy Trinity won or lost. All they heard was the declaration of victory.

Mr. Schmitt excitedly burst into the station and sounded the siren. Outside, Sheriff Huffman sounded his car siren, then quickly redesigned the rolling scoreboard:

FINALS UPDATE HERE
GAME OVER: WE (2) THEY (1)

Back at the stadium, the players' frantic screaming tapered off, then stopped once Mary Agnes Connelly entered the dugout. In the calm, Powers sprang into action, directing everyone to back up except for Mary Agnes and Moriarity, who still cradled Murphy's head in his arms. The rest of Murphy's body lay straight and lifeless on the dugout bench.

Mary Agnes directed Cooper to fan Murphy with the scorebook, then Anthony and Orlowski to strip Murphy of his windbreaker, uniform shirt, and T-shirt. She calmly told Spider to go call for the ambulance. She then began to compress the area over Murphy's heart, hoping to jump-start it back into action.

During this commotion, Murphy had ascended from his body, beyond the dugout, and high above the field. He wasn't flying, more like slowly soaring upward high enough over second base to remove him from the pandemonium regarding what he hoped would be futile lifesaving attempts.

Where Murphy had elevated to was quiet, serene, with a breeze that gently rocked him back and forth as he weaved around the infield, fully and gratefully resting in peace. He was relieved and happy.

Suddenly he felt Ryan's presence, even before he looked over and noticed him also soaring alongside him. Ryan was smiling. No words were spoken, but Murphy felt his peace and tranquility. The two soared together over the stands, where Katherine was being consoled as she wept uncontrollably. If only he could somehow reach out to her, to O'Connor and the others who were frightened and sorrowful. No one should be crying for him. He was in a much better place. He was relieved to be in this new element, somewhere everyone needed to know and experience. There should be no tears or no heroics to bring him back to life. He was happily resting in peace.

Both Ryan and Murphy sailed back up again, high over right field, where a groundskeeper slid open a door and an ambulance burst onto the field, siren wailing, strobe lights circling. It raced to the Holy Trinity dugout. Murphy and Ryan followed the ambulance to the dugout, where Moriarity, Powers, and the rest of the team gathered around his body.

Murphy's body was quickly placed on a stretcher, which the paramedic and driver then slid into the back of the ambulance. Moriarity and Powers jumped in with the stretcher. In the stands, someone helped Katherine to her feet and led her to the exit to drive her to the hospital.

For the second time that afternoon, a paramedic began, or in this case continued, chest compressions to revive a dead coach from the Holy Trinity baseball team. The driver slammed the hatch shut and made his way back to the parking lot.

Murphy began to notice that he was sinking from the sky, slowly at first. He looked at Ryan with perplexity. He was even more confused by Ryan's smile, which had changed from one of serenity to one of slightest irony, even amusement. Murphy was falling farther away from Ryan now, faster and out of control.

Then Murphy felt the ambulance drop off the curb onto the parking lot. He now also felt the heel of the paramedic's palm pushing steadily into his bare chest. Though he wasn't wearing his glasses and thus couldn't make out the faces of the three individuals surrounding him, he did clearly make out the mop of red hair that shook as his star pitcher sobbed. And then he heard Moriarity speak.

"I killed Coach Murphy," Moriarity said between sobs.

Murphy had always believed God would take him immediately after he had fulfilled his mission of leading Holy Trinity to victory in the Finals. There comes an end; there has to be an end for everything.

But now it was clear that the end was not winning the Finals; it was winning over Moriarity. Murphy's life would not be complete until he was as successful with Moriarity as he had been in the other areas of his life. Upon his death, Murphy would stand in judgement before God and be sent on to heaven or hell based on his performance in this one area. Now there was no doubt in his mind that God would keep him alive at least until Moriarity matured and they won the Finals together again next year to prove it.

"I'm not dead yet," Murphy finally said through the oxygen mask.

"No," Moriarity sobbed, "but you're gonna be!"

"I'm freezing," Murphy said, turning to another individual beside him, hoping this person would be more helpful or at least more optimistic than Moriarity. "And can someone get me my glasses?"

"Thank God," came a devout and relieved voice that Murphy recognized as Powers's. A moment later, after Powers slid Murphy's glasses into place, he actually recognized Powers's relieved face.

A paramedic completed the trio of caregivers gathered around him. The paramedic stopped compressing Murphy's chest, sat back, and breathed a sigh of relief. Powers quickly draped Murphy in his T-shirt, uniform, Holy Trinity windbreaker, and woolen jacket.

Murphy focused on Moriarity, who had blown his nose into his hand and wiped it on the back of his uniform pants. He sniffed hard to try to prevent the need for another deposit.

Murphy knew for certain he would coach at least one more year of baseball at Holy Trinity. And Murphy's decision would become Egg's decision as well. As for Ryan, Murphy knew God had made his final decision.

This was as good a time as ever for Murphy to announce his decision. *It's time to begin*, he thought.

"I'm coming back to coach again next year," Murphy said. "And I want you two to be my captains." Murphy breathed the sweet oxygen from his mask as deeply as he could before continuing. "We could be even better next year than we were this year. I expect more than ever that we'll win the Finals again."

Then Murphy pulled off his oxygen mask, waving off the paramedic who urged him to keep it on.

"I want you to start pitching," Murphy said, focusing on Powers. "I wonder who'll catch for us when we throw you. Any ideas?"

Moriarity and Powers looked at each other in amazement. As shocked as they were at Murphy's astonishing escape from the clutches of death, they were even more stupefied that he seemed to be inviting them to participate in a discussion regarding the betterment of the team. The old men had never asked their opinion about anything. In fact, if a player ever volunteered an opinion, the old men would have done the exact opposite.

For the rest of their short trip to the hospital and amidst the wail of the siren, Powers and Moriarity offered suggestions on who might be the backup catcher as well as who would play up the middle: second base, shortstop, center field, and even left and right field.

"You really think we could be better than this year?" Moriarity asked as the ambulance pulled into the drive alongside the emergency room. "We're losing so many seniors."

Murphy nodded with confidence and a tiny hint of an arrogant smirk that told Moriarity he was foolish for not seeing what was so painfully obvious.

"We still have to work hard. Nothing like this ever happens by chance. Toward that end, I want you two to schedule a practice for tomorrow . . . say, three o'clock."

The ambulance jerked to a stop. With lifesaving urgency, the driver popped open the ambulance hatch.

"You can slow down," Murphy told him. "I'm fine."

A moment later, the driver and paramedic hoisted Murphy, still on the stretcher, from the back of the ambulance and whisked him inside the emergency room. Moriarity and Powers followed on the heels of the paramedic.

Egg was waiting there inside with a doctor. Both Egg and the doctor were relieved to see Murphy and hear that he had simply had another spell—though this one had actually taken him to the other side.

"You call them spells," the doctor said. "I consider them warnings. It's exactly like baseball. You only get so many strikes before you're out. From everything we heard about your condition at the baseball field, we thought we had lost you too."

In a single, silent glance, Egg and Murphy shared a well of sadness for Ryan's death.

Moriarity didn't understand until Powers' eyes began to fill with tears. Moriarity suddenly looked around for Father Ryan, who was one and the same as Murphy and Egg. Moriarity couldn't recall seeing one without the others.

Ryan was gone. Moriarity bowed his head and began to sob again.

"I killed Father Ryan!" Moriarity moaned.

Nearly everyone who had come from Cottage Park was now on the field, tentatively, pensively celebrating and congratulating the players and one another. There still was no update regarding the condition of the old men. Reporters from the *Des Moines Register*, KCCI News 8 in Des Moines, and WHO Radio jostled about as well, interviewing the players.

Before his team could board their bus and return home to Davenport, Jordan Houston wanted to get a Holy Trinity uniform shirt. He was willing to swap it straight-up for his uniform. He removed his uniform and presented it to each Holy Trinity player as if he were a salesman with a priceless Picasso. He expounded on his last name spelled out across the back, above the number 15—which, he explained, his coach had reserved for him because he knew that was the number of his favorite NBA player, Earl "The Pearl" Monroe of the New York Knicks.

Houston removed his hat as well, offering it as an alternative option. Free of the hat, Houston's hair mushroomed up and out. He primped it nonchalantly, unaware that any boy from Cottage Park would have traded his hair for such an afro in a heartbeat.

It was unusual for Houston to be unsuccessful in nearly anything (except school), but he wasn't having any luck with a uniform exchange, even with the $60 his coach had even given him as an overdue graduation gift. Even so, none of the Holy Trinity players would consider such a deal.

Each player swore he would gladly give Houston his uniform, but there was this matter of their coaches, who were more likely to part with their very own limbs than give up a Holy Trinity uniform. Houston was fascinated with the loyalty these boys had toward their school and town. He finally put his uniform back on.

Houston was ready to join his teammates for the bus ride home when a man stepped up at home plate, clapped his hands loudly, and asked for everyone's attention. The man was dressed in a full dark suit and tie with the standard footwear for old men in Cottage Park, black wingtip shoes. Underneath his coat he wore a black Holy Trinity Baseball T-shirt further accentuating the differences between him and the people around him. Houston guessed he was an undertaker, or perhaps an undercover policeman from the small town. He was drenched in sweat and looked tired and anxious. The crowd stilled as the man clapped his hands for attention. Houston listened intently for some clue to the man's purpose at the game.

"Thank you," Wilson said once it was quiet on the field. "I am Hugh Wilson, the principal at Cottage Park Holy Trinity School. Thank you for joining us at today's game with Davenport East." Wilson pointed a hand directly at Houston and led the crowd in applause. "You guys were terrific. You have given us a performance that we shall never forget."

Wilson parted sweat from each eye and continued. "I have some important updates about our coaching staff, who unfortunately cannot be here with us for this momentous event in Cottage Park and Holy Trinity history."

Wilson thought for a moment and couldn't resist the opportunity to cement the ending of the old men's tenure at Holy Trinity.

"As you know, this was the very last game for our coaches at Holy Trinity. We are so grateful for their years of service." He cleared his throat. "A few moments ago, I communicated with Katherine Murphy, the wife of our head coach, Al Murphy. They are in the emergency room at the hospital. She wants you to know that Coach Murphy is fine. He and Egg will spend the night at the hospital for observation to make certain they're ready for the trip back to Cottage Park tomorrow. I'm certain they're on their way to a full recovery."

There was scattered applause, but it quickly faded when Wilson's expression turned somber.

"I do have sad news about Father Ryan, however. He collapsed in the parking lot and passed away in the ambulance about forty minutes ago on his way to the hospital."

"Fuck!" T. J. growled angrily. He shook the state championship trophy as if strangling its last breath.

Wilson stopped speaking but pretended not to hear the loud profanity nor see the clear display of rage. Out of the corner of his eye, he saw Mrs. Jones console her son.

He also noticed McKenna slump over and sob. He too was consoled by his mother. She gently talked over him as he cried.

"Why?" he asked himself and anyone around. "Why didn't I go with Father Ryan? I knew something was wrong with him. I could have saved him!"

Wilson swallowed. It was uncharacteristic for Cottage Park men—particularly the always stoic McKenna—to express grief so publicly.

Wilson next looked out to the pitching mound, where Spider hugged Margaret. She also wept.

"He's lying," Spider whispered. "No way he's dead and gone. He's here right now." He moved his mouth to nuzzle her ear. "Let's name our baby Ryan," Spider said, moving next to kiss tears from her eyes.

And then with no plan for how or where he would raise that baby, and no vision of the future other than how far he could see from the pitching mound upon which he and Margaret stood, he took her hand and dropped to one knee. All his life, he had lived by a creed: real joy was so rare and elusive—once located, it needed to be secured, nourished, and expressed regardless and sometimes especially in spite of time and environment. Surrounded by grief, Spider squeezed Margaret's hand and looked into her eyes as she desperately bailed tears in order to see him.

"Yes," she said. She nodded her head vigorously and repeated this confirmation over and over again while he stated his intentions.

"My previous life ends today," Spider said. "From this moment on, I live only for you. I'm begging you—please marry me."

Those who witnessed the engagement proposal, including Anthony and Orlowski, charged in. They hugged, lifted, and twirled the bride and groom around. The crowd began to turn away from Wilson, gravitating toward that celebration.

Wilson was losing control. Crowd management during life and death transitions had always been Ryan's purview. People followed him as if he were a shepherd or their father. There would be no replacement for Ryan. The naming of a new priest probably wouldn't happen in the near future.

Like it or not, Wilson had to be that replacement for the here and now. Again he clapped his hands loudly and called all back to him.

"Let's have a moment of silence," he said when all had regathered. After a respectful pause, he said, "Let us say a decade of the rosary."

He quickly reviewed the association of rosary mysteries to days of the week. It was Saturday, which meant the Joyful Mysteries should be meditated upon. From the five Joyful Mysteries, he randomly picked his favorite, which hearkened back to a more pleasant time.

"The third Joyful Mystery is the Nativity of Jesus in Bethlehem," Wilson said reverently. Wilson then led the crowd in prayers: an Our Father, ten Hail Marys, and a Glory Be.

As he had done minutes ago in the stands with the Burnettes' grandmother, T. J. calmed himself in respect for Ryan. He bowed his head and said his own prayers as the united voice of Cottage Park rose around him.

After the Glory Be, Wilson began the Prayer for the Poor Souls in Purgatory.

"Eternal rest grant unto him, O Lord," Wilson said.

The crowd responded, "And let perpetual light shine upon him."

Wilson and the crowd then responded together, "And may the souls of all the faithful departed, through the mercy of God, rest in peace. Amen."

Houston remembered Ryan as the coach who had come out onto the field without shoes. It was unimaginable that a coach would do such a thing, let alone a holy man. And now he was dead.

Still lingering amongst the Cottage Park crowd, Houston too had bowed his head while listening to the prayers. He knew how to bless himself at the end. Even though he had never been in a Catholic church or taken any religious instruction, he had learned the sign of the cross as a ritual before every free throw. He thought it was cool. And it worked. He shot the best free throws on the team.

"All right," Wilson said. He looked at his watch and grimaced. "It's 6:00 p.m. I've been informed that the staff here at the stadium would like to close down for the evening. It's been a long day for them, and we thank them for their hospitality during this trying time. So let's finish everything up and move on. The *Des Moines Register* is here to take our team's picture. I'd ask Coach Cooper to gather his team around home plate for the photo."

Houston watched, confused, as the young coach tried to summon the team. But he didn't seem to know his players, and they didn't seem to know him.

Then things really got out of hand when T. J. yelled out in direct defiance to Coach Cooper's efforts.

"No way I'm taking any kind of picture without Coach Murphy and Egg!" T. J. said.

He wanted to add, but thought the better, that if everyone really had to take a picture and do it right, they should also bring Ryan back and lay him out on home plate. Dead or alive, Ryan was still part of the team.

T. J. clutched the championship trophy close to him. "You will never get me or this trophy in any kind of a photo without at least Egg and Murphy. And Powers and Moriarity too. No photo without the whole team."

All of the players and even some citizens chorused their agreement throughout the crowd. Just as many voices, particularly parents of the players, groaned in impatient disagreement.

"Wait a minute!" Wilson seethed at T. J. "You're not even—" He hesitated, then bit his tongue.

What he wanted to say was, *You're not even enrolled at Holy Trinity. How in the world can you purport to represent this school in any way? I might not even let you enroll this fall, given your behavior today and in the past. It'll be easier for me to put you on a school bus and send you twenty minutes away out in the country to a consolidated public school that's equipped to work with behavior students like you!*

But he couldn't verbalize even one single word of his internal rage. The whole world was watching him now. He had very nearly slipped and announced, with reporters present, that T. J. wasn't enrolled at Holy Trinity. The representatives of the Iowa High School Athletic Association wouldn't even take the time to do an investigation. They'd simply hand the championship trophy over to the Davenport East pitcher who was standing there, still watching them, for some reason. They'd tell him to bring it back to his teammates, who were now heading for their luxury bus.

This was all the old men's fault. It was doubtful that they had given out, let alone collected, eligibility and insurance forms for T. J. to participate with the team. Even now—when they were all retired, one was dead, and another was close to it—they still haunted him and made his baseball experience a living hell.

"You're not even," Wilson repeated, this time slowly and deliberately, ensuring none of the angry residue should seep into his expression, "aware that the Burnette family needs to leave for the bus station in an hour. Plus, I know you boys are hungry," Wilson also said deliberately, trying to not let on that the old men had *not* fed the team today. "We have good news that Father Ryan had set up a big family-style supper at McDonald's for all of you. So we need to finish up here so we can begin the celebration. Please, let's set up for the team photo."

Orlowski stepped in front of T. J. to shield him. "Coach Murphy was very specific that T. J. was responsible for this trophy." He turned and pointed to the trophy for emphasis. "So I think we should honor T. J.'s belief that we not take the picture without all our teammates and coaches." Orlowski now turned to Coach Cooper. "I mean you no disrespect, but the real coaches were the guys who stuck with us from the time we were in first grade. I think we can wait a day for a picture and take it when everyone's back home." Much to Wilson's dismay, Cooper nodded in passive agreement.

No one thought to call Murphy and Egg at the hospital and ask them how to solve this particular dilemma. If they had, the old men would have responded that they would rather light their hair on fire than be in any kind of self-serving photograph, even if it did commemorate an event they had spent their lifetime trying to achieve. And that was if they had even answered the phone. Moriarity had taught Murphy how to use the television remote, which neither Murphy or Egg had in their home. Their plan was to flip through as many stations as possible to catch the sports news coverage of their championship. Given all this, it was difficult to predict how he would have reacted to the sheer bedlam playing out on the field in his and Egg's absence.

Houston took it all in. Several involved dads were pretty much of the same opinion as Wilson, that Holy Trinity needed to line up and take their photo now so everyone could move on. The players argued as strongly against the photo, but Houston sensed their will was slipping.

Houston found this sociological episode of great interest. But Coach Razz eventually caught his attention and pointed to his wristwatch and their teammates that had drifted away to their bus.

Houston nodded to Razz, but held up his hand to signal a little more time. He had longed to jump into the Cottage Park fray all along. It was now or never.

Houston had routinely negotiated conflicts where the death of a beloved gang member was still fresh in the minds of those who had weapons and craved to use them. He knew death, grief, and the ache and disarray lingering in the wake of any loss. And most importantly, he knew how to make it better—at least how to get people communicating and living with each other again. He knew he was blessed in this and many facets of his life, and he knew he was required to put those blessings to work.

Houston cut right into the epicenter of the heated discussion. He headed straight for T. J.

"I want you to trust me," Houston said as he took his arm. "I know what I'm doing."

He led T. J. directly to home plate. "Those old guys you want in the picture? They'll be heartbroken if they open up the *Register* tomorrow morning and don't see your picture front and center on page one. Am I right?"

T. J. nodded.

"Stay here," Houston said before he went right back into the maelstrom.

Now Houston had to garner the trust of the other leader, Orlowski. Again he strode directly into the middle of the group. He politely excused himself to Orlowski's father, who was berating his son that this foolishness had to stop now.

Houston placed the palm of his hand over Orlowski's heart. "Do you trust me, brother?"

Orlowski nodded, more so in the expression of, "Yeah. Why not?"

Houston took Orlowski by the arm, as he would a loved one. He led him to T. J., then asked both players to kneel.

"Shortstop!" Houston yelled out.

Anthony now joined the trio at home plate. Houston positioned Orlowski to T. J.'s right, Anthony to his left. He instructed T. J. to keep both hands on the trophy. Orlowski was to place his right arm around T. J. and his left hand on the trophy. Anthony same thing, different order.

"Outfielders!" Houston yelled next.

The fielders quickly approached.

"Right field, right here," Houston said, hugging and then positioning McKenna directly behind Orlowski.

He took McKenna's hands and placed one on Orlowski's shoulder, one on T. J.'s. Spider was to be directly behind T. J. with both hands on T. J.'s shoulders. Jack put one hand on T. J.'s shoulder and one on Anthony's.

By now, the fathers and other adults had formed a semicircle, admiring Houston's political and choreographing efforts.

"Third base! First Base!"

Houston placed one of Jack's hands on Anthony, the other on Jeff. McKenna would do the same with Orlowski and Stephen.

"Rest of the players, gather around!" Houston said, placing a proportionate number of players in the front and back.

There was a noticeable grumble from the players when Houston next called Coach Cooper over. Houston stopped and admonished them.

"Photographs are for the future. This man is your coach for the future, so all you crumb crushers need to give him your full respect if you want to come back here next year."

"Anyone else?" Houston called out as if the train was preparing to leave the station.

"Me!" Wilson said, stepping forth from the crowd and dutifully falling in line with Houston's commands. It was a relief that at least one person was helping him bring order from the chaos. "I'm the principal."

Again there was noticeable murmuring, this time from the seniors on the team. Houston ignored the discontent. If he had a chance later, he would take the seniors aside and share his own wariness and reservations about including a school administrator in the photo. But compromise was the heart of diplomacy, so in Wilson would go. He had placed Cooper on the far left back row, so he added Wilson to the far right back row.

"Now," Houston said, standing in front of the team like a maestro, "you guys are a team. The best team in Iowa. And teams are tight, so move it in closer. Come on," Houston barked. "Asshole to belly button!"

Houston continually waved his hands to bring the group even closer together. Then he stopped for a moment to admire his work and take his own mental picture. It was nearly perfect. At last, he turned to address the audience that had gathered behind him.

"Television first, followed by newspapers, and then family shots," Houston called out.

As the professional photographers set up their cameras to begin taking pictures, Houston circled around back behind the team, then inserted himself directly into the middle of the back row. Now it was perfect.

The *Register* photographer took several shots in rapid-fire succession. Each photo accurately captured the Holy Trinity players: hungry, angry, and tired. They looked as if they couldn't wait for this chapter in their life to be over, exactly like the photos of the previous Holy Trinity teams that had graced the "Special Finals Baseball Edition" of the *Chronicle*.

One player, however, was different from every other player in that photo and in all those old photographs. It was Jordan Houston. He was smiling and in most of the photos laughing.

After the last of the team photos, no one saw Jack and Jeff Burnette slip away with their parents and leave the stadium. As the entire town celebrated on the field and became one body, the Burnettes all but evaporated. There wouldn't be an emotional good-bye. The silent exit was a ritual handed down over generations in a community that ached over good-byes and mourned the passage of its beloved youth.

But Jack had a Greyhound bus to catch, and he was running very late—so late that the family drove right by the McDonald's where Kossuth County cars were already filling up the parking lot and stacking onto the street. They continued straight west, almost to the Des Moines River, where the bus depot was located.

Once there, Jack quickly hugged his mother, shook his father's hand, then shook Jeff's.

"I'll write—I promise," he said, then immediately boarded the bus.

Seated near the front on the window side, Jack then practiced another Cottage Park good-bye ritual. He never once looked out the window, even as Jeff and his parents slowly walked alongside the bus as it rolled from the parking lot on its destination south.

The rest of the team eventually made it to McDonald's. Even Moriarity and Powers joined them, courtesy of their first ever cab ride. As far as they knew, it was the first time anyone from Cottage Park had ever ridden in a cab. They reunited with their teammates as if they'd been apart for years.

Ryan had been correct about the one-of-a-kind all-you-can-eat buffet. Despite all his baseball heroics, Orlowski's greatest feat in the Finals was consuming two large Cokes, three large french fries, nine cheeseburgers, and three servings of baked apple pie.

Anthony watched as Orlowski pinched mustard and ketchup stains from his lips, leaned back in the booth, and groaned in pained ecstasy. Orlowski closed his eyes. After a few moments of silent bliss, he belched loudly.

"You ready to go?" Anthony asked Orlowski.

Now that he had tasted freedom, he was eager to keep going down this path of newfound independence. And that path was now leading him out of the confines of the crowded McDonald's booth.

During the McDonald's buffet, Anthony hadn't eaten or even touched any of the food set before him. He had merely watched Orlowski in his all-you-can-eat conquest.

And as Anthony had watched Orlowski, Mr. and Mrs. Civilla had watched Anthony from across the dining area. They sat very much isolated from the rest of Cottage Park—and even from each other—as they nursed their coffees. Through longing, mournful gazes, they watched their youngest son stand and walk by and around well-wishers to escape McDonald's and his family.

Outside, Anthony awaited his new family, the Orlowskis, for the exodus from Des Moines.

At about ten o'clock, the celebration came to a reluctant end. Without thinking, families announced their usual rationale for leaving any Saturday night activity: "Mass in the morning."

Then they realized that for the first time in Cottage Park, there would be no Mass in the morning. Mass often seemed, especially to the youth, like an ordeal and imposition. But now Mass was suddenly and silently eulogized, much like Ryan himself. Like so much of Cottage Park, Mass was now best understood in its loss.

This temporary nostalgia was vanquished by Powers's and Moriarity's frequent exhortations that there would still be baseball practice, a captain's practice, as usual, in the afternoon. They smiled to themselves, holding the secret that Murphy and Egg would coach the practice and would be returning for another year as their coaches. Out of respect, Powers and Moriarity would let the old men announce their comeback to the Holy Trinity baseball team.

Cooper looked up upon hearing the word *practice*. He had been sitting at a booth with his wife and two little boys, who giggled as they shoved french fries in each other's mouths.

"Are you sure you're up for this?" Cooper asked with some concern for them but mostly for himself. "So soon? It'll be at least a couple of weeks before I can get my family moved up there." He gave his head a shake. "Don't you guys ever take a break from baseball?"

"Never," Moriarity and Powers responded at the same time. They waved to Cooper before joining their families as they left McDonald's.

One by one, cars pulled out of the parking lot and headed back to Interstate 35 North. McKenna was the last to leave McDonald's. He had waited to ensure that each player had gone home with his family. Seeing no one else from the team or Cottage Park remaining, he checked the booths for anything left behind. Finding nothing, he joined the procession back to Cottage Park, driving the bus home himself, alone.

— CHAPTER THIRTY-THREE —

Countdown to the Finals: 365 Days to Repeat

THE NEXT DAY, THE HEARSE CARRYING RYAN picked up Murphy and Egg at the hospital and started the journey to Cottage Park. About every twenty minutes, Egg politely, almost meekly, asked the same question, as if getting his bearings for the environment he found himself in.

"Now . . ." he said for the third time. "Where are you taking me?"

"We're going home," Murphy said loudly in hopes that Egg's comprehension difficulties might be rooted in a loss of hearing. "Back home to Cottage Park." He hitched his head back to the coffin behind them. "We're taking Father Ryan to Stangler's Funeral Home. You and I need to start planning for a big funeral."

Egg responded the same way he had the first two times: he nodded as if he should have known better, as if it were all making sense to him now, and as if he wouldn't be troubling Murphy with such silly questions in the future.

"Right, right," Egg said hurriedly. "On the way home." But after a few moments, he stated apprehensively, "But we're not going in the right direction."

And for the third time, Murphy and even the driver assured Egg they were, in fact, going in the right direction. Soon, they said, he would see Cottage Park, and all his questions would be answered. But the questions still came.

Murphy had his own questions for Egg, though he wasn't yet prepared to ask them. His questions were even more basic than Egg's persistent query of where they were going next. Did Egg remember the man who lay in the coffin behind them? Did Egg even know Murphy? Had it registered with Egg that Holy Trinity had finally won the Finals?

Murphy was most alarmed about that last question. The Sunday *Des Moines Register* sat on Egg's lap basically unopened. Normally, Egg would have pored over the *Peach* sports section, reading the article about the game out loud. He would have repeated and then explained and elaborated upon key facts to anyone within listening range. He certainly would have had the same questions Murphy had—such as how and why Jordan Houston was in the huge Holy Trinity championship photo adorning the front page.

Murphy had seen other older people in Cottage Park experience similar memory confusion. It'd happen after a hospital stay, a trip, or any significant interruption to their familiar routine of life in Cottage Park. Sometimes those people snapped back to their old selves after returning home and readjusting. In other cases, if they'd been stricken by a stroke, even a minor one, they were never the same again.

Eventually, Egg's questions tapered off. Murphy appreciated the familiar silence between them, especially after they drove through Fort Dodge and onto Highway 169 North. Murphy would break the silence to announce each town they passed through—Humboldt, Saint Joseph, Algona, and Burt—and remind Egg of the baseball adventures they had experienced in each place. Egg seemed to recognize the landscape now as they got even closer to their destination. Now his questions stopped altogether.

And then they were home again. Two signs, more like small billboards, greeted visitors to Cottage Park. They stood nearly seven feet from the ground and were twice that size in width. They were close enough to each other that one could walk the distance between the two, yet far enough away that a speeding car on Highway 169 could easily see the community's singular achievement: baseball championships.

Murphy asked the driver to pull over so he and Egg could review the signs. The first sign, the one bedecked with the American and Iowa flags, showed the years the American Legion and Holy Trinity teams had captured a state championship. Someone had already amended the board to show 1974 for yesterday's Finals victory. The other sign also displayed Holy Trinity and American Legion championships but included Cottage Park's semi-pro baseball team as well. That board had also already been painted over from twenty-one to twenty-two spring, fall, and now summer state baseball championships.

Satisfied, Murphy and Egg took their seats in the hearse and directed the driver downtown toward Stangler's Funeral Home. Each streetlight on Main Street had been wound in crepe paper from top to bottom in the red and black school colors of Holy Trinity.

"Wow," the driver exclaimed as he slowed in front of the darkened Five Star Theatre.

The marquee had changed again. This time, it would remain unchanged for at least the next full year. It read: We Won the Final Game!

Similarly, the vacant storefronts had changed. Once covered with poster-sized Holy Trinity schedules, many storefronts now displayed today's *Des Moines Register* front cover and the *Peach* section, proclaiming Holy Trinity's mastery of the Finals. The large banner draped across the front window of the closed-down Vern Van Oosbree's Variety Store had also been amended to exclaim: Countdown to the Finals: 365 Days to Repeat!

"End of the line," the driver said as he steered into the looping driveway in front of Stangler's Funeral Home.

As Egg and Ryan gathered their bags and Ryan's, the driver quickly stepped inside the funeral home. A few moments later, Art Stangler and the driver returned with an aluminum bier on wheels. After they slid the coffin onto the bier, the driver left them to return to Des Moines. Murphy held the door as Stangler and Egg wheeled the coffin to the air-conditioned comfort inside.

After they stopped in the lobby, Murphy lovingly reached his hand out, laid it upon the coffin, and held it there.

"I guess we need to start arranging the funeral," Murphy said.

"Actually," Stangler said, "that's not necessary. The bishop's secretary called me first thing this morning and said he's handling everything. They're looking at a burial in Sioux City. He's calling me back tomorrow with the finalized plan."

That remark would have generated an angry tirade from the old Egg. Instead, this Egg studied the coffin and appeared as if he wanted to leave.

It fell upon Murphy alone, then, to summon an appropriate reaction to this news that outsiders were stepping in—and considering a burial outside Cottage Park. Anger bubbled up inside him. He scowled and shook his head.

"Before you do anything, you run any of their plans by the both of us," Murphy said tersely to Stangler. "You got that?"

Stangler was fifty years old. Ryan had baptized him, and the three old men had coached him. Like nearly everyone else in Cottage Park, he was uncomfortable and unskilled in direct confrontation, especially with the old men. He gulped and bobbed his head until Murphy's glare turned back to solemn reverence of the coffin before them.

The trio was silent for several moments. Stangler knew the old men could stand there in that silence, taking up his time indefinitely. He felt the need to say something that would move them on and out of the funeral home. Some kind of a prayer might bring closure. But what? Ryan had always led this sort of ceremony in the past. Exactly what prayer do you say for a deceased priest?

As Stangler saw it, Egg was next in line to say or do something to honor the moment.

"Egg, would you like to say a few words?" Stangler asked.

"I don't really . . ." Egg said, hunching his shoulders.

"Hold on a minute," Murphy said, reaching into Ryan's duffel bag.

There, underneath Ryan's clothing, he felt for and found a Championship Baseball Ryan had made up for an upcoming baptism. However, this ball was different from any other he had signed and autographed over the years and decades. Instead of reading "We Will Win the Finals," Ryan had changed the message to "We Won The Finals . . . Undefeated 1974."

"This goes on display with Father during the wake," Murphy said.

Stangler hesitated. "The bishop—"

"No," Murphy quickly and angrily interjected. "The bishop will come and go in one day. I'll be here forever."

Murphy firmly placed the Championship Baseball into Stangler's hands as if expecting him to deliver a strikeout pitch with the bases loaded in the seventh inning.

"And make sure that ball gets to Marty McKenna before you close the lid and bury this man."

Murphy waited for Stangler to nod in approval, then he fished back into Ryan's bag. This time, he brought out a bottle of Jameson Irish Whiskey. He handed it to Egg.

"You know what to do with this."

Egg took the bottle and held it up to the light. He swirled it around, then stopped to watch minute bubbles float in suspension and suddenly disappear. In the liquid light, a glowing golden chalice emerged. However, he could not find the words to explain his vision. He was confused about why Murphy had given him the bottle.

Murphy waited impatiently. The old Egg would have known what to do. Murphy had hoped handing him the bottle would channel the old Egg. He wanted to kick-start that person again, like pushing a car down the street and popping the clutch to get it started.

Murphy reluctantly took the bottle back, opened it, and tipped its contents until the liquid covered his pointer finger and middle finger.

"Father Ryan used to say this was the closest any of us would ever get to Ireland," he said. He traced a Celtic cross over the top of the coffin. "He also told us that when he died, he didn't want to be buried. He wanted us to sit him up in the dugout and let him stay that way forever, like the Celtic warriors used to do."

Murphy studied Egg, hoping for some kind of reaction, hoping Egg would come back from so far away, from where he seemed to be only observing this scene.

"Egg, there's a prayer I would like you to read," Murphy said. "You wrote it. This is a good time for you to read it to us. Give me your wallet."

Egg handed over the overstuffed collection of newspaper articles, holy cards, drawings, and poems to Murphy.

For decades, Murphy had tried to keep and thus protect Egg from his own fiery emotions, from the tension and anger that often resulted in a fight. But now he wanted to light the fire of some kind of emotion, anything that could destroy the sinister invader that had overtaken his friend: indifference.

Murphy found the poem Egg had written after Denny died. Egg produced it regularly, often reading it to help himself and other grieving families who had lost loved ones before their time. Murphy unfolded the paper and handed it to Egg.

Egg looked at the typewritten words. They did look familiar, but he couldn't say from where. He looked again at Murphy, who nodded for him to begin. Egg read the words hesitatingly in the beginning but then with growing confidence.

Hear and Answer Me

Remember O most gracious Virgin Mary that never was known,
Yet even you have turned from the sorrow I have shown.
And here I believed you best to understand
What it's like to bury God's Son made man.
My son too walked the water, calmed the seas.
So you must hear and answer my pleas.
Show my son risen, now free of this world's stain,
Let me see him laughing and running the bases again.
Take me to heaven, if heaven there be.
I'll meet God myself and know her plan for me.
I'll thank God for life but curse her for giving
Mankind's death seed known since our first living.
We carry that seed, watch it take root and start growing,
Understanding it bears fruit at the time of our knowing
That we'd lived lives full of dreams and God's glory.
There'd be blessings, long lives—or was that just a story?
I've carried my death seed knowing all along,
My children would bury me.
Grandsons and great-grandsons would carry me,
all handsome and strong.
But my son is gone.
I can't live with my memory.
Take me to heaven or take hell from me,
Or down by the river, where grief floats away merrily.
Rivers move forward; they never look back.
Never retreating, always on the attack.
Make me a river where my tears can flow.
The river will hear and answer me so,
so to the river I go.

Murphy paused at Egg's last words, then gently received the paper from Egg. He folded and placed it back inside the menagerie of Egg's billfold, then returned the billfold to Egg.

After a few moments, Egg spoke softly. "That's a nice poem," he said.

It wasn't the show of emotion Murphy had hoped for, but there was still time. There was still hope. Memorial Field and baseball practice was next. Perhaps he would see the old Egg emerge in the familiarity of his Holy Trinity baseball team.

"We should go," Murphy said.

He took the whiskey, removed its top, and gulped down a mouthful. Murphy's eyes and sinuses seemed to clear. His heart seemed to rev up. He felt like a new man.

He handed the bottle over to Egg, who repeated the silent ritual before passing the bottle on to Stangler, who did the same. Murphy declined to take the bottle back from Stangler.

"Keep it for the wake."

Murphy then picked up his and Ryan's duffel bags. Egg carried his own. Together they set off for Memorial Field.

Outside, the weather was quickly and dramatically changing. A cool dry breeze carrying the first hint of autumn rolled fluffy white clouds overhead. They cast billowing shadows at Murphy's and Egg's feet as they carefully stepped along the sidewalk that was often cracked, sometimes even heaving from roots that raised the concrete in sheets.

When they reached Memorial Field, the large wooden door leading inside the ballpark was already open. Cottage Park was their home, and the ballpark their house. Murphy again watched for some kind of acknowledgement from Egg. But there was no flicker of anticipation nor words spoken. There was only the sound of baseballs popping as they were caught and thrown over and over again.

The two men passed by the ticket booth and the concession area as they made their way to the gate to the field. Murphy opened the gate for Egg, and they headed for the dugout. There, they both slurped from the porcelain fountain. After long drinks, they seated themselves on the bench. The state championship trophy the team had won the day before was also sitting on the bench.

The fifteen players playing catch on the field ran over to see them. T. J. picked up the trophy and presented it to Murphy.

"We didn't say anything before the game," T. J. said, "because we didn't want to ruin your speech, but the whole team dedicated this to you, our coaches."

His words were met with polite applause from his teammates.

Murphy accepted the trophy. It was a large wooden model of the state of Iowa on an elevated platform. Along the base, bold gold letters read "State Champions 1974." A gold batter was poised and frozen in a hitter's stance. A plaque entitled "Summer Baseball Class 2A" listed Murphy as coach and Ryan and Egg ("Egg Gallivan" was actually engraved on the plaque) as assistant coaches. Then came all the players' names. At the very bottom was the name T. J. Jones: Scorekeeper.

Murphy studied the trophy and pointed to Egg's name. "Do you recognize this guy?" he asked.

Egg nodded and smiled broadly.

Murphy smiled himself. Egg appeared to be catching on to what mattered most in life: baseball. He handed the trophy over to Egg. T. J. then presented Murphy the scorebook from the Final game, and sat down alongside Egg.

Murphy opened the scorebook for a glance. "I'll calculate statistics for the Finals later tonight," he announced.

He found the faces of the three incoming freshmen, one of them Wilson's oldest boy, Jim. These boys had never practiced with the varsity team. He spoke to them as his primary audience.

"Egg and I accept this trophy on one condition: that you get us another one to keep it company next year. Otherwise, we don't talk a lot around here. You can ask your captains about that and everything else we'll teach you in order to win the Finals next year and every year after that."

Murphy looked for and found his captains, Moriarity and then Powers. He was especially pleased Moriarity was fully attentive and focused.

"We work hard all the time. And dammit, we win. We're undefeated. We're planning to keep it that way in the future." He paused. "All right. I'm all talked out."

Murphy did not and would not announce he and Egg were revoking their retirement plans and returning as coaches. It was simply not needed. People in Cottage Park used a certain expression whenever someone stated the obvious: "Even the dog on the street knows." No one—not even Wilson, but especially not the dogs on the street that greeted Egg on his daily walk across Cottage Park—had ever truly believed the old men would retire.

Murphy called out to Moriarity and Powers. "Get these guys playing pepper."

As the players broke for the field, Murphy singled out T. J. "Coach Cooper will keep score for us this year. That means we need you out in right field."

"I gotcha," T. J. said to Murphy, echoing the words of confidence and reassurance that Moriarity had often exclaimed.

He started out onto the field but immediately returned and patted Egg on the shoulder.

"You did it, Egg! I'm proud of you."

T. J. delighted in Egg's smile. It was like the one he had displayed when Anthony waltzed him around McDonald's.

When he first met Egg, T. J. had thought the old man's face might crack should he ever smile or be happy in any observable way. Now it seemed he smiled all the time. T. J.'s plan to rescue the old man had worked.

Since Ryan's bequest of his car tied T. J. to Egg and Cottage Park indefinitely, T. J. decided to go ahead and make the best of his stay there. Earlier that morning, he had strained to complete ten pushups. Tomorrow he was determined to do at least eleven. He could already feel the muscles forming in his arms. He committed to making himself bigger, stronger, and faster.

T. J. reached out to show Egg that newfound strength. He shook Egg's hand firmly, then dashed from the dugout to one of the pepper groups.

Now all the players were on the field except one: Jeff, whom Murphy noticed making his way over to make his own announcement. Murphy knew this would not be an easy or a happy announcement. Jeff had picked this time to quit the team.

Murphy also knew he could never allow Jeff to utter even a single word of this announcement. Nobody had ever quit his baseball team. Nobody good, anyway. He had a canned presentation prepared for such occasions. He needed it once every few years, whenever a player such as Jeff was tired of the baseball grind in Cottage Park and wanted to try something new.

Normally, Murphy would have sent Egg to supervise the pepper groups. Instead, he kept Egg near him. He knew there was power in numbers. Egg would play a role in diffusing Jeff's polite plea to break the bonds that bound him to Holy Trinity baseball.

"Say hello to Holy Trinity's new leadoff man," Murphy announced proudly to Egg.

Egg placed the state championship trophy down on the bench and dutifully stood to greet Jeff and shake his hand. Again, Egg smiled pleasantly, as if he might be meeting this young man for the first time.

"I've been coaching for . . . forever," Murphy continued to Egg. "And I've never seen a player run the bases as fast as Jeff did yesterday. You missed out on a real treat."

Murphy then turned his gaze to Jeff.

"Your brother was our leadoff for three years. I'd never put a sophomore at leadoff until him. I think it's interesting that you'll also be a sophomore this year. You're already bigger than him and faster. It won't be long before you're stronger than him too. Now we'll have three more years with an even stronger leadoff man."

Murphy next opened his duffel bag and took out his baseball uniform: pants first and then shirt. He draped them over the bench and began to take his shoes off. All the while, he gabbed to Jeff in such a continuous and rosy stream of prognostication that Jeff could find no break in which to interrupt him.

"I have to apologize to you, Jeff. All this season, I've misread you as a power hitter. You're the opposite. You're a guy that slaps the ball and gets on base. Egg and I will show you how to chop the ball. We'll also work on your switch-hitting as soon as I'm finished changing here."

"Thanks, Coach," Jeff said nervously and dubiously.

He knew Murphy had sniffed out his intentions. From this point, Jeff had to negotiate like a man.

"And thanks for a really great season," he continued resolutely. "I'll never forget it. But I'm a runner."

Without skipping a beat, Murphy manipulated Jeff's words as he reclined back on the bench and yanked off his pants, followed by his shirt. "Oh, we'll have you running those bases more than you've ever run in your whole life. That's a promise."

Murphy stood now in just his boxer shorts and a loose white T-shirt, knowing his frail appearance would draw sympathy.

"You'll have to accept my apology and trust that I know what I'm talking about. Once we work on your new batting stance . . ."

Murphy grabbed a bat and now modeled exactly the pose: low crouch, bat nearly straight back, front leg nearly horizontal to the back leg. According to a passionate Murphy, this stance—which Jeff had never seen employed by any baseball player in the world—would immediately turn Jeff into a hitting machine.

Jeff studied Murphy holding the bat—or did the bat hold him? He appeared to have no flesh or bones, not a single muscle on the loose pale skin that hung like smoke around the bat. Jeff feared that the growing wind might at any time lift and carry Murphy away.

Murphy handed the bat to Egg and sat down to catch his breath. After a moment, he grabbed his uniform pants and pulled them over one leg and then the other. With the pants hitched around his waist but not yet buckled, Murphy stepped into his black loafers, picked up his uniform shirt, and put an arm into a sleeve. Jeff held the uniform so Murphy could slide his other arm into the other sleeve.

Murphy then returned to the bench to conserve his energy and strength. He motioned for Jeff to sit back on the bench, between him and Egg. Jeff did so.

"You need to understand . . ." Murphy said, breathing heavily.

He placed his open palm over his heart as if he were reciting the Pledge of Allegiance. This pledge, however, would not go to the flag of the United States but to the activities playing out on the field before the trio in the dugout.

"My heart," Murphy began, "is so broken that I really have no heart at all." He took his hand and waved it slowly over the field as if he were blessing it. "My heart, Egg's mind, Father Ryan's soul—"

Murphy stopped at his own mention of Father Ryan. His canned presentation suddenly changed in intensity and authenticity. He took the hand that had blessed the field and used it to push off Jeff's knee and launch him up the step of the dugout.

"Grab my cap." He pointed back to his duffel bag, where the cap laid across the top.

Jeff brought the cap to Murphy, who was using his right hand like a visor to scan the sky above them. Murphy took the hat, secured it tightly over his head, and continued to search the sky.

Jeff also looked up.

"Do you see a red-tailed hawk anywhere up there?" Murphy asked.

Jeff saw no sign of a hawk or any kind of a bird. Instead he marveled at the clouds that surged like waves across the sky. The sun hid behind the clouds, peeking playfully, shooting out rays straight and strong across the whole length of the sky.

"Well, he's up there," Murphy continued. "And the rest of the town is all right here." He looked back over the field. "All our hearts, souls, and minds are on this field. My heart," Murphy implored, circling his arms together as if capturing the action on the field and ingesting it into his body. "This is what keeps me alive."

His voice began to quiver. His eyes welled with tears. He pinched them away before they could run down his cheeks.

This was obvious and real grief that someday or somehow, Jeff and other boys of Cottage Park might run from Memorial Field, that they might run instead to other sports or simply run away from the passion and pride for Holy Trinity baseball. This emotion and these tears were real—but they were also undoubtedly making an impression on Jeff. Murphy knew he needed to close the deal.

"If you run away from this"—he looked up at Jeff, his voice strong and stern again—"you kill us all."

Murphy let the words sink in a moment.

"Did you hear what I said?" he continued.

Jeff nodded.

"I said *us all*—that includes you. You're one of us. You kill us all. And don't think you can run away from yourself either. You'll kill yourself."

Though the temperature was a comfortable seventy-two degrees, the blustery wind now chilled Murphy. Jeff saw goose pimples cover Murphy's arms. Murphy looked back out onto the field, wrapped his arms around himself, and shivered.

Jeff descended to the dugout, retrieved Murphy's windbreaker, and helped him into it. Even then, Jeff could tell Murphy was still cold. He stepped back into the dugout and returned with Murphy's heavy woolen jacket, which he also helped Murphy into.

Like the other players, Jeff was learning that he was now responsible for Murphy's care, physically and emotionally. Helping Murphy into his uniform and coats, he reflected, was not unlike a father ensuring his son was properly dressed before sending him out to play in the snow.

Murphy suspected he had pacified Jeff's threat to leave the team. Still, he didn't want to have this discussion again. Not at the end of next season or any other time. So he continued his presentation with a reference to a place he seemed to know with some degree of familiarity.

Murphy said, "If any of what I've said is untrue, God can strike me down to hell forever." Murphy placed his arm around Jeff to steady himself. "Now, enough of this nonsense. We've got work to do. Egg," he said, calling down to the dugout. "Come on. Bring the bat. Let's work on the new batting stance for Holy Trinity's new leadoff hitter."

Egg did as he was instructed. As the trio made their journey to home plate, they were joined by the holy ghosts of Ryan, who moved alongside Murphy, and Denny Gallivan, who moved alongside Egg—seemingly steadying and supporting them.

Murphy also held onto Jeff as they walked, partly to steady Murphy's own gait; partly to encourage Jeff's trust; and partly to restrain the boy, should he suddenly decide to bolt away.

"We'll teach you to bat from the left side of the plate," Murphy said. "Once a game, probably at your first at bat, we'll have you drag bunt down the first-base line."

Murphy's eyes, now dry and clear, brightened at the thought: the left-handed ruse and a surprise bunt. Just the sort of sucker punch combination that might knock the air out of an opponent long enough for Holy Trinity to get on the scoreboard first and lock up victory before a game barely even started.

Jeff associated each stride toward home plate as one more advance deeper into a swamp that would suck him faster and farther under murky slime if he should offer any effort of resistance. He was now clearly and officially locked into at least another year of playing baseball.

Here he was, like so many others, asking himself what had just happened. How and why had he failed in his determined quest to quit the team? What, if anything, could he have done differently? How do you beat these old men at their game?

He momentarily wondered if it would make a difference if Murphy were to actually die and go away. But Jeff quickly reconciled to the sad fact that Murphy's spirit and memory would somehow continue to haunt and guilt and damn him into playing baseball at Holy Trinity forever.

For his part, Egg was completely living in the mindfulness of the moment. It seemed he had forgotten the past. He definitely wasn't thinking about the future. His full attention was now on those steps toward home plate. Nothing else in the world mattered to him. He was in the company of friendly people, in a familiar place, and doing a rewarding activity with youth all around him. He felt a sense of peace and quiet joy.

Murphy's mind, however, freely raced back and forth, from past to present to future. His primary concern was Egg. He still hadn't come around. Not yet, at least. Hopefully once Egg got back into his routine and back into the sureness of life in Cottage Park, he would be his old self again. Cottage Park had its own unique ability to heal people.

Murphy knew his performance with Jeff—his performance over the whole season, actually—had been on the dramatic side. But it had also been very effective. If necessary, he would employ the same tactics or whatever else it might take to keep Holy Trinity winning throughout the year and at the Finals all over again next season.

At least everything he had said was true, or partially true. Murphy didn't actually believe God would strike him to hell forever. However, maybe God would set him up in some sort of time-share arrangement. He considered himself, at his core, to be a devilish angel. He was an attendant of God, sometimes celestial, who occasionally resorted to devilish means to a sacred end. In this case, threatening Jeff with varieties of death— Murphy's, Cottage Park's, and of Jeff's very soul—if he should not remain a member of the Holy Trinity baseball team.

Some would argue, however, that there was no angel in Murphy's demonic makeup. They'd say he had sold his soul to the devil a long time ago. They claimed he was, in fact, the real deal, complete with pitchfork and horns.

The person who now knew him best—his wife, Katherine—would possibly agree. Probably so if she knew Murphy had gone directly to his first love, Memorial Field, instead of reporting to her once he had arrived in Cottage Park. Murphy could only hope she would buy his line that he wasn't really "coaching" but merely "helping" Cooper until he landed on his feet at Holy Trinity.

Arriving at home plate, Murphy situated Jeff in exactly the same stance he had modeled a few minutes earlier. He grabbed Jeff's legs by the knees and planted them just off the plate. He then studied the pose, walking around and looking Jeff over from top to bottom and back over again. Then he stopped and gently cupped Jeff's chin, moving the boy's head degree by degree, as if adjusting an antenna on the back of a television to get better reception.

"A big part of this new stance is having both eyes looking straight onto the ball," Murphy said. "No more looking only out of the left eye for you."

Murphy nodded in appreciation of his handiwork.

"All right," Murphy said to Egg. "I think we're ready for the bat."

Egg looked over the wooden Louisville Slugger with the signature of Carl Yastrzemski etched into the barrel. He stroked it to remove dirt and dust. Satisfied it was now ready, he presented it to Jeff, who took it and clenched it at the end of the handle.

"No!" Egg said. He took Jeff's hands and inched them upward on the bat. "You need to choke up. Remember—you'll be chopping at the ball."

Murphy was startled by Egg's emphatic and angry response. The simple act of sharing a baseball bat with a youth seemed to rekindle a flame from cold ashes.

Jeff cocked the bat as if he were preparing to face a pitcher.

"Do you ever watch Joe Morgan for the Reds?" Egg now reached both hands under Jeff's right elbow and slowly lifted it up and down as if pumping water. "This is how Joe Morgan gets all his power. We'll get you all the power you want by cocking this elbow."

As Egg continued the batting tutorial, Murphy turned to study his new team. They were already working hard. He was certain they would be a very, very good team in the upcoming season. With Moriarity pitching, they could and should beat anyone.

Murphy realized that even a nitwit like Cooper probably couldn't screw up this team. Still, Murphy would definitely not miss one moment of the team's upcoming journey—in large part for selfish reasons but also for Moriarity. If that made Murphy evil, so be it.

Hugh Wilson, of course, would testify that Murphy was unquestionably some variation of the supreme personification of evil. So would the Iowa High School Athletic Association, which would be enraged to know Murphy was now preparing to illegally coach his first full practice, as he always did, nearly ten months prior to the official starting date of May 1, 1975—the day all Iowa high schools would begin their baseball season and annual quest to win the Finals.

— AUTHOR'S NOTE —

Uncle Tommy

IN APRIL 1945, MY FATHER AND HIS CLASSMATES at St. John High School in Bancroft, Iowa, were startled by the sound of a church bell somberly ringing at the nearby Catholic church. The parish priest rang the bell at his first knowledge of the passing of one of his parishioners—one bell for every year of that person's life. On that day, the bell rang twenty times. Though he hadn't been officially notified, my father as well as all his classmates knew that his brother Tommy had been killed in the war.

Uncle Tommy, for whom I am named, wrote to my father in February 1945. He told my father not to drink, smoke, or join the army. "I've seen all the world I want to see and would settle for Iowa any old time," he wrote that last time. The rest of the letter was filled with pleasantries of life at that time in the Philippines. Soldiers had been ordered not to share the grim reality of the war for fear of upsetting their families. Two months after writing the letter, he was shot to death in an ambush as he was following a tank unit through a narrow pass in Luzon en route to Baguio in the Philippines.

They called him a hero. But the people of Bancroft, the "Garden Spot of Iowa," a town of 727, had another reaction. It was captured by Harold Clark, editor of the *Bancroft Register*, in a poem entitled "Tommy."

Tommy

Don't say a world moved, a nation rose on Tommy's death.

Just say he smiles no more and he is cold as winter's breath.

He is no more. Though he was youth, his story ends.

He did the things he must for home and friends.

And that is all.

Don't say he gave his life, or sought the light of some ideal.

At twenty, men don't wish to give a thing so real.

Just say his life was snatched before the start.

Because the world said, "Do your duty. Bare your heart."

And that is all.

Don't prate of mock heroics.

Only briefly say

He did the thing he had to do.

He fought that day.

To live. He lost a game he'd hoped to win.

Because conventions say, "You fight or sin."

And that is all.

Won't say we're proud he died for this, our cause.

Or that there's compensation in applause

From fellow men.

Just say we love him now as then

And pray youth won't be sacrificed again.

Let that be all.

World War II
Killed In Action

Pvt. Thomas A Murray
Pvt. Thomas A Murray. son of Mr. and Mrs. W. A. Murray of Bancroft, died in action on Luzon, Philippine Islands, April 16, according to an announcement received Wednesday of last week.

Murray Killed

Pvt. Thomas Murray, son of Mr. and Mrs. W. A. Murray of Bancroft, was killed on Luzon in the Philippines, April 19. The above message was received this (Wednesday) morning by his parents from the War Department. Details of his death are not known.

Tommy entered the service on July 26, last year, and was home on a short furlough at Christmas time. He left for overseas duty shortly thereafter. It is known that he had seen considerable action from letters received from him during the winter months.

He is survived by his parents; one sister, Mrs. Eileen Kelly; and four brothers, Lt. (jg) Joseph, Pfc. Donald, and John and James at home.

Uncle Tommy had been exempted from the draft for severe juvenile arthritis, but he insisted on joining the army. Upon enlistment, he chose one of the most dangerous positions in the war: operation of a man-portable flamethrower.

The famed and historic Bancroft Memorial Baseball Park—which opened for play in 1948 on land in part donated by my grandfather, Art Murray—is dedicated to Tommy Murray and all soldiers who sacrificed their lives for this country.

— ABOUT THE AUTHOR —

Tommy Murray is a retired teacher from the Minneapolis Public Schools. He is the author of one other novel: *The Empty Set*. Murray is married to Mary Ann, and they reside in Shoreview, Minnesota. They are the parents of four adult children, all of whom are baseball and softball legends in the Shoreview area.

Tommy Murray with his coach and father, John Murray
Photos courtesy of Carlos Grados Family Photography, Minneapolis

— ACKNOWLEDGMENTS —

I wish to thank the following professionals at Beaver's Pond Press: Angela Wiechmann, my editor; David Rochelero, my proofreader; Alicia Ester, my project manager; and Athena Currier, my designer.

I would also like to thank my sons, John Curran Murray, for storyline contributions, and Joseph Raymond Murray, for technical assistance.

Lastly I would like to thank Bill Dudding for his friendship and endless work to keep baseball alive and strong in Bancroft, Iowa. You can join Bill in this effort by making a contribution to:

Bancroft Memorial Ballpark Restoration Fund
P.O. Box 475
Bancroft, Iowa
50517